HEROIN(E): ENTROPY

A NOVEL BY

GORDON X. GRAHAM

It’s always nice when a pawn checkmates a king

Table of Contents

Prologue 9
PART I 11
Chapter 1 12
Chapter 2 16
Chapter 3 21
Chapter 4 33
Chapter 5 38
Chapter 6 47
Chapter 7 57
Chapter 8 63
Chapter 9 68
Chapter 10 75
Chapter 11 86
Chapter 12 95
Chapter 13 101
Chapter 14 107
Chapter 15 116

Chapter 16 125
Chapter 17 134
Chapter 18 138
Chapter 19 143
Chapter 20 150
Chapter 21 156
Chapter 22 174
Chapter 23 179
Chapter 24 189
Chapter 25 192
Chapter 26 204
PART II 212
Chapter 27 213
Chapter 28 232
Chapter 29 238
Chapter 30 250
Chapter 31 254
Chapter 32 264
Chapter 33 271
Chapter 34 280
Chapter 35 295
Chapter 36 306
Chapter 37 318
Chapter 38 326
Chapter 39 334

Chapter 40 345
Chapter 41 357
Chapter 42 375
Chapter 43 389
Chapter 44 398
Chapter 45 404
Chapter 46 417
Chapter 47 434
About the Author 439

Prologue

Your world is not real.

It's a synthetic dimension created for the enjoyment of others. Others who seek to manipulate you in order to secure political, social, and financial domination of issues most important to them.

Like clockwork, events on your planet have elapsed in concrete, sequential patterns of the numbers twenty-three and seventeen, similar to the ten yards needed to accumulate a first down in American football, or more appropriately, the fight for the middle four squares in chess required to successfully enact victory. Like an illuminated lighthouse on a stormy inner harbor, the number twenty-three, along with its lesser sibling, seventeen, gives my Opponent and I esoteric signals on how to proceed forward in our game—a game that will decide the fate of mankind.

These numeric patterns embedded in all variants of time, life-altering events, and even chromosomes, give me and my combatant specific signals on how to proceed forward in your world and in this game that controls humanity for our enjoyment.

My Opponent and I exhibit the most consistent, yet inconspicuous control over two particular humans. Ms. Nina Sullivan, a nascent copier salesman from Laurel, Maryland, and her ex-lover, Konrad Hunter, have been chosen to execute our game. Together, these two will weave through cataclysmic, society-defining events that have in the past, and will in your future, seismically affect life on Earth.

To accentuate the circular, often inverse, and artificial nature of what you humans refer to as time, let's end this introduction and slip back into Nina and Konrad's dimension, where a woman is fighting against a ruthless killer to keep her family alive.

PART I

Chapter 1

Please stop staring at me like I'm Heinrich Himmler. I'm only partially responsible for this mess, thinks Nina, causing my Opponent to smile in adoration. Although he can't control her actions, nor talk to Nina in any capacity, my enemy can certainly read her thoughts.

Nina Sullivan, the prosecutor's most important witness for a drug kingpin on trial for conspiracy to commit murder, looks at the ground within the witness booth, ashamed at her role in a multi-state sophisticated synthetic heroin operation.

A sketch artist, sitting uncomfortably in a wooden chair at the back of the dank room, gently draws Nina's bright blue eyes by repeatedly overlapping small, misaligned circles. Every courtroom row, usually empty during most murder trials in Anne Arundel County, is filled to capacity with Nina's coworkers, media from around the world, and last but not least, extremely intimidating members of the defendant's extended family. The diverse audience is visibly on edge. The defendant's lawyer looks over his left shoulder toward his brooding client before resuming his inquiry.

The accused criminal, a powerful underground syndicate head charged with neo-genocide, nods softly toward his representation, who stands in front of an anxious Nina. “Based on an interconnected web of circumstantial evidence and conjecture, you're comfortable sending the defendant to prison for life?” he asks, staring at two attentive African-American jurors from Baltimore.

It was at this point, right after the silver-haired prosecutor repeatedly objected to his opponent baiting Nina, and immediately before an Australian reporter in the crowd titled his article: “Nina Sullivan: Vigilante or Criminal?” that I realized we'd found the right human to observe, scrutinize, assist, educate, and most importantly of all, fuck with.

Barely over a year before Nina connected the dots in Annapolis, my Opponent and I witnessed another young woman fight for respect thousands of miles away in the state of Washington.

February 17

Bellevue, Washington

Thousands of miles from the mid-Atlantic region, the town of Bellevue endured another depressing, stereotypically rainy afternoon.

"I'm home, Auntie," shouted a drenched Agatha Phillips, entering the modest foyer of her aging relative's two-story, two-bedroom row home.

"Can you please take these dirty dishes to the kitchen for me?" moaned a creaky voice from upstairs. Having just finished her cashier shift at the local Whole Foods, the millennial shed her raincoat and dejectedly looked up the dilapidated wooden stairs. A single mother living off federal assistance, Agatha barely had enough time to take care of her infant daughter, finish her associate's degree at nearby Roosevelt Community College, plus work two menial jobs to make ends meet. Obeying the request of her deceased mother's sister, Agatha quickly climbed the staircase.

"Work or home, it never stops," she muttered.

Once reaching her Aunt Helen's bedroom on the second floor, the exhausted mother opened the door to find her only child asleep, comfortably nestled on top of her most trusted relative. "She was full of energy earlier, but just passed out ten minutes before you arrived," whispered Helen.

"What's my baby girl been up to?" asked a weary Agatha, softly rubbing her child's wispy blonde hair.

"Crying for you mostly—until I fed her lunch, that is."

"Well, when Sophia wakes up, please whisper to her that I found a new apartment for us. Now she can finally have her a room all to herself."

"I'm so proud of you for handling your business, honey."

"It's been a long road, but I finally see the light at the end of the tunnel," replied Agatha, dirty plates in tow. Happy to see her healthy daughter, Agatha kissed her forehead before jogging back down the staircase toward the trash bin.

After taking a step inside the kitchen, Agatha was shot in the left side of her skull by a .45 slug from a SIG-Sauer handgun. Crumpling to the floor like a wilted dandelion, we watched—on the edge of our seats, as they like to say—as the unidentified killer briskly exited Helen's home. No neighbors witnessed his exit.

The single gunshot caused Agatha's aunt to flinch and then instinctively clutch the baby's mouth in order to muffle her crying. After hearing the familiar creaks of her rickety veranda, Helen took a deep, exaggerated breath and then knelt in front of the window to try and ID the murderer. Unfortunately for her dead niece and Bellevue law enforcement, she saw nothing more than a quiet, empty residential road.

Helen tearfully said to herself, "There's only one man on this planet who wanted her dead. But if I tell the cops, he'll kill me next."

Chapter 2

After quickly exiting one of BWI's terminals, a weary, downtrodden traveler finds a pale, burly Caucasian man about twenty years his senior. In his hairy, meaty hands, the individual holds a handmade sign reading "MR. ADAMS" in bold lettering.

"I'm FBI Southeast Regional Detective Charlie Adams. Are you Lieutenant Patrick?"

"Yeah. Do you want to head straight to the station or go eat?" responds Patrick after tossing the sign into a garbage can.

To Detective Adams, Maryland's humid October resembles New Orleans weather in the winter. As he pulls his unmarked police vehicle into Nick's Chophouse in Rockville, Patrick breaks the small talk about their non-existent family life with a probing question on the death of the serial killer's latest, and hopefully last, victim in Maryland.

Unsure of whether to divulge his theories on the serial killer to a complete stranger, Detective Adams changes the subject by stating he has to text message his wife to tell her he landed safely. Forty-five minutes later, after blitzing through a crabcake sandwich and cranberry whisky, Adams finally opens up to his cordial and attentive host.

"I hate to say it, but if this killer didn't leave Baton Rouge like I think he did, we'd be up to thirty corpses by now," says Adams.

"Is that so? Why?"

"You know, I've only been doing this for a decade, but I've never seen a more inept, bureaucratic police department overrun by incompetent homicide detectives in my life. The Baton Rouge PD was a nightmare."

"Whoever this killer is, if he's indeed stalking the DC area, he won't have the ability to fly through traffic like he did in Louisiana. Even if he happens to kill late at night, we'll trap him with roadblocks. There'll be nowhere for him to escape," confidently responds Patrick.

"What gets me most, from what I observed briefly in Sierra Vista, and more so in Baton Rouge, is the undetermined profile of the murderer. I mean, who exactly is he?" questions Detective Adams.

"I also spoke to that Sierra Vista sheriff via the phone; are we in agreement that that the Arizona homicide was the killer's first?"

"Yes, that's what I believe: murder one occurred in Arizona, and five in Baton Rouge, including one double homicide. Although one death was by a handgun, our suspect usually uses a muffled assault or sniper rifle," answers Adams, who at this point hasn't figured out that this murderer was also responsible for the killing in Bellevue.

“The realist in me tells me that his recent killings show the signs of a psychopath—someone who is getting cockier and more brazen as every day passes,” theorizes Patrick.

“This isn't just about murder, or revenge. This megalomaniac is bent on spreading as much chaos, fear, and paranoia as possible. And, oh yeah, he seems to have the power of invisibility,” surmises Adams.

The next morning, October third, less than a year after Agatha’s murder, Patrick and Adams step on an unoccupied business property. With its location in the middle of a modern, upper class, residential neighborhood, this Texaco, where yesterday's anonymous shooting took place, is the county's largest refueling station. Underneath a red overhang are twelve gas pumps in a conventional four-by-three setup.

The dozen refueling outposts, now empty because of the yellow police tape wrapped around them, congregate around the nucleus of an enclosed, door-less billing depot. The depot houses a cash register and credit card approval machine on top of a lanky metal table.

“Inside that outdoor office is where our most reliable witness was stationed after the shooting.”

“Where is he now?” responds Detective Adams, walking briskly toward the office. “Our observer, Zachariah Milani, is currently undergoing a psychological evaluation at Shady Grove Adventist. From what my boys tell me, he's in serious shock and could be there at least a week.”

Montgomery County's most decorated police lieutenant momentarily leaves Adams’ side to focus his attention on the tangled car wreck at the gas station's entry/departure area.

Patrick, his pulse quickening, adeptly snaps photos of the bloody, shattered windshield of the crashed Focus.

Behind him, a uniformed Montgomery County Police Department officer jumps over the chalk outline in front of a gas pump and approaches the FBI detective standing by the external cash register.

"Detective Adams, I read the case file on your recent work during the voter recount in Florida; thanks for winning the election for us. If I can be of any additional help while you're in Maryland, please don't hesitate to ask," says Officer Michael McGary. With a build and profile resembling the fittest members of Adams' Iraq War battalion, the young, low-ranked officer takes off his cap and extends his open palm.

"Just tell me how this taxi driver was killed, son. In this line of work, never let politics get in the way of your job," responds Adams, not shaking the outstretched hand.

"Mr. Milani, whom I personally spoke to at the hospital, gave us what we believe is an accurate account of what happened. Yesterday, a self-employed East-Indian taxi owner was getting gas, via pump number four, at 3:52 p.m. Then, he suddenly dropped due to a .223 bullet entering his skull via his nasal bone. Once inside his body, the bullet exploded in his brain cavity."

Intimidated by Adams' cold stare, McGary looks down before continuing. "Right afterwards, a frightened customer, specifically a seventeen-year-old female named Makiah Wilkins from nearby Langley Park, jetted off in fear with the gas nozzle still in her car tank. In a state of hysteria, she unintentionally plowed directly into a compact carrying two local kids, also wearing no seat belts, killing both drivers and the one passenger instantly."

"This is the sniper's second East Indian victim," adds McGary when Adams doesn't immediately respond.

Staying quiet, Lieutenant Patrick continues to survey the empty station.

After a long pause, Detective Adams finally speaks. "This guy must be invisible or not human, because your force should have more solid leads based on one simple fact: incommensurable from any of the murders in Louisiana, this is the only crime scene related to this case I've seen in a high traffic area with dozens, if not hundreds, of bystanders and drivers around as this man was killed. Yet you don't have a single decent witness? This bullshit won't fly with me, Lieutenant. Get your act together!"

The lieutenant ignores Adams' rant while reading a text. "Detective, unfortunately we have to reschedule that meeting between you and the chief."

"What the fuck? Please don't tell me it's another one," responds McGary.

Chapter 3

Much earlier in the day, a late-model Buick sedan sits alone in a medium-sized, nondescript Montgomery County office complex. Covered top to bottom in modern, reflective silver windows, the 500,000-square-foot facility houses more than a dozen multi-national, vertically integrated businesses. Next to the large, modern lobby of the four-story building's only first floor office is a pair of glass doors leading to an equally humongous expanse. On top of the pristine, Ferrari-red carpet of this large room sit two-dozen industrial copiers of various sizes and speeds. This salesroom, always buzzing with activity during normal business hours, is half the size of an American football field end zone. Against one wall of the salesroom rests a coffin-sized gray machine, capable of emitting 135 paper copies per minute. This useful contraption, at a retail cost of well over $110,000, is sold directly to Maryland businesses by this conglomerate's regional, mid-Atlantic sales force. On the wall of the red-carpeted room, above the eight-foot-long apparatus, reads a sign stating the company's motto:

efficienTECH: THE REPRODUCTION EXPERTS

Maryland's efficienTECH sales force, a diverse bunch of local men and women ranging in ages from twenty-two to fifty-five, theoretically are hired to spend their time finding and securing business for their employer.

Beyond the salesroom is another enormous space containing dozens of cubicles surrounded by partially enclosed offices. Because it's Monday morning, and well before 9:00 a.m., Colin Esposito, a senior account sales executive representing Howard County, sits alone at his cubicle near the office's rear. Resembling an extra from *The Sopranos*, Colin gazes at his car, still sitting unaccompanied in the parking lot. He rises from his desk, scurries to the four-by-twelve stack of mail slots in the room's corner, and quickly sticks his chubby Italian hand in each of the forty-eight slots. Dressed in a tacky, olive, double-breasted suit, he voraciously inspects every corporate document addressed to his co-workers. As he steals commission opportunities, Nina Sullivan, directly affected by his thievery, prepares her mind, soul, and body for work.

Twenty-three miles east of Colin, and located inside a top-floor, two-bedroom/two-bathroom apartment within a recently built apartment complex in North Laurel, she struggles to get dressed. Built prior to the real estate-fueled global recession, the three-story housing complex contains twelve apartments crenelated by two outdoor staircases. Each semi-private domicile, especially Nina's on the top floor, boasts a panoramic view of the awe-inspiring, heavily wooded landscape.

"Fuck, I'm going to be late again," mumbles Nina, slipping on her black Yves Saint Laurent pumps.

Living alone in a modern, expansive apartment gives Nina the privacy she craves, but it also breeds laziness into the psyche of the stunningly attractive, mid-twenties American female. The shielded sunlight from the gray, misty morning contrasts well with her dewy complexion, shoulder-length jet-black hair, and turquoise eyes. While standing in her bedroom, Nina quickly zips her thigh-length black skirt before buttoning her slightly too-small blouse. While using her handheld mirror to apply pink lipstick on her naturally pouty lips, Nina tries to ignore the news broadcasting from her fifty-inch rear projection television.

Yawning while pressing the "mute" button, Nina twists her head toward a bulletin board she nailed into the wall well before making the recent Samsung purchase with her fourth credit card. The bulletin board contains a Jamaican flag, New York Knicks banner, and a picture of the "twin beams of light" World Trade Center memorial.

"I can't wait till the NBA season finally starts," remarks Nina.

Nina, who is 5'8, with a thin, athletic build, looks at her watch, groans, then walks out of her bedroom and toward her kitchen, located past the expensively decorated living room. Now in front of her dishwasher, Nina chews the remaining fifth of a week-old cranberry muffin and then grasps a hand towel. As the microwave's timer, heating her bowl of oatmeal, counts down—twelve, eleven, ten—Nina squints at an unidentified flying object escaping the low-lying clouds, headed straight toward her closed balcony door.

A bird, unaware of the clear barrier, flies full speed into the glass barricade. After momentarily flinching at the violent impact, Nina decides to take a closer look.

Now on all fours on her living room carpet, Nina taps the glass door to see if she can awaken the rattled animal without directly touching it. The medium-sized, brownish-gray bird, most likely a female House Sparrow, now lay on its side on the wooden balcony floor, barely alive, but still breathing. Nina gasps as the bird slowly rotates its head ninety degrees and looks directly into her eyes.

* * * * *

Seventy-five miles north, inside a decaying apartment within a ten-story public housing complex in Pennsylvania, a mounted wall clock indicates the time of 7:30 a.m. Nina's widowed mother, Mrs. Jane Sullivan, inhabits this particular residence, on the wrong side of a stereotypical, depressed Rust Belt wasteland. In living quarters much smaller than her daughter's digs, Nina's birth mother struggles to stand in the humble kitchen of her dusty, one-bedroom shithole.

Mrs. Sullivan's face is severely bruised and her jaw is swollen as if someone struck it with a dull metal object. Tears roll down Mrs. Sullivan's plump, Gaelic cheeks as she struggles to stir cornmeal porridge. Without warning, she grasps her chest and collapses to the ground, splattering a spoonful of porridge across the floor.

While Mrs. Sullivan's body twitches on her kitchen floor, Nina, no longer inspecting the fallen animal, tries to eat before attending her weekly sales forecast meeting. "Fuck!" she screams, attempting to pull the hot bowl out her microwave. Unaware of her mother's faltering health in York, she runs her burnt index finger under faucet water. After sighing at her watch, she tiptoes back to the balcony door armed with a spoonful of instant oatmeal.

Again in doggy-style position, Nina gingerly sticks her arm toward the injured bird. Startled, she drops the silver spoon as the animal prepares for flight. Barely making it over the metal balcony fence, the Sparrow slowly ascends toward the overcast sky.

As Nina finally starts her ignition to drive to work, Konrad Hunter, her most trusted co-worker, lazily accelerates south on Route 270 South, headed toward the same destination. Unlike Nina, Konrad, a subtly smooth, intelligent hustler in his early thirties, welcomes the beginning to the work week. Cool and composed, he lowers the seatback of his high-end import sedan to further accommodate his gangly legs. Prior to joining efficienTECH ten years before the sniper murders, Konrad was a standout wide receiver at the University of Maryland.

But once Konrad tore his right patella tendon during an on-field collision a few months into his sophomore year, he immediately focused on his impending post-graduate career. The slim, agile, 6'4 North Philly native used his sterling smile—along with relationships with boosters who'd paid him to choose Maryland over Georgia, Oregon, and Michigan State—to secure an executive sales position with efficienTECH. His gregarious personality, combined with an innate ability to read people, has given him national acclaim as a transcendent salesman.

". . . on Friday, Chief Macklin, head of the Maryland leg of the serial killer investigation, has advised citizens to be on the lookout for a . . ." states a monotone radio news announcer from Konrad's car speaker.

April 11

Sierra Vista, Arizona

A few years after lower Manhattan's controlled demolition, and some time before Nina took the witness stand in Annapolis,

Billy Ray Braun quietly practiced his awkward putting stroke, on Sierra Vista Country Club's manicured practice green. Only located about fifteen miles north of Mexico, this pristine piece of Arizona property isn't immune to undocumented workers traveling northbound through its acreage.

"I never seen a wetback dressed like that before. Better text management."

Billy Ray took another swig of his Lone Star beer before retrieving his cellphone from a stationary golf cart. Searching the barren desert landscape with his bloodshot eyes, he was unable to find the individual he assumed was in the US illegally.

"Damn, they're fast." Playing alone as usual, he plopped into the covered, battery-powered vehicle and began his short commute to the first tee.

After watching a pair of members tee off, Billy Ray jumped out of his cart. As he strapped on his golf glove, he was immediately shot in the spine by the hollow tip from a long range, military-style rifle.

The powerful gunshot, which caused a golfer in a nearby sand trap to cower in fear, instantaneously broke Billy Ray's back in half before exiting through his chest. The gunshot was so mercilessly violent that after it withdrew from his body, it burrowed a hole within his golf bag between his two hybrid rescue irons.

* * * * *

Almost five months later, and 1300 miles east of Braun's termination, Ashimanya Chopra stood behind a translucent window opposite a routine customer.

"Why do you always come in just before closing?"

The frustrated customer silently fumed as Ashimanya meticulously inspected the bills from his last habitué of the night. He then slowly put the liquor purchase in a brown paper bag: the same size used by Jamaicans to encapsulate beef patties.

Immediately after the infuriated man departed his establishment, Ashimanya turned off the main light inside his store and lowered the storefront's steel gate. As he walked out the back door, he was shot in the otherwise barren parking lot behind his store via close range from three projectiles exiting a polymer Ruger SR40. After his crooked corpse fell to the wet pavement, the masked assailant shot Ashimanya a third time in the head without remorse.

I accept full responsibility for these murders. The thing is, in your dimension, there were multiple parties that caused these deaths—outside of the dog whistle villains from the NRA and executives at Rockstar Games, I mean.

* * * * *

Two weeks after I directed Ashimanya Chopra's execution, Kelly Grace was shrieking at an emergency responder on her new cellphone.

"Ma'am, can you see the gunman?"

"No, she was just outside, taking down posters on the front window for the night; then she got shot . . . I'm at the Bottle King liquor store in Brownsfields . . . bring help now!"

Poor Kelly Grace was fatally struck in the tailbone by a singular .223 Remington cartridge. She never stood a chance.

The gunshot fully severed her spinal cord in half seconds before exiting Kelly's chest cavity and finally creating a small hole in her workplace front window.

As if she were diving into a pool, co-worker Marissa Jones ducked behind a four-foot pyramid of Cabernet Sauvignon wine jugs and struggled to dial 9-1-1.

"It's just us two in here before closing . . . who would do something like this?"

"Ms., officers are on their way. Please stay where you are."

I'm one of many in my world. Although I have certain abilities that astound your species, I cannot control, nor anticipate a human's ignorance, or it's twin brother; free will.

So, to my Opponent's glee, I sighed as Marissa ignored the operator's warning and scampered toward the liquor store's anterior fire exit. Once her full torso was exposed, she was immediately fired upon via the same long-range rifle that just killed her co-worker. The projectile quickly ripped through Marissa's kidney before finally settling in her right tricep.

* * * * *

A half mile from Marissa's dead body, fragmented brain tissue from a South Korean skull was splattered in front of a dilapidated Beauty Depot store. Like most of the previous murders I've described, Hyung-Soon Lee's exploded face suggested that the weapon of choice is likely military grade.

* * * * *

Half a block east of the yellow police tape blocking the media, Charlie Adams, the Southern Regional District's highest ranking, Federal Bureau of Investigations officer, huddled around Conway's defunct frame with a few members of Baton Rouge's Police Department.

"First off, from what the hole embedded within Conway's suit jacket tells me, this looks like the work of an experienced gunman—not a random killer or a disgruntled, recently laid-off employee with an axe to grind."

"Charlie, what makes you say that?" asked a local officer.

"Like the other connected murders in your city, this was obviously a long-distance shot instead of a drive-by shooting. But more than that, the killer did his homework by prepping his vantage points minutes, possibly hours, before he pulled the trigger. Any untrained eye can also see, by the way his abdomen twists abnormally from his hips, that this victim was paralyzed before his heart stopped beating. This sick fuck likes paralyzing his victims by shooting them in the middle of the back before watching them die."

Detective Adams added, "He's definitely had military or domestic terrorism training. Look at the way the .223 perfectly perforated his aorta and membrane surrounding his heart before exiting his body. It was a perfect bull's-eye. I'm calling this into Quantico as a regional serial killer."

Six days later, and eleven hundred miles northeast from Louisiana's last sniper killing, Malayali Singh, a content, East-Indian taxi driver working within an edge city in Maryland, was suddenly shot dead while pumping gas. The fragments of the .223 projectile initially ripped through his wrinkled copper skin and then propelled through his left lung. A young female waiting for her gas tank to fill, adjacent to Singh's corpse, let out a bloodcurdling scream at the top of her lungs and jumped into the driver's seat of her beige Focus. Agitated and confused, she accelerated her car away from her gas pump while it's still receiving gas.

The woman's overwrought action caused the hose to keep its nozzle locked into the sedan's refueling opening, ripping the hose's end away from the pump's foundation. Resembling a hungry snake biting a frightened boar, the woman's small import sped past the sniper's latest shooting and toward the entrance/exit of the mid-sized gas station.

"No!" screamed the gas station manager. The frantic seventeen-year-old drove her Focus into an incoming Civic, instantaneously crumbling and exploding the compact car's engine upon impact.

The severity of the heinous, long-range execution at the Montgomery County Texaco on October 2, combined with the reflective, life-ending accident between the green-eyed witness and several children in the Civic on the same property sent the collective mood of the mini-city of Rockville into a hapless tailspin.

After a DC Affiliate gave word that a.223 shell casing was found at a Maryland crime scene, Detective Adams immediately boarded the first available plane out of Baton Rouge and flew to Baltimore-Washington International Airport; located about a half-hour north of the nation's capital. Subsequent to fitting his muscular frame into a fist-class window seat, Adams tried to find similarities between the lone killing in Arizona, and four subsequent shootings in Louisiana.

Via his laptop, Adams typed. . .

(Long Range) Victim #1 – April 5: senior citizen Billy Ray Braun in Arizona; a prominent member of the local Militia Minutemen, who lived on the rugged outskirts of Sierra Vista. Braun had many enemies in the Arizona community; none were violent.

(Short Range) Victim #2 – September 5: Ashimanya Chopra, the Baton Rouge Liquor Store owner who by all accounts, was an honest and hardworking member of his community. Chopra's business was located in a high crime area, plagued by drug dealing, muggings, robberies and other forms of violent crime.

The detective then writes condensed, brief sentences on the other remaining four murders, to seemingly innocent Louisianans, he adamantly believes were carried out by the uncaught killer.

I chose Adams because he has a quiet, modest, peripheral persona that masks his intensity and moral fortitude. He reminds me of the roles Matt Damon often plays. And akin to the fictional character Roy Miller, played by Damon in the war film *Green Zone,* Adams was an army chief warrant officer. He served during the pubescent stages of Operation Desert Storm and again briefly for a few months during the post-2000 occupation of Iraq. After working for his country, Adams decided on the burgeoning field of domestic terrorism so he could be closer to his young wife and son, now based in New Orleans. Until now, his highest profile continental project occurred in 2000, when he led a secret team of FBI officers to investigate voter fraud in Florida during the recent Bush-Gore Presidential election.

"Is he sadistically evil or does this serial sniper think this a game? And how did he manage to quickly evade Baton Rouge downtown traffic so easily? It just doesn't add up," types Adams before giving up and shutting his laptop.

Chapter 4

A few minutes northwest of DC sits Rock Creek Regional Park, one of Rockville's most popular destinations for tranquility, exercise, and family activities. Ms. Angela Ramos, a thirty-four-year-old El Salvadorian paralegal working her way through law school, takes a seat on a concrete bench parallel to Needwood Road, the park's main artery for four-wheel travel. Refusing to buy a car to ease her travel needs, Angela relies heavily upon public transportation to supplement her exercise routine. After using Rock Creek's expansive and challenging wooded trails to complete her daily, early-morning five-mile run, she drops her petite, diaphoretic frame on the bench created exclusively for waiting bus passengers.

Dressed in nothing more than running sneakers, compression shorts, and a yellow tank top, Angela removes a damp bus ticket from her left sock and looks at her watch. Casually glancing to her left, she sees an inconspicuous vehicle traveling northeast toward her, coasting on the empty road. Not thinking anything of it, Angela stands and stretches her arms toward the cloudy sky.

As the approaching car slows down, a man in its passenger seat takes notice that Angela is the only person in the immediate area.

Angela tilts her head southwest, twisting her arms and torso in sync. While executing a perfect triangular yoga pose, she screams at the top of her lungs and freezes in fear.

Approaching Angela, at a rate of about ten miles per hour, is the tip of a muffled black automatic rifle.

Sticking out the passenger-side window, the gun lets out three quick shots—*bap bap bap*—squarely directed at the left portion of Angela's rib cage and diaphragm. Two of the three .223 bullets immediately fracture Angela's torso, mercilessly killing her.

Realizing that the third gunshot went awry, the shooter, next to the driver, shakes his head in disapproval. He doesn't notice the infinitesimally small strand of blond hair that catches a quick glint of sunlight before floating out the window and onto the sidewalk, but luckily for him, neither will the crime scene investigators. The two serial killers, seconds after conspiring for their ninth murder on this cross-country murder spree, agree that they're also in need of some exercise and meditation.

A few minutes after the killers depart Rock Creek Regional Park, a frightened bus driver calls 911 to report a dead body located at the apex of his route.

* * * * *

"The bus driver who reported the murder saw no sign of the killer, nor did he see any footprints into the wooded area surrounding the park road," says Patrick to Adams. A half-hour after Angela Ramos' expiration, he and the detective are back in Patrick's cruiser, desperately trying to get to the park.

"Where are these roadblocks set up, Tommy?" asks Detective Adams while texting an update to his commanding supervisor, FBI Associate Deputy Director Alex Henson.

"Chief already set up three on Route 200 North, plus a few more northeast of the park. He also stationed officers at all park exits, with another half-dozen spread south and southwest of the park on Crabbs Branch Way. He's not going anywhere; we'll catch him today."

"Radio your chief and tell him to meet us at the closest checkpoint. This is spiraling out of control." By 10:00 a.m., about two hours after the Ramos murder is validated via local police dispatch, a few national television correspondents, who've periodically been reporting the string of unsolved murders in Louisiana, interrupt their regularly scheduled programs on the mid-term Senate elections.

It was at this interval, on this specific time and date, when the movement took a zig-zag course—a path that no pig could anticipate.

I had ideas of making the Chosen One a rapper, but that seemed too artificial, even within a manufactured world constructed for our enjoyment. No, making my most powerful piece an MC would be too mainstream. Too contrived. My general needed to be someone that no one expected: a person who didn't yet have a following.

Anyway, I'm getting ahead of myself. Wolf Blitzer, host of his eponymous CNN show, comes on the air much earlier than usual in order to report the death of Angela Ramos and the murder's purported connections to the Baton Rouge, Sierra Vista, and Texaco shootings. Within a studio located inside Manhattan's Time Warner Center on Columbus Circle, Wolf stares directly at a teleprompter.

"Good morning everyone. Instead of starting today's show with an interview of state senate hopeful John Ricketts of Fargo, North Dakota, we instead turn our attention to the suburbs of Washington, DC. There, yet another heinous murder is suspected of being connected to the killings in Louisiana and Arizona. These murders suggest, I repeat, *suggest*, that a serial killer may have traveled through the South and into the mid-Atlantic region, targeting unsuspecting victims. Let's go live now to Joe Johns at a checkpoint set up at Maryland's Route 200, locally known as the Inter-County Connecter."

Joe Johns, a decorated correspondent, stands to the left of a makeshift barricade on Route 200. The partially open palisade, identical to six others circumscribing Rock Creek Park, siphons off three lanes of bumper-to-bumper highway traffic between two standard patrol vehicles. Staring into a stationary camera, Johns forcefully speaks into a handheld mic inches from his soft, brown chin. "As commuters waiting in line angrily beep their horns in frustration, a Montgomery County Police Officer shines a flashlight at the driver of the foremost vehicle in line at this emergency checkpoint. At the same time, a member of Montgomery County's K-9 unit directs his German Shepherd around the same car to sniff out anything that could be suspicious. So why is this checkpoint, along with half a dozen others like it, surrounding Rock Creek Regional Park here on the ICC in Rockville, Maryland, one of Maryland's busiest highways?"

A CNN video editor rolls pre-recorded footage from crime scenes in Arizona and Louisiana, then Johns continues to speak. "For that answer, we need to go back to March of this year, at the Sierra Vista Golf and Country Club in southeast Arizona. That's where, while preparing to tee off from the course's first hole, a seemingly innocent man was shot from a long-range distance by a .223 bullet. Fast forward to seven months later and 1300 miles east: five more unsolved murders in Baton Rouge, Louisiana, also from an unidentified assailant using a long-range rifle to discharge .223 cartridges into innocent, ordinary citizens who were doing nothing more than walking down a street or closing up their local business. According to Montgomery County police sources, only a week after the latest Louisiana victim was shot in broad daylight, Malayali Sengupta, an immigrant taxi driver from here in the suburbs of Washington, DC, was anonymously shot and killed by a long-range bullet while filling up his cab at a nondescript Texaco gas station. The murder of Mr. Sengupta occurred only three miles from where I'm standing here, where the shooting of Ms. Angela Ramos . . ."

Chapter 5

Cutting off the news report, Konrad pops a CD into his in-dash, six-disc player. Back at Maryland's efficienTECH office, Colin sits again at his desk, peacefully stroking his neck while inspecting stolen client leads. About 2000 feet from his location, Denelle Coleman, who's the district office manager, casually walks through the front door.

Denelle was born and raised in Owings Mills, an unincorporated community north of Baltimore. Equally quick-witted and insecure, she resembles a youthful version of Grace Jones. Rocking a ratchet, ultra-tight sky-blue business suit, completely inappropriate for the office, she turns on the overhead lights in the lobby and salesroom.

"Morning, Denelle!" shouts Colin.

"Are you here stealing leads again?" shouts back Denelle.

At 7:55 a.m., Nina finally reaches her destination. She sees her most trusted friend and co-worker, Konrad, get out of his sedan and grab documents from his trunk.

* * * * *

Almost five years before I contacted Nina, Konrad successfully recruited her to work at efficienTECH. When she was a student at New York University, she, like most of NYU's 5,000 graduating students, attended a job fair near Washington Square Park in Manhattan's West Village. Nicknamed by her peer's as a "Sternie," in reference to her undergraduate affiliation to the Stern School of Business, Nina mostly sleepwalked through her first three and a half years in college—an unfortunate result of too many late nights clubbing in the Meatpacking District. One of only a few high-school graduates to escape York's meth-addicted populace with an academic scholarship, Nina squandered most of her Wall Street and Fortune 500 opportunities with her 2.3 GPA. But to Nina, heterosexual men, hypnotized her physical assets, would always be there to help her get ahead.

When Nina initially saw the sharply dressed Konrad near the end of the 20th century, he was the lone efficienTECH representative stationed at his NYU Job Fair booth. With his wide grin and athletic build, Konrad stuck out to Nina like a lighthouse to a wayward ship desperate to navigate stormy waters.

As Nina secretly watched on from the swamped Google booth twenty yards from efficienTECH's, Konrad used his height, along with his onyx eyes, to interrogate each student sincerely interested in his company.

"Before I give you my resume, tell me exactly how efficienTECH salesmen are compensated? What's the base salary? Tell me exactly how your sales commission structure works," said a quirky male student familiar with eT's products.

Konrad, enraged by the direct question, emitted a low growl before relaxing his stance as if a life-altering incident buried deep within his mainframe allowed him to achieve Zen. Putting his hand on the slightly shaken boy's shoulder, he responded, "Poindexter, how many companies here have propriety rights on all their technology?"

"Umm . . . not sure."

Sensing weakness, Konrad then went in for the kill. "Other than the 'holier-than-thou' pharmaceutical companies, and trust me they're not hiring in this economy with all the lawsuits they're getting *from the deadly side effects of their anti-psychotic schizophrenia pills*, and a few bloated software firms with hundreds of thousands of mindless drones based in Silicon Valley, no company drives industry innovation more than we do at efficienTECH."

"OK, that's not what I asked you though."

As more NYU students, interested in the interaction between Konrad and the twenty-one-year-old, congregated around the booth, Konrad subtly waved Nina over while continuing his argument. Nina then abandoned a line for kids wishing to submit their resume to Eli Lilly and walked toward Konrad. "Because we at efficienTECH have propriety rights for all of our equipment, we're the only company in our marketplace that can directly sell our equipment. We don't have to accomplish business-to-business sales via a third-party vendor; that's why we have a stranglehold on our competition. When a small-, medium-, or large-sized company is looking for a one-stop wireless solution for their document management, faxing, and copying needs, the only place they can turn to is efficienTECH."

Nina, now standing next to Konrad, butted in. "I don't understand: Don't Canon, Xerox, and Minolta do the exact same thing you guys do?"

"Excuse my French, miss, but fuck no! Those guys suck, and let me honestly tell you why," he said, smiling at her before continuing. "Canon makes decent copiers, but their machines can't read Apple software, rendering them useless to graphic design, fashion, and architectural firms. Xerox machines are way overpriced in relation to their ability, plus their maintenance contracts are actually more expensive than the equipment you're buying."

"Really? I didn't know that," said Nina, feigning interest while batting her eyelashes. Ignoring her, Konrad momentarily turned his attention back to the finance major.

"Ever been to Best Buy with thoughts of buying an entertainment system and an employee tells you that the only way you can buy that $2000 big screen you're drooling over is if you fork over another $2500 up front for future damages related to normal use?"

"No; no I haven't," admitted the NYU student.

"Well that's how Xerox does business. Their arrogance has lead efficienTECH to expand 400 percent over the last three years. We've whittled Xerox's market share to under 17 percent. And last but not least, if you decide to try and pitch Minolta's piece-of-shit boxes, you'll end up unemployed and dragging your feet at another job fair weeks later. Konica Minolta's turnover rate is the highest in the industry."

Konrad then momentarily turned to Nina and said, "Ms., please give me a moment of your time once I'm done with him. I'll only be a second." As Nina smiled and nodded her head in approval, Konrad finished his conversation with the young job seeker.

"The only reason I exist in this matrix is to maximize profit. So trust me, our compensation package is higher than any of the companies I just mentioned. Our Manhattan office boasts more NYU grads than anyone else in the industry. And now that I have your information, someone from HR will contact you if we're interested. Adios."

After politely taking a dozen more resumes and waiting for his audience to disperse in search of other opportunities, Konrad finally acknowledged Nina in the corner of the small, carpeted, red booth accentuated with eT paraphernalia.

"Hello, my name is Konrad Hunter. I'm a sales director at efficienTECH. But I'm not based in New York; I work out of our Maryland office. What's your name?"

Nina jumped off the chair she was sitting on and cautiously extended her open palm toward Konrad.

"Nina Sullivan. I'm a junior business major."

Konrad laughed before sipping from a bottle of water.

"What?"

"Usually students proud of their GPA state it right after saying their major."

As Nina fidgeted uncomfortably, Konrad continued. "Don't sweat it; grades aren't everything. Where are you from?"

"York. York, Pennsylvania. It's about a half-hour south of—"

"Harrisburg. Don't sweat it; I know where that is. I'm from North Philly. What are your plans tonight?"

"I don't have classes on Friday—so I'm free for the night," quickly replied Nina.

"They put me up in a suite at the Cooper Square Hotel. You wanna get some drinks later?"

* * * * *

Five blocks east of Washington Square Park later that night, Konrad cursed at his $25,000 Devon Steampunk watch.

"I knew she wouldn't come; it's already quarter to ten." After slipping into pressed, matte-gray jeans, a black cashmere sweater, and a pair of "Bred" Air Jordans, Konrad sat in a leather chair next to a large, and equally expensive, mahogany table. He then unwrapped a ball-like plastic wrap, holding an eighth ounce of a powdery substance, before hearing a cacophonous knock at the door. "I already put the room service plates and silverware outside; thank you."

"It's me, Nina. Open up; it's cold out here." Konrad stuffed the drugs in a desk drawer faster than Sean Penn in *Carlito's Way* and sprinted to the door. Flabbergasted at Nina's size-two hourglass figure, Konrad momentarily lost his train of thought.

"Are you gonna let me in, big guy, or what?"

After sharing sixteen lines of pure Molly, Nina and Konrad braved the winter cold and took a cab to No Malice Palace in Alphabet City, where Nina ordered two glasses of Moscato at the bar before grabbing Konrad's cold hand and directing him to a velvet couch in a candlelit corner. Once seated, with her shapely, exposed legs crossed, Nina, still very much lit off Ecstasy, happily explained her background.

“I know I look high class, but I was born with nothing and grew up with nothing.”

“Tell me your story, Mommi.”

“Do you want the sugar-coated, cookie-cutter story I usually tell strangers, or the truth?”

“Whatever you’re more comfortable with. *It’s your world, Nina.*”

“My father, whom I've never officially met, left my mother and me when I was seven months old. Supplemented by food stamps and welfare, she supported us by working two jobs at a time; usually one was at the local Walmart while the other consisted of making bagels every morning at the local bakery. We were poor, but always had enough carbs.” Nina laughed before motioning the waitress for two shots of Goldschläger.

“I grew up surrounded by 'urban rednecks'—a kaleidoscope of poor, uneducated sub-humans who vented their pent-up animus at being left behind economically and socially. Race wars were a way of life in high school, so I always felt pressure to escape that environment plagued by crime and high unemployment. After a really good SAT score, I was fortunate to get a full ride to NYU. I still have to work part-time at the library, but I'm very blessed for what I have.”

“Even with everything you faced in York, you still couldn't survive one day in North Philly,” responded Konrad.

“You'd be surprised.”

“I came from a broken family too—crack-selling everywhere, my pops in and out of Frackville for everything from aggravated assault to grand larceny. It's all about making a conscious decision, hopefully at an early age, to ignore those evils and try as hard as possible to do things the right way. Once that moral fiber is instilled in you at an early age, hopefully by a parent, teacher, coach, whomever, the rest is easy. I mean, I thought I was going to be the next Marvin Harrison growing up. Blowing my knee out at twenty-one derailed my lifelong dream of playing in the NFL, but that fire, that self-determination inside of me, got me through that low point and carried me toward success at efficienTECH."

"Frackville, huh? That's maximum security. I'm sorry."

Konrad, suddenly quiet, looked at the expensive Oriental rug beneath his feet and sighed. Nina edged closer to him and put her palm on his reconstructed patella tendon.

"I definitely thought you were a former athlete when I saw you today; you're so tall—not to mention you have a really nice body . . ."

Konrad quickly got up, brushing off the advance. "I'm headed downstairs to the bathroom, then calling it quits for the night."

"But we just got here."

"Sorry; I got a long day tomorrow. Be back in a few."

Downstairs, inside a dimly-lit washroom stall, Konrad crushed two blue pills of Viagra on top of the toilet paper holder. He then used his gold American Express card to expertly combine it with the leftover coke from the teener he bought from a bellhop yesterday.

"You can't wear a dress like that and think I'm not going to fuck you. Come on now," he mumbled.

Back upstairs on the lounge's main floor, Nina's BFF finally texted her back.

“Unfortunately, it's how the real world works.”

Nina was still reading the first text when her phone went off again three times in quick succession. “Yes, sleep with him.”

“Look at the bright side, at least he's good looking.”

“If this happened to me, my recruiter would look like Alan Greenspan.”

Nina fired back, “Are you sure? I never have sex on the first night.”

Her phone beeped again. “Unemployment is at an all-time high for college grads, so make sure he's definitely going to hire u before getting undressed . . . And he sounds like a complete dog, so use a condom!!!”

When Konrad climbed the stairs from the basement level bathroom a few minutes later, he couldn’t stop starring at Nina’s bubble-shaped ass. As she turned from the bar and smiled in his direction, Nina’s cleavage, accentuated by her tight, defined six pack and hard nipples, nearly drove Konrad to the point of ripping her beige dress off and bending her over a bar stool.

“I know I’m being forward, but do want to continue this night at my suite?”

“At least let me pay the tab so I don't feel like a complete hooker.” Nina responded before laughing out loud.

It was that mischievous, carefree cackle that immediately made Konrad fall head over heels for her.

Chapter 6

Montgomery County Police Department Chief Davis Macklin, a darker, slightly overweight, and short-statured middle-aged African-American male, not to mention the purported leader of all that's well and just in Montgomery County, leans on the hood of his unmarked Ford that's parked thirty feet from Johns' location.

“How's your fishnet working?” asks Adams after a terse shake of his hand. He studies Macklin for a moment, observing the dark circles beneath his eyes and the way his back is carefully turned away from the news vans across the street, and then shifts his gaze to the hundred-plus vehicles behind Macklin impatiently waiting to pass through the police's gauntlet.

“I would have caught him by now if I knew who the fuck 'him' was. Look at all this rubbernecking; we're causing traffic jams that rival what you'd regularly see on 495. I can’t wait until this hits the evening news,” replies Macklin.

As soon as the serial killers reached Maryland, the public, due to a cunning, multi-pronged attack executed by my

Opponent while I focused positive energy toward Nina, began to align public frustration with Macklin's face.

Let me explain how my immortal enemy did it.

The mainstream media, initially enamored with Macklin's gregarious, boisterous personality, immediately associated his face with the manhunt for the serial killer and the government's attempt to alleviate its burden on the public, much like they did with Mayor Ray Nagin after the Hurricane Katrina disaster in New Orleans. Macklin certainly didn't help his image as a savior by immediately conducting an impromptu press conference after the first Maryland killing and personally recommending that suburban Marylander's carry on their life as usual so as to not give the killer the power he craved. But when Angela was killed in the serenity of Montgomery County's most popular park, a small group of prominent reporters, all on Cheney's payroll, started creating a scapegoat. Their tactics were so subtle that no one, not even the viewers at home or the scapegoat himself, noticed how they pushed the public view of Macklin a little more toward the negative with each update.

Even though many outranking officials were also desperately searching for the killer, Macklin's press conferences became the de facto standard for all things related to the killings as federal officials refused to publicly comment on the case. The Cheney administration, in accordance with the international and domestic intelligence community, decided that until there was an apprehension, it was best to state that President Cheney publicly commenting on the snipers would only "compromise" the ongoing investigation. The White House Chief of Staff, Bison Sealy, then instructed producers at all three major news cable stations to focus on the Chief for investigation updates; not them.

"Turn him into a folk hero. Make him the story, not us," ordered Sealy.

"Even though we don't have much to go off of," Lieutenant Patrick adds, stepping out of the car, "I told every officer on this case to be on the lookout for a twenty-something male, most likely Caucasian, in a used domestic vehicle. The getaway car could show wear and tear associated with cross-country travel. Unfortunately, our men haven't seen anyone deemed suspicious." As the three investigators temporarily divert their attention to Johns wrapping up his interview with a member of highway patrol, Macklin puts his smallish hand on the left shoulder of the melancholy federal detective.

"Like Patrick told you, I'm more than qualified to solve these crimes as quickly as possible. No one wants to see innocent people murdered, but I'm actually glad your perp came this way. I've been chief of police here for ten years, after serving as the chief constable in Beaverton, Oregon, where I received my master's in public administration."

"Not to start a pissing war, Macklin, but you'll always be underneath the supervision of the Federal Bureau of Investigation, which I represent. Currently, our role is to watch the day-to-day actions of your department, especially in regards to your ability to collect damning evidence for this case. Because as you know, this scumbag will obviously also be charged on the federal level: murder-one. I'm not here to tell you how to do your job. However, further missteps won't only result in you losing congressional earmarks."

Macklin, slightly taken aback by Adams' attitude, stays quiet while the federal detective continues his rant. "And Chief, if you bungle this investigation in the name of personal fame, purposely or by accident, I'll personally see to it that you're brought up on obstruction of justice charges. There's no star of this story. Let's honor those who've perished by quietly doing our job, then go home to our worried families. OK?" Adams then excuses himself and enters Patrick's unmarked vehicle to have a private conversation with his supervisor, which prompts Macklin and Patrick to turn their backs to him, giving Adams privacy during his conversation.

"This asshole's definitely seen one too many action films, because he's playing the role of an uptight FBI rep to a tee," says Macklin.

* * * * *

"Where do we stand now that you're up and running, Charlie?" says Adams' supervisor, Alex Henson, from an office phone in his Oklahoma City corner office.

"Macklin's more competent than anyone at the Baton Rouge PD, but that's not saying much. However, between him and Lieutenant Patrick, who's second in command here, I think they'll be able to spread a strong enough net around this county."

Back in the Midwest, Henson stands and looks outside his eighth-story window. The delicately trimmed roses at the memorial, standing where the now-defunct Alfred P. Murrah Building once stood, reminds him that domestic terrorism always affects the public more than violence abroad, no matter how many troops and civilians are killed in international wars.

"It's important that we stay on the same page in the coming days," continues Henson.

“What do you mean?” asks Adams, fiddling with the in-car police scanner.

“We've been instructed by the White House to appear ghost on this operation, first and foremost because of everyone's inability to catch our target. Plus, I want the general public, and the Montgomery County Police Department, if necessary, to think that this is Macklin's case—and his alone. When shit hits the fan again, the public needs to think that he's the head of operations. It’s the only way to prevent panic—we can’t have this entire country thinking that not even the federal government can keep them safe.”

“There's another gunshot victim at the Sunoco at 1600 Auburn Avenue,” calmly states an EMT dispatch through the radio.

Adams immediately turns on Patrick’s car and types the gas station address into the car's navigation system.

“We’re just getting word that . . . unfortunately, we have somewhat of a repeat of what we saw at the Texaco station yesterday,” says Adams, bringing Henson up to speed.

While driving away from the highway checkpoint, Adams sees Macklin speak into his phone. “Hello, Nicole; I need specifics. Tell me how many dead; then I need to know if my boys on the scene apprehended anyone,” states Macklin through the lieutenant’s car speaker.

Nicole Freeman, Montgomery County's highest-ranking EMT official and Macklin’s confidant, surveys the carnage at the Sunoco gas station.

“Excuse me, this is Charlie Adams of the FBI's Southern Regional District. I know that you’re not an officer, but can you please give me your best description of the new crime scene?

Lieutenant Patrick told me you often assist officers in this manner, and I want to get a medical professional's assessment of what's going on."

"Nicole's better at assessing crime scenes than most of my detectives," chimes in Macklin. "Go on, Nicole, tell Charlie what you see. We'll both be there in ten minutes."

"Hold on, an officer just handed me some identification," says Nicole, reading a laminated card in her hand.

"What we have here is a large blond woman, tagged Ms. Jane Henderson of Bowie, Maryland." Nicole places a sheet over the stiff body of the deceased 5'10 female. "Identical to the East Indian killed at Texaco yesterday, Ms. Henderson was struck by a long-distance shot in the back. But, unlike the circumstances surrounding the death of Mr. Sengupta, she was the only customer at this gas station before she was shot. The only possible witness, a gas attendant working the afternoon shift, was inside the station garage while the murder took place. To my knowledge thus far, there were no cars getting gas when the victim was killed."

"Describe the property, along with the crime scene, in further detail," demands Adams.

"The corner of the Sunoco property contains an automatic air pump and an industrial-strength vacuum. From the sucking apparatus attachment on the car floor next to Ms. Henderson, you guys will probably ascertain that she was bent over, cleaning her right rear car seat. There is a small wooded area, northwest of the property, which seems like the location she was shot from by this ninja sniper."

No, he wasn't a ninja, although his tactical brilliance became noteworthy when the killer shed blood later that night only a few blocks from the White House.

* * * * *

A few hours after Ms. Henderson perished, around a quarter after seven, Mr. Emmanuel Pierre exits a local public bus east of the Anacostia River in the Good Hope section of Southeast DC. The short, stocky Haitian prepares to walk a few blocks to his home in an often-ignored section of the nation's capital. Before zipping up his gray fleece to his neck, the forty-six-year-old stretches his arms and yawns. Happy to be on the last leg of his commute from a warehouse an hour north of Washington, Pierre stands underneath a streetlight to gain some artificial light.

Just as he raises his right hand to light a cigarette, a high-powered, long-range bullet crashes through his palm near the base of his thumb.

The cartridge wallops into Pierre's chest cavity, near his left collarbone, before turbulently ripping open a major artery and vein. Killing him instantly, the .223 then fragments within his rib cage, shoulder, and collarbone tissue. Unlike the previous murders, two hours pass by before Pierre is found deceased on the cold black pavement of Eaton Road SE. Eight and a half months after his first murder in Bellevue, the elusive serial killer, desperately pursued by the FBI along with several state and local police departments, remains uncaught.

The next morning, around twenty-five miles away, Chief Macklin attempts to quell public outrage. Nervously shaking his coffee cup like he has Tourette's, Macklin peers out the window of his corner office and surveys the madness outside. The jittery head of the police department, responsible for the welfare of all 990,000 citizens of Montgomery County, slams the door to his office and kneels to pray to a god he's not even sure he believes in. The blind desperation of faith is what binds all these characters, regardless of whether they're being manipulated by my Opponent or me. Trampling the fifty-yard fescue lawn serving as the border of Montgomery County's 50,000-square-foot police station/holding center/courthouse, production assistants and cameramen prep their equipment for their impending close-up of Macklin's worried face. Simultaneously, reporters, who've traveled from around the world to become another member of the growing lynch mob, put makeup on their chiseled faces in order to hide their forehead wrinkles and dark eye circles. Behind the busy press contingent, local, regional, and national news trucks, with raised digital communication antennas, are scattered along the road in front of the colossal criminal justice compound.

It is now 7:45 a.m., on Monday, October 8. Coined by the local DC media, the "Serial Sniper" is repeatedly described as an individual who murders repeatedly without regret or emotion and seems to enjoy killing most from a long distance via sniper rifle.

"Chief! Are you in there, Macklin? May we have a word with you please?" asks Lieutenant Patrick.

Detective Adams, also worried about Macklin's mindset, stands next to the lieutenant as he brusquely knocks on Macklin's closed oak door. "Chief, before you speak to the media again, we'd like to go over the leads that came in yesterday," pleads Adams. Macklin, finished with his brief words for my good friends God, Jesus, and the Holy Spirit, cracks open his door to let only Patrick into his office.

"Meet me by the podium outside in ten minutes," growls Macklin before slamming the door in Adams' face. Patrick, no longer interested in playing peacemaker between the two stubborn men, plops a stuffed manila folder onto Macklin's cluttered desk.

"On each of the sixty or so pages within that binder are the more than two thousand tips we've received from local citizens on so-called sniper sightings. And that's just from the weekend," says Patrick. He attempts to elucidate the best leads moving forward, but changes his mind after observing his supervisor's fragile state. Macklin, now slumped in his broad leather chair, palms his head with his hands while staring at the ground.

"Wow, look at those piranhas out on the lawn. I count at least fifty more reporters out there today than were there last Friday. What am I going to tell them this time? After searching every inch of this county with a fine-toothed comb, we've got no clue where this killer is, nor do we have any idea about when he'll strike again. The only information we've gotten from the finally completed autopsy is that based on the accuracy of the shootings, this killer has got to have some sort of military background, but half those reporters out there already published that information based on common sense alone. Every mayor in the area, even the non-racist ones I've broken bread with, says I'm in way over my head."

"I think we should look at this from a different angle. We need to analyze this case from a 3-D perspective."

“What do you mean?” asks Macklin, breaking three packets of sugar into a cup of stale coffee. Staring out his window and looking down at the dozens of satellite antennas sprinkled like trees across the department's front lawn, Macklin feels like a European king who finally realizes his subjects want to send him to the guillotine.

“For instance, what other investigations are being labeled high priority by our detectives?” asks Patrick.

“Why?”

“Call it a hunch, and maybe I'm wrong, but this Sniper homicide case could possibly be connected to another case in another division.”

Macklin grabs a couple of notes he’d scribbled for his press conference, opens his office door, and motions for Patrick to walk through it before he does.

“I don't know, but I doubt this serial killer is also running a prostitution ring through a Asian massage parlor—or better yet, hosting an underground poker tournament. Lieutenant, if you don't get your shit together and stop overwhelming me with these bullshit theories, both of us will be nothing more than a footnote in this investigation, unceremoniously fired for incompetence.”

Chapter 7

Two after weeks after their inebriated, passionate one-night stand, Konrad, after purposely ignoring Nina's desperate voicemails and text messages for a month, verbally guaranteed her a sales position to begin once she graduated.

Using connections established during Konrad's decade-long run as a top-tier salesman at efficienTECH, he secured a salary for Nina of $150,000, plus a signing bonus of $25,000—more than four times the starting rate for her peers. However, after several years of reaching her quarterly sales projections, Nina has failed to complete any transactions to any small, medium, or large-sized businesses in her newly designated territory of Montgomery County, Maryland.

Further complicating Nina’s life, other than the fact that a serial killer has been murdering unsuspecting citizens in her territory, is that she's spent most of her savings on extravagant retail therapy and unnecessary, week-long vacations to Melbourne, Paris, Hokkaido, and Rio. So when Nina, on the morning of Monday, October 8, 2002, pulled her late-model

BMW M3 into an empty spot next to Konrad's car, she had a lot to be concerned about.

“You're late; what happened?”

“You wouldn't believe me if I told you.” Clearly depressed, Nina begins walking to the office complex with her closest friend.

“You’d be surprised at the things I believe. Anyway, I don't have to worry about this job; you do. You're so lucky Kreesha's as lazy as you are.”

“I had to deal with Mom this weekend, so don't start with me. OK?” While walking, both salesmen see their district sales manager, Kreesha Mason, a half-Irish, heavyset black female in her early-fifties, drive her late-model Mercedes sedan toward her reserved parking spot.

Under her leadership, the Maryland branch has been a venerable cash cow for the entire company, regularly selling their equipment for two to three times the suggested list price. Recent technological advances by eT's Innovation Department in both wireless and 3-D imaging have caused most of Kreesha's sales team to easily rack up client re-sales and breeze past their third-quarter forecasts. As the two approach their workplace, Kreesha's most trusted salesman momentarily weakens his inquisition.

“Didn't your mom check out of the hospital last night?” asks Konrad. After asking about Mrs. Sullivan, Konrad curls his right index toward her only child, then works to button up Nina's business suit. “You know you can't expose that much skin inside our office. What are your numbers this month? I heard you're at, like, 25 percent of goal.”

Ignoring Konrad's question, Nina looks in the reflective door and views Konrad's conservative interpretation of her business attire.

“I really hope Kreesha doesn't give you your notice today. But she may, because you're the weakest link in our district.”

To escape interacting with their boss earlier than usual, they both walk through the office complex lobby, adorned in gray marble, and toward a glass door marked “efficienTECH” in red.

The lobby is empty except for a Salvadorian janitor in his mid-twenties mopping the floor. Nina, taking notice of the young man's pride in completing his work properly, acknowledges the minimum-wage worker with a heartfelt smile. Konrad, irritated by the worker's baggy, outdated hip-hop style clothing, ignores him as they finally reach their office. Once inside, both eT employees barely acknowledge Denelle quietly sitting at her workstation behind the front desk. The duo walk toward their cubicles in the office's rear section. Denelle peers her head around the connecting hallway, then shouts, “Nina, when Kreesha fires you on Friday, can I take your pencil sharpener?”

Nina, used to ribbing from her abrasive co-worker, shrugs off the comment and walks to her designated mail slot in the bullpen. “Why the fuck don't I have any leads?” she says a little too loudly, pulling her hand out of the empty slot. “I manage the largest and most affluent county in the state of Maryland.”

“Watch your mouth, Ms. Sullivan; we don't talk like that here,” responds Kreesha after tapping her on the back. Somewhat startled, Nina clenches her teeth to muffle an acidic response. Seeing out the corner of her eye that her phone is ringing, Nina jogs to her cubicle, picks up her office phone, and then presses the flashing voicemail button.

* * * * *

Approximately two hours earlier, Nina's childhood friend knocked loudly on the front door of her mother's York apartment. "Mrs. Sullivan! Mrs. Sullivan! It's Bartolo from downstairs. I'm here to check up on you; are you OK?!" he yelled.

After hearing no answer, he kicked down the door and violently stormed into Nina's childhood residence. Oblivious to the loud *boom* behind her, Nina's mother, a heavyset Caucasian woman in her early sixties, sat at her dining room table, transfixed on snorting her next line.

The unknown drug, the end product of dozens masticated prescription pills carelessly arranged on the kitchen table's corner, sat in a small mound next to ten two-inch-long stripes in front of the zoned-out female.

Mrs. Sullivan didn't even acknowledge her intruder, willfully ignoring the SWAT-like entrance while continuing her destructive drug habit.

"Bitch, didn't I tell you to open the fucking door when I knock?!"

Bartolo then grabbed Mrs. Sullivan by her graying ponytail and used the butt of his gun to pistol whip her face. Unrelentingly violent, he forced her forehead against the dilapidated wooden table, sticking his gun at the back of her skull and clicking the safety off his weapon.

A half-hour after Bartolo stormed into Mrs. Sullivan's residence and mercilessly assaulted her, he was inside a phone booth in front of a busy Cracker Barrel not far away. A half-dozen of Bartolo's friends, of similar age and social disposition, surrounded the young Puerto Rican as he left a voicemail for his childhood friend.

* * * * *

When Nina, after cursing aloud about her suspected theft of new business leads, finally receives his message at her cubicle, nearly two hours has elapsed since her mother's turbulent episode with Bartolo. Knowing that making quota will be extremely difficult without the leads Colin stole, in addition to Kreesha's ambivalence regarding the matter, causes a frazzled Nina to ignore most of Bartolo's message about him checking on her mom.

Seeing that her weekly sales forecast meeting is about to begin in the conference room, Nina quickly hangs up her phone before she hears her childhood friend lie by saying, “Yo, I banged on the door for like fifteen minutes; no one came. I wouldn't sweat it; I'm sure your mom's fine.”

A few minutes later, Nina and Dave Palmer, an efficienTECH salesman responsible for driving new business in Anne Arundel County, quietly sit together at one the end of the large, modern conference room table.

“Nina, I was wondering, you know, if you're free . . . umm, if you'd like to shoot some pool with me, and maybe get some drinks afterwards.”

“Didn't Hunter tell you? I'm a nightmare sober, and a whole lot worse when drunk. Trust me, I’m doing you a favor by saying no.”

Denelle, without acknowledging Dave and Nina, walks into the room and places a handful of PowerPoint presentations on top of the table's opposite end. Konrad sneaks in the conference room behind Coleman and smiles while putting his hand on her thigh.

“Hey, Konrad . . .” slyly replies Denelle, provocatively arching her back.

Dave shakes his head in revulsion. Nina points her index finger to her open mouth and pretends to gag. “Keep that hate up, Nina,” replies a suddenly serious Konrad. Denelle, somewhat embarrassed, quietly retreats to the front desk.

“I can't believe you hit that, Hunter.”

“Yo, she doesn't shave her bush. It's like a jungle; sometimes it makes me wonder how I keep from going under!” roars Konrad, who does his best Grandmaster Flash impression for emphasis. Nina, still very much stressed, can't help but laugh.

While the efficienTECH employees raucously debate the structure of Denelle's vulva, the country's most pursued criminal suspect exits his parked Chevy Caprice. A few dozen miles from Nina's office, and much closer to Macklin's location at MCPD headquarters, the serial killer walks lightly into a patch of woods behind a Rockville middle school.

Chapter 8

The killer is an athletic, wiry, middle-aged man. While Nina was at work, the sniper was dressed in black hiking boots, green military-style pants, and a zipped black fleece. Walking toward his pre-determined destination on a public school's periphery, he held a stuffed, medium-sized duffle bag. After looking over his shoulder, the killer quickly retrieved a pair of metal hand spikes from his satchel and used them to scale an imposing oak tree. The murderer then silently hopped from the tree's trunk and straddled a thick branch fifteen feet off the ground.

Back at efficienTECH's Maryland office in Rockville, more of Nina's coworkers meander into the conference room.

Nina, in order to alleviate her own anxiety, pulls out her Palm Pilot and begins to play electronic spades. After cleaning crumbs from her second chin, Kreesha finally starts the meeting. "As you know, this is the last week to turn in orders so you can get your machines delivered by Devil's Night. Regardless of everything going on inside and out of this office, there's no reason not to be selling. We're in danger of losing grip of majority market share because, as you know, Xerox introduced a new box last month to compete directly with our fifty-page-per-minute all-in-one machine. Headquarters chewed me out all day Friday, so you know what rolls downhill."

Kreesha swallows her last confectionary bite, hardens her face, and continues.

"Again. There's no reason for any salesperson in this room not to be selling."

Nina, knowing that Kreesha is indirectly referencing her, nervously adjusts her sitting position. "From what I see here, some of you are desperately in need of a sale. Remember, in order to reach quota, all orders have to be in by Friday at noon. Let's go over what everyone is working to close this week."

Gabriella Francisco, a twenty-four-year-old Caucasian saleswoman representing Baltimore County, is the first to speak.

"I'm picking up a deal for two ET5000s this afternoon. That should easily get me to my quarterly goal."

Colin, not to be outdone, butts in.

"Kreesha, I'll be at 200 percent of goal by the end of the week. Don't even sweat it."

"That's great, you two. Especially you, Colin; you're really killing it. Maybe I should raise your quota."

"Or you could lower Nina's. That would eliminate dead weight," quips Colin. Everyone in the room, except for Konrad and Nina, begins to giggle. Nina, trying to remain composed, ignores Colin's wisecrack and continues to play cards on her personal organizer. As Nina electronically cuts a nine of hearts with a jack of spades, Konrad intercedes.

"Look, Colin, your fat ass doesn't have to duck sniper shots while doing cold calls like Sullivan."

"Not to mention all the client leads you continuously steal from me. Care to comment, douchebag?" adds Nina.

"Trust me, no efficienTECH employee is stealing business opportunities from another co-worker. It's one big family here, and everyone benefits when their coworker is successful." responds Kreesha.

"Everyone knows you fucked your way into this company, Sullivan. So it's kinda funny, and ironic, to see you fucked when sex can no longer advance your career," says Colin, smiling.

With the precision of a virtuoso, Nina hurls her Palm Pilot at Colin's puffy face. The Treo 650 disintegrates on impact, instantly breaking Colin's nose and chipping his two front teeth.

Meanwhile, in a more densely populated section of Montgomery County, the FBI's most wanted suspect tightly grasps a Bushmaster rifle. Satisfied with the shot he just fired from the tree branch, the serial killer smiles while softly jumping to the ground. After tiptoeing through the wooded, trail-less area accounting for his most recent escape route, the suspect nods to his accomplice located behind the steering wheel of their getaway vehicle. Their car is located in a residential parking lot designated for commuting via the Maryland Area Regional Commuter (MARC) train line. In desperate need of a shower and warm meal, the two psychopaths, satisfied with their work, leave the uninhabited parking lot and escape into routine, mid-morning suburban traffic.

Minutes later, after the two serial killers make their way to a YMCA in Silver Spring, Nina stands outside of the chaotic efficienTECH conference room, biting her nails. Two hardware technicians, along with Kreesha, lead a dazed Colin from the office hallway and toward the first-floor bathroom opposite the eT entrance. Before walking into the lobby, Konrad turns to Nina and says, “What the hell's your problem, Sullivan?! He was only joking.”

Nina passively looks at Colin, who looks like he's on the verge of losing consciousness.

“Go make some colds calls, and get out of my sight. You have till noon on Friday to close a deal or you're fired!” shouts Kreesha.

Konrad grabs a few rolls of paper towels and industrial cleanser from a cabinet below the kitchen sink and begins to spray and pat down a trail of blood approximately ten yards long, originating from the disbanded meeting and winding all the way to the lobby. Cleaning on all fours, he delicately motions to Nina that he'll call her as soon as possible. “It's best you leave—like, right now,” he says under his breath.

As Nina drives away, Kreesha stands with her oldest executive in the men's washroom. In a motherly fashion, she attempts to wipe Colin's blood off of his stained, tan dress shirt. “What's wrong with you; why didn't you fire her on the spot?” he asks.

“Take it off and hand it to me. I'll drop it off at the dry cleaners during my lunch hour,” replies Kreesha in a warm, southernly fashion. “I hate to admit it, but if I fire Nina this late in the year, then hire and train a new rep for her territory, I'm not going to have anyone to nurture and close her previous opportunities by December 31. Our board of directors is extremely cutthroat, and after a theoretic drop in sales, I could definitely see them deciding that there's too much overhead for us to remain open. After efficienTECH sales decreased 15 percent in Southern California last summer, headquarters closed the San Diego office mid-year with no warning to the staff—not even an e-mail sent to their district manager. At the end of the day, they could decide we're dispensable and close us down, too, then sell our product wholesale through established retailers like Staples and Office Depot. I can't give them that option by firing Sullivan. So, Colin, you see how the negatives of doing so, at least at this point, far outweigh the positives of letting that crazy bitch go."

Chapter 9

Back in North Laurel, Nina hastily enters her apartment, tripping over a pile of junk mail slid through the front door letter slot. Exhausted, tired, and depressed, Nina strips off her jacket and skirt and then slumps on the couch.

Meanwhile, inside a dirty living room within an off-campus apartment, blocks away from UMD, a quirky electrical-engineering student relaxes with his roommate by playing his Sega Dreamcast. The sixth-year English major, Anthony Chen, perfectly content with missing his fourth class of the day, hallucinates off the last tab of acid he just licked. Dazed and confused, he tries to stand from his friend's upright futon but ends up stumbling into his outdated television. Brian Tucker, an aspiring computer programmer, softly pushes Anthony to the ground with his heel. “There, that'll teach you to try and test me at NBA 2K; you'll never beat me when I use the Lakers,” says the inebriated senior, tossing the video game controller at Anthony's back. Clearly tripping, Anthony relocates his undersized, Taiwanese-American body toward to the living room's corner and crawls into a ball.

“Marshall, come here right now!”

Brian and Anthony giggle as their third roommate fails to appear upon command.

“Lord, why have you always cursed me with demonic roommates?” says the stressed student to himself while banging his surprisingly large fist on his IKEA bedroom dresser.

With a pencil stuck in between his skull and left ear, Quincy Marshall, self-nicknamed “iQ” for his aptitude at retaining information at a genius-like level, angrily appears from his small bedroom located at the opposite side of the dingy, first-floor, off-campus apartment. Eager to take a break from studying, the struggling undergraduate student, resembling a younger, lighter version of Konrad, mopes his way toward the living room.

“Wow, you two are fucked up. You know I have to get my problem sets finished before class; what’d you guys want?”

“Go to the kitchen, boil me the rest of the mushrooms on the counter, and then bring us two cups of tea. Do it now,” orders Anthony.

“Stop irritating me; I can't afford to not finish my homework before tomorrow's Chem lab,” angrily responds Quincy.

“And I can't afford to cover you for rent again; don't you remember that you owe me for four months?” In a vain attempt to his assuage the hysterical nineteen-year-old, Quincy softens his face before responding to Chen's inquiry.

“I told you, I'll find a decent job and pay you back once mid-terms are done.”

“Stop being full of shit. No one told you to take Organic Chemistry and study for the MCATs during the same semester. That's suicide.”

Quincy, realizing that he's fighting a war he can't win, stands down and asks for mercy.

“It's only early October; please just give me till November to repay you two. I'll figure out a way how; don't worry.” Brian, also experiencing the same paranoid delusions Anthony's experiencing, shows his acquaintance no sympathy.

“I'm tired of your shit. Come up with the $1500 you owe by the end of the week or get out. Now go get us our ‘shroom tea, Marshall, and add honey to mine.”

Quincy, needing to stay calm in order to finish his schoolwork, walks past the kitchen and slams his bedroom door before locking himself inside his alcove.

* * * * *

As Quincy puts on his headphones, Mrs. Sullivan tolerantly sits in the grimy waiting room of the Leader Heights Healthcare Center in York. It’s a quarter past one—a couple hours after Nina broke Colin's nose. Mrs. Sullivan, unaware of her only child's violent actions, struggles to maintain consciousness as she, and hundreds of Pennsylvanians, wait for their socialized medical evaluation. The threadbare Leader Heights waiting room is packed with older, lower-income Caucasians and African-Americans, along with a sizable minority of undocumented Latinos—all anguishing from a variety of ailments including emphysema, obesity, heart disease, cancer, and diabetes. In order to keep the procession of patients orderly, four police officers, moonlighting as armed security guards, stand at both passageways of the large, fenestra-less room.

Behind a bulletproof glass partition at the room's north side sits a young Dominican-American female. An hour and half after Nina's mother writes her name on the waiting list, the young woman blankly announces, “Mrs. Sullivan? Mrs. Sullivan, the doctor will see you now.”

Nina's mother finally begins to receive the medical attention she requires, as her daughter is stretched on her living room sofa, fixated on the blood stain the fallen bird left earlier on the balcony’s glass door. Nina, wearing nothing more than pink cotton panties and a long Yankees t-shirt with the last name “SORIANO” embroidered on the back, is on the verge of taking a midday nap when her cellphone rings, abruptly interrupting her impending slumber.

“What do you want?”

“Do you know the serial killer shot someone else this morning?”

“Are you serious? Don't fuck with me like that, Hunter; it's bad karma.”

“No bullshit, it was a little kid this time. Eight years old—outside a middle school in Germantown.”

“What the fuck?”

“It's crazy, I know. I haven't officially heard that the boy's dead yet, but he's now in critical condition, fighting for his life.”

Nina shakes her head in disbelief as her ex-lover continues. She grabs her remote and turns the TV to CNN.

Meanwhile, back in York, the front desk attendant at Leader Heights rudely claps for Mrs. Sullivan to walk faster. Struggling through a crowded hallway, which acts as a main artery for dozens of exam rooms, Nina's mother puts her hand on the wall to maintain balance as an overwhelmed doctor motions her forward. Mrs. Sullivan, once regaining her breath, walks inside the ten-by-ten-foot windowless box inhabited by two medical professionals.

Patiently sitting on a metal stool in the room's corner, a stone-faced nurse instructs Mrs. Sullivan to disrobe behind a shielded partition, adorn a disposable hospital gown, and step on top of a scale. As she does, the primary care physician standing next to her smiles and says, "Mrs. Sullivan, you must really love us. We just discharged you yesterday for your depression and perceived elevated heart rate; now you're back to see us eighteen hours later. Please be honest with us and tell me the truth: How did you get that large bruise covering your eye and cheekbone?"

The nurse gently tugs at Nina's mother, who's now naked except for a flimsy paper robe covering her overweight frame. She then motions for her to sit on the wax-paper-covered exam table. Mrs. Sullivan, sighing in a manner similar to her daughter when trying to relieve stress, remains silent as the doctor washes his hands and then puts on a pair of plastic gloves.

"I'm only here to help you, Mrs. Sullivan," gently adds the concerned physician.

"I slipped out of the wet tub this morning and accidentally banged my face on the floor as I tried to grab the sink."

The attending nurse quickly writes on her log book that Nina's mother's injures are probably the end result of blunt force, but could also be self-inflicted in order to legally secure more painkillers. The nurse, a portly lady slightly older than

Mrs. Sullivan, gives a handheld magnification instrument to the inspecting doctor, who in turn uses it closely view one of Mrs. Sullivan's pupils.

The doctor finishes inspecting Mrs. Sullivan and then moves on to her medical history chart. “Atrial Fibrillation . . . mother of God, we just discharged you yesterday for overdosing on your arthritis medication. Mrs. Sullivan, I'm weary of giving you any more meds; can we trust you not to overdose again?”

“Sir, you see I've been . . . I've been very stressed lately. Some family issues have really gotten me down. I’m doing better, though—this was just an accident.”

“Your addiction to pain medication isn't the answer. It wouldn't surprise me if you had someone punch you on purpose to get another prescription,” replies the nurse.

The doctor dissents the nurse's opinion. “Although that could be the case, with your face in this condition, I can't in good conscience let you leave here without at least a few days’ worth of something strong enough to at least make this sort of eye-socket injury bearable. If you need any more, though, you’ll need to come back when this prescription runs out—unfortunately I don’t think it’s a good idea for you to have a longer-term prescription just now. If you continue down this perilous path, I’m afraid the next time I'll see you will be in a morgue.”

Nina, back in Laurel with a bowl of chopped salad in her hand, opens her front door and lets Konrad enter her premises.

“What was that all about this morning? Why'd you snap like that?”

“efficienTECH will never own my attention or emotions, Hunter. It's just a job to pay the rent. Nothing more, nothing less; let it go.”

“Really? Just a salad? I’m such a better chef than you, even if I only have processed ingredients to work with.”

Konrad takes a seat in front of Nina's TV, grabs her lunch, and begins to eat.

Chapter 10

In Rockville, outside MCPD headquarters, Chief Macklin wavers behind a podium in front of eager reporters. Ten feet to the right of Macklin, outside the widescreen view of cameras documenting his incompetence, stoically stands FBI Detective Adams and EMT Nicole Freeman along with a preoccupied Lieutenant Patrick.

"Unless directed otherwise, don't make a public statement on the debacle this afternoon—or in the future. This directive comes directly from the White House," reads a text message in Adams' inbox, sent seconds ago from Director Henson.

"Today . . . today it went down to the children," begins a clearly shaken Macklin into a cluster of black television microphones, each designating a local, national, or international conglomerate media outlet.

The Chief wipes drops of sweat off his forehead, then struggles to continue as his eyes water. Nicole, wishing she could console her mentor and closest confidant on the police force, painfully watches him commandeer his first press conference of the week. She begins to sob as Macklin momentarily loses focus of his hastily prepared speech. But as flashbulbs illuminate the facade of Macklin's resolve, the embattled chief continues. “Someone is so mean-spirited that they shot a child. Now we're stepping over the line, because our children don't deserve this. So parents, please do your job tonight. Engage your kids; tell them every day that you love them. We're going to need our community to stay as strong as ever, because shooting a kid . . . I don't know; I guess it's getting to be really personal right now.”

* * * * *

Back in North Laurel, Konrad finishes the last morsels of Nina's lunch while Nina stuffs two crushed nuggets into her four-inch-long glass pipe. “I like Macklin. He reminds me of Carl Winslow from Family Matters.”

“Yo, you get that zip from York? Did Bartolo mail it to your work address again?”

“Yeah, he also sent me some grams of ketamine last week, but it didn't come in today—unless Colin stole it.”

While taking the burning pipe from Nina, Konrad refocuses his attention on the television. “You're crazy. Everyone knows that brother's a joke. The public has absolutely no confidence in Macklin.”

Nina's attention zig-zags between different subjects that, on the surface, bear no relation to each other. She replies, “Yeah, Bartolo's good like that. He also stops by my mom once in a while to check up on her.”

Konrad inhales the powerful NYC Diesel and exhales through his long, thin nose. "No question, that's what friends are for. You know you broke Colin's septum this morning, right?"

"This country spends billions to find a so-called terrorist, who's supposedly hiding somewhere in the Kush mountains, but can't even find a domestic one minutes away from the nation's capital. You know, maybe this maniac is a NFL fan, because he never kills on Sunday. Think about it," responds Nina.

"All of this, Nina, all of this chaos and strife in the world, from Maryland to Kabul to Nigeria, boils down to two sides. Two sides controlled from a different dimension."

"Go on, Alchemist; I'm listening." Nina puts the television on mute and then buries her inebriated head underneath a sheet.

It's at this specific time, on this specific October afternoon, that I feel my Opponent, who I'll only give the attention he craves when necessary, plug in the soul of Konrad to our dimension and officially designate him the leader of new rebellion, with powers enabling him to accomplish whatever he desires. Jealous that he didn't find Nina first, my Opponent found the next best human to designate as his most powerful chess piece opposite Nina in this global game of world domination—her first true love: Konrad.

"In society, here on planet Earth that gives life and death to the most docile and savage human beings, there are two types of people, irrespective of their age, religion, or race. Every person in this world, regardless if they're conscious of it or not, belongs to one of two camps, two organizations, two squads," begins Konrad.

"You mean like the Ravens and Redskins? What the fuck are you talking about?" casually responds Nina.

Nina grabs a Dos Equis lager from the fridge and plops back on the couch at the opposite corner of Konrad's nestled location.

"The football analogy could work, especially when describing the general manager that hires and fires members of their respective roster. But let's also describe this power struggle in chess terminology, for transparency and clarity. Now each team has their own operatives, or players, who work in in unison to defeat the other team, similar to how chess pieces work."

"The sensi is hitting you harder that you think."

"Listen to me," he responds, slurring only a little. "The vast majority of operatives behave in a manner indigenous to their side, which, for simplification, I'll regard to as characteristics, ideals, and ambitions that are strictly black and white in nature. But this game isn't standard chess, but a variant of the game mastered by Kasparov and Capablanca; so an operative may end up being a combination of both colors, or traded from one side to another while this game unfolds. General managers that represent the interests of both organizations have the power to manipulate this character to each sides' benefit."

Konrad pauses his rant for a moment to take another deep hit.

"Moving on, the characteristics of both the Black and White side are obviously more salient than their designated shade. For example, all mercenaries, objectivists only interested in making money by any means necessary, rep the Black side. Conversely, all progressives, wanting only harmony, fairness of opportunity, and equality of mankind, advance Unitarian goals enveloped within the White side."

Nina attempts to change the channel, but can't pull away from viewing the teary-eyed Chief Macklin still standing in front of MCPD headquarters.

"Go on, this is interesting," she says, still not looking at him.

"The Black side is controlled via a triage of evil. This triangular organizational structure consists of the music industry, mainstream movie conglomerates, and Wall Street, which I'll also refer to as corporate America. In a macro sense, Hollywood actors, along with Zionist directors, use film as a medium to convince members of the White side to consume—both directly via blockbusters and sequels and indirectly through a self-metastasizing celebrity culture. This equation has also been enacted to create a herd mentality. These particular sections of the triumvirate work hand-in-hand with other facets of corporate America to elicit ideals that condone violence, unnecessary pantophagy, materialism, and hyper-sexuality. From a popular actor advocating credit card use via TV commercials to a director producing a video game that encourages rape and vehicle theft, it's all scripted and disseminated by the Black side."

"How does the music industry fit into all of this?"

"A significant minority on the White side are brainwashed by mainstream and independent artists alike: influenced by songs that embrace vanity, self-obsession, immortality, and desecration of family structures essential for social harmony. This is done in order to convince White-siders to eschew their embedded values and join the ranks of the other side. It's a never-ending struggle."

Nina presses pause on her DVR remote before finally turning and gazing into Konrad's eyes.

"That's the same bowl I use DMT for, and I'm sure you accidentally smoked some remnants of it. That's why you're bugging out."

While Konrad's thought process expands centrifugally, he curls into a tight ball and clutches a pillow sewn by Nina weeks ago.

"Alright, I'm sorry. Continue your point and stay calm," says Nina.

"Wall Street banks make up the third, and most clandestine, member of the Black side's triage. Their whole goal, and meaning for existence, is to increase the death rate of those on the White side. They do this via a variety of methods, including—"

"OK, Nostradamus, which side is the serial killer on? Since you can read into the future, what agenda does he have?"

"That's to be determined I guess. But I'm sure his pharmacist would be able to know," says Konrad, who smiles while re-straightening his tie.

Now that his upload is complete, Konrad stands and walks to the kitchen to make some coffee.

* * * * *

"Do you know that if Kreesha weren't so desperate to make her district quota, she would have fired you on the spot this morning?"

“There are definitely other ways for one to get their point across. On another note, Ronnie's driving down from Greenpoint Wednesday night.”

Ronnie Bryant, Nina's former career adviser and a Brooklyn native, is a business professor assistant at NYU working toward his doctorate. A few years older than Konrad, the trustafarian is the only son of a hedge fund manager in Manhattan.

“Damn, I forgot. What ignorance is he trying to get into?” casually asks Konrad.

“His boyfriend bought him a Porsche for his birthday, so he wanted to drive to DC and experience Howard Homecoming. But since that isn't for a few weeks, he was thinking of hitting up one of those bro lounges in Georgetown and maybe taking in a Wizards game the next night,” responds Nina.

Back at Police Headquarters in Rockville, Chief Macklin walks away from the outdoor podium on top of the entrance's uppermost front steps. On his way to his assembled, makeshift team of Adams, Patrick, and Nicole, the shaken chief keeps his head down while ignoring stinging questions from established national reporters.

“Have you made any contact with the serial killer?”

“How come you haven't released a composite sketch of what the murderer looks like?”

“What role are the federal and state government playing in assisting the manhunt of the killer?”

Back at the younger Sullivan's apartment in North Laurel, Konrad stares at Nina, then stands.

"Get up"

"Why?" replies Nina, still sober.

"You've worked that PWI account all summer. Let's go squeeze an order out of them, so Kreesha can get off your back. They're located just outside of Damascus, right?"

"In this war zone? There's been three, possibly four unsolved murders by long range assault rifles in my territory this month, and you think *now's* a good time to do cold calls?"

"Look, bitch. While you were here, probably taking a nap, Kreesha and I begged headquarters to keep you on board. They only relented from firing you, pursuing criminal charges for assaulting and breaking Colin's nose earlier today, and finally suing you for breaching eT's conduct code after I told them you had a high-six-figure order from PWI headed their way in a few days. If you don't close that deal by Friday, you're looking for a new job in this recession come Saturday. And don't dress like a slut, either; their gatekeeper won't let you past the front desk if you flash too much skin. Meet me downstairs in ten minutes, and bring your stash; we can smoke on the way back here."

Nina, used to his sometimes erratic, almost bipolar behavior, realizes that if she doesn't go with him, she'll definitely be on Monster.com this weekend searching for a new job; she throws on some work clothes, locks her apartment, and joins Konrad in his car.

Fifteen minutes later, at around 2:46 p.m., only a few hours after Bartolo assaulted Nina's mom in York, the two are headed west on the Patuxent Freeway, fighting through mid-afternoon traffic toward their destination.

"Hollywood lies to us, all day
The question is what does your culture say
Where's your culture at?
Who's your prophet?
What history guides your spiritual logic?
It starts with a story, then it's hypnotic
Then any myth that comes along, you just adopted it
Why?"

The greatest rapper of all-time plays through Konrad's speakers.

Located in the driver's seat, Konrad turns down the KRS-One track, then asks, "What's really troubling you? You usually make your yearly quota by August."

Before Nina can muster an answer, Konrad dry-swallows six ephedra pills.

"I think this over-hyped sniper drama has made my mom crazier than usual."

"Stop being myopic; your mom doesn't get high because there's a psycho killer on the loose. Your mom gets high 'cause she's a fucking crackhead; that's what crackheads do."

"Leave me alone."

"What!? Calling you up every night, drunk and high. All she does is bleed your money. She's nothing more than a fucking parasite."

"Oh, you don't know, man? About they programs?. . .You still watching Lindsay, you don't see that low hand?" interjects KRS.

"You look great, just be yourself and you'll be fine," says Konrad eight minutes later, ushering Nina toward an underground office door demarcated "PHARMACEUTICAL WHOLESALE INCORPORATED."

"Lancaster's only a half-hour east from home, and I was thinking of taking some classes at Franklin and Marshall, then eventually getting my master's in Public Policy somewhere back in NYC. Plus, I'm the only family Mom has since dad left us years ago."

"You've got too much talent in sales. I'm not letting you leave me at eT," quietly retorts Konrad while entering PWI's threadbare lobby.

"Thanks for your support, but it's not your choice, Konrad."

Oh, the paradox of free will and the irrelevance of time. Two concepts intertwined within these two, on multiple levels, now and forever. My Opponent and I both notice that Konrad enjoys delivering pain while Nina's psyche savors receiving it.

So even though I know she can withstand an abrupt greeting, I choose a more indirect, proven method in order to say hello

Chapter 11

At the other end of the mostly empty, dusty, depressingly sterile twenty-by-ten-foot room sits a homely woman in her late fifties behind an unlamented wooden desk. The gatekeeper, Ms. Ashley Simmons, looks up from her modern desktop computer and then smiles at the patiently silent salesmen. Konrad, not wanting to destroy the chemistry between Nina and her contacts, retreats to the corner of room and sits in a tacky, uncomfortable chair. He then peruses through a stack of outdated gossip and nature magazines while Nina and Ashley banter in a friendly, superficial manner.

"Hey, I haven't seen you here in almost a month; how are you?"

"Hi, Ms. Simmons. My co-worker and I were in the area and decided to stop in and see Curtis. Is he in?"

"Sure, let me see if he's free." Ashley picks up her standard black office phone and dials the office of PWI's Information Technology manager, Mr. Curtis Sharpton.

* * * * *

Thirty-seven miles from Konrad and Nina's location, in Montgomery County's adjacent province of Prince George County, Quincy dispassionately waits in line at the Bursar's office, located within the immaculately landscaped South Campus of UMD. Desperately seeking relief from his most recent financial aid statement, the Cali native quickly departs the grumbling thirty-person queue as a financial aid officer motions him over to his partitioned booth.

“Good afternoon, how can I help you?”

“Hello, I . . . I need to get an extension for my student loan debt ceiling,” responds Quincy, stuttering a little as he looks toward the ground with his shoulders slumped.

“Sure, I just need you to sign some paperwork. Student ID please?” As the Officer inspects Quincy's account, the timorous pre-med student twirls his keys in his right hand.

“I'm sure you probably know this already, but it seems that you've already overdrawn your account. Until you remedy this with a sizable deposit, your balance won't cover tuition for the upcoming spring semester. And obviously, you won't be able to register for new classes until this debt is resolved.” Quincy, while remaining silent, squirms as a second financial aid officer approaches.

“I'm sorry, but our records indicate your account is ten months past due. Is there anyone that can help you resolve this matter so UMD isn't forced to expel you?” Embarrassed, Quincy slowly backs away from the window and then leaves the Bursar's office without responding.

* * * * *

Back in Damascus, Curtis strides into the waiting area of PWI's headquarters. Curtis, a homely looking white male in his mid-forties, smiles at Nina. Dressed in casual, Walmart-brand attire, the fifteen-year employee of Pharmaceutical Wholesale Incorporated ignores Konrad but greets Nina with an inappropriate hug. “Hi, Nina; this is an unexpected surprise,” he whispers into her ear.

Politely extricating herself from his clutches, she says, “My associate and I were just in the area and decided—”

“You could have called and scheduled a meeting, but it’s fine, we can talk for a half-hour or so. And at least you'll be safe from all the violence outside. I'm surprised there aren't any bullet holes in your business suit.”

At this point, Curtis finally acknowledges Konrad's presence in the corner of the stale waiting area. “Unfortunately, due to corporate policy, we're only able to let in salespeople we know past the front lobby . . . no offense.”

Konrad jumps from his chair and extends his hand toward Curtis. “Konrad Hunter. Regional sales director—”

Without shaking his hand, Curtis turns toward Nina and adds, “Also, because of terrorism concerns, we've had to beef up our security around here. Ashley, keep Ms. Sullivan's clearance active until the end of the year; that should be more than enough time for us to conclude business.”

As Curtis verbally blocks Konrad from encroaching any further on PWI property, a smallish, East Indian man exits the metal door separating the lobby from the office's main section.

Without acknowledging Curtis, Nina, or Ashley, the aforementioned individual, dressed in a lab coat, glances nervously at Konrad and leaves PWI's reception area. Konrad, uninterested in hearing Curtis' discursive lecture on PWI's corporate history, market share, and future ambitions, says, "No problem. I'll wait in the car," before turning around and leaving. A few minutes later, both Nina and Curtis casually walk through a twenty-foot-wide concrete hallway. On the left side of the commuter room, covering its entire length, sits an elevated, slightly tinted plexiglass window about fifty yards in length and fifteen feet in height. Nina, taken aback by PWI's inner workings, stays quiet while Curtis affably ushers her to his office located at the couloir's opposite end. But what's on the window's opposite side, easily covering the entire length of the hallway, makes her momentarily forget the swirling thoughts inside her head.

"You've never taken me past this room before," says Nina while Curtis unprofessionally puts his hand on her thigh. Caught off-guard by what her eyes view, she arches her back away from him while pressing her nose against the plexiglass. As her escort remains giddily silent, she watches hundreds of thousands of small pills machinating through four large silver processing machines. At the end of the humongous machines are robotic arms attached to steel pillars. Each arm extension, approximately ten yards in length when fully erect, has a giant scooping apparatus fastened to its end.

"Wild stuff, right? As you probably surmised, computers run that whole room. Each day, we get industrial size quantities of various types of prescription medication delivered here from the largest pharmaceutical companies in the world. After our quality control team properly tabulates each order, a rough estimate of hundreds of thousands of pills are placed at the beginning of the conveyor belt. From there, the robotic arms scoop tens of thousands of pills off the belt and puts them in specified plastic bags encased within oil drums at the room's westernmost point," says the excited IT manager, pointing to green oil drums arranged in dozens of clusters against the antiseptic room's far wall.

"Wow. For the most part, what type of pills do you distribute to the immediate area?"

"The vast majority of our Paxil, one of our top five imports, is distributed to Walter Reed in Bethesda. The soldiers back from duty use it to help with their depression and posttraumatic stress disorder. As I'm sure you know, PTSD is a huge problem after our recent invasion of a sovereign nation in the Middle East," answers Curtis, referring to the Iraq War.

Now upstairs with Nina, Curtis opens the glass door to his sleek, ultra-modern corner office, noted for its expansive, western views of Little Bennett Regional Park. While smiling at Nina, he chaperones her to his mahogany leather sectional pinned into the far corner of a pair of floor-to-ceiling window panels. Curtis then grabs a pair of water bottles, along with his laptop, and pretends to fall into a couch seat next to her.

"We also ship out large consignments of Vicodin throughout the Mid-Atlantic region. However, eighty-eight percent of PWI's shipments in the immediate area consist of morphine—in its pill form, of course. I can't make a direct correlation to what's happened in this region lately, with this madman on the loose, but we've seen an uptick in orders to Montgomery County hospitals and pharmacies since the serial killer shot his first Maryland victim this month. Unprovoked, unapologetic violence is good for business, I guess."

Konrad, six floors below, desperately sprints twenty yards toward the same retreating Indian employee who just exited the PWI lobby. Resembling a Tanzanian cheetah, Konrad uses acute angles to swiftly navigate through parked vehicles and trip the middle-aged man from behind. This violent motion, which occurs in between two dimly lit rows of parked cars, causes the 5'5 male to tumble face-first into the underground, oil-stained black top, simultaneously spraining his jaw and wrist in the process.

Konrad picks up the injured man by the back of his collar and raises him to his knees.

“Didn't you get my message? You knew I was fucking coming, right?” whispers Konrad in the East-Indian's left ear while using his right hand to choke his Lilliputian neck.

“Nadir, I told you I need my shipment now!” screams Konrad at a decibel level that would make eardrums bleed.

Dr. Nadir Jayaraman, a PhD-accredited engineer, chemist, and biologist, originally from the East Indian state of Karnataka, grabs his sore jaw while wiping gravel off his forehead.

“Konrad, I told you that I can't do it myself anymore. It's the truth,” whines Nadir. Konrad stands and easily hoists the terrified scientist to a height of seventy inches; causing the doctor's painfully thin legs dangle helplessly in the air.

“Wrong answer!” shrieks Konrad after quickly surveying the underground enclosure. Double-checking that only he and his detainee are in the immediate area, Konrad twists Nadir's frame in a 360 motion and then painfully cracks his neck by shifting it abruptly to his collar bone.

Nadir, between soft cries of agony, mumbles, "Neither you nor I have the ability now to get your shipment—not with PWI's updated security clearances . . ."

Back upstairs, Curtis, not picking up Nina's red-light signal, leans unethically close to his designated eT rep and then places a spreadsheet printout on her lap. "As I initially stated during our first meeting in July, I'll personally guarantee that our firm can reduce your electrical and document production operating costs by 35 percent," softly says Nina. Trying to take small breaths of air to avoid Curtis' halitosis, she wishes that Konrad had been allowed to fully accompany her to this unscheduled meeting so that they could collectively close this account together, even if it meant sharing the commission and quota revenue with her grumpy ex-boyfriend. "I've been with my organization for almost half a decade and feel that your firm would be the crown jewel of my client list. Are you looking to make a purchasing decision today?" she adds.

"Well . . . to be honest, I'm still waiting to hear from our chief technology officer at our headquarters in Seattle. That should take no longer than a few weeks. In the meantime, I see no reason why we can't get to know each other better."

Nina nimbly removes Curtis' palm from her lower thigh and quickly grabs her belongings.

"I understand where you're going, and will take what you've said under consideration. Please keep me in the loop over the coming weeks, and we'll set up another meeting detailing our installation process."

Ten minutes later, Curtis and Nina reenter PWI's first floor entrance lobby. Still politely conversing with one another, they see Konrad, who's back in the lobby corner chair, say sternly into his cellphone, “No excuses; take care of it now.”

There's no physical evidence on Konrad's frame of his thrashing of Nadir, who immediately drove away after Konrad sent him sprawling toward the blacktop for a second time.

As Ashley looks on, the awkward-looking IT manager kisses Nina's cheek, and again completely ignores Konrad's presence. Disgusted for different reasons, both efficienTECH employees exit the office complex, then walk by themselves back to Konrad’s sedan. “You know, times are desperate enough for you that sleeping with him would have not only kept you employed, but given you at least twenty K in commission. Those twenty g’s would have erased your personal debt and really helped your mom out.”

Before Nina can respond to Konrad's harsh-but-honest assessment of her reality, she gets a call from Kreesha on her cell. “Hi, I meant to call you and apologize,” begins Nina. “I just got out of a great meeting with PWI. And I'm pretty sure, barring any unforeseen circumstances, that I'll be able to close them for a six-figure order by Friday.”

“Nina, do you know how much grief headquarters has given me over you the last seven hours?! A promise is a promise. If you don't get that business in four days—” trumpets Kreesha.

Before the twenty-five-year copier sales veteran can continue, Nina hangs up her phone in disgust. “I can't worry about her; it'll work itself out in a few days I'm sure.”

“She's going to make your life a living hell this week,” warns Konrad. “Mentally prepare yourself for it, because this isn't a normal verbal or written warning based on weak performance. For you, this is life or death.”

Nina, feeling unusually lightheaded, puts her seat to “cool” by pressing the passenger seat comfort button located to the right of the car’s center console.

“I can't stop sweating, or catch my breath, and my skin feels clammy. Why do I suddenly feel so faint?” says Nina.

Konrad, genuinely concerned, reaches into his glove compartment and grabs a second bottle—this time one marked “Vitamin C.”

“I don't know why, but while Curtis was hitting on me I kept thinking about your lunchtime diatribe regarding the two sides, locked in a chess match, constantly fighting throughout all aspects of society. It was so random.”

Konrad, restraining comment, pulls his car into a gas station to refuel.

This particular Lukoil has a hundred-foot-long tarp extending between both drive-in entrances. Hastily constructed to safeguard customers from the uncaught serial killer, the plastic shield is anchored by concrete poles on its lower corners.

“Which side are you on, Konrad: Black or White?”

“Huh, what are you talking about?” responds Konrad, refusing to make eye contact with his passenger.

Chapter 12

Back in York, Mrs. Sullivan is alone in her gloomy, unkempt apartment. Nina's past achievements, from her youth gymnastics trophies to her NYU Certificate for Outstanding Achievement in the field of psychology, litter the homemade mantle above the broken furnace; as much as dust and cat hair cover the cold, wooden ground. The dual decrepit polyester couches covered in clear plastic are too large for Mrs. Sullivan's railroad-style living room, causing them to face one another at an uncomfortably close distance.

Nina's biological mother, ignoring the stench of spoiled food emanating from the kitchen, is lying stretched out on the filthy carpet close to an open window acting as a visual, auditory, and free-flowing canvas of jeopardous urban life. Turning away from watching young men on the corner selling crack, Mrs. Sullivan, in a drug induced stupor and barely grasping reality, picks up her portable phone and then slowly dials Nina's home number. After eight rings, Nina, who's also lying alone in her top-floor apartment, reluctantly picks up her phone.

“Hi, Mom; how are you feeling this Monday night? Bartolo left me a voicemail that he checked up on you this morning.”

Nina feels drained, which seems unusual to her after taking a two-hour nap minutes after Konrad dropped her off. Too dizzy and lightheaded to stand, she gets on her hands and knees, then crawls four feet to retrieve the TV remote from the living room carpet.

I'm in the best shape of my life and quit cigarettes five years ago. Why am I so short of breath for no reason? thinks Nina, clutching her chest. Even with the air conditioning at full blast, Nina’s still experiencing some of the same unwarranted perspiration issues that plagued her a few hours back in Konrad's car.

On Nina's TV, with the volume set low, is the Monday Night Football halftime show for the game between the Raiders and Chiefs. Al Michaels, the longtime announcer for MNF, interrupts the injury report and gives an update on developments concerning the local serial killer.

“Welcome back to Monday Night Football. Although my partner and I usually spend this time dissecting action from the first half, I'd be remiss if I didn't notify you of developments with regards to the recent, horrific events in the southern and mid-Atlantic regions of this country. Unfortunately, as of 10:15 p.m., we have no positive news to report. Local and state authorities, spanning twenty-three hundred miles, have communicated that an anonymous gunman has killed random, unknown citizens in Arizona, Louisiana, and Maryland and that most of his victims were via long-distance assault rifle. According to the lead investigator, Chief Davis Macklin of Montgomery County Maryland's Police Department, all leads have turned up empty, leaving officials unsure if, when, or where the serial killer will strike again. Preliminary results by the police conclude that at approximately 9:15 a.m. EST this morning, a pre-teen child, whose name is being withheld, was shot below his waist via a long-distance rifle. The young man is in stable condition, and by all accounts, should pull through. If you have any information regarding this case, please call this anonymous hotline at . . ."

Back in York, Mrs. Sullivan pops opens a standard-size, plastic orange prescription bottle—the successful end result of her most recent visit to the Healthcare clinic. She removes five Percocet's from the bottle and arranges each ten-milligram pill in a perfect line on top of an unfurnished, two-foot high glass table squeezed between both chesterfields.

"Oh. I must have been in the shower when he came by, darling."

Back in Maryland, Nina lowers the volume on her television to an inaudible level, then crawls to the balcony door and pulls it open to let in some fresh air.

"Are you sure? He told me he knocked on your door around seven. You usually wake up around six."

Finally getting her bearings after breathing heavily and grabbing a doorknob for stability, Nina propels herself to two feet, exits the musty living room, and grabs a bleach-based cleaner from underneath the kitchen sink before painstakingly wiping the small circle of avian blood from the balcony door's exterior. Her elevated wooden veranda, empty except for a pair of worn running sneakers and a clay ashtray, provides Nina the ability the ability to fully embrace the sweet, yet slightly chilly October air.

Back in Pennsylvania, Nina's mother carefully arranges eight lines of pulverized pain medication.

"My body is still worn out from last week, so I got up a little later than usual," says Mrs. Sullivan.

Nina's mother puts her phone on mute and places her right nostril a few centimeters from the table. After insufflating three two-inch lines, Mrs. Sullivan resumes her diluted conversation with her daughter.

"Hey, did you get my most recent medical and prescription bills in the mail yet? I sent them over late last week." Nina's mother wipes her clogged nose with the back of her hand and sniffles worse than Donald Trump at a debate before resuming her attention toward lines three, four, and five.

"How much do you need, Mom?"

"I don't have the paperwork in front of me at the moment, but it's only around $2800 I believe. I wouldn't be such a nag, dear, but it's just that I need to cover my prescription refill for the rest of the year. You and I both know I'd be dead without my painkillers."

"I don't know, Mom, it's just a lot to handle right now, especially with you not working. Yes, it was just a simple cashier job at Walgreens, but every little bit would help right now," says Nina. Now inside her apartment again, she laboriously opens up three bills on her modest kitchen table.

"When do you need your medical expenses taken care of by?" asks the younger Sullivan while inspecting the second bill, this one a car note from BMW America. Upon opening the bright orange envelope, Nina gasps at the first few sentences of the letter.

"After sending you three prior notices requesting your monthly lease payment for your E46 BMW M3, we are still seeking remuneration for your outstanding debt in the amount of $4,175.19. Be advised that continued avoidance of this matter will result . . ."

"Mom, you just got your medication refilled a couple hours after your last hospital visit last week. It's only Monday night; what's really wrong with you?" inquires Nina, who's unaware of Mrs. Sullivan's visit to the clinic earlier today.

"Who died and made you head of this family?! If you didn't run away from me, like your goddamn father, I wouldn't have to call you during emergencies to take care of me!" shouts a heated Mrs. Sullivan, while banging her closed fist on the table, almost causing the hoisted glass slab to crack in half. Remnants from the compressed Percocet residue lurch helplessly into the air, causing the dimly-lit living room atmosphere to cloud a bit.

Nina, somewhat tone-deaf toward her mother's antics at this point, opens up her last targeted letter beneath a pile of junk mail; it's a puffy, light yellow envelope from Leader Heights.

"This is incomprehensible. Your healthcare center express mailed me on Saturday. They're stating that, because Pennsylvania's Department of Public Welfare deemed your recent hospital visits unnecessary, and that you owe over $15,000 in healthcare costs. How could you make so many visits without consulting me? This is crazy. I'm on a basic medical plan with Cigna, and my credit is already shot. How am I going to be able to pay for this?"

Nina's mental pain, different than the nausea she felt earlier, creeps through her skull like the blunt smoke in a hot-boxed Volkswagen.

"Paulo Coelho said that while life sequentially gives us challenges, the Lord continues to bless us, and give us courage. Use the courage my genes gave you to fight through this week, and you'll be fine," advises Mrs. Sullivan.

Chapter 13

“When you're by yourself, with no one left to depend on, it’s the little comforts in life you learn to appreciate,” whispers Nina.

Seven hours after ending her conversation with her rambling, drug-addled, oscillating mother, Nina soothingly curls her cotton-covered toes into the lush beige carpet beneath her feet. Dressed head-to-toe in silk pajamas, Nina yawns while sitting in one of the four chairs at her isolated, square wooden kitchen table. Located five feet away from the elevated wet bar attached to her walk-in kitchen, the table is located directly in front of the quiet apartment's mail slot. As opposed to Monday, the Tuesday morning sky is bright and cloudless. The generic, vacuous walls surrounding every inch of the penthouse’s interior happily absorb the moderately-warm October air. Nina Sullivan, her mood matching the outdoor temperature, ravenously makes her way through a steaming bowl of cinnamon raisin oatmeal while keying into her open laptop. As usual, her living room television is on; this time it's turned to CNN correspondent Dana Bash, who's filling in for seasoned veteran Carol Costello.

“Welcome to CNN Newsroom on this Tuesday, October 9th. So where exactly is this Serial Sniper? Is he still in the state of Maryland?”

“They're never gonna catch that motherfucker, because he doesn't exist. He's a ghost,” mumbles Nina, dialing her cellphone.

“Good morning, efficienTECH Solutions.”

“Hi Denelle, it's me. How are things?”

Colin, wearing a hastily-fastened splint, covering a visibly fractured nose, slithers around the corner of the hallway connecting the employee bullpen to the front lobby, then discreetly tiptoes behind Coleman.

“Hey, Nina, what do you want? Have you been arrested yet? I thought you'd be in lockup by now,” purrs Denelle before flinching away from Colin's cold hands on her neck.

“What's going on in the office?”

“Stop beating around the bush and get to the point; I'm busy,” responds Denelle. Unrelenting in his thirst for flesh, Colin softly nibbles Denelle's right ear with his coffee-stained teeth.

“OK, is Kreesha or Konrad there yet?” asks Nina in a more authoritative tone.

Konrad is at the opposite end of the office, verbally massaging one of his clients frustrated with a faulty copier.

"Kreesha left to get her car serviced, but your boyfriend's at his desk. Colin's here too if you want to apologize."

"Hunter's not my boyfriend anymore; stop acting like we didn't break up three years ago. Just please tell the boss—"

Before Nina can continue bantering with Denelle, she's bestirred by a booming, thunderous knock at her entryway.

"I know, I know. You're doing telemarketing from home again, right Nina?" asks Denelle.

Instead of responding, Nina instinctively turns off the volume on her portable phone so that pressing its buttons won't create additional sound. Still seated at her kitchen table, approximately ten yards in front of her front door, she softly closes her laptop. With her face glued to the closed entrance door, Nina stands, then squats toward to the ground effortlessly, like Æon Flux. As if there's a fire spreading through her top floor apartment, Nina gently gets on all fours and then crawls underneath her small dining room table, easily wiggling her size-two frame through the three other chairs pinned beneath her makeshift, at-home workstation. "Does Ms. Nina Sullivan live here at 8-5-9-6, Russett Green East, Laurel Maryland?"

Now hunched to the side of her front door, Nina carefully looks through her small glass peephole and gasps at what she sees outside.

Two tall, stocky Caucasian men, covered in black sweatpants and black bandanas, furiously eye the exterior of Nina's ingress. The man closest to the door unhinges a long, black flashlight from his waist clip, then angrily raps it against the alabaster wood directly above Nina's interior viewing point, causing her to recoil in fear.

"We need to speak to you immediately, Nina Sullivan! Open up; we know you're in there!" bellows the posterior member of the two-man crew.

In order to formulate their next course of action, both men, their cleanly shaven skulls expunging perspiration, huddle together, equidistant from the barrier separating them from Nina. The first 300-plus pound man to roar Nina's name directs his associate toward Nina's car, which sits comfortably in the parking lot adjacent to the sheathed outdoor staircase constructed in between parallel apartments with the modern, fully-occupied, three-story housing complex.

"Shit," whispers Nina, twirling her black hair with her right thumb and index finger to calm her nerves.

"We should just break into her whip, tow it back to headquarters, then let this bitch sort out the paperwork on her own," says the second repo man to his partner. This particular stooge, who looks like a younger, taller version of the actor Michael Chiklis, then points to the clipboard in his left hand. Nina frantically runs into her walk-in bedroom closet, disrobes, then puts on a long business skirt, dress shirt, and Nike running sneakers.

"Alright, Sullivan, think!" says Nina to herself.

The first man, who could pass as a husky neo-Nazi, takes his pallid left earlobe off Nina's front door and then removes his police-grade electronic Taser from his jacket pocket. He then softly murmurs, "She's inside."

Trying to ignore the next round of thunderous bangs at the door, Nina scratches the back of her head while momentarily looking at the TV that's currently broadcasting a local NBC news edition.

“Here, among pictures and flowers honoring the life of Malayali Sengupta, blood stains still mark the spot where he died while pumping gas in this quiet, Montgomery County community,” says a stone-faced female correspondent.

Dumbfounded by the senseless violence and escalating madness around her, Nina diverts her attention toward the stubborn blood residue left on her balcony floor by yesterday's injured bird. Then, without a second thought, my girl takes flight. Nina takes off her belt and grabs her car keys from the dining room table.

“If she doesn't come to the door in two minutes, I'm jackin' her M3 in four.”

“Luckily there's no other residents outside, so we'll be able to avoid a commotion from any residents looking to post this on YouTube.”

“I'll be there in a second, just making myself decent!” yells Nina before taking a step outside and slamming the balcony door between her and the interior section of her apartment.

Except for her missing five-inch Givenchy stilettos, Nina's all dressed for work. Her arms tiring, she uses her thick leather belt, to precariously hang three feet off her plastic balcony guard rail. Nina, now two and a half stories from the soft, yet partially muddy, manicured lawn below her dangling feet, struggles to swing her right toe toward the second-floor apartment balcony railing: a dwelling that's inhabited by an amiable young family who work as programmers at NSA headquarters four miles east in Fort Meade.

Back by Nina's entrance, the shorter of the two men repeatedly strikes his metal flashlight on Nina’s barricade.

“Stop being stupid; you'll arouse her neighbors. You know how insecure girls are; she's probably just putting on her makeup.”

Approximately fifty feet away, Nina dangles precariously in purgatory, dangerously twirling between the second and third floor like a circus performer. Nina's left toe now touches the second-floor apartment's balcony gate just as her sweaty grip on the leather belt loosens.

Unable to stretch her lean body any further, Nina bangs her shin on one of the twelve parallel plastic posts designed to keep her neighbor's young children from falling to the ground.

“She's downstairs!” Both repo men, ecstatic to finally see their target, frantically run down the three flights of empty stairs and toward Nina's crumpled body on the property’s opposite side. Grass stains greener than a Celtics road uniform cover Nina's tan skirt as she struggles to regain consciousness.

“See what the Black side made you do, Nina? I'm here to help, so use your inner strength to rise,” I say to her, finally breaking my silence.

Chapter 14

"Lucky for you, all your internal organs are intact, and remarkably, you didn't break any bones. Grab your keys, slightly to the right of you—that's where you dropped them before hitting the ground. Do it quickly, then hobble as fast you can to your car. Your adventure has just begun, and our assailants will be here soon."

Shrugging me off as an auditory hallucination, or specifically a DMT-induced flashback, Nina, for some reason, intuitively disagrees with the unrecognizable thoughts in her head and pats her hips for the cluster of metal previously in her right skirt pocket. Like two un-neutered, wild Spanish bulls blindly entering a bullfighting arena, the two men accelerate toward Nina, quickly approaching her location on the grassy knoll parallel to her apartment complex.

Wanting to bring her along slowly, I stop giving her instructions and let her figure out an escape route by herself.

In my dimension, the definition and concept of time bears no similarity to the way you understand it in yours. Pointing out this difference in time accumulation between our two dimensions is important, because chess moves made by my Opponent and I create changes, some slight, some substantial, to your world that have in the past, and will in the future, alter your current concept of reality.

Anyway, back to Ms. Sullivan. Before Nina can toss her two essential belongings in the passenger seat and plan her next move, her taller tormentor haphazardly belly flops on the car's front hood.

"We've been ordered by BMW Financial Services to repossess your black M3! Step out of the vehicle and sign this release. Then vacate the premises!"

"OK, OK; I give up. Let me just get a pen, then I'll wind down the window."

Nina quickly opens the embedded compartment within her center console and rummages through some small, unremarkable paper items mixed with candy and gum wrappers. Nina, photogenic from our viewpoint in any situation, maintains eye contact with the growling attacker inches away the vehicle's windshield wipers. Flashing her trademark smile while using her healthy right hand, she searches the metal floorboard beneath her coupe's passenger seat.

"That's right cunt, it's all over. Step out of your car and hand us your keys. Jimmy, try not to leave a crease in her front hood while keeping an eye on her. I gotta take a minute to catch my breath," says the smaller of the two men, standing to the left of Nina's car.

A bolt of adrenaline rushes over Nina, making her forget about the stinging pain in her left ankle and collarbone. In one swinging motion, she inserts her car keys into the ignition with her left hand, twisting it slightly to the right so that only the vehicle's electrical system is functional.

Before Jimmy, still positioned on Nina's car roof like a helpless beached whale, can warn his friend about her next move, Nina grasps the once-hidden spray bottle, cracks her driver's side window a few inches, and sprays three squirts of car cleanser into his eyes, impressively repelling half her opposition.

“She fucking pepper sprayed me!”

Andrew, a burly, 6'1 man in his early forties, recoils a few feet from the German sports car, dislocating both kneecaps as he drops onto the empty parking space to the left of Nina’s BMW. Jimmy lifts his shins off the M3’s front bumper and braces his sneakers against the concrete wall marked “RESERVED PARKING” directly behind him.

Nina, chillingly unemotional, uses her left foot to press the clutch, turns on the engine, and then shifts her sports car into reverse.

* * * * *

Back in Rockville, Kreesha says, “I believe I did the right thing by giving Nina four more days to close an account. But long term, what do you think I should do with her?”

“Stop being so diplomatic and just fire her today, boss,” says an unsympathetic Colin in between chewing remnants of his fried pork sandwich. Seeing right through Kreesha's specious argument, Colin's southern equivalent from Georgia concurs.

“Breaking another coworker’s nose, regardless of circumstances, is unacceptable. You must have incredible pull at headquarters, Kreesha, because if an episode like Monday's incident happened in Atlanta, our district manager would have called the cops and had her brought up on felony assault charges," says Daniel Evans, a heavyset Mississippian about five years older than Konrad.

"Not that it's an excuse, but the officers 'round here seem busy enough trying to solve more serious crimes. I'm not condoning her actions, Colin, but we both know you're at least partly at fault for thieving her leads. At least admit that you're partially culpable," serenely replies Kreesha, before adding a few minutes later, "At least for now, Nina's the only person I know who can deliver some sales to this company. She's been in embedded in Montgomery County's business scene for years."

Kreesha Mason is an interesting lady, worth telling you more about, I believe. A 1980 graduate of the small, historically black college of Coppin State University, Kreesha resides by herself in a gated community in Columbia, Maryland: a bustling, planned suburban city of about 100,000 residents located squarely in between DC and Baltimore. After graduating near the top of her class, Kreesha, a focused woman intent upon breaking through much thicker glass ceilings than exist today, endured numerous incidents of harassment—some still too painful for her to speak about openly. From coworkers lynching stuffed monkeys in her cubicle in 1989 to a married supervisor exposing his flaccid penis during a late-night meeting in the mid-nineties, she's experienced more than her fair amount of corporate-related drama.

Her former husband of fifteen years, who left her and their only child the year of President Bill Clinton's re-election, was a moderately successful part-time real estate agent who squandered Kreesha's life savings on a volatile mix of alcohol, cocaine, and frequent weekend gambling trips to Atlantic City and Montreal. Beyond the emotional scars of a failed fourteen-year marriage, Kreesha's ex-husband beat her with alarming regularity while they were together. During a particularly violent episode, in which Kreesha's ex came home one Sunday morning after nine-hour drug binge at a popular DC nightclub, he beat her legs and rear with an ice-covered tree branch, right in front of their shaken daughter, to the point that Kreesha had a restraining order issued against him in the winter of 1993.

“Let me ask you two this, with an untargeted serial killer at large, are you willing to cold call Montgomery County so I can meet my raised sales estimates before our fiscal year finishes?” asks Kreesha to both men beside her. “Because if you have another solution to this dilemma, let me know. I'm fresh out of ideas on this end.”

Colin, remaining quiet, looks at Konrad’s occupied workstation via a floor-to-ceiling window separating the conference room from a congregation of cubicles.

Back in North Laurel, before directing her car toward the parking lot exit, Nina suddenly stops her vehicle, causing Jimmy to predictably roll off the BMW like jostled snow from a SUV's rooftop, immediately crashing his right shoulder into the apavement. He rotates a few feet on the ground, rumbling to a stop right in front of his partner. Nina reverses a car length and winds down her driver's side window.

“Is attempted assault part of your job description? Do you get off on illegally chasing defenseless women in public? Don't you think you deserve what you got?” screams Nina.

Out of the corner of her eye, behind a nondescript, second story window diagonally across from her apartment, Nina sees a burlap curtain close shut.

“Authorities will be here in a few minutes, but if you immediately call in medical assistance for these two fallen men, they won't rat you out, because they're partially culpable for your three-story fall,” I tell her in an authoritarian voice I can feel she thinks is from a male.

A chill rushes up Nina's spine. The small hairs on the back of her neck stand perpendicular to her skin.

“Drive to an area, not too far from here, where you think your car can blend in. You'll only be safe if you leave in half a minute,” I add, knowing that she can handle the increased pressure.

Back at efficienTECH's Maryland office, Kreesha continues to censure her two co-workers.

“Colin, stop being so self-righteous before you continue to criticize Nina. Everyone here knows what you're up to once work gets out.” Colin, his cheeks blood red, reclines his head into the plush, black, Humanscale Freedom Task Chair, holding his jellyfish-like frame.

“Why can't Nina be more like Konrad? He's easily our hardest working sales rep. I've seen that guy do cold calls on the weekend and holidays,” says Colin, changing the subject.

Kreesha, sitting at the end of the long, black marble table in the meeting room's center, rotates her chair seventy-five degrees and looks toward her most trusted co-worker. Konrad, still on his desk phone, and oblivious to her stare, works to finish closing his third deal of the infant week.

“OK, let’s move on. Colin, this afternoon I need you to drive to the state courthouse in Annapolis to meet with their office manager. Bring Gabriella for backup, because it's potentially a seven-figure deal.”

North of Maryland, another racially mixed group, albeit much younger, make their way through the dusty, urine-stained lobby of Mrs. Sullivan's public housing complex in York. Nina's exhausted mother tries to ignore the raucous group of five men aged eighteen to twenty-five.

Dressed in a kaleidoscope of oversized Starter jackets, baggy jeans, and knockoff Air Jordans, the men, four of whom are on parole for offenses ranging from aggravated assault to felony drug possession, focus on Mrs. Sullivan waiting patiently for the dilapidated elevator to arrive.

The pack's self-appointed leader, Bartolo Maldonado, reaffirms his alpha position while eyeing Mrs. Sullivan's vulnerable disposition. “Wow, playa; you really fucked up her face,” whispers one of Bartolo's friends.

“Fellas, leave me alone so I can get back to business with this crackhead. Go wait outside at your usual lookout spots, and text me if you see anything suspicious.”

While Bartolo's friends hurriedly exit the building, Nina's mother presses the plastic elevator button, illuminating it bright orange. Before making any sudden moves toward his victim, Bartolo scopes the dusty, doorman-less entranceway for any bystanders and/or future witnesses. After concluding that there are none, hc prudently approaches the same woman he viciously assaulted a little over twenty-four hours ago.

"Are you going to beat me up again, Bartolo?" screams Mrs. Sullivan at the top of her lungs. "Your mother would be proud; God bless her soul." Bartolo approaches, zombie-like and undeterred by her plea to his pathos.

You see, during this past Labor Day, hours after a family barbecue on the outskirts of York, Mrs. Maldonado succumbed to internal injuries accrued during a late-night domestic dispute with Bartolo's intoxicated father. Occurring in an apartment a floor above Mrs. Sullivan's, the fatal attack left Mrs. Maldonado with three-inch stab wounds to her arms, groin, and stomach.

According to rumors heard by Mrs. Sullivan, the origin of the argument began when Bartolo's mom blamed her husband for their only child's bipolar disorder and his extensive history as a juvenile delinquent.

The morning after the national holiday, awakened from his slumber by distant, agonizing screams from his mother, Bartolo ran into the Maldonado's modest kitchen only to watch in horror as his mother agonizingly bled to death while his now-imprisoned father looked on and laughed. On his own, and with his family in shambles, Bartolo had nowhere to turn—until a cryptic, tax-free business opportunity arouse in September that enabled the unemployed youth to work in his immediate area.

While never directly meeting his employer, Bartolo quickly agreed to provide two specific services: (1) conduct minor reconnaissance, and (2) forcefully intimidate Nina's mom while selling her heavily discounted prescription drugs.

Now, in present human time, Mrs. Sullivan arches her neck upwards to see what floor the elevator is on. Bartolo taps her on the shoulder, immediately making the emotionally troubled woman jump in fear. “You didn't tell your precious daughter about yesterday, did you?” Nina's mother rolls her emerald-colored eyes toward the lobby's rotted ceiling, the end product of decades of asbestos-induced decay.

“No, no, of course not, Bartolo.” stammers Nina's mother. “She's too stressed out as it is, handling my medical bills, plus work and all. She has no problem with you; why are you asking about her?” Not mustering up enough courage to outwardly defend her only child from Nina's twisted, demented childhood friend, Mrs. Sullivan rubs the still-swollen bruise on her cheekbone as her eyes begin to water. Bartolo, conflicted in his emotions, balls his fist to strike Nina’s mother again, then relents as he remembers that his strict orders from out of state indicate to keep Mrs. Sullivan terrified, but alive; failure to do so will result in his own death.

“Listen, you fucking welfare parasite, it's outta your hands at this point. So if you want your eighties at this new, discounted rate, keep your fucking mouth shut.” Bartolo subtly removes a plastic-wrapped bulge from his boxers then places a bundle of ten eighty-milligram oxycodone pills in Mrs. Sullivan's shaking right hand.

“You're not planning to hurt my only child, are you?”

Chapter 15

Quincy, sitting inside the drab, concrete-laden, three-story chemistry building located at the corner of Regents and Stadium Drive inside the picturesque University of Maryland campus, struggles to maintain attention at his late-afternoon, 600-student Organic Chem class.

More boring than a historical fiction novel with an ambiguous plot, Quincy loses interest in the lecture and turns his attention to the Diamondback crossword puzzle on top of the tray-sized laminated oak desk. At the bottom of the coliseum-shaped auditorium, Quincy's professor, Dr. Elmo McElroy from the marsh-filled, Chesapeake Bay banks of Easton, places a new transparency slide on the projector.

The figure contains two angular sketches facing opposite of each other. Two parallel lines, approximately two inches in length, connect the outsides of both L-like illustrations.

"Figure eight point one. In an ethylene molecule . . ." Professor McElroy then uses his sharpie to draw a circle around the entire mirror image of C(2)H(4), before continuing.

". . . As you can plainly see here, the two carbon atoms are connected by a double bond, causing each atom to lie in the same plane." After engraving his initials in the aging wood underneath his notes, Quincy doodles two grumpy faces in his notebook. Instead of following his teacher's orders, which require inking a pictogram of the flammable gas hydrocarbon, Quincy, further deviating from his instructor's lecture, draws a circle around both rudimentary faces, then draws two lines bridging both images.

"Man . . . all in all, I need about $10,000 to pay off financial aid, hire a tutor for the MCATs, and pay rent," mumbles Quincy.

A transfer student from Pepperdine University in Malibu, Quincy has always been a naturally gifted learner who scores in the top percentile of his class, regardless of the subject material. Born and raised in the sun-soaked Republican enclave of Orange County, Quincy is the youngest son of Floyd Marshall, a chemical engineer for a consulting firm in Irvine, and Nancy, a personal trainer at a Gold's Gym in Anaheim. Around the turn of the century, Marshall eschewed his two older brother's paths of military service via the Air Force. The black sheep of his cookie-cutter family, Quincy instead decided to parlay his prodigal talent in indoor volleyball and secured a full athletic scholarship at Pepperdine.

Near the conclusion of his sophomore spring semester, Quincy got greedy and decided he wanted more.

Colluding with his girlfriend Rebecca Mathews, a thirty-two-year-old athletic trainer and teacher's assistant from the Kinesiology department, Quincy decided that he wanted some extra spending money to "fit in" with the clique of trust-fund babies and spoiled heiresses on Pepperdine's campus.

"I was taught that hard work equals success, but it's easy to become disillusioned when you see all this conspicuous consumption around you," vented the then business major to Rebecca one day after volleyball practice.

One of the few African-Americans not playing basketball on campus, Quincy took solace in expressing his frustrations to her; she had been the first girl to teach him how to kiss—along with other relationship subtleties that he'd had no prior knowledge of.

On one particularly gorgeous LA afternoon, while rehabbing the middle blocker's sprained ankle in the Athletic Center whirlpool, Rebecca proposed that the two share an eight-ball of cocaine, along with a bottle of merlot, at her quaint, rented off-campus townhouse in nearby Thousand Oaks.

A few days later, the statuesque, trim blonde from the wealthy Silicon Valley enclave of Saratoga hosted Quincy at her humble abode for an intimate dinner for two. It was that night, before the two copulated, and after they insufflated liberal amounts of nose candy, that Rebecca convinced Quincy they could turn a sizable profit by selling small amounts of bath salts, Adderall, Ritalin, meth, coke, and other illicit drugs to Quincy's teammates and classmates.

Initially hesitant of Rebecca's plan, Quincy eventually agreed to only carrying weight of infinitesimal amounts.

Slightly a year later, back at his Chem lecture, Quincy's doodling is interrupted by an unkempt, scraggly neo-hippie trying to sneak into class via the open door adjacent to the seated professor. Before heading up the lecture hall staircase to take a seat close to Quincy's, the barefoot student quickly removes his hooded sweatshirt, revealing a black t-shirt with a large white bull's-eye on it. Around the bull's-eye, in large, capitalized letters, are the words "KILL BLUE DEVILS, DC SNIPER, NOT PEOPLE!"

As Quincy struggles to absorb the last lecture during his stressful Tuesday, Mrs. Sullivan finally walks into her apartment door, barely escaping another beating from Bartolo. She immediately grabs her handheld phone and dials Nina's cell.

"Ms. Sullivan, if you look above, you can see that the headliner of this particular Bentley is trimmed in Alcantara, which nicely accentuates the black carbon finish on the dash and center console," says Greg Rogan, Automotive Sales Consultant at EuroMotorcars in Bethesda, Maryland.

"Now, this vehicle is a significant upgrade in price from your M3; you're aware of this, I assume?" inquires Rogan before smiling at his first customer of the day. Nina sees that her mother is trying to reach her and puts her cellphone on mute.

"I have some time to kill, how about taking me on a test drive?" responds Nina.

Now barely off campus after his Chem lecture, and sitting in the left pew inside a lonely, cherry red booth at the unhygienic College Park grease pit appropriately named Ratsies, Quincy stares at dozens of basic, bulimic Long Island sorority girls all dressed in black or gray yoga pants, form-fitting hooded sweatshirts, and headbands acting as a stopgap for their collinear ponytailed hair as they cross Route 1 from Fraternity Row.

Quincy takes a small bite of his soggy cheeseburger and then tosses it back toward the table. "It's funny how love can make your decisions for you, rational or otherwise," writes Quincy in his diary before pressing his isosceles nose against the chilled, clear glass.

* * * * *

A few years before enrolling at Maryland, Quincy, nineteen years old and a sophomore at Pepperdine, secretly moved out of his dorm room shared with a similarly aged, copacetic Samoan winger from the varsity rugby team and into his girlfriend Rebecca's place, where their first official date occurred.

The crux of Quincy's agreement with his former Samoan roommate, Ualesi Sale, was the genesis of his West Coast problems—and also the beginning of his untimely exit from California.

In order to escape any suspicions of a lax academic disposition from his obsessive, but loving parents, Quincy supplied Ualesi with a bionic monthly dosage of Human Growth Hormone along with an ounce of Quincy's favorite hybrid strain: Skywalker OG Kush.

"From now on, I'm gonna sleep at Becca's crib to keep the local pigs running in circles, but I wanna do transactions in this bedroom to maintain a continuous presence on campus. In return, I'll give you 65 percent off the Barry Bonds juice, OK, Ualesi?'

"It's strange, because you definitely don't need to sell drugs to get ahead in life, Quincy. Even though we've only been friends for half a year, you're easily the naturally smartest person I've ever met. And although volleyball isn't really working out, I don't think flooding this college with illegal narcotics is the answer," replied Ualesi before turning his attention to his paused video game within the roommates cramped, shared dorm room.

"In Samoa, we have a saying: 'Ia fili e le tai se agava'a.' It means: *Let the wind choose as to the quickness of a canoe.* I'm not going to rat you out, but someone eventually will once they figure out how easily you can be replaced. It's the nature of the drug trade."

"I'm just the middleman for the only supplier servicing this school, and he has no reason to give me up to the cops; Becca has too much info on him. I'll never have anything incriminating on me that could lead to more than a possession charge, and making $10,000 a month is more than our starting tailback gets from bookies. So what's the downside?" replied Quincy before hugging Ualesi goodbye, running down a couple flights of the dorm emergency stairs, and tossing his belongings into the back of Rebecca's convertible.

A year and a half later, after a confluence of self-created athletic, personal, and legal setbacks, Quincy found himself approximately 2700 miles from home and alone in College Park, desperately trying to dig himself out from under the mess he created in Malibu. Determined to positively turn his life around as a Terrapin, make his disconnected parents proud of him, and become self-sufficient via a chemistry degree, Quincy tried to ignore the fact that his tuition and living expenses were spiraling out of control.

In present time, back at Ratsies, Quincy scrolls through his cellphone to inspect a fresh text message, which states:

"THIS IS AN EMERGENCY MOBILE ALERT . . . PLEASE BE ON THE LOOKOUT FOR ANY SUSPICIOUS WHITE BOX TRUCKS IN PRINCE GEORGE, MONTGOMERY, PRINCE WILLIAM, AND HOWARD COUNTIES . . . SUSPECTS OF THE RECENT SNIPER SHOOTINGS ARE LIKELY TO BE IN A VEHICLE OF THIS TYPE. THEY'RE ARMED AND EXTREMELY DANGEROUS, SO PLEASE USE CAUTION . . . FOR

ANONYMOUS TIPS, PLEASE CONTACT THE MONTGOMERY COUNTY POLICE."

Quincy quickly disposes his oily lunch in the receptacle bin with hopes of catching the next metro bus traveling north toward his apartment located in a shady Greenbelt neighborhood behind the jeopardous Beltway Plaza Mall.

* * * * *

"The check for this garage is gonna bounce as soon as the landlord cashes it," says Nina, precariously pulling her tuned German import into the empty, one-car cavity.

Back at his place, Konrad rips open a Chinese take-out packet of soy sauce and aimlessly pours it on a half-cooked piece of grilled chicken.

"So let me get this straight, how many times did you run over the repo guy again?" replies Konrad into his cellphone before laughing hysterically.

"Let it go; what's done is done. Damn, this has been a strange and long day. I can't believe it's already half past eight."

Back at Konrad's townhouse, located in an isolated suburb on the western edge of Montgomery County, Warren Barber, and Eric Andrews slouch on his albino-colored, ten-foot-long leather couch. Shaped in a formation reminiscent of the only move a knight can make in chess, the sofa, along with its two denizens on top of it, hunkers in the corner of Konrad's immense living room, which is easily three times the square footage of Nina's. Konrad, who's entertaining two friends from the rugged

Baltimore neighborhood of Elwood Park, removes his dinner from a George Foreman grill and puts it in a toasted potato roll.

“Three days . . . three days and it's a wrap. Based on Kreesha's ridiculous deadline, I just don't see myself working at efficienTECH any longer than Friday.” Nina, her speech slurring and heart rate slowing, yawns as she reclines her driver’s seat.

“She’s close to committing suicide. This could become a reoccurring problem,” says my Opponent, stating the obvious.

“Get her to your player’s domicile; it’s time to bring her closer to the truth,” I respond.

Now across the street from her apartment complex, Nina presses her remote garage door opener, which slowly closes the large, pulley-mounted door behind her vehicle. With the BMW's naturally-aspirated engine at idle, odorless and colorless carbon monoxide continues to slowly emanate out of the car's aftermarket exhaust system.

Nina electronically winds down both side windows, yawns, then softly rests her skull on the steering wheel's temple. Back in Dickerson, Konrad sips a Red Stripe before responding to his suicidal ex-girlfriend. “Oh, I just remembered. I got a word in for you this afternoon with management, so looks like things aren't as dire for you as you think.”

Nina's hazy eyes open immediately. Straitening her spine, Nina takes her cellphone off speaker, then places it in front of her trembling mouth.

“Don't fuck with me.”

“I'm serious. Come over; I'll give you the details in person.” Obsessed with the neoteric, laminated black wooden floor installed last week, Konrad pulls a yellow canister from underneath his sink and begins to clean a spot where his unruly friend just decided to use as an ashtray. "I feel sorry for your kids," says Konrad, while cleaning Eric's blunt residue.

"Fuck yo floors. You can afford another one, you greedy piece of shit."

"Eric's over there?" Nina asks.

"Yeah. Warren, too. Hurry up before dinner gets cold."

Nina, no longer interested in taking her own life, opens the garage door, reverses her black BMW out of the garage, and then directs her vehicle toward the highway.

"Something strange is going on with me, Hunter, and I don't know who else to turn to," says Nina, accelerating on a four-lane road not far fr

om Interstate-95 South.

Konrad smiles. While breaking lime-green buds of Kush with his newly manicured fingernails, he says, "Let's not go into details about this over the phone. OK?"

Chapter 16

Dickerson comprises mostly of wooded expanse littered with pockets of single-family, ranch-style homes. A little over a year ago, Konrad keenly snatched one such property for a little over $30,000 at a Montgomery County real estate auction for foreclosed properties. Unbeknown to outsiders, his traditional, colonially-designed four-bedroom home recently housed an intricate, illegal underground Moonshine distillery in its multi-level, three-thousand-square-foot basement.

Konrad, once joking to his real estate lawyer that he would turn the lower floors into an abattoir, spent twice the house's purchase price on interior and exterior security upgrades—none of which are visible to naïve visitors. While cleaning dishes in his impressive kitchen, he instructs his lackey Warren to cautiously answer the front door after the doorbell rings.

"Tuck your nine in the back of your jeans, just to be safe," barks Konrad. Warren, with a black bandanna thinly tied across his cleanly shaved, chocolate-colored head, quickly opens the front door after peering through the peephole.

"Long time no see, Nina. I didn't think Konrad would ever get you over here."

Nina, also dressed in lounge gear with purple NYU sweatpants matching her heliotrope Air Max's, hands Warren a fresh six-pack of Guinness. Before standing on her tippy toes to kiss Warren on the cheek, she replies, “Yeah, it's been a while. After growing up in York, I try and avoid the sticks at all costs.”

Konrad, trying his best to ignore Nina's hourglass figure enhanced by subtle, yet unnecessary liposuction, washes crumbs off his soapy palms from the kitchen sink.

“Shuffle the cards, Eric. We got a long spades game ahead of us.”

Forty-five minutes later, the eclectic group of four sit in a square at a retractable poker table in Konrad's den.

“Who are your ten best rappers of all time, Nina?” inquires Eric, trying to get her mind off of her stressful day.

“Off the top of my head and in no particular order: Big, Nas, KRS-One, Mos Def, Common, Ghostface, Raekwon, Styles P, Jadakiss, Sean Price, and Roc Marciano. Was never really a Pac fan, and Jay fell off in recent years.”

“That’s eleven, and you didn’t even put Marshall in there. Wow,” observes Eric.

“Why, because he's white? Em stopped making good music since he left Rawkus,” adds Nina before focusing her attention toward Konrad.

“Damn, it's desolate out here, Hunter.”

“I still deserve my forty acres we were promised, but I guess fifteen will do for now,” responds Konrad, referring to the forty acres of land emancipated African-American slaves were promised after the conclusion of the Civil War.

“So you're content with your life?” asks Nina.

“Absolutely. Like Costanza said, ‘It's all about mastering your own domain.’ That domain being the environment you inhabit—the personal environment that interacts with you in a day-in, day-out basis. Once that's accomplished, you'll can rapidly expand your domain, and before you know it, you'll be the most important person in the universe.”

“Konrad, we're not reality show stars, real estate magnates, or politicians. We sell copiers for a living.”

“Like, for example, when I rule the world, the first thing I’d do is create whorehouses on the sides of highways, next to rest stops. The prostitutes would be paid for and subsidized by the government as a service to men who need healing.”

“That could be the most vile, sexist statement I’ve heard in my life. Why would any rational person be OK with that?” passively asks Nina, who's heard these statements for years.

“Listen, the vast majority of crimes, white collar or otherwise, are committed by men who're sexually frustrated. Eliminate the frustration, you eliminate the crime. Likewise, if you ever wanted to exponentially increase the murder rate, all you’d have to do is make some minor adjustments to the distribution, application, and in some cases, the inherent chemicals of the main connector to violent crime: illegal drugs,” adamantly responds Konrad.

“Plato once said that ‘love is a serious mental disease.’ It seems crazy now, but it’s impossible to quantify how madly I was in love with you when I first moved down here from Manhattan,” says Nina before inhaling and then passing a lit spliff to Eric.

“Answer me this, partna, why do you call Nina names like 'babydoll' and 'sweetie pie' when you were the one who dumped her?” inquires Warren.

“Long story short, I wasn't as balanced mentally as I am now. But do yourself a favor and change the subject,” angrily responds Konrad.

Almost five years ago, days after signing her contract cementing her position as an efficienTECH senior marketing consultant, Konrad asked Nina to be his girlfriend during an admittedly unromantic lunch at an Applebee's in Columbia, Maryland.

“Hey, do you want to take our relationship to the next level?” he had asked, seemingly out of nowhere. “It seems like our natural evolution is giving us the ability to forge a stronger alliance regarding corporate, as well as personal, growth.”

“I'm sorry. Did you just ask me to be your girlfriend?” responded Nina. Surprised, yet overjoyed with emotion, she quickly said yes.

A week later, Konrad moved Nina out of her cockroach-infested room inside a decrepit, three-story home. Glad to be out of the dicey neighborhood bordering the two PG County towns of College Park and Berwyn Heights, Nina blissfully shacked up with Konrad in his apartment in vibrant Adams Morgan, DC.

“I definitely thought you two would have gotten married after you moved into his crib in Northwest” continues Warren before taking a quick drag of his delicately rolled, hash-oil infused, white owl blunt, which is being passed counterclockwise while Nina’s joint rotates in the opposite direction.

“Why'd you two separate a year and a half later?” asks Eric, eager to keep Konrad’s annoyance level high. It’s no secret that both Eric and Warren have a crush on Nina. And after repeated rejections by Nina for sex, both friends are using this opportunity to drive a deeper wedge between her and her ex-lover. While a smiling Eric deals a fresh set of cards to the game's three other participants, Konrad, trying to keep his temperament calm, avoids eye contact with Nina as both continue to reminisce about their complicated past.

Even casual observers could notice that Konrad had significant interest in Nina once she started working at efficienTECH, even though he played it off initially by not returning her calls after their initial sexual encounter in NYC. Not long after their initial 'honeymoon' stage dissipated over the course of a few months, the two became inalienable partners, spending nearly all of their time together between work and home. Attending everything from pro-immigration rallies on the steps of the Supreme Court to Knicks/Wizards games at the Verizon Center, the two opinionated souls seem destined for a life spent together.

However, nine months after unceremoniously asking Nina to be his monogamous partner, Konrad began to change. Soon after a routine mellow trip off magic mushroom tea with Nina while watching the cherry blossom parade from the extended southern border of the White House, Konrad felt hampered and disturbed by secret, subtle symptoms of schizoaffective disorder. Nina, always looking for the positive traits in everyone she felt was worth caring for, decided from the outset to brush off Konrad’s sometimes sudden, abrupt personality changes and instead focus on how much he’d helped her escape her turbulent past.

Schizoaffective disorder, yes that's it, is the affliction a doctor at George Washington University hospital said he had. Nina begged him to see a psychiatrist after Konrad repeatedly told her of his hallucinations; his attending physician concluded that much of his mental issues stemmed from his chaotic upbringing in North Philly.

In reality, our reality, Konrad was chosen for greatness by my Opponent once I started focusing in on Nina at NYU, and his "disorder" was my Opponent's preferred method of communicating with him. I'll say exactly more about who we are once I officially introduce myself to Nina, but as for why my Opponent chose Konrad as the Black side's chief-in-command, his combination of traditional educational intellect, street smarts, athletic ability, unwavering mental mindset, and socio-economic awareness really made him the perfect option for my enemy. Although his mood was generally elevated and stable, hourly, continuously reoccurring visual, auditory, and even tactile hallucinations clogged Konrad psyche—even more so once Nina moved in with him.

During one particular late-night hailstorm, while Nina slept comfortably next to Konrad in their king-sized floor-bound bed, Konrad looked away from an early morning rerun of Syracuse winning the NCAA Men's Basketball Championship on television.

"Did you just see those red and white flashes in the corner of the ceiling, Nina? It looked like a miniature firework."

"What you're witnessing has nothing to do with physics . . . But let me ask you a question: Is this life causing you joy? Or do you want more?" my Opponent asked him.

At that moment, I wanted nothing more than to chime in to stop Konrad from ruining his relationship with Nina—their tangled web is what makes this game so interesting. However, rules of our game prohibit me from directly conversing with Konrad or any other member of the Black side. Likewise, in no uncertain terms can my Opponent explicitly speak to Nina, or any of her associates.

However, soldiers of both the Black and White side can disseminate information, or misinformation, about the enemy's intentions, goals, and ambitions without fear of reprisal from me or my Opponent. For millions of centuries, my Opponent and I have strictly adhered to this game clause, and breaking it would result in an unfathomable punishment, more severe than your human mind can comprehend.

Although I'm neither male nor female in the traditional sense, my Opponent made sure to directly contact Konrad in a distinctively male, racially anonymous American English voice inside his perplexed skull. When my Opponent did reach out to Konrad for the very first time, he literally jumped out of bed and woke his beautiful girlfriend in the process. Konrad then rushed out of their unpretentious bedroom and into their railway-shaped, baroque-style bathroom.

"What flash are you talking about? I don't see any lightning outside," purred Nina, rubbing the rheum discharge from her eyes.

Embarrassed, and unable to verbalize what was happening inside of him, Konrad threw water on his face. "Can you please turn up the air conditioning? I can't stop sweating for some reason."

"You're probably just coming down with the flu due to this unpredictable DC weather. Grab a bottle of water from the fridge, take some Benadryl from the cupboard, and come back to bed."

“Don't be alarmed, but prepare for the future; we have much to inform you of,” my Opponent continued.

His Kafkaesque, monosyllabic voice began to make Konrad tremble in fear. Konrad hunched his head underneath the running faucet as Nina, still in bed, pulled the covers over her naked body.

“Remember, you have to meet with Kreesha before work to discuss increasing your bonus. Come back to bed, you know you have a long day ahead of you,” said Nina, yawning.

* * * * *

Now, back in Dickerson years later, Konrad, unfazed by Eric and Warren’s attempts to unnerve him, scans through popular articles on Google News and reads that neither Chief Macklin, nor federal authorities, have any substantial leads or motives for the current local killing spree. Looking to shift course away from the tenor of his thirsty friends, eager for an obvious, yet impossible threesome with Nina, Konrad superficially changes the subject.

“Do you want to know what really happened during that morning meeting with me and Kreesha? The 7:00 a.m. one that I had to rush to the day after that crazy hailstorm years ago?”

Nina, immediately familiar with Konrad's reference from a day thirty-four months ago, replies, “That was a day after you saw a ghost in our bedroom, right?”

“It wasn't a duppy, Nina; it was a small light flash, almost fluorescent in appearance, bursting out of the ceiling,” says Konrad.

“I had something akin to your experience earlier today. Remind me to tell you about it later,” continues Nina, while looking at the three spades in her hand.

“You are now running on reserve battery power,” says Konrad’s computer.

“Don't worry, bitch; you gonna live,” replies Konrad, plugging in his laptop. Warren and Eric uncontrollably giggle as Konrad clears his throat, then continues.

“Lord have mercy, Kreesha was in a world of hurt that morning. Once in her office, she told me she was secretly stealing revenue from another district to make quota, plus rewriting new, high-end business contracts to re-route commission to herself.”

Chapter 17

Encapsulated within the complexities of many corporate pyramid schemes is the foundational premise of how some lucky, well-connected sales employees are paid handsomely, while other, less fortunate workers toil through ignominious new business leads, cold calling campaigns, and dead-end networking events to hopefully get customers, both large and small, to buy their products at an inflated price. Like other variations of pyramid schemes, especially regarding insurance agents selling voluntary benefits, the pay structure for efficienTECH sales reps differs not only on how many products they push, but how far they're willing to go in order to screw over the customer. EfficienTECH, accepting this reality, doesn’t rate members of their sales force on how much they overcharge a particular client or group of companies, but on the amount of revenue that particular sales executive generates for the company on a quarterly and yearly basis. Obviously, the more tenured a salesman is at efficienTECH, the more they're expected to sell. Not to bog you down with minutia, but to further clarify, Nina’s job status is in flux because she's sold well under $50,000 worth of efficienTECH hardware for the last three quarterly business cycles of the calendar year. On the other hand, Konrad isn't under nearly as much pressure to find new business because of an internal “golden key” policy known as “Ship-ins.”

In a nutshell, Ship-ins are when a salesman from a different efficienTECH branch closes a deal with a company desiring to disperse recently acquired hardware to a sister office in another region, which of course is inside another salesman's territory. In instances such as this, even though executives like Colin, and to an even larger degree Konrad, did none of the grunt work, often lasting six months to a year, they still get revenue credit for a deal that places sold hardware in their territory; revenue that is counted toward their monthly, quarterly, and yearly quota. In addition to their salaries and deal-related commissions, each particular efficienTECH salesman, at any level, receives a bonus if they surpass their yearly, agreed upon, sales quota with the firm.

On the other hand, Kreesha’s payment equation is more traditional with her $300,000 salary much higher than anyone in the Rockville office. However, her incentive-laced deal with efficienTECH stipulates that her team must sell a certain number of industrial printers, copiers, and fax machines in order to meet her estimated total district net revenue of well over seven figures. Failure to do so over the course of three to four quarters in a row will lead to her termination.

“It doesn't make sense that Kreesha would steal from her employees. There hasn't been much turnover in the sales department, which is rare in copier sales, and over half our crew generally make quota every month,” states Nina.

“That morning we spoke, she immediately requested that we go into an empty stall in the men's bathroom, because she was paranoid that efficienTECH had hidden microphones spread throughout the office. After making sure no one was in there, I ushered that horse-faced bitch into an empty stable in the far back corner and locked the door behind us," responds Konrad.

"'I'm stealing a quarter million a year from you and your coworkers, and I think the board of directors are on to me. You gotta help me find that amount to recirculate to my sales team before tax season, or I'm going to prison,' she tells me."

"Is that why you broke up with me, because you were unable to tell me about Kreesha?"

Konrad ignores Nina's question and keeps rehashing the incident.

"“Why are you telling me this?" I asked.

"“I don't know who else to turn to. After applying over half a dozen times for senior positions, I'm continually being denied a promotion to executive vice president."

"“So stealing money from the very people that keep you employed . . . that's your answer to discrimination?' I asked her."

"Number one: how could you have participated in, or been witness to criminal acts without reporting her? The Konrad I know and loved for years would never have resorted to theft to ever justify or condone anything. And second, she must have done a great job stealing from us, because no other reps have told me of an unexplained dip in their pay structure. My commission percentages have also remained constant, so what gives?" says Nina, briefly interrupting Konrad's story.

"How many times have you blue-balled clients to close a deal, or told a CFO that you had hungry kids that wouldn't get fed if she didn't sign a contract? Honor, class, and decency flew out the window as soon as you started climbing the corporate ladder," retaliates Konrad.

"Nina, you sell copiers for a living at 300 to 500 percent of what they cost to make—usually to struggling small business owners who can barely keep their head above water during this recession. Stop acting like you're better than us," adds Eric.

"I still can't believe we just ran a Boston on you!" says Warren, indicating that he and Konrad collected all thirteen books of the last round, cementing their victory over a disinterested Nina.

While scooping up the last four cards off the table, Konrad looks Nina directly in the eyes, then says, "Come with me, so I can finally tell you why we broke up. I need to show you something."

Chapter 18

Chief Macklin sneaks a fifth of Hennessy into his large styrofoam cup before screaming, “Come in!”

“You ready for the meeting in your tactical room, Chief? I want to introduce you someone who may get under your skin, but please don't rip my head off; I had no say in the matter,” says FBI Detective Adams with a sullen Lieutenant Patrick behind him.

After both men enter Macklin's office and shut his door, Patrick, his hands in his pockets while looking down at the dusty gray floor, adds, “Other than a serial killer uncaught in your own backyard, it's probably your worst logistical nightmare come true.”

With a little over a day to tone down his personality in front of the overwhelmed, and understandably increasingly irritable Macklin, Adams has now struck a more conciliatory tone with the media's anointed sniper investigation head.

“The state police sent their highest-ranking officer to assist our team,” says Patrick while an unusually quiet Macklin gathers his notepad, pen, and secret alcoholic drink before leaving the room with his contemporaries.

* * * * *

Jonathan Dobkins, the reigning superintendent of the Maryland State Police for the last twenty years, waits by himself in the MCPD's Tactical and Elevated Threat Meeting Room, which, by initial inspection, very much resembles efficienTECH's Maryland conference room. But unlike the place where Nina hurled her palm pilot at Colin only thirty-six hours ago, this space has a direct telephone and video link to the twenty-three other county police departments, the Baltimore and Washington DC police department, and instantaneous access to other clandestine and paramilitary agencies in the area like the Secret Service, Department of Homeland Security (DHS), Federal Emergency Management Agency (FEMA), and even CIA headquarters in Langley, Virginia.

"You're in my seat; get up," calmly instructs Macklin to Dobkins, who jumps into another one of the fourteen black leather chairs docked at the otherwise empty, rectangular marble table. Much worse than yesterday's pissing contest between Macklin and Adams, the tension between Macklin and Dobkins is palpable, for reasons that go back to last decade.

The true, living embodiment of the so-called "Wyatt Earp Syndrome," Dobkins still enjoys driving an unmarked car to autonomously break up underage, alcohol-fueled, high-school backyard parties. "There's no feeling in the world like pointing a gun in the face of a punk-ass teenager; I'd do it for free," Dobkins unwittingly told an Internal Affairs informant a few years back.

In the late 1990s, the Highway Patrol division of the Maryland State Police, along with their counterparts farther north up the coast in New Jersey, were embroiled in a racial profiling scandal that reached the highest levels of both organizations. In conclusion, secret testimony from rank-and-file troopers to tenured majors and lieutenants in both states revealed there was an established process in place that encouraged illegally pulling over, harassing, and often erroneously arresting young black males for no reason other than the amount of melanin in their skin. After both the *New York Times* and *Baltimore Sun* ran exposés detailing this prescribed practice, and subsequent cover-up, of systematic racism in both departments, the FBI (before Adams joined) essentially cleaned house in both organizations, forcibly making higher-ranked officers resign or take an early retirement. An ingemination of discrimination lawsuits soon ensued in both states, causing Maryland and New Jersey to implement written reforms and policies stating that "No individual may be detained based on race, unless that individual matches the description of a specific suspect." According to prior conversations between an FBI inquisitor and Macklin, Dobkins was the architect of such Maryland highway traffic policies specifically targeting innocent African-Americans. Because the MD State Police has jurisdiction over the Montgomery County Police Department, Donkin's henchmen were able to run roughshod on the two main arteries through Montgomery County, Interstate 270 and 495, stopping and frisking innocent citizens in Macklin's own county.

Macklin, who held Patrick's current position at the time, was powerless to be anything more than a bystander to the Highway Patrol's heavy-handed techniques of discrimination and intimidation. And because of his cozy relationship with Michael Steele, the powerful Republican lieutenant governor in a historically corrupt Annapolis state senate, Dobkins was not only able to avoid prosecution, but also retain his position as Maryland's top cop.

"How many innocent Blacks and Latinos have you mercilessly accosted this week on my highways—all in the name of stopping domestic terrorism?" asks a terse Macklin, gritting his teeth while sitting in Dobkins' original seat.

"Since I got here from Baton Rouge, we've swerved off topic way too many times. Superintendent, what have you and your men been able to come up with in regards to that white box-truck tip from that student in College Park . . . by some kid named Quincy Marshall?"

"That turned out to be a false lead. But yesterday morning, some seventy-year-old from Wheaton saw a Caucasian male in his mid-thirties enter a bread truck with the front tip of a shotgun hanging out of a long, polyester bag. Although he broke a statute forbidding him from carrying a weapon less than one hundred yards from their town hall, it turns out the guy was only trying to protect himself while making deliveries," calmly replies Dobkins, before adding, "A bigger problem is that troopers stationed at checkpoints statewide have no foundation upon who, or whom, they should be looking for."

"I'm sure you'll use it as an excuse to harass as many of us Negros as possible," remarks Macklin before taking an extended gulp of his Hennessy-infused Pepsi.

* * * * *

Jumping back to Dickerson, Konrad leads Nina down a staircase, which connects the second to first floor.

“Wow, you could really turn one of those bedrooms into a gym or entertainment room, and if you did it right, it wouldn't come across as tacky. I'm very impressed, Hunter.”

“Hey before you leave, let me show you the basement. As you know, a couple of rednecks used to run an illegal moonshine distillery down there,” says Konrad, opening the basement door.

“Quarter to one, and you still haven't told me about how Kreesha is getting away with all this. And did really you dump me because you're gay? Everyone knows you’re a down-low brother,” replies Nina before yawning.

While trotting down the darkened basement staircase of his impressive mini-mansion, Konrad says, “I hear your mom didn't answer the phone when you tried to reach her yesterday. That can't be good.”

“Hey, how the hell did you know about that?”

Chapter 19

Warren, tightly grasping an all-steel, 9mm Desert Eagle in his left palm, softly pokes Nina's lower spine, then motions her to continue to walk down the charcoal-black gateway.

"Don't make any sudden moves to the front door Nina; this is for your own good."

Nina stands, paralytic in terror as her life is directly threatened for the second time in a little over fourteen hours. Konrad, inches away, whispers, "Why do you think I'm fucking that insecure primate Denelle? For the exercise? Do as you're told, and get downstairs."

Nina's knees buckle as she momentarily loses balance.

"Acting syncopic won't alleviate your predicament, so just try and stay calm," I tell her, trying to ease her initial pain. Nina suddenly stiffens her vertebrae and fights the urge to cry.

Not knowing how exactly to react with a gun pointed at her back, Nina nervously takes a rubber band from her pocket to put her hair into a ponytail.

"Do that again and Warren will blow your fucking hand off. No more sudden movements while you navigate the darkness.

Until you reach the light switch to the bottom step's immediate right, use the guardrail to get down."

“What the fuck happened to you? First white collar crime, now kidnapping, Hunter?”

Following instructions, Nina’s silhouette slowly disappears as she descends into the darkness.

“All right. Once you hit the lights, turn around in a circle; please don't try and run anywhere. There's no exit on this floor and no neighbors within two miles to hear any screams for help.” Konrad smiles as Nina hits the greasy beige switch, finally exposing her to his villainous wonderland.

Nina rotates her body in a 360 degree motion, slowly absorbing her dreary, musty surroundings in Konrad's sunken, homemade factory. The entire room's a 4000-square-foot imprint, more than twice the size of the floor above it, and is completely covered by a large ventilation hood that turns on when Nina hits the switch.

“That aluminum hood above your head is used to eradicate evidence of vapors when we cook. Before we get to how I paid for it, pretend it's your first day at high school Chem lab all over again, and grab one of the four gray rubber aprons hung up on those hooks to the left of the stairs. Then put on those waterproof gloves and plastic goggles tucked inside its front kangaroo pouch,” instructs Konrad.

Nina takes a second look at the barrel of Warren's 9mm handgun pointed at her head and stays quiet while following Konrad's orders. Upstairs, Eric leans forward on a rustic leather chair in front of a desktop computer. In a hidden room on the second floor, Eric focuses one of the basement's security cameras on Nina's shaking hands as she quietly slips a protective smock over her neck, then fastens the waistband behind her slim waist.

Increasingly unstable emotionally, she turns away from Konrad and takes a second look at the coffin-like room in front of her. Running against, the length of each gray wall, which is composed of stacked, gray concrete blocks, are steel tables along embedded wash sinks, each one about four feet in height.

On top of each of the four, linked metal tables are dozens of industrial blenders, micro-mil grinders, glass and plastic mixing tubes, Bunsen burners, cryo-safe cold boxes, microwaves, incubators, magnetic stirrers, calculators, pipette controllers, burettes, homogenizers, vortexers, thermometers, unfolded cardboard boxes reaching the twenty-five-foot ceiling, analytical balances, crucibles, refrigerators, dry ice makers, spring scales, pizza and conventional cooking ovens, incubating turntables, pencils designed to accurately discover the pH level of various surfaces, iceboxes, benchtop fume hoods, compound microscopes, and desiccators—all neatly dispersed amongst thirty or so randomly placed plastic buckets, pails, and trays.

A large silver table with large metal sieves on top of it sits prominently in the room's center underneath a large hanging light usually reserved for hospital operating rooms.

In the room's nearest corner are ten plastic containers the same size as oil drums, each identically stacked in a level, tenpin-bowling arrangement.

Konrad strides to one of the drums farthest from the wall, then opens its round lid.

"Here's my problem," says Konrad, shaking his head in disapproval.

Inside the steel container are hundreds of thousands of small tablets no larger than a typical Molly pill. Konrad grabs a fistful of tablets, then brazenly shows them to the ex-girlfriend he just threatened to murder.

"Well, OK . . . that can't be aspirin, asshole. It's getting late, what are you really trying to accomplish by having me down here?"

"This is much bigger than you and I. With these chemicals, I'm going to start a revolution through unmitigated entropy, and in doing so, reclaim my kingdom.

"Before Warren gets bored and puts five in your ribcage, crouch underneath that table and pass that plastic thingamajig marked 'Acetic Anhydride.'"

Nina quickly gets on all fours and crawls underneath the exposed island.

"What are those pills composed of? Ecstasy, Meth, Ritalin?" apprehensively asks Nina while retrieving the six-and-a-half-gallon smooth-neck glass carboy marked "AA" in triangular black tape.

Konrad momentarily turns away from Nina to retrieve a large, restaurant-grade spice grinder from a wall opposite of Warren's location at the bottom of the stairs.

"With nationwide restrictions tightening prescription drug abuse across the board, I've decided to take advantage of a new emerging market. On another note, have you ever asked that voice in your head a direct question? Don't you want to know it's age, or if it's male or female? And what right does that voice have being there anyway? Theoretically, if it's a schizophrenia symptom triggered by stress and trauma, why is it so positive instead of telling you how fat and stupid you are?"

After berating Nina, Konrad tosses a hundred or so pills into the spice grinder and turns it on, causing an earsplitting, grating sound to reverberate throughout the sound-proofed basement.

"I don't even know where to begin . . ." cautiously says Nina.

"Remember that PWI account you worked all year and visited yesterday?" asks Konrad.

After Nina quickly nods her chin in agreement, she asks, "What chemical is that?"

"Acetic Anhydride. No, I'm not making Krokodil. But you're barking up the right tree."

Konrad uses a wooden spoon to roughly pour the foul-smelling, clear chemical from the glass carboy into his now-liquid consolidation. "I first started visiting that Pharmaceutical Warehouse Incorporated location years ago—about three months before you graduated from NYU. Well, after a night of heavy drinking at the Eighteenth Street Lounge, Curtis let me in on a little company secret over pancakes at IHOP."

"'You know, in addition to distributing popular name-brand and generic prescriptions to pharmacies in the area, our Maryland branch also has a research and development division unbeknown to its shareholders and even most of its employees,' Curtis told me.

"After casually prying for more classified info, he went on to say that this secret R and D division was solely created to try and discover scientific alternatives, healthy and otherwise, to popular street drugs like methamphetamine, cocaine, and even LSD. The codename of this branch was officially branded Crimson, Black, and White after its director's alma mater, but subsequently changed to just Black and White to avoid confusion."

"You mean, like the colors of the metaphysical sides we talked about yesterday?"

Hypnotized by the toxic soup between his exposed, lean muscular legs, Konrad puts the hoodie of his oxford gray sweatshirt over his cleanly shaven head, then picks up the bucket and momentarily places it on the basement's center table. As Konrad pours the bucket's rising, oatmeal-like contents into a three-foot high, spheroidal enamel pot on top of one of the four corner stovetops, he continues speaking. "Do you remember that East Indian guy that bolted out of PWI's office lobby and toward the parking garage while you were talking to Curtis?"

Nina, trying to act as unafraid of Konrad and Warren as possible, takes a seat on an empty stool next to the island, then nods her head in agreement.

"That's Nadir Jayaraman, head of the Black and White division at PWI. I definitely don't, but some minions in his office refer to him as 'the Creator.' Nadir is the one who officially facilitated the voice in your head for the last two days, and, because there's no antidote, for the rest of your life."

"Nina, let him continue. Indoctrination isn't easy, and before we get started, there's a lot you need to understand," I whisper.

"Stop hyperventilating, and let me explain this to you as concisely as possible. Number one: What's happened to you will improve your life in innumerable ways, both seen and unseen; just like it has to me. There was a one in seven billion chance that this could have happened to you, so like me, consider yourself lucky," says Konrad. Warren looks at his watch, then gets on his knees and begins to pray toward Konrad.

"I am the reincarnation of Amun-Ra. The King and Father of all Gods, Lord of all Thrones, and most importantly, Lord of Truth whose shine is hidden. I am the power that lies within each human's DNA, and each human's mind. Simply put, I am using Konrad Hunter's flesh and bone to recapture my kingdom and rule earth as I please," states Konrad, who obviously isn't a present reiteration of the past Egyptian King of all Gods and symbol of universal force in Ancient Africa. However, my Opponent is a master of deception, and told Konrad that he did indeed possess the soul of Amun in order to raise Konrad's confidence and gain his trust. As you can tell, I'm taking a more subdued, less insane approach to boost Nina's ego.

"What . . . what does that make me?" stutters Nina.

"Stay strong, and play it straight. You're just as powerful as he is," I remind her.

"Not sure. Isn't this the part where you, *the villain*, tell me how you plan to take over the world?" asks Konrad. While Warren is praying, Nina grabs the 9 from his waistband and points it at her head.

Chapter 20

As Nina squeezes the trigger, preparing for her head to explode, Warren lunges at her ankle, causing Nina's equilibrium to momentarily fluctuate. The gun explodes right above her temple, with the bullet ricocheting into the ceiling-mounted chemical hood.

"Death will never be an option, because you and I are immortals!" screams Konrad at the top of his lungs.

Defeated, Nina hunches over a table, hugs herself, and begins to sob.

"The voice is all-seeing and knowing. He used Nadir's greatest creation, officially called x-2317, as the most reasonable way to reach out to you and Amun-Ra. Using this power, Konrad was able to formalize a way to not only help Kreesha sneak that missing quarter mill back into efficienTECH's coffers, but also create a foolproof, money-making operation to rebuild his kingdom without the foolish authorities catching wind," ominously says Eric through a hidden speaker. "Not soon after 9/11, Nadir, along with his small team of dedicated scientists, secretly researched creation of an artificial alternative for the powerful drug Morphine, without using opium as its base. What initially began as a PWI attempt to wean the First world off its dependency for Opium from the Golden Triangle and Afghanistan grew into something much, much more."

Warren, taking pity on Nina, lights a pre-rolled blunt, takes a hit, and then hands it to her.

"Ending your life is impossible now. Now the fun begins; cheer up."

"I won't bore you with the complexities of molecular specifics, but after fourteen months of using chemical-combining methods, typically found during the preparation of artificial sweeteners like Equal and NutraSweet, then an additional six short months of testing the side effects of mice who ingested x-2317, Nadir accomplished the unthinkable: creating a homespun substance, much cheaper than imported black market opium, that can be used as its own powerful, artificial opiate, or as a substance chemically identical to Morphine," says Konrad.

After exhaling marijuana exhaust for ten seconds into Konrad's cleanly shaven, taut, poreless face, Nina hands the joint back to Warren and says, "Or heroin: the one hard drug you failed to mention so far. Isn't this what this operation is all about?"

Konrad carefully puts the flame below an enamel pot on low, then pulls out his cellphone and taps the glass screen a couple of times, electronically starting the basement's air-filtration system. Connected to an aluminum duct leading toward a hidden, four-by-two-foot, above-ground pipe a few acres behind Konrad's backyard, an eclipsed, inverted fan starts spinning silently above Konrad's head.

“Do you know that since Monday afternoon, your IQ has shot up approximately 75 percent? This is chess; you don't have to do want he wants. Keep attacking, and create your own power play,” I remind her.

Konrad elaborates.

“After the Others established contact with Nadir, they instructed him that they were focusing on a male and female, of different human races, to engage in geopolitical, economic, and social jousting, all for their viewing pleasure. When Curtis drugged your glass of water at your meeting yesterday, your nervous system was laced with all the medicinal advantages x-2317 has to offer.”

Nina lunges toward a couple of empty glass burettes, grabbing them before Warren can react. She then violently smashes the thin, cylindrical tubes against a metal table next to Konrad and presses the broken glass against the right side of his neck. Warren jumps from the stairs, cocks his retrieved weapon, and then points it directly at her back.

“Don't shoot her! I knew this was going to happen,” shouts Konrad as he arches his jaw away from the benign, superficial cut below his right ear. “You've never gotten in a physical fight in life and have no training in martial arts. Yet here you are, immediately targeting my external jugular vein with a handmade weapon, which, if applied with a little more pressure, could kill me instantaneously. This is what x-2317 did to you, babydoll. Your ability to read and react to stressful situations has been amplified in ways you're not even aware of.”

“If I’m your enemy, why are you telling me all of this?”

“Who would Mikhail Tal enjoy playing more: a novice or another grandmaster?”

“Huh?”

“I’m bringing you up to speed to make this game more interesting, but I’ll never tell you everything I’ve been taught,” elaborates Konrad.

“You getting all of this on tape, Eric?” barks Warren.

Three floors up, in one of Konrad's converted bedrooms, Eric focuses the closest of the basement's eight cameras on Nina, who's seconds away from slitting Konrad's throat.

“Come on, Nina, put the burette down, you're not built for life in prison. And then who'll take care of your mom? We both know she can't go on without you.”

Nina relinquishes pressure of the broken glass against Konrad's skin, then rips a segment of paper towel from above the sink and passes it to Konrad. “Never underestimate me,” she says, her eyes glaring like a caged lion.

“You're in too deep to go to the pigs now. You see, even though x- 2317 has a similar chemical makeup to morphine, opium, and heroin, it has one major side effect based upon the sex of the user.”

Because I had the option of choosing Nina to begin our game from the White side before my Opponent could pick his most powerful piece on Earth from the Black side, I had to agree to handicap Nina in some manner to account for my Opponent having one less human to select from.

Konrad, trying to keep Nina focused on how he's able to turn x-2317 into synthetic heroin, quickly picks up a clean pot next to the one that's boiling and then sticks it into Nina's stomach, causing her chiseled core muscles to flinch, then contract. Nina, remaining quiet, takes hold of the filled pot as Konrad continues.

"As I began to touch on earlier, there are fundamental, and of course biochemical, differences between x-2317 and our synthesized version of heroin. The feelings of dizziness, lethargy, moist skin texture, and unexplained confusion you felt Monday afternoon and evening were all because of x-2317. Now, the reason I resorted to creating synthetic heroin off of what, for argument's sake, we'll call synthetic morphine is because x-2317 doesn't attack the bloodstream the same way traditional morphine, opium, or mass-produced oxycodone does." Warren smiles while ashing the end of his joint into the concrete floor, then again points his handgun toward Nina.

Konrad looks at his watch, smiles and says, "You see, the first wave of temporary side effects for x-2317 commence instantaneously and last quite a few hours. But the euphoric, itchy wave of warmth that flows through every inch of your body, like you're on cloud nine, well that doesn't begin for thirty-six hours."

Nina carelessly puts the closed enamel pot on the island then grasps the table's sharp corner to maintain balance.

Konrad picks up the pot from the center of the room and places it on top of an opposite-wall corner table next to three plastic, gallon-sized bottles marked "Hydrochloric Acid," "Caffeine," and "Sodium Carbonate."

"Don't worry, the intoxication x-2317 provides will be gone by the time you wake up. x-2317 is now permanently in you; there's no turning back," I add.

In her catatonic, drug-fueled emotionless state, Nina begins to visualize, from a third-eye, elevated vantage point parallel to her apartment complex roof, herself dangling off her penthouse balcony, dozens of feet above the grassy knoll, by nothing more than a thin leather strap. As Nina views this, the hallucinatory version of herself momentarily glances away from the second story ledge she aimed to grab with her toes and smiles toward Nina's elevated viewpoint before chanting, "Don't worry, I was never going to hurt you . . ."

Nina, still watching the hallucination, is handling this onboarding process worse than Konrad, and is close to permanently losing consciousness. Knowing that Nina's on the verge of losing her sanity, I momentarily interrupt her x-2317 side effect and tell her, "Nadir only exists to assist; never hesitate to use him as a resource—regardless of the risks involved."

"Take her home, Warren, and make sure she stays hydrated. On the way, tell her about how she'll serve me," orders Konrad to his assistant. Konrad then grabs the wobbly Nina by the neck and forcefully shoves her face into a mound of synthetic heroin on a table.

Chapter 21

"Once I realized the economic opportunity synthetic heroin presented, I immediately reached out to your childhood friend Bartolo, who put me in touch with Tavon Ayala at the Baltimore City Detention Center," says Warren to Nina from his driver's seat.

"Fuck . . ."

"Yeah, Nina, *that* Tavon."

Her head pounding, Nina recalls a front-page *Baltimore Sun* article she read last year about the infamous drug kingpin.

Tavon Ayala is the de facto mid-Atlantic leader of the BCM, or Black Commando Mafia: a wickedly violent prison and street gang originating from inner-city Oakland in the 1960s. Isaiah Taylor, while wrongly incarcerated at the San Quentin California State Prison for the 1987 murder of a young woman, a witness-less crime historians later believed was carried out by the Zodiac Killer, decided, along with cellmate Elijah Harris, to form their own organization as an alternative for the fragmented Black Panther movement. Using tenets from Marcus Garvey, along with philosophical beliefs from Marxism, Harris and Taylor founded a movement initially focused on altruistic goals of (1) eradicating racial discrimination, (2) affirming sanity, hygiene, and self-respect while behind bars, and (3) forcefully dismantling all three branches of the federal government.

Nearly forty years later, BCM morphed into one of the country's most ruthless and violent street gangs, with over 100,000 associates located from city corners to prisons stretching from California to Maine. Mr. Ayala is easily the most powerful inmate at the City Detention Center in East Baltimore, which rat-infested accommodations closely resemble the worst global prisons from 'Locked Up Abroad.'

Ayala orchestrates all East Coast regional business matters for the BCM.

Although extortion, contract killing, money laundering, and racketeering are all major forms of revenue for the Black Commando Mafia, the majority of their profits are from importing, then distributing, bulk quantities of heroin, methamphetamine, cocaine, and marijuana to large and mid-sized cities in Pennsylvania, Delaware, Maryland, and Northern Virginia. Nina, with her newfound photographic memory, remembers reading a third paragraph in a Sunday edition years ago while Konrad served her breakfast in bed.

"The growing influence of Mexican cartels in heroin production, and their sophistication of smuggling routes across the border, and through all arteries connecting cities around this country, is truly mind-blowing. This has led to an unexpected consequence on the streets of Baltimore. Local dealers, sized out of high-grade heroin, are increasingly using cutting agents such as rat poison and battery acid, instead of staples like starch and lactose, to not only increase their supply, but as retribution for addicts that only turn to them after failing to score purer, slightly more expensive heroin from Central American pushers," stated the article.

“In retaliation for their tactics, members of MS-13 paid a hefty sum to B-more homicide detectives, almost seven figures worth, to trap the established black dealers in a sting operation for ten kilos of Colombian white. This is how Ayala got locked up. Of course, this hasn't stopped Ayala from continuing to manage regional BCM operations from behind bars while awaiting appeal to his fifty-year sentence,” says Warren.

Warren checks the rearview mirror for law enforcement, takes a deep breath, then continues to drive on the empty highway.

“That's where Ayala and our story meet. You see, synthetic heroin, with x-2317 as its base, is much cheaper to produce than the real stuff. It's also just as addictive and undetectable to drug-sniffing dogs.”

* * * * *

“A C.O. I got on payroll snuck in your shipment, and I personally tested your h on a couple crackheads in my cell block,” bragged Ayala during a face-to-face prison meeting with Konrad a few years back.

“Not only can users not tell the difference between the synthetic and real heroin, but it's going to be a lot easier to send it up to states like Vermont, New Hampshire, and Maine, where tough restrictions on oxycodone and Percocet have forced consumers to further explore the underground black market. We will charge four, possibly five times of what's fetched down here for a normal packet of black tar,” added Ayala.

Konrad let Ayala take control of the conversation and stayed quiet while the convict continued speaking.

"I also have people on the outside—brothers that tell me you have no gang affiliation and by all appearances are a stand-up North Philly cat with a normal nine-to-five and no criminal past. Your father was murdered in a drug deal gone wrong, and your mom is wandering aimlessly around Broad Street willingly sucking dick to get her next fix. Yet you were able to avoid the gang life growing up and used your athleticism as a way out the hood. But your bodyguards, Warren and Eric, are Crips, so why not distribute through them?"

"It makes business sense for me to give this opportunity to everyone. The Central Americans and Mexicans don't want any part of me because they've got the purest, all-natural product on the street. To them, it makes no sense to introduce a commodity to the marketplace that's competing directly with something they've already got the majority of addicts hooked on. As for the Crips, and any other rival gang of yours, they don't have the leader of their regional organization locked up like the Black Commando Mafia does. I've contemplated offering them side deals to sell small quantities of synthetic heroin in the DMV. But after deep reflection, I've devised a better plan. Mr. Ayala, I'm giving you the opportunity to take over distribution of my product through the upper New England region. And by the time you get out of here, which could be before you turn forty if paroled, you'll be rich enough to buy the Ravens."

* * * * *

“So Konrad's a drug kingpin now?” asks Nina in present time.

“Amun is using Konrad's opportunity in order to recapture his kingdom. The other dimension has decided this is just. The other dimension has decided this is fair.”

“Get your hand off my thigh and tell me exactly how he's getting away with all this.”

“One Sunday night a month, within his lab, Dr. Nadir quickly cooks up a massive quantity of x-2317 then deposits over 600,000 tablets in two nondescript oil drums outside his office. After bypassing lax security around the loading area due to a guard change close to midnight, Eric tiptoes through the desolate PWI facility, loads the drums onto a forklift, and then drives it to an unmarked white box-truck Warren has in neutral. With Ayala's people already stationed in Burlington, Manchester, Albany, and Portland, we distribute synthetic heroin to unaware zombies in those four states. Our smack is so good we got addicts hitchhiking from Philly, Boston, and even Staten Island to get it. Even though it's as dangerous to the system as regular heroin, our product hasn't been cut with any dangerous adulterants and is more addictive than what junkies were using previously.”

“Konrad wouldn't have just let you tell me all this. So what's the catch?” asks Nina.

Nina, fully reclined in the passenger seat, graciously receives an unopened bottle of water from her driver and then uses it to try to damper her ongoing, vivid visual hallucinations. “You know, when Konrad took x-2317, he ended up spending the first week in bed staring at the ceiling while asking his internal voice who was going to win every upcoming NBA game so he could bet on it. From what he's told me, the match between you two doesn't work like that. You only get internal advice when your life is being threatened. *The more life-threatening risk you take, the more money you get.* You're not an immortal, like Supergirl or the Hulk in comic books, but x-2317 has already modulated your central neurotransmitters, allowing your muscles and tendons to become much more aggressive upon command."

"If I'm so powerful, why anger me by torturing my mom?" Seconds before Warren left, Konrad ran to Nina's car and gleefully revealed how easy it would be to execute Mrs. Sullivan if Nina disclosed Konrad's night job to law enforcement.

"You haven't decided how you're going to build your empire yet, so Konrad's going to do all he can to prevent you from getting to his level. And everything was running smoothly until that asshole decided to leave Louisiana and continue his killing spree in this state. That forced PWI to upgrade their security since the start of October, and that's cut into the time Dr. Nadir has to cook x-2317," responds Warren.

"Hey, look ahead. I think you got a problem."

Warren, with the inebriated woman beside him, downshifts the M3 to fourth gear while Eric follows two car lengths behind the BMW in his Alpine white, Mercedes S65 AMG, limo-tinted and riding on twenty-two-inch, gloss-black, five-spoke rims.

"Better patch in Eric and boss on the three-way," adds Warren before gently rubbing Nina's greasy forehead. He then adds, "Konrad didn't kill you tonight because you're the messiah for the White side. He's afraid your death would anger the other dimension to the point that they permanently disable his powers. You may feel differently, and could view killing him as the ultimate sign of your victory. In order to add excitement, the other dimension has not yet defined what the game's final objective is—only the parameters in which you two can play."

Konrad picks up the phone, interrupting Warren's accurate explanation of this important fact regarding our game.

"Yeah, Konrad, patch through Eric for me; the queue for a checkpoint is beginning just ahead . . . Yeah, I'm guessing it's for the sniper, too."

Eric double-flashes his high-beams to indicate he's aware of the situation as Nina's car approaches one of Dobkins' twenty-four-hour checkpoints.

Still in his basement in Dickerson, Konrad puts a spoonful of his completed synthetic black tar heroin on a scale.

"Take the phone off speaker and pass it to Nina," Konrad orders.

A few hundred yards in front of Nina and Warren, FBI Detective Adams sits on the hood of one of the six eastbound police cruisers.

On the opposite direction of the identically formatted, two-lane highway headed west is the same setup: six Montgomery County Police Department vehicles with their overhead lights on, also stationary, and equally split on each shoulder of the toll-less road. Superintendent Jonathan Dobkins, head of the westbound checkpoint, looks across the fifteen-foot-wide, miles-long stretch of grass acting as a barrier for both sections of the purposely obstructed road.

Back in the passenger seat of her own car, Nina slightly regains her consciousness, and partially winds down her window while receiving Warren's mobile phone.

"You're going to be our new driver for completed batches of synthetic h. Each week, you're going to pick up a few kilos from my place and drive it to our contact at BWI. Warren will fill you in on the details," says Konrad.

At this point, it's important to clarify what signifies a victory for either me or my Opponent. Simply put, the game ends when either side stops, or completes, the majority of these twenty-one events from occurring. The brilliant author Dr. John Coleman, who was an unaware gray, Nadir-like character from a previous twentieth century game between our predecessors that ended in a draw (10.5 – 10.5), unknowingly wrote our game's parameters in his book *Conspirator's Hierarchy: The Committee of 300.* Past games have disclosed these immutable game parameters through acclaimed paintings, music, and other less direct works of exalted literature, like haikus. These twenty-one events are:

The creation of a One World Government, with one single church and one single currency, under either side's control.

The total destruction of every nation's identity and national pride, because only then will people accept one super-national world government.

The destruction of every religion, especially Christian denominations. The only exception being a new "religion" of their creation.

The establishment of thought-control techniques, with the goal of creating self-reliant, human-like robots who respond to external impulses and direction.

The destruction of industrialization, with the exception of the world's computer and service sectors.

The legalization of drug usage and normalization of pornography throughout society.

The depopulation of the world's largest cities by any means necessary.

The suppression of all scientific development, except for advancements which serves the purposes of either the White or Black side.

The premature death of three billion people by the year 2050—either through regional warfare or through starvation and sickness in under-developed nations.

The demoralization and destruction of society's working class via large-scale unemployment.

The forcing of society to be completely reliant on government agencies like *FEMA (or the Federal Emergency Management Agency)* during times of crisis.

The introduction of new cults that clandestinely support either side's desires.

The creation of an autonomous, Zionist state by financial means.

The creation of religious sects that specifically exist to carry out thought-control experiments for the benefit of either perspective side.

The circulation of ideas that undermine all existing religions with denominations over one million followers.

The collapse of the world economy by any means necessary.

The takeover of all domestic and international policies of earth's greatest superpower, the USA.

The enhancement of current multi-national organizations, like the United Nations and the International Court of Justice.

The destruction of each nations sovereignty by any means necessary.

The creation of a falsified international terrorism organization used to instill fear around the world.

Complete control of America's education system in order to manipulate it to benefit the advancement of an eventual one-world government.

Both Nina and Konrad will have their entire lifetime to complete accomplishment of these twenty-one goals—with respective help from myself and my Opponent, of course. Whichever victor completes the majority of these tasks will have the option of dying a natural death on earth or joining us in this dimension where death does not exist and where they can compete in their own multi-dimensional games if it so pleases them to do so.

Now that that's out of the way, let's turn our attention back to Nina, who's still stopped at the police checkpoint with Warren.

"Your strength is returning . . . use confusion as an asset; it's your best weapon at this point," I remind her.

Three hundred yards from her location, Adams removes the night vision binoculars from his weary, bloodshot eyes, turning his attention away from Route 28 West and toward his designated stretch of road—also constricted by a semi-open, siphoning auto barricade.

“You see anything suspicious on my side, Dobkins? I can't find anything abnormal on your cnd—othcr than morc than a few disgruntled drivers beeping their horns and giving your boys the finger,” inquires Adams into his walkie-talkie, his voice hoarse after being up the last sixty hours. Nearly two days after arriving in Maryland, Detective Adams has yet to find any indication of where his killer could be. Footprints left yesterday near the MARC station, thought to possibly be those of the serial killer after he wounded his most recent and youngest victim, don't match footprints left at crime scenes in Louisiana and Arizona.

“If pigs ask where you're coming from, tell them the truth: that you're driving a friend home after a night of domestic drinking and card-playing,” says Konrad, now back on speaker in both cars.

“Those are MCPD and State Trooper cars ahead, sprinkled with a couple unmarked Impalas. This ain't no DWI checkpoint,” observes Eric.

Eric then presses an obscure button on his car dash, usually reserved for activating the front seat heaters. Instantaneously, a metal, airtight stash box, with just enough space to house a pair of inverted, size-thirteen Jordans, escapes from underneath the beige leather-bound glove compartment via two parallel, pressurized pumps. By a more conventional method, Warren also conceals his weapon by moving his handgun from his lap and into a rear pocket attached to the backside of the front passenger seat.

Remembering what her internal guide suggested, Nina uses the skills she learned in her weekly Muay-Thai class and throws a quick-hitting, southpaw hook to Warren's cheekbone, causing him to momentarily lose control of the steering wheel and consequently lurch the car toward the highway's emergency lane.

Dobkins notices the M3 swerve, then nods toward a couple state troopers on Route 28 West. As cops slowly let interrogated citizens, the highlight so far being a man dressed as Batman in a Lamborghini convertible, accelerate from the cluster of cruisers partially blocking both directions of the highway, Dobkins radios to Adams

“There's a black BMW, with aftermarket headlights and a carbon fiber hood, about ten cars back from where your Eastbound checkpoint begins. It'd be best to check it out.”

Adams darts away from his roadblock onto the plush, manicured pasture between both directions of the highway, then squints in Nina's direction.

“Jonathan, there was a recent court order banning you from indiscriminately pulling over law-abiding Marylanders. This is my only warning: don't use trying to catch this psycho as another excuse to abuse the Fourth Amendment.”

Dobkins, dressed in full Maryland State Police regalia while sitting on the hood of a parked squad car, continues to stare at the tinted window hiding Warren's bruised jaw.

“She just popped me in the mouth, Konrad; please let me return the favor,” says an angry Warren.

Outside of the European vehicle, Nina’s sports car catches a supervising officer’s eye.

“Fairfax chink gangs soup up German coupes like that M3, so make sure my boys pull it over when it gets to your queue,” says Dobkins to one of his state troopers via a walkie-talkie.

Adams taps the shoulder of Officer Michael McGary, who's inspecting an expired vehicle registration card from a pulled over, dilapidated beige Diamante belonging to a mid-fifties, visibly nervous redneck from Western Maryland.

"Hey, Michael, unless there's truly something suspicious going inside that car, make sure you don't search that black BMW approaching the checkpoint," whispers Adams into McGary's left ear.

"She's not gonna make a fuss in front of Montgomery County's finest, because if she does, Mrs. Sullivan will be dead by sunup. Just act normal, everyone," instructs Konrad over the speakerphone.

The roadblock line for Maryland Route 28 East slowly inches toward a vicinity between two diametrically opposed black and white Dodge Chargers with "MCPD" emblazoned in red and blue on their side doors. Behind both cars are a couple of unmarked Ford Crown Victoria's in navy blue and beige. The Crown Vics are the cars of Adams and Lieutenant Patrick, who surreptitiously dozed off in the backseat of his vehicle.

Conversely, the setup is the "bizarro world" opposite on Route 28 West. Two Maryland State trooper cruisers, split at an approximately seventy-degree angle, wait to inspect thirty-five to forty cars, also impatiently composed in a single, slow-moving line. The green and black Crown Victorias, also fitted with oscillating blue and red lights, display the Maryland state flag emblem on their side door. Behind the two trooper vehicles, common to drivers accustomed to routinely seeing them during organized, I-95 speed traps, are two unmarked Ford Mustangs in stealth black with limo-tinted windows.

Eric, now fifth in line, echoes Konrad's sentiment. "I spoke to Bartolo before this conference call; he's willing to spend years in prison if need be. Nina's not going to say a word. Just stick to Konrad's story, and we'll be in Laurel in no time."

Konrad, the cunning raconteur, stops talking just as Officer McGary, under the directive of Detective Adams, takes over the duties of quizzing drivers at the line's beginning.

"Turn off your phone and radio so you can give me your full attention; I don't want to keep you here longer than necessary. OK, for starters, sir, I need to take a look at your license and registration. A more thorough investigation of your vehicle may follow."

McGary then shines his illuminated flashlight toward Nina.

"Your passenger's eyes are dilated and she's sweating profusely even though you have the air-conditioning on. What were you two up to tonight?" asks McGary to Warren as both Adams and Dobkins watch from a distance.

Warren turns down his stereo, puts his phone down without turning it off, then tactfully takes the registration card and proof of insurance from Nina, who, moments earlier, retrieved both documents from a leather case in her glove compartment.

"The car is mine, officer. I got really drunk at a friend's house, and my friend is driving me back home," says Nina.

"Why would a serial killer be out here in the middle of the night using this state's busiest roads? Did that coon Macklin hatch up this plan? He's a fuckin' idiot," adds Warren.

Momentarily shocked at the audacity of the young black male in the luxury car's driver's seat, the rookie cop points to an empty patch of grass next to Patrick's halted car.

"Park next to that Ford on the side of the road over there, then turn off the engine. Do not exit your vehicle for any reason!" shouts Officer McGary at a level loud enough for both Konrad, who's still quietly listening on Warren's enabled speakerphone, and Eric, who patiently waits in the second queued car, to easily hear.

Konrad texts Eric and tells him to drive directly to Nina's apartment, then wait for Warren and Nina's arrival.

"He looks like he wants to bash your skull with his billy club. What did you do that for?" asks Nina while Warren drives her car to its ordered location.

"You still don't comprehend how powerful you are, how x-2317 has transformed all of us, regardless of which side we fight for. You and Konrad are no longer constrained by draconian, feudal measures implemented and maintained to hold back society's progress," observes Warren while turning off the headlights.

Ten feet away from their location, Adams ducks behind Eric's departing Mercedes and gets in McGary's face.

"I specifically told you not to give them a hard time, officer. Why'd you disobey my orders?"

Dobkins quietly looks on from the highway's opposite side.

"The thug in the driver's seat started complaining about the line's pace and lack of leads in the sniper investigation."

Officer McGary then places Warren's license, along with Nina's registration card and proof of insurance, in the open palm of Detective Adams' hand.

"Go back to inspecting cars waiting at the queue, officer; I'll handle this."

"The shorter one, who just grabbed your license from that cop, definitely doesn't look like one of Montgomery County's own. He's got a swagger to him; I can feel it," says Nina, still seated in the M3 passenger seat.

"Even though you and I are on different sides, x-2317 shields us from petty disagreements with the wealthy's personal security force. He won't do shit to us. Watch and learn," remarks Warren.

"Adams thinks he's Melvin Purvis; what the hell is he up to?" inquires Dobkins out loud, referring to "Little Mel," the famous FBI agent who tracked notorious criminals like Pretty Boy Floyd, John Dillinger, and Baby Face Nelson.

"Good morning, Warren," says Adams, while extending a handshake to the skeptical, and yawning, personal escort for Nina.

"We've committed no crime, have no criminal history, and yet you detain us against our will. I've been harassed by the state police on this road before, but your style is too relaxed to be one of Dobkins' Klansmen. Who are you?" directly asks Warren, who's extremely familiar with the Maryland State Police's heavy-handed practices based on numerous run-ins with them in Baltimore County.

"My name is Charles Adams, and I'm the Federal Bureau of Investigation's lead detective for our regional southeast district. What brings you out here these few hours before sunup?"

Adams, who regularly experiences recurring flashbacks of his two tours of duty in Iraq, remembers how this impromptu interrogation feels eerily similar to a situation he commandeered during a routine stop and frisk in the country's northern region.

A few years ago, during a busy, weekday afternoon in Kirkuk, Adams' regiment of six soldiers dispersed a few dozen roadside stand operators who were protesting the war in the middle of the city's main avenue.

“Routine shit; we were conducting traffic clean-up operations like this on a daily basis around the country,” he told his mandated army psychiatrist at Walter Reed Hospital right after debriefing his supervisors at the Pentagon.

“Then, before you know it, two kids, one male, and one female, no older than twenty-five, walked up to my Sergeant, and . . . without uttering a word, they detonated an IED, right in front of him. The blast instantly blew up my most trusted soldier and released enough shrapnel to amputate both legs of a communications officer standing five meters to the left of me.”

Back in Maryland, in the eyes of Nina and Warren, Adams can easily see the same indescribable look of anger that he saw in both suicide bombers.

“Before we leave, then decide whether to call my lawyer to sue the county and state police for harassment, tell me what progress you've made on the sniper case.”

“That's classified information that you're not privy to, miss.”

“You know, insanity is defined by performing the same functions, day in and day out, while conceding the same negative results. Yet you're out here again, trying to retrieve a needle from a haystack. I bet you thought it'd be easy to find a killer in this state, but now you're beginning to realize how diverse, yet segregated, Maryland is. Unless you comprehend these dynamics, Charles, you'll never be successful in apprehending your suspect," Nina replies.

Instead of devising a bogus excuse to detain Nina and Warren, Adams signals good-bye to the duo while memorizing the car's license plate.

"Did you see the look on his face after you and I finished dressing him down? Fuck the police; I told you they wouldn't do a damn thing," says Warren, casually massaging Nina's left breast.

"Words can't explain what's going on inside my head. Just get me home in one piece, and you'd better not fucking try anything."

Chapter 22

"I got Ritalin for all your scholastic worries. Only twenty-five a pop," says a text message instantly delivered to a cellphone.

The SMS, delivered by a random weed dealer Quincy found off backpage.com, flashes inside his software application designed to collect conversations without leaving an electronic footprint.

As he steps off the otherwise-empty red-and-white University of Maryland campus bus at the corner of Regents and Campus Drive, Quincy casually types, "I don't do drugs; stop contacting me."

Quincy momentarily looks south at the flower-adorned roundabout proudly displaying the letter "M" in bright, harmoniously colored tulips, then prepares to make the short trek toward the chemistry building.

Operation Sudden Drop, or OSD, as members of the Drug Enforcement Agency refer to it, was a recent Pepperdine University drug ring foiled by both state and federal officials. It's also the reason Quincy currently resides in Maryland instead of California.

“We're going to rob every one of those spoiled, spoon-fed douches in those frat houses,” said Rebecca while driving past Pepperdine University's abbreviated version of Maryland’s frat row two years ago.

After turning off the Pacific Coast Highway, Rebecca drove past the off-campus properties of Sigma Chi, Delta Tau Delta, Sigma Phi Epsilon, and Psi Epsilon: the five chapters that compose Pepperdine's Interfraternity Council.

“We've only pushed quantities below the statute of 'intent to distribute.' You know that, right? Once we cross that line, and venture into the territory of mid-level drug dealer, then theoretically, we could be locked up until our fifties. And I ain't going out like that.”

“Cheer up, honey. We'll stay below the radar; trust me,” responds Rebecca, momentarily taking her hand off the car's stick shift to twist Quincy's curly, obsidian locks with the precision of an urban hairstylist.

As two weeks passed, near the middle of Quincy's third fall semester at Pepperdine, he and Rebecca began to steer, then up-sell, their client base toward purchasing higher quantities of oxycodone, Adderall, cocaine, heroin, meth, and hashish.

“I'm basically just attending classes and studying while rehabbing my injury with the Athletic Department, Mom. No need to worry about me up here,” lied Quincy to his mother during a past phone conversation.

Instead, Quincy, always with the Karissa Shannon-lookalike Rebecca draped on his arm, searched high and wide to expand, and eventually transition, his clientele from the occasional, once- or twice-a-week buyer to prospects interested in purchasing a quantity of product ten times larger than the average, or previously average, sale. When not spending money for bi-monthly, extravagant trips to cities like Honolulu or Vegas, Quincy and Rebecca pitched their illicit menu everywhere in Malibu.

From various social, academic, and athletic Pepperdine organizations located in the 90263 to Malibu beach parties hosted by professional athletes and entertainers, Quincy and Rebecca went everywhere to try to snag a customer with the ability to purchase four to five figures worth of drugs per transaction. The madly-in-love couple, acting with the aggression of a chess player who just successfully gambitted their rook, finally found their mark after two weeks of cold calling.

With their supplier's blessing, Quincy finally discovered their Beluga whale inside the hallway of the Graziado School of Business and Management.

Jeremy Emanuel, son of powerful super-agent Ari Emanuel, immediately took a liking to Quincy when first meeting him after his Business Ethics lecture.

"He had such a calm, open demeanor about himself. It's kinda hard to describe, but it's like Quincy effused a Zen-like, reassuring quality when he asked me how my day was going. And his girlfriend, looking like a model out of a Victoria's Secret catalog, was really cool too—much more engaging than most of the stuck-up bitches on campus," said Jeremy during a future taped conversation privately observed by his lawyer and the Pepperdine University Provost.

"We were both done with classes for the day, so being somewhat lonely, I invited him and Rebecca back to my place to smoke and listen to me spin some Barrington Levy records."

After following Jeremy to his multi-million-dollar duplex near Paradise Cove, he and Quincy discussed a wide array of topics, ranging from President Cheney's "War on Terror" to the Clippers' chances of repeating.

"You've heard the story before, Quincy: rich, aimless, and disillusioned son of Hollywood big-wig seeks a rush to disrupt his falsely presented, idyllic Southern Californian lifestyle," said Jeremy during his uninterrupted harangue.

"My father's formula for delivering blockbuster hits is falling apart at the seams. Casting decisions are now instantly being bashed on Twitter due to an increasingly diverse population uninterested with today's homogenous, manufactured movie stars. I'm afraid that I'm not going to be able create the same successful films my father did in the eighties and nineties. The paradigm has shifted, my friend, and I need a plan that enables me to maintain this lifestyle."

"What if I told you Quincy and I have an unlimited supply of the purest heroin in California? Here, test the quality yourself," said Rebecca, handing Jeremy a rolled one-hundred-dollar bill.

"I'd say, you now have an opportunity to grow your business through me, as the third and final member of your team. That's what I'd say as that individual," replied Jeremy, who, after a couple lines, rambled his intention to partner with the entrepreneurial couple.

Back in present time, after tightening the straps of his North Face backpack, Quincy strolls up Regents Drive, taking in the unmatched beauty of the desolate campus at 7:15 a.m.

“Hey, my brother, can you make it out to our church meeting this evening? We'd be glad to have you,” says an eager Nigerian exchange student, dressed in Dockers and an obnoxiously bright-red University of Maryland sweatshirt.

Blocking Quincy's path with a broad, ivory smile, the chemical engineering student forcefully gives the Pepperdine transfer a pamphlet, stating the principals of the ICOC, or International Church of Christ.

“No thank you, my man, no thank you,” politely responds Quincy, well aware of the cult controversy that exploded on campus a few years ago. As he puts on his headphones, Quincy glances at the trunk of a mature oak tree to his right. Stapled to its bark, at a height of about five and a half feet off the ground, is a flyer for one of the few legitimate bars in College Park. The ad reads

“CORNERSTONE GRILL AND LOFT @ *7325 Baltimore Avenue is hiring this week for the following staff positions: Bar back, Bouncer, and Bartender. Looking to hire ASAP. Stop by for more info.*”

Quincy looks in both directions before snatching the flyer from the tree.

Chapter 23

"Sorry I'm late, you two. That PWI account, the one that Nina's been working on for months? I need it closed ASAP in order to make district quota. Let's talk about how we can help her."

After closing the conference room door behind her, Kreesha then asks, "Also, Colin, have you heard anything, like around the office, about Nina trying to reach out to any other co-workers? You know, about what happened on Monday?"

"I wish I had some good gossip to share, but she's been a ghost since trying to kill me on Monday. And for your information, my wife and I are filing a civil lawsuit against you—and efficienTECH."

"You don't want to do that, Colin, you're basically a vice president around here," Konrad chimes in

"What does that make you, Konrad, Monica Lewinsky?" retorts Colin.

"Let's put aside the fact that you've illegally stolen over five dozen leads from Nina since the start of the fiscal year. Leads that have netted you over $60,000 in commission. That's not only a clear violation of efficienTECH corporate policy, but also possibly makes you criminally negligent in denying Nina's career advancement," states Kreesha.

"But, but boss—"

"In light of these facts, but because you're obviously still traumatized by Monday morning's events, I've decided to give you a rock solid, five-figure prospect. This time it's in Northern Virginia; in Alexandria."

"What's the name of the company, and what's their occupation?"

"The company's name is Northern Virginia Auto Recovery. It's an easy deal to close," says Kreesha, referring to the business that tried to recover Nina's BMW yesterday.

After another five hours cut into the dwindling hump day, Nina blindly grasps her buzzing alarm clock from her bedside dresser, then hurls the small plastic device against the room's far wall, shattering it upon impact. While keeping her forehead planted against the pillow, she releases the bedroom blinds, sending them crashing against the dusty windowsill inches away from her elevated mattress. The instant darkness of the room reassures Nina's other four senses, giving her the trust to finally open her eyes and embrace the future.

Nina arches her neck at her DVR cable box, which flashes the time 3:06 p.m. in neon green.

"Last night didn't happen. It couldn't have. I don't even remember walking into this apartment last night."

Nina unlocks her mobile phone. Finally mustering enough energy to pivot her legs from underneath the bedspread, she walks toward her balcony, eventually gets on her knees, and unhinges the black belt used in yesterday's escape.

"What the fuck. Not one message from Konrad—or Kreesha for that matter."

Nina inspects the only text that entered her inbox within the last sixteen hours.

"Get ready for dinner in DC, then drinks at some place called Cornerstone in College Park. I heard there's a lot of ass there, so be ready to leave by 4 ;)" states the periphrastic message from Ronnie.

"I'll just get him loaded so he'll be too hammered to get a hotel room. Then I'll cook him breakfast and see how long he can stay until this all blows over," theorizes Nina while turning on the faucet of her walk-in shower.

"For at least the next one hundred seconds, keep the water temperature as cold as possible. I'll be finished updating your mainframe in a few minutes," I tell her.

Because her body fat content is under ten percent, it's easy for me to activate her enhancements wirelessly. Nina's hardened body begins to shiver uncontrollably, making her striated oblique muscles clench and contract at a pace matched only by her quickening heart rate.

Nina grabs a razor, looks at the ceiling, and then brings the shaver to her left wrist.

"I'll assist whenever possible. But there's no instruction manual on how best to benefit, and supplement, your decision-making process. Remember what Warren told you last night, and use it as your mantra."

Calculating that Nina would be on the verge of suicide, I cleared up traffic on 95 South so that her friend would arrive early.

“Nina, c'mon, open up. It's me, Richard Howell,” shouts Ronnie, referencing the alias he always gives strippers.

Bartolo I can see, but there's no way Ronnie's in on it. He's a socialist from Greenpoint living well off his daddy's handouts, so what's five figures to a thirty-eight-year-old hipster with no direction? thinks Nina, trying to elicit my response.

Once hiding the butcher knife in the hallway closet, Nina smiles and opens the door.

“I know efficienTECH doesn't define 'work from home' as taking bong hits and watching soap operas all day,” says Ronnie after giving Nina a tight bear hug. Dressed in covertly expensive True Religion dark blue jeans, tightly laced black converse sneakers, and a light gray $825 Saint Laurent hoodie covering his frail, 5'8 frame, Ronnie tosses his overnight bag on the couch.

“The last thing your coke-bloated face needs is another night on the town, so promise me you'll take it easy this evening. And chill out. I'm only selling industrial copiers, not a manual for immortality.”

As Nina decides what color heels to wear, Ronnie twists a clump of hair from his three-inch-thick, dirty-blond beard.

Turning on the television, he proclaims, “I'm sick and tired of hearing about this Serial Sniper. On every news station in Philly, Delaware and Baltimore, each announcer kept regurgitating the same abstract drivel off the same stale press release. Macklin and his crew have no idea where that psycho is; you can tell from the bullshit they're trying to feed the public.”

Bypassing the mainstream news channel, Ronnie turns to HBO, which is playing his favorite stoner movie: *Fear and Loathing in Las Vegas.*

"I wonder what Thompson would think about this serial sniper," says Ronnie.

Nina emerges from her bedroom in a simple black tank top, white jeans the same size as Ronnie's, and bright red, four-inch Louboutin heels.

"Who is this, Hitler?" curiously asks Ronnie, while holding a black-and-white picture of a mid-twenties Eastern European man dressed in military garb.

"Stop being stupid; it's my biological father. I never met him, of course, but before he emigrated to Philly in the 1950s, my dad was a colonel in the Polish ABW., which is their version of the FBI. Kazimierz—Kazimierz Luczak was his name."

Now in his brand-new, metallic-gray Porsche Turbo S, Ronnie and Nina fight through traffic on the Baltimore-Washington Parkway headed toward DC. Stuck in traffic by the Bladensburg Route 450 exit, he again brings up her father.

"What kind of work did your pops do once moving to the states?" asks Ronnie.

"He became a homicide detective for the Philadelphia Police Department. A few years back, using an efficienTECH contact, Konrad e-mailed me a .pdf file detailing each case he was involved in. Most of his work focused on Philly's Italian Mafia, specifically targeting Angelo Bruno and his associates during the late '60s," responds Nina.

* * * * *

"Yeah, I remember recently watching a National Geographic special about the 'The Gentle Don.' He definitely wasn't killed mildly though," comments Ronnie a few hours later, while splashing tabasco sauce over a dozen oysters.

"Yeah, getting shot in the back of the head with a shotgun while sitting in a car in front of your home is bad enough. But if your killer ends up in a body bag in a random car in NYC, with three hundred dollars stuffed in his anus, then that's a whole different story," adds Nina's friend from Brooklyn.

"From combing over Luczak's personal files, I found out that once his predecessor retired to Italy, and the Sicilian Cosa Nostra appointed him head of the Philly Mob, Bruno disallowed his crew from distributing heroin, and other serious narcotics, within city limits and southeast Pennsylvania, preferring to collect revenue via more traditional methods like racketeering, loansharking, and illegal bookmaking. Obviously, that caused tremendous tension among his Underboss, Capo's and of course, the man who orchestrated his death: his consigliere Gastone Capronigro. My father was working with the NYPD and FBI in finding out exactly who killed Bruno, and Capronigro as well, when his captain suddenly ordered for Luczak to transfer to another police department with no jurisdiction over the Philly mob or be dishonorably discharged from the force," says Nina.

"Wow. So the mob conspired with the police to get your father off their backs. That's crazy, but I bet those relationships probably still exist today. How does that explain you being born and raised in York?" inquires Ronnie.

"I'm not sure. Dad mysteriously disappearing on Mom while she was pregnant with me jumpstarted her oxycodone and meth addiction. I'm sure it was the biggest reason why she started stealing prescription pads from doctors in order to satisfy her cravings."

"Maybe I should just run away from Laurel, resign from efficienTECH over e-mail, and stay with Ronnie in Brooklyn until I can rationally plan my next move without fearing Konrad or his people killing me. He's got enough money to support me for at least half a year," Nina thinks.

"Konrad has already prepared for it and will kill your mother if you leave Maryland," I warn her. Ronnie motions for the Old Ebbitt Grill waitress to bring the check and snaps his finger in front of Nina's face.

"Hey, stop zoning out for a sec. Do you wanna get dessert or move on to College Park? I don't want to keep you out too late, especially because Konrad will be there."

Nine miles northeast, Quincy walks back toward campus after a quick shower underneath grimy, undrinkable, PG-county water at his apartment.

Increasing his pace, Quincy takes his phone off speaker and presses it to his ear.

"Yeah, Dad, you'll be proud of me today. I just got another job, which I think should cover my credit card bills for tuition and MCAT expenses this year."

Quincy jogs south on Baltimore Avenue right past Ritchie Coliseum.

"You're not selling drugs again, are you, son? You'll give your mother a heart attack. But I don't understand your age group; maybe you get a kick out of doing that type of thing," says Floyd Marshall from his quiet home in Orange County, California.

“No, Pops, what happened at Pepperdine was just a blip on the screen. All that garbage from Malibu is in the rear-view mirror now. I got a job at this bar and lounge off campus; everything is great.”

“Are you still communicating with that white whore, Rebecca? Do you realize how much that girl destroyed your life, Q? What's going to happen when you try to get a real job and your prospective employer sees your criminal background? Even though you don't have to still wear that tracking bracelet around your ankle, that mugshot of you will be around forever. Do you understand the gravity of what I'm telling you, son?”

Before writing to the University of Maryland Dean's Office, and subsequently meeting with their Office of Undergraduate Admissions to formally apologize for his past legal transgressions, Quincy had to convince his probation officer that he wasn't a risk to toxify a somewhat identical environment to the one he helped degrade in Malibu.

“Your actions, although indefensible, were no less common than what goes on at many college campuses around this country. Although I suspect you, and your accomplice Ms. Mathews, acted as a middle point for a tidal wave of illegal and prescription narcotics flowing into Pepperdine, our surveillance team was only able to charge you and her with possession of a controlled substance, thereby giving your presiding judge incredible leeway in sentencing,” said Officer Joseph Burnett, the presiding parole officer for both Rebecca and Quincy.

The precipice for Operation Sudden Drop accidentally began late last winter when Quincy, apparently too caught up with his illegal activities, forgot to appear in court to declare his innocence on a DUI misdemeanor. That court date disappearance led to a warrant being issued for his arrest. And since he wasn't pretending to live on campus anymore, a couple Los Angeles County sheriffs, in collaboration with their doppelgangers from Ventura County, consequently knocked on the front door of Rebecca's off-campus apartment in Thousand Oaks to serve a warrant for Quincy's arrest.

Fortunately for Quincy, they found no one home as he was on campus, rehabbing his gimpy knee at the Runnels Swimming Pool with Rebecca. But unfortunately for her, the four attending sheriffs decided to knock down her front door with a battering ram. After noticing that her townhouse's external hydro meter seemed to be extensively tampered with, the four sheriffs stormed into the three-floor residence and discovered the presence of a full-scale marijuana grow operation in Rebecca's basement. Forty-eight plants, in four rows of twelve, contained an equal amount of the powerful strains Kosher Kush, Bubba Kush, Tahoe OG, and Master Kush.

“Ms. Rebecca Mathews is only growing Indica strains, instead of Sativas, because of the shorter grow time. This is a fairly sophisticated operation with a professional lighting and watering system,” later wrote LA County Sheriff Timothy Lang in his corresponding police report.

Embarrassingly captured a few afternoons later, Rebecca was arrested at the Malibu Country Mart while helping Quincy pick out a new wardrobe at the Ralph Lauren store. After a lengthy and heated interrogation, Rebecca soon confessed to running the grow-op. However, she refused to implicate Quincy as an accomplice. Agreeing to the prosecutor's offered plea bargain of thirty-eight months in a undisclosed, Level I prison, Rebecca's non-admission of Quincy's hand in them not only growing 120 ounces of marijuana per crop, but also transporting dozens of kilos of high quality cocaine, molly, meth, and heroin to Jeremy's place in Malibu, gave Quincy a legal reprieve.

"The county detectives kept asking her if she had anything to do with a couple of Ecstasy overdoses at the Electric Zoo in Nevada, because the girls that died there were sophomores at Pepperdine. But thankfully, she didn't crack," Quincy said when first explaining his previous life to his Maryland roommates.

"So, are you going to pick things back up with Rebecca once she gets out?" asked Quincy's Asian-American roommate while taking seconds of baked mac and cheese from the casserole dish on top of the trio's makeshift dinner table.

"No, definitely not. Even though she'll probably be out next spring for good behavior, I promised my heartbroken parents that I would never speak to, or see, her again," added Quincy yesterday night after his roommates agreed to let him live with them another month—rent free.

"I don't know, son, your mother is worried about you. You haven't been home in ages and hardly call," says Mr. Marshall as his son, in present time, crosses over the College Park intersection of Knox Road and Baltimore Avenue.

Fourteen miles west of Quincy's job, Chief Macklin exits the Robert A. Pumphrey funeral home in Bethesda.

Chapter 24

"This is the second open-casket wake we've been to in as many days. These killings make me wanna vomit, Davis," says Nicole as she and Chief Macklin, surrounded by a moving octagon of eagle-eyed officers, make their way to the chief's chauffeured limousine.

In between Macklin and his curbside destination stand a throng of reporters, eagerly waiting for a fresh quote.

"Chief Macklin! Chief Macklin! You've been noticeably silent since Monday afternoon's press conference and your PR team didn't release a statement today. Are you and your girlfriend any closer to catching the sniper?" asks a frustrated *Washington Post* reporter.

EMT First Responder Nicole Freeman, Macklin's most trusted confident since his recent separation from his wife of thirty years, falls behind Detective Adams and Lieutenant Patrick, who are also quietly headed to a waiting limo.

"Please, Malik, have some respect for the deceased," responds the despondent chief, referring to the *Post's* tenured investigative journalist standing amongst his impatient peers. Malik Allen, a twenty-five-year-old graduate of George

Washington University and Wilde Lake High School in Columbia, has published daily, labyrinthine, multi-page articles on the regional sniper crisis since it infected the DC area last week. Personally affected by the killer's path of destruction, Malik was a nephew of Emmanuel Pierre, the Best Buy employee officials believe was killed by the serial killer in Southeast DC.

"In respect to the family of Ms. Ramos, the chief won't be answering any questions at this time," interrupts Patrick.

"Unnamed sources in your own department have stated that the recent all-points bulletin your force put out for the white box-truck turned out to be, and I'm quoting here, 'both an exhaustive and demoralizing waste of time that probably diverted attention from finding the sniper sooner than later.' Care to comment on the discord within your own department, Chief?" asks Allen, unafraid of the eight uniformed officers surrounding him who look like they're on the verge of beating the 5'9, 150-pound Haitian-American into a bloody pulp.

"It would be irresponsible for me to respond to unnamed sources, Malik, and we'll convene a new press conference tomorrow morning in order to bring the public up to speed. Have a good night," tersely replies Macklin before being escorted into the rear cab of the open black Lincoln.

Nicole, now sitting in the rear corner passenger seat of the extended limo, cracks open a tinted window, then nervously lights a menthol cigarette.

"It was only a matter of time before leaks started spreading out of your department. I'd bet for anything that it was that weasel Dobkins behind it," says Adams as the limo exits the funeral home behind the flashing lights of a moving patrol car.

The MCPD motorcade then makes a quick left onto a congested Wisconsin Avenue before eventually getting on Route 410 toward police headquarters.

"Someone has to be protecting this serial killer. Is it that far-fetched to believe he could have radical, deranged sympathizers in the area? If he didn't, and he's working alone, then why'd he come to my state instead of just continuing up north to a more heavily populated region?" wonders Macklin out loud.

"The thing that I don't get is that unless he's the Terminator, he must be sleeping and eating somewhere. Where does he shower? Where does he get his exercise? He fits the profile of ex-military, so repeating a daily routine is obviously important to him. We've combed through every motel, hotel, extended-stay suite, and homeless shelter in the area and found nothing," adds Adams as their vehicle speeds on the East-West Highway toward MCPD headquarters. He then smiles while scrolling through the last of his e-mails.

"Chief, as soon as we get back to the office, please set up a press conference for tomorrow morning. President Cheney has fast tracked a $5,000,000 reward for specific information leading to the immediate, live capture of the sniper. That should quicken up the pace of this investigation."

A few miles away, another domestic sedan pulls to a stoplight.

"I don't think I can get a good shot, sir. Not in this light."

Chapter 25

Renzo Vincent motions to his mentor and guardian, Blake Rice.

The Aruban boy takes his right eye from the scope attached to his bolt-action, M40 sniper rifle, then quickly shimmies his wiry-strong, 5'5 frame from the center crawlspace separating their car's rear seat from the trunk.

“We'll try again later tonight, son. Don't forget to disassemble your rifle before joining me in the passenger seat, soldier,” replies Blake, raking his hand through his thin, wispy blond hair.

The forty-one-year-old arches his back, trying to keep his aching spine as upright as possible.

* * * * *

It was only nine months ago that Blake, a retired, medically-discharged Navy SEAL, met Renzo while vacationing by himself at Eagle Beach on “One Happy Island.”

"Beads, incense, spices, whatever you're looking for, sir. I've got whatever you're looking for," said the bare-chested, tanned young man many months ago to a US vacationer temporarily residing at the acclaimed Bucuti & Tara Beach Resort.

"Shouldn't you be at school right now instead of trying to sell me trinkets on this private beach? And how do your parents feel about all of this?" politely inquired Blake before yawning and stretching on his beach towel.

Blake took the impromptu Caribbean vacation after his wife, citing irreconcilable differences, divorced him and took their months-old daughter cross-country to live with her Aunt Helen in Bellevue, Washington. "Sir, I'm just trying to put some food on the table for my mother and I. We don't have much," pleaded Renzo.

The heterosexual ex-officer slowly took a sip of his rum punch, admiring the teenager's eight pack and sculpted upper body. Blake extended his hand toward Renzo, the first time any American vacationer had done so in Renzo's six years of pitching products. "I'm Blake, Blake Rice. Nice to meet you, son. What's your name?"

"People from your country always talk down to me like I'm less than human; I guess you really can't judge a book by its first ten pages," said Vincent, smiling and grasping Blake's strong, open palm. "My name is Renzo, sir. Renzo Vincent."

"You're in great shape, Renzo. Are you the next Caribbean track star?" politely asked Blake, patting the dark blue padding on the reclined beach chair beside him.

Over the next five hours, while the blistering Aruban sun roasted their skin and the two dined on belchi di pisca, Renzo gave Blake an honest account of his turbulent childhood.

Like Nina, Renzo grew up never meeting his father. When Renzo's mom felt he was old enough to comprehend the irrational evil of others, she told him that his birth was the product of an unknown Dutch vacationer who had impregnated her during a prostitution incall at her modest residence in the Aruban capital of Oranjestad. All Mrs. Vincent knew about Renzo's father was that he was on the island for a day during his week-long, southern Caribbean cruise.

"Did you know the Dutch enslaved this beautiful country for many, many years, Mr. Vincent? In fact, slavery is the foundation of Western Civilization."

"No. I didn't."

"Well, we're in a new millennium now, and that mentality is dead. Your future is clear and ripe for opportunity. The world is much bigger than Aruba. Do you understand?"

"Yes, yes sir."

Blake wasn't the first man to seemingly try to steer Renzo in a more positive direction; he had received similar encouragement from his teachers, soccer coach, and pastor. However, Blake was the first Caucasian American man to approach the bi-racial teenager in this manner, and within the course of a few hours, the impressionable and vulnerable youth was hooked on every word uttered by Blake.

As Renzo told his brief life history of being a relatively well-adjusted, poverty-stricken boy only arrested twice for stealing candy and trespassing, it wasn't just the Mid-Atlantic, straight-shooting delivery of Blake's elocution that entranced

Vincent. It was the fact that Blake was the first human he met that shared his rare, blueish-green eye color.

"For your skin tone, your eye color is very rare, Renzo. You should be proud of your all-seeing eye, not ashamed of it. Let me ask you a question: have you ever been to the United States?"

"No. No, sir, I haven't. But I'd like to; there isn't much opportunity for me here, sir."

"Well, if you're interested, I want you to come back home with me for a couple of months to do some freelance work. Your mother, where does she live? I want to speak to her on how I can help," said Blake, finally getting up to stretch his finely tuned, 6'1 frame.

"Well, she's at work right now. She's got a double shift as a maid at a resort on the other side of the island and won't be back home until sun-up tomorrow," replied Renzo, eager to disassociate himself from his mom. His other siblings are spread throughout the island, also trying to hustle small keepsakes to scrape by.

"What kind of work are you talking about? And how much does it pay?"

"Some undercover government work targeting the bad guys. Nothing dangerous, and you'll be back home in a few months. And for accompanying me on this all-inclusive adventure, you'll be paid $100,000. $50,000 now, which I'll advise you to deposit in a Panamanian bank to avoid taxes, and another $50,000 after our mission is completed. To seal our agreement, I'll buy you a dirt bike tomorrow afternoon. You can lock it up in storage and can play with it when you get back."

Renzo, who had never held more than fifty dollars in his hand, immediately agreed to Blake's amorphous employment offer.

The next day, after fulfilling his promise to buy Renzo a new dirt bike, Blake rented a four-wheel all-terrain vehicle, and the two set off on a day trip throughout the island. After quickly riding adjacent to Aruba's western coast and visiting the Balashi Gold Mill Ruins, then stopping for lunch at Coral Reef Beach, Renzo took his new best friend on a scenic tour of Arikok National Park.

Letting his newfound, quiet-yet-confident protégé take the lead, Blake marveled at Renzo's mature leadership skills as he first navigated the two through the remarkable, unmatched beauty of the Quadirikiri and Fontein caves, then toward Jamanota Hilltop, the highest point in Aruba.

Afterwards, they finally stopped for drinks at an outdoor café at Boca Prins, a small protected beach on Aruba's southeastern shore.

"Wow, that was quite a ride, son; words can hardly describe how beautiful your country is. Its interior reminds me of Cabo San Lucas, or some parts of Arizona. Would you like to see Arizona sometime, Mr. Vincent?" softly asked Blake before munching on a handful of spiced yucca chips.

"I'm not a lazy Aruban, sir. If you have temporary work for me in America, and can guarantee my safe return by the end of August so I won't miss any school days, then I'm interested in being your employee. And exactly what type of 'freelance' are you talking about?"

Blake knew, after studying and searching for an apprentice outside the US, that Aruba enjoys a higher living standard than most other Caribbean nations. Many of the island's children, regardless of circumstance, learn up to four languages and often proceed to college in the Netherlands. However, Mrs. Vincent had kicked Renzo out of their decrepit one-bedroom tin-roof home on the outskirts of Oranjestad after the third time she caught him stealing florins from her purse, forcing him to move into a shelter for wayward youths.

While watching the sun set over the angry Atlantic Ocean, Blake, who strikingly resembled the eclectic actor Hugo Weaving, finally divulged his own plan for societal change via his philosophy, which he's coined *The Audacity of Fear.*

“We've only known each other for twenty-four hours, but I feel there's something more to you; and that there's much more to life than this small island. You, like me, are an end product of a society hell-bent on rewarding others for irrelevant and unspeakable acts while discarding those who have the unavoidable misfortune of being born from a certain region of the world, or in your case, having a higher percentage of melanin in your skin than others. My life hasn't been lucky, but I wasn't afforded the same tribulations you've experienced. And although not being born rich, I, at one time, felt an innate responsibility to uphold and defend the vales of well- connected, plutocratic individuals determined to stop society from progressing.”

“Go on,” says Renzo.

“Renzo, I'm a retired Navy Special Warfare Command officer who, around four years ago, started realizing that, to make a change in the world, I had to stop being a brainwashed soldier and be the change that earth desperately needs to evolve. Let me ask you a question, have you heard of the broken windows theory'?”

“No. No, sir, I haven't.”

“Well, around twenty years ago, two scientists theorized that serious crime, primarily in major cities in my country and around the world, would decrease if law enforcement agencies focused attention on eliminating petty crime, specifically vandalism, thinking that doing so would decrease more serious crime. Essentially, the premise was to scare non-violent criminals straight. Championed by those using this theory as an excuse to incarcerate low-level offenders of color, implementation of the broken windows theory is morally wrong, but its embedded argument, that fear is the foundation of all social interaction, is 100 percent true.”

“Your last sentence contradicts itself. Please clarify your theory, sir.”

“There are yings and yangs throughout society. In this world, forces at opposite ends of their specific spectrums, when analyzed correctly from another dimension, are intrinsically bound to each other in ways that mere mortals could never comprehend or accept. Individuals and events, that at first appearance seems to be inverse, are in fact working together to achieve their respective goals.”

“Give me an example where this is true.”

“OK, what if I told you that, because of how technically interconnected I know this world is, a minor increase in targeted, serious crime will lead to a decrease in poverty, racism, and overall human suffering?”

“Go on.”

“Renzo, what I am about to divulge is factual. It may be hard to digest at first, but you must believe me when I tell you that it was not by accident, or happenstance, that we met yesterday for the first time. Everything that happens in this world is pre-determined to happen, whether it is negative or positive in nature. Due to your inert politeness and respect of elders, you failed to ask me what I did for a living. After growing up a listless and aimless teenager from a nuclear family in America, I decided to enlist in the Navy to try and find some direction in my life. Twenty-four hours before a stressful beach jumping followed by a search and capture mission in central-east Africa for supposed terrorists responsible of a Kenyan mall attack, my commanding officer ordered my regiment of six soldiers to take a small pill with the imprinted indentation 'x-2317.' The tablet was no larger than an average-sized aspirin tablet."

"What happened after you took the pill?"

"In my bunk that afternoon, within an off-shore US battleship floating on the Indian Ocean about 1400 miles north of Madagascar, I started to feel the standard nausea and disorientation associated with putting anything foreign in your body; it almost felt like I drank some really cheap liquor laced with codeine. Anyway, after waking up the next evening, my team and I jumped in a modified combat raiding craft. We headed to shore to capture our targeted suspects while they slept in their homes, then deliver them to a safe airfield for deportation to Guantanamo Bay in Cuba. Now, although all stealth missions have inherent danger, I could have completed that particular expedition blindfolded. While they were asleep in their barracks, not only were we able to successfully capture our ten suspected combatants in their heavily guarded compound, but amazingly did so without using any maps or GPS programming."

"So how exactly did you get to your location once hitting the beach?"

“After giving my brothers and I the rundown of our opponents’ location in the ship’s briefing room, our sergeant declared that having any maps or locating devices could indicate our US affiliation, but that the experimental pills we took would give us *all the navigation we need,*” answered Blake, giving a truthful account of what happened during his brief and only stay in Africa.

“So how did you find the bad guys?” excitedly asked Renzo. His heartbeat quickening, Blake hadn't felt this much excitement since he read *The Illuminatus! Trilogy* on the plane ride to Aruba.

“I know this sounds strange, but as soon as our boat hit the beach, a voice, unheard by my team members, started speaking to me. This voice had no clear dialect, and no distinct sex or age either. What it did, though, was give me specific directions on not only where the insurgents were located, which was five miles off-shore through some thick and treacherous jungle, but also painstaking details as to where each of the ten suspects were sleeping inside their compound.”

Over the next twenty minutes, Blake gave an accurate account of a Pentagon- and White House-approved clandestine Navy SEAL mission that successfully ended without one mishap.

Blake, enthralled with Renzo's magnetic attraction to his past, continued his story.

“After hijacking a truck at the insurgent's compound, we delivered our targets to our final destination dozens of hours away from the beach at an unoccupied airstrip normally reserved for military drones in Arba Minch, Ethiopia. While leaving Africa in an unmarked Gulfstream IV rendition aircraft with our suspects in hand, a fellow soldier aggressively complained to our sergeant; that he was not properly informed of possible side effects that taking x-2317 could cause. 'Is x-2317 a combination of organic chemicals, or did I just ingest a miniature microphone with global positioning capabilities?' he asked."

"What happened next?"

"Once the flight landed in Cuba, all six of us were detained and debriefed individually by CIA doctors for forty-eight hours. As a twenty-plus year veteran of the armed forces, it was the first time that I felt like the enemy. The whole situation felt like we were the criminals instead of the enemy combatants we just captured."

"Stay focused, and finish up strong, soldier. The young man will soon become a valuable asset to your movement," an associate, playing his own chess variant game in my dimension that intersected mine, told Blake.

That "associate" was conducting his own exercise, and for viewing entertainment, we decided to later intersect our narratives.

"For some reason, which I'm still not clear about, those physicians came to the conclusion that each one of us were suddenly unfit to be soldiers anymore and that we all suffered from extreme schizophrenia. The doctors then strongly recommended that we be banished from the military immediately," continued Blake as his eyes began to water.

Vivid memories of being handcuffed in arm and leg shackles filled Blake's head. Minutes before he and his band of brothers were escorted by armed gunman from the infirmary to the same Gulfstream they flew in from Africa, Guantanamo prisoners already stationed there couldn't believe what they were seeing. Taking a break from playing soccer behind an electric fence, they cackled at the dehumanized former SEALs, forcibly restrained and receiving the same daily, inhumane treatment they faced as the soldiers boarded a different, unmarked plane headed to the US.

"After we landed at Naval Air Station on the Chesapeake Bay in Maryland, all six of us were forcibly remanded to an uninhabited airport hangar in a far, remote corner of the immense military instillation. There, CIA lawyers informed us that we were all, effective immediately, medically discharged from the Navy. Upon signing a release indemnifying the military from all responsibility including, but not limited to, our ingestion of x-2317 less than seventy-two hours before, we would all receive a lump sum, tax-free payment equal to an additional five years of service, plus a hazard pay bonus, for our seamlessly successful mission in east Africa."

"So, instead of complaining about x-2317, you took the money. I think most people would say they have an annoying voice in their head telling them to do wrong or right. What makes you so special?"

"Another good question son, and I apologize for not answering your earlier ones as I felt it was first necessary tell you my past. I can say with absolute certainty, after researching it intensely, that I do not have schizophrenia or any other related mental disorder. Days after I was disbarred from the military, I hired a general practitioner to come to my former home in Maryland and give me a thorough check-up. The doctor, a good woman from the Baltimore area, found that everything inside me was working correctly; I exhibited no signs of posttraumatic stress disorder, nor any other mental disorder for that matter. Unfortunately, my now estranged wife felt differently, as she filed for divorce and fled to the state of Washington only a few days after my return from Cuba."

"I apologize for your suffering, but, sir, for the last time; how does this concern me? You can be honest, so stop holding back what's on your chest, and tell me everything."

Blake, wiping away authentic tears, retrieves five opened envelopes from his knapsack.

"Son, each one of the five soldiers who took x-2317 along with me committed suicide only a few weeks after I got my physical exam. They all wrote suicide letters to me before taking their life; here, take a look."

Chapter 26

Before commenting further, Renzo rapidly unfolded each of the five one-page letters and eagerly scanned through each handwritten document.

"Brother, we're on the precipice of a new global beginning, starting and ending with you . . ."

Another one, buried within its second paragraph stated: ". . . x-2317 provided the clarity that once was missing. It's been decided among us that you begin the revolution, Blake . . ."

The last one Renzo could stomach reading, from a soldier named Trevor S. Gilmore, was signed in blood. Directly above his full signature, Gilmore wrote, "x-2317 has declared you the first leader of a new undertaking: a clandestine movement advocating chaos as a more rational, direct method in achieving the goals we've always thought we were upholding. My communicator from the other side told me that the rest of us soldiers were no longer of any use to the dimension controlling us because they had suffered too many losses and were going to most likely lose their matches, which has intersected with yours."

"Is that why they all killed themselves. Because a voice in their head told them to do so?" asked Renzo.

"For my brothers in arms, the mental strain of being told to commit suicide every hour of every day, in return for peace, prosperity, and tranquility with their family in another dimension exactly resembling Earth, with no recollection of what happened in Africa and Cuba, became too much for them to bear. So, one by one, over the course of a month right after we all got back from Guantanamo Bay, they all took their lives," responded Blake.

"Why haven't you committed suicide then?"

"My voice has told me stay alive, and to keep fighting, because my victory depends on exposing what my brothers went through, and in the process, destroying the power system responsible for the pain and suffering x-2317 has brought us."

"You mean by bringing down America's government, right?'"

"Yes."

"We're only two people though. How are we going to do that?"

"Be patient, young one. You're not mentally prepared for that answer yet."

Renzo, desperately grasping for meaning in life after always feeling discarded, unwanted, and marginalized, felt an internal need to help Blake's cause, begin a new adventure, and of course, make more money in a three-month span than he'd seen in his lifetime.

"For $200,000, not $100,000, I'll work for you for three months. I need half that amount before we leave this island, and the other $100,000 upon my return. Every month after the first three months, for whatever reason, that I have to stay in the states to complete our mission, you will pay me an additional $10,000 per month. All work expenses, sustenance, and lodging are also to be covered by you during my stay in America. Is this clear, sir?"

Blake, overjoyed by Renzo's unemotional professionalism, shook his head in approval.

"Now, before we sneak you out of here, son, and begin our intense training mission overseas, answer me this . . . Have you ever shot a rifle before?"

The next afternoon, the duo nervously walked through tinted sliding doors at the sleek, modern, and busy Queen Beatrix International Airport. They then headed straight to a targeted, corner kiosk in front of a seated boarding agent underneath a ten-foot wide, florescent blue sign for the low-cost carrier Spirit Air Lines.

"You know you could have said goodbye to your mother, son. I'm sure she would've liked to see you before you left," said Blake, adjusting his sunglasses before pulling his Orioles cap over his cropped hair.

"She's not even gonna notice that I'm gone. Plus, as soon as I land, I'll make arrangements to get her half of everything you pay me."

"That sounds like a great idea, son. I'll even help you compose the letter instructing her how she can withdraw money from the account we set up this morning. But in the meantime, I need you to be quiet and let me do all the talking. Regardless of what this woman asks you, look the ticket agent straight in the eye. And only nod your head up and down, or left to right, when she asks you a question. Am I making myself clear?" asked Renzo's mentor.

Blake grasped the handle of his titanium-colored carry-on as they reach the booking desk of twenty-eight-year-old Janelle Stuyvesant, a lifelong Aruban national and employee of Spirit Airlines for only six months.

"Stay calm and remain focused, this is only the precursory step of our super-secret operation. Also, be aware that operatives from the other side, when studying how best to attack you during a future pursuit, will analyze security camera recordings of this conversation," warned an associate from my dimension, speaking directly to Blake in his head.

"Good morning, Miss. We're flying on your 3:30 flight. Here are our e-tickets," unhurriedly said Blake while handing Janelle a printed e-mail confirmation of his airborne itinerary.

Renzo, not as composed as his unofficial guardian, couldn't help but stare at the three security guards, armed with M-16 assault rifles, who were curiously inspecting the snake line behind them.

"You'll both be in the exit row, so remember to study the handheld pamphlet provided to you on how to assist the crew in case of an emergency. Can I please see your identification?"

Blake handed two stolen Canadian passports to Ms. Stuyvesant and held his breath.

A few years before his aforementioned mission in Africa, Blake studied how Ahmed Ressam, an Algerian Al Queda member who briefly lived in Montreal and applied for political asylum there, managed to transform stolen Canadian passports into valid identification documents for other Algerians.

And after receiving all five post-mortem letters from his comrades from Operation Catch and Collect months before flying to Aruba, the voice inside Blake's own head told him to temporarily get over his wife leaving him and make an impromptu, eight-hour drive from Maryland to Toronto. Once crossing the border and renting an apartment in London (Ontario), Blake then used classified files he stole from a hacked CIA website and discreetly networked with suspected Middle-Eastern terrorist cells loosely connected to Ressam, knowing that these individuals had detailed knowledge on how to procure and falsify the two documents he just handed to Janelle.

Without arousing the suspicion of Canadian Security Intelligence Service officials, Blake rented an apartment in Ontario for a month under an alias from a previous mission before Operation Catch and Collect, then quickly established contact with one of Rossum's associates.

After paying Farid Abdul $25,000, or one percent of his Navy SEAL discharge buyout, Blake secured two fictitious Canadian passports: one stolen from an Alberta man roughly matching Blake's description, and another fabricated one; approximating Vincent's height and weight. What Renzo would find out hours after they landed in Canada, and what Aruban and US authorities would never discover, was the painstaking precision and planning Blake put in to ensure Renzo's safe departure to North America.

“That's a strange request, Leonardo. But hey, my tentacles reach far and wide. Money talks, so I can make it happen. I can do what you want for an additional $25,000. What height, weight, and skin-tone are you looking for again?” said Abdul to Blake over cheeseburgers, fries, and Molson Dry at the Real Sports Bar & Grill across the street from the Air Canada Center in downtown Toronto.

While oblivious fans took in the Raptors game on one of the bars dozens of Vegas sportsbook-style, flat-screen TV's, Blake, using an alias, told Farid that he needed a young Columbian drug courier, who matched Renzo's presumed description, to escort to Aruba. “All I need is the boy's body for part one of a two-part flight. Of course, I won't be flying to Columbia, and will bring a new friend with me back here to Canada.”

The plan, which was seamlessly executed, followed as Blake's temporary accomplice, using his real passport and help from paid informants, took a short two-hour flight from Oranjestad to Bogota right after arriving from Toronto while Blake stayed in Aruba to search the country for a new flying partner matching the courier's description. Days later, 50,000 Canadian dollars, delivered in small, unmarked bills, was given to Farid in exchange for two round trip e-tickets and instructions on where in YYZ to meet the young Columbian named Sebastian Ramirez. After landing in Aruba, and before Ramirez left for his flight to South America, the already-experienced fifteen-year-old coke courier, who was around the same age as Renzo, discreetly handed his fake Canadian passport to Blake for him to later doctor slightly, which Blake did hours before leaving Aruba by gently ripping off the passport photo of Ramirez and expertly replacing it with a new picture of Renzo. So when Janelle, a well-paid informant used by the Norte del Valle Cartel to facilitate the flow of pure cocaine into Aruba, recognized Blake by his lime-green polo shirt, whom she was instructed by her underboss to be on the lookout for, she smiled and breathed a sigh of relief.

“The skies are clear from here to Canada. Custom lines are notoriously slow at Toronto Pearson, but my friends up there ensure me that you'll be on your way without any hassle. And due to a couple last-minute cancellations, I've upgraded you two to business class, free of charge. Don't forget to visit our duty-free shops before you leave, and here are your boarding passes.

You and little Johnny have a great flight," said Janelle, before pointing the direction to their departing gate.

Renzo, with this being the first time that he'd left his sun-soaked homeland, much less been on an all-expense-paid flight in business class, could hardly contain his excitement.

As Blake handed him his glass flute with his unfinished mimosa minutes after their ascension into the sky, he said, "Drink up, son, and enjoy your comfort. Once we land, we will abstain from alcohol and consumption of pork and processed red meat."

Renzo fiddled with small buttons on the television ingrained in the headrest in front of him.

"Sneaking you through customs was the easy part, and I've been assured by an associate that we'll be fine passing through immigration once we land. There's so much corruption in the Navy now, with admirals being implicated in various pay-to-play schemes, so we'll be safe and incognito long before anyone notices what we've done. Try and get some sleep though, because after exiting Pearson International, we're immediately renting a car and driving across Canada to our training facility on the outskirts of Coquitlam, British Columbia, which is a relatively small suburb close to Vancouver. You and I are going to take turns driving. It'll be good practice for when we go live."

"Vancouver; that's a funny name. How far is it from Toronto, sir?"

"About 2700 miles."

Grinning from ear to ear, Blake reached into his leather knapsack and retrieved a small paperback book of about 200 pages. "Here is *The Art of War* by Sun Tzu. Your first assignment, which you'll be tested on once we reach our driving destination, is to memorize and digest each theme of every one of its thirteen chapters. And you need to absorb Tzu's teachings, to the point where you can recite a summary of any one of those thirteen chapters to me instantaneously and upon command."

Blake handed Renzo his blanket, fully cognizant that this catered flight is the last taste of luxury he'd ever experience.

PART II

Chapter 27

Approximately three years after Renzo and Blake safely passed through international customs upon landing in Toronto, Nina and Ronnie finally make their way out of DC and into the Cornerstone Grill and Loft in College Park, Maryland. Now at the front of a fifty-person line, extending past Cornerstone's more gentrified neighbor, R.J. Bentley's, Nina and Ronnie have sobered up considerably since their sybaritic four-course meal.

"What's the crowd like in there tonight?" asks Ronnie as he excitedly hands his New York state license to Quincy's large, delicate hand.

"The normal congregation, mostly comprised of frat boys and sorority girls. There are a few athletes in there, unwinding before the big Thursday night game against Florida State though. Is it just you and your girlfriend?"

Quincy gravitates his eyes toward Nina's infectious smile.

"Ronnie's my gay boyfriend, silly. Join us for a shot later, OK?"

"It's my first night at work here, but I'll try to meet up as the night progresses," says Quincy, ushering in four sisters from Tri-

Delta. After getting change back for the $20 cover charge Quincy inflated to make $10 off each partygoer, Ronnie escorts Nina through the maze of revelers drinking and smoking outside Cornerstone, and through its brown, large front doors.

“Hey, did you happen to visit Konrad's new place yet?” shouts Ronnie as the two finally enter the bar's first floor interior.

“Yeah, why?” Nina quickly buys two glass test tubes from a scantily-dressed waitress, each pipette filled to the brim with fluorescent green jello shots. While letting gelatinous liquid effortlessly slide down her throat, Nina can't help but notice the seemingly endless number of hundreds in Ronnie's hand.

“I heard he just finished remodeling his basement,” says Ronnie, as he counts the twentieth Franklin in his left hand.

“What else did he say?”

Ronnie pulls out a Parliament from a carbon fiber case, then slowly lights the cancer stick. “Ease up and enjoy yourself tonight, mamacita. With everything that's going on, it could be our last.”

Cornerstone, a more refined establishment created from the figurative ashes of its rowdier, destructive, and borderline lawless predecessor The Vous, is an aesthetically pleasing, two-story bar/restaurant. When packed, it can easily fit nearly 300 loaded bacchants. On the first floor of the relatively upscale lounge, parallel to the south wall of approximately thirty feet, is the main bar, where Nina patiently waits to order among a throng of sweaty students. The interior walls of Cornerstone contain signed jerseys of UMD's most famous basketball stars, including Stevie Francis, Juan Dixon, and the late, great Len Bias. Where Ronnie silently stands by the front door to best absorb the environment alien to his uptight, collegiate experience at

Wesleyan, are two large open safari windows encased within glass cinderblock, each one designed to let in cooler air while giving outside customers the ability to listen to the base-heavy music originating from inside.

Diagonally opposed to Ronnie, Cornerstone's resident DJ succumbs to the fifth female request for Akinyele, and finally plays “Put It in Your Mouth” After finally getting the blitzed bartender's attention, Nina pays for her order and walks back to Ronnie with a vodka Red Bull in each hand.

“Konrad just texted me and said he's going to meet us here in about an hour or so to relieve work stress.”

Is Ronnie in on it? thinks Nina. I gleefully stay quiet.

Looking through the open window, Nina catches Quincy starring at her, which causes Nina to bashfully put her back toward him and face the bar inside.

“You know, you're just wasting your time pursuing Konrad. He's not gay.”

“Of course he is; he just doesn't know it yet. Tell the truth: you're still in love with him, right?”

Before she can respond, Ronnie and Nina hear “Fight!” screamed by an unknown male, who’s standing on Baltimore Ave. outside.

Nina immediately looks over her shoulder once again, just in time to see Quincy, along with a couple bouncers from the rugby team, run up the outdoor stairs constructed next to the bordering bar, named Bentley’s, and head directly to Cornerstone's second floor.

“I'm going to start a conversation with that cutie who let us in. He must be around 6'6; he looks a few inches taller than

Konrad." Ronnie, brushing aside Nina's alternate-dimension theory she drunkenly divulged five minutes ago right after shared Jägerbombs, grabs her thin waist and navigates his way through the tangled mass of humanity on the dance floor.

Lines of uncut, raw cocaine are gently manipulated four hours later. Like Jordan and Pippen angrily deciding who would guard Kukoc during the Dream Team's '92 Olympics run, the two angry coworkers stand together, huddled in the handicapped stall of a first-floor bathroom. The dimly-lit lavatory is the same one Kreesha used to hopelessly clean blood from Colin's suit on Monday.

"Don't be greedy. Pass me some."

"Are you still sure you want to bring Nina on board?" adds Kreesha before using a piece of toilet paper to wipe her runny nose.

"Stop asking me about Nina; I've got her under control. Instead, tell me more about my money. Have you taken the appropriate steps to launder it through Geneva yet?" replies Konrad.

"Yes, storing our millions in Switzerland gives us a bit more anonymity to safely manipulate our money worldwide; even more than via the Caribbean. Following your instructions, I also created one for Mr. Ayala per our agreement with the Black Commando Mafia. This is the third time I've told you this; stop being so paranoid, King."

Konrad casually drops his drawers and begins to urinate toward the toilet.

"The cash we make in New England has to be cleaned via BCM's Canadian brokerage contact who turns the millions of US dollars into Bitcoin currency, then into Canadian dollars before it's finally deposited in Switzerland. For this fee, Ayala's charging us a 16 percent tax on top of every dollar we make during synthetic h exchanges at the airport, which is really smart, considering that BCM marks up synthetic 300 percent the price of wholesale . . . I know we need a new alias to handle exchanges for us at BWI, but why don't we hire someone off the street, or subcontract a gang member through Warren's underworld contacts? I mean, Nina's got nothing to lose, why won't she rat us out?"

"Enslaving my immortal's most powerful enemy, while Bartolo itches to kill her mom in York, is organic progression in my book. And if shit hits the fan, I've already put together a game plan on how to frame her for all our activities, including forging Nina's signature regarding her ownership of a dummy LLC fictitiously designed to launder money from our operations to her over billing past clients to shelter illegal funds acquired from synthetic heroin transactions. It's like we're playing chess, and I just forked her queen and king. Nina's unable to rescue society from synthetic heroin because her mother's being terrorized by Bartolo. While concurrently, she doesn't have time to comprehend how x-2317 has improved the way her brain works and made her superior to normal humans."

"I fail to see why guys like you find her attractive. She's just like the rest of these white girls running around thinking they're black without actually having to deal with the racist bullshit we do in this world. First it was tanning beds, next came the Botoxed lips, and now it's the endless squats and leg presses to make their ass big. And if that doesn't work, they'll get butt implants. Talking about implants, that reminds me, remember to follow up with Nadir after you leave here. While you were closing that deal at your cubicle, I got an urgent text from him for you to call him immediately."

"Tomorrow, give Nina a lay-up deal she simultaneously closes with Colin, then split the revenue amount and commission equally to their respective quotas. It's imperative that everything at efficienTECH, from our co-workers' perspective, appear as placid, equitable, and translucent as possible."

"That ugly cunt is so unpredictable. Just be careful playing with fire, OK?" responds Kreesha.

Konrad, now outside and into the cool and clear October night, cautiously walks 500 feet through the same parking lot he lambasted Nina in on Monday. Pacing through the dimly lit and nearly vacant property, he nervously keeps his head on a swivel, as most Montgomery County citizens do in light of the sniper's killings. A four-door sedan in the far corner of the parking lot with its engine and headlights off escapes Konrad's view as his scurries to his own vehicle. From inside the car's front seats, two individuals curiously watch Konrad remotely open his car lock, start his ignition, and quickly drive away. After driving the speed limit on MD-32 East for about three miles, Konrad makes a sweeping right turn onto an onramp for the state's main transportation artery: Interstate 95.

"Talk to me, doctor," Konrad says into his Bluetooth set. "I was tied up in meetings all day and unable to take your call. What's up?"

"Happy to finally get a hold of you, Most High. Everything is going smoothly here at PWI. Money works wonders, and I've greased enough wheels to avert management suspicion about the extraneous x-2317 processed," nervously says Nadir from the rooftop of one of the ten buildings that make up PWI's Maryland location.

Momentarily ignoring his phone conversation, Nadir looks at the uninhabited outdoor corporate dining area five floors down. The busy lunch-time alfresco space, now unoccupied by any human because it's half-past eleven, is immediately adjacent to the building Nadir's standing upon. Quickly wiping the fog inside his spectacles with his lab coat sleeve, Nadir sees a Cinnamon Teal duck. It meanders from the wetland brush surrounding the artificial, three-mile wide pond just west of two dozen wooden picnic tables below his feet.

"Time is money, Doctor Death. I check in with other agents also employed to PWI every day or two, and they tell me all faucets of our operation are running smoothly. Why are you about to tell me otherwise?" responds Konrad.

The duck, once on the trampled grass behind a table closest to the still, moonlit water, hops on a table and stares directly up at Nadir, causing the fragile psychopharmacologist to jump back in fear. Desperately grasping the metal doorknob for the only gateway to the 5000-square foot rooftop, Nadir awkwardly tries to keep his balance.

"How long have you been under the influence of x-2317? I mean, after Curtis stole the experimental tablet from my lab, exactly when was the first time you ingested it?" asks Nadir, whom my Opponent and I directed to never take x-2317. We orchestrated this to have him truly only exist as a gray character, used by both sides as struggle to accomplish the majority of twenty-one tasks earlier described.

"A few years after the turn of the century. The exact month, nor day, is not your concern. Why?" responds Konrad.

Unable to find any more crumbs on the picnic table, the inquisitive, reddish-brown bird arches his neck to look at his new, shy friend dozens of feet above him. The highly respected fifty-five-year-old, an honored graduate of Harvard, and esteemed board member at Johns Hopkins Hospital, inches to the rooftop periphery before dangling both his legs over its edge.

"Right, that's about a half-month after I personally created it myself and administered it to, administered it to . . ." stammers Nadir as he tightly clutches his cellphone to his ear.

Gray characters, like Nadir for example, can be traded from the Black side to the White side, or vice versa, in exchange for the death of a member of the side receiving the gray character. These trades can occur without Konrad or Nina's knowledge, or consent for that matter.

"No one's going to die tonight, Doctor; please stay calm. You have my word, as my esteemed mentor and business partner, that I will never again enact, nor imply, any violence toward you or your family. Please stay calm, sir," says Konrad, with a smirk on his face.

"You promise?"

"You've taken x-2317 and created the narcotic version of Equal, except that doctors and other health officials can't tell the difference between our product and real heroin. From a geo-political perspective, if we enter business relations with cartels down south, our product can destroy Afghanistan's stranglehold on the entire industry. Do you realize how powerful this will make me?"

"Stop kissing my ass for a second, and listen very carefully. Based on a month-long research analysis I just concluded this morning, there is one catastrophic, long-term, irreversible side effect to half of anyone who has taken x-2317, or for that matter your, not my, creation of synthetic heroin by injection."

"I already know that women who ingest x-2317 lose the ability to conceive and that I've lost the ability to impregnate. The Others created this to eliminate spawns from complicating our war. So what are you talking about?"

"I'll spare you the chemical, biological, and molecular specificities on why this is so, but based on my calculations, which I re-tested twice this evening to make sure, I can absolutely conclude that 50 percent of all x-2317 users, no matter their physiological disposition, or whether they've only taken it once or one hundred times, will develop tendencies consistent with homicidal maniacs, serial killers, and mass murderers within the next five years. Yes, this means this could be the case for either you or Ms. Sullivan."

"You haven't administered x-2317 to anyone else other than Nina and I, correct?"

Ignoring Konrad's last question, Nadir continues.

"For those that take synthetic heroin via injection, their future is twice as dire. Even though a synthetic heroin user doesn't get the same psychological and mental enhancements that an x-2317 user receives, synthetic smack ballistically aggravates x-2317 side effects by 200 percent. This means that any user injecting synthetic h will inherit irreversible, severe homicidal tendencies within two and a half years regardless of their sex, age, or race," truthfully rambles the chemist.

The duck five stories below the stumpy, suicidal, middle-aged Indian-American, clearly fascinated by a human attempting flight, happily gives Nadir instructions on how to fly by flapping his wings.

Twenty miles east from Nadir's location at PWI, Konrad, close to his destination in College Park, sighs at the approaching Beltway traffic jam one hundred yards in front of him. He then turns on the car's air-conditioning to try and keep his heart beat normal.

“This means, in a little over two years—”

“How many people have taken synthetic heroin since you created, mass-produced, and distributed it to the northeast this year?” screams Nadir.

Momentarily putting his phone on mute, Nadir opens up a scientific calculator, and tabulates Konrad's estimations.

“On every Friday afternoon since late August, we've hand delivered one hundred pounds of synthetic to our Fed-Ex contact at BWI. As you obviously know, one hundred pounds equates to about forty-five kilos or 45,000,000 milligrams. On average, first-time users purchase 20 to 30 milligrams of synthetic during their first buy. By contrast, a long-term junkie, also intent on delivering their high intravenously, will need upwards of 100 to 300 milligrams in order to feel normal enough to avoid withdrawal.”

Reminiscent from scenes in *Back to The Future* films, Nadir jumps up, unbuttons his white lab coat, and maniacally runs in a figure eight pattern, causing his new friend to immediately retreat to his safe habitat of the tranquil pond.

“This is what I feared . . . At the minimum, we have 1.8 million cases to deal with. Answer me this, King, how many new users do you gain a week, and how many degenerates using your drug are repeat offenders?”

Unintended consequences of a complicated game that causes more chaos the more my Opponent and I try to control the outcome.

“Interesting . . .” mumbles Konrad.

“I can't hear you. What did you say?” responds Nadir.

“For starters, let me remind you that no user can tell, to any degree, that my product is any different than black tar heroin distributed to them via Mexican drug lords. Ayala's pushers don't even know that what they’re dealing is artificial. Since this summer, we've seen a 57 percent uptick in rate of sales.”

“How did you figure that number out?”

“Our product leaves Maryland by late Friday afternoon, and once it touches any major city in our targeted Northeast locations, no more than two hours later, it's broken up to four bricks, each one weighing twenty-five pounds. Each brick of synthetic heroin, now in the hands of four of Ayala's most experienced and trusted couriers, are shipped by ground to the four largest cities in Maine, New Hampshire, Vermont, and upstate New York. From there it's slightly stepped on, with what I've been assured is harmless powdered milk, and then immediately sold on city streets by midnight Saturday. What used to last Ayala's dealers until Friday afternoon is now only lasting them until Monday night, regardless of if competing dealers try to undersell us by pushing real Colombian or black tar heroin. I've cooked 318 kilos for seven past shipments to New England. And since the second week of synthetic h distribution, Ayala's dealers only deal with trusted, repeat junkies to avoid police interference. So I can definitively say that based on top of your initial, accurate estimate of 1.8 million new synthetic heroin users who tried it for the first time in late August, you can add another 450,000 new junkies that tried it for the first time in early September, all confined to the sixteen largest cities in the four regions I just mentioned. So that's about 2.3 million synthetic heroin users, give or take 50,000 junkies here or there."

"Umm, you probably need to add a few more Navy SEALs to that number," responds Nadir.

"What the fuck are you talking about, Doctor?"

"Here at PWI, we just don't handle mass quantities of prescription drugs for distribution to local hospitals and pharmacies. As you know, we've also branched out to explore new ways chemicals, created organically like opium, or mixed together in a lab, can manipulate and control humans. About a year before you met Curtis, while exploring tax breaks for moving our Maryland PWI branch to Washington DC, we were approached by the federal government, who were interested in creating a pill soldiers could take—"

"Have you told them about me and the Others who control this world from another dimension?"

"No. Of course not, King. They are too simple-minded."

"Proceed."

"I'm not sure about the exact date, as it's all a blur now, but a few months before you met Curtis I was alone, reading the *Post* on my laptop in Starbucks, as I do every Sunday morning while drinking my large, Jamaican Blue Mountain coffee. Anyway, a nondescript male, of average height and build, dressed business casual as I was, sat in the wooden chair next to mine and introduced himself. The coffee shop was near empty as usual, and initially, I didn't think much of this man's presence," recanted Nadir to a captive Konrad.

* * * * *

Years ago, Nadir awkwardly shook an unknown man’s extended hand; the stranger smiled, then said, “Good morning, doctor.”

The mysterious, unknown individual then immediately pointed to Nadir’s laptop screen.

“I see that you're a big fan of the brilliant Russian scientist Igor Smirnov. Smirnov's research was well ahead of his time, and his book *Psychotechnologies* will be a fascinating read, don't you think?”

“How did you . . . how'd you know I just purchased that book from Amazon two hours ago?” immediately inquired Nadir, startled and angry that someone he's never met before could know about his most recent American Express purchase.

“Don't worry, Dr. Jayaraman. My friend at the National Security Agency assures me, with absolute certainty, that your personal computer's hard-drive is clean and doesn't contain any videos like kiddie porn—videos that could keep you locked up in federal prison for a very, very, long time. You know what they do with people like you in jail, right?”

“I have young kids, and would never desecrate a juvenile in that manner. What . . . what are you talking about?” asked Nadir, his voice trembling.

Dolan grabbed Nadir’s laptop, typed in his laptop password, then went to Gmail, where he typed in Nadir’s username and e-mail password. Once inside Nadir’s personal inbox, he clicked onto an e-mail folder marked “Child Pics” with hundreds of draft e-mails, each with dozens of attached, unspeakably horrific .jpeg photos of compromised kids.

The accomplished doctor stared in horror.

“I never created that folder; where did all those photos come from? I didn’t take those!” Nadir recoiled from his seat, nauseous from what he was being forced to view.

“Because you have distant relatives in India that live in the same region as the terrorist Khalistan Zindabad Force, President Cheney’s recently passed Loyalist Act gives me the ability to inspect your e-mail to see if you have contacted any of their operatives. While doing so, I stumbled upon this visual cesspool.”

“But, I didn’t take or post those pictures. This is illegal; I know my rights.”

Dolan motioned Nadir to look across the room and forced the doctor to stare at one of his associates, who cocked his automatic weapon, removed it from underneath his table, and pointed it directly at Nadir’s head.

“OK, get to the point. Who are you, and what do you want from me?”

The man then handed Nadir his business card, and said, “My name is Benjamin Dolan, and I'm a Central Intelligence Agency operative of over fifteen years. The Technology Manager at your office of employment, Pharmaceutical Warehouse Incorporated I believe it's called, recently submitted paperwork to the IRS about moving your Maryland branch within city limits. Of course, a company like PWI, that possesses vast amounts of harmful chemicals, requires an intense security check before moving into our nation's capital, which led to our paths serendipitously crossing.”

Nadir’s knees began to shake. “To my recollection, our CEO discussed the move at our last quarterly meeting, but the move from Rockville to DC is far from definitely happening.”

“Its perfect timing that your co-worker Curtis did apply for your re-location, because an opportunity has arisen for you to help the welfare of our country.”

“I'm a . . . I'm a proud American, sir. How can I be of service?”

“That's the spirit; there's no time to waste. We are soon deploying six of our finest, most experienced soldiers for a mission in East Africa. These men, all experienced special operations soldiers, need your specific help and expertise in order to complete their highly complex and dangerous objectives.”

“Continue.”

“The CIA has plenty of doctors, chemists, and physiologists on its payroll, but none of them have conjured advanced development of x- 2317. While perusing through each file on your hard drive, no matter how immoral and illegal they were, I happened to read your almost-finished thesis detailing the wide-ranging benefits of x-2317. Spare me the fastidious details of the mosaic biochemistry involved in this application. Instead, quickly tell me about how x-2317 can make my men invincible warriors, unrestrained by outdated requirements like telecommunications and technical guidance.”

Dolan grabbed Nadir's cup of expensive coffee from the table and took an extended gulp.

“Think of x-2317 as an organic hardware upgrade to the world’s most complex computer; this, of course, being the human brain. x-2317 enables the mind, of anyone, regardless of their previous intellect, to make decisions that almost seem godlike in nature."

"Keep talking, I'm listening."

Nadir removed a pencil from his jacket, preparing to scribble on a white and green Starbucks' napkin.

"For example, say one of the soldiers for your African mission needs detailed, topographic information on the fly to complete his task, whether that be for a search and rescue or stealth assassination. And to successfully complete his operation, which I assume would take place under the cover of night, only continuous information from a GPS can equate to success. Now everyone's brain has the ability to absorb and regurgitate directions based on the amount of times and how often they've traveled a specific route. x-2317, ingested twenty-four hours before its effects take hold on the brain, will in this instance give your soldier the ability to absorb a detailed, three-dimensional map he would usually study for hours at a time, days before his mission. Then this soldier can accurately calculate and accommodate any plot variation, no matter how dire the situation. Obviously, it can make your soldier a more efficient killer as well. He'll seem almost invisible to the opposition as he can use his newfound intelligence to evade pursuers quite easily. x-2317 innumerably ramps up the decision-making ability of its user to levels never seen before in humans."

"So it's like tuning the engine of my Audi to increase its horsepower just by rewiring the software and installing a few computer chips. Is that a fair analogy, doctor?"

"Of course. But just like tampering with the engine of your Audi immediately voids the factory warranty, x-2317 can eventually invalidate the warranty of a healthy person's life.

More tests need to be done to eliminate ghastly side effects before its safe to administer to people. Of course, this could take years, if not decades, to complete."

"What kind of side effects are you talking about? I swear, if you're lying to me, I'll jump across this fucking table and rip both limbs from your shoulder sockets"

Before continuing, Dolan nodded at another average-looking Caucasian man seated at a booth on the other side of the coffee house. The two Starbucks employees behind the counter, also CIA agents posing as baristas, stopped making coffee in the near-empty store and stared toward Dolan.

"At this very moment, I have three undercover agents in this place currently watching us, plus a court order possessed by the store's owner to conduct matters of National Security within his property. And all four of us have young children, the same age as those subjects in your banned videos. Now let me repeat myself, what are the side effects of x-2317?"

"Well . . . now that I think about it, the side effects would be manageable. You see, any female that takes x-2317 will immediately cease the ability to have children. Men that take x-2317 no longer have the ability to procreate. Unfortunately, these effects are lifelong and irreversible. More testing has to be done, but for now, the only other discernible side effect that I can find in male participants is acute schizophrenia. Women who take x-2317 will develop schizophrenia as well, but of a much milder variation."

Nadir, because of his precarious positional ranking, is only contacted by a Voice from my dimension when absolutely necessary. He only calls Konrad "king" out of fear of retaliation from Warren, Eric, and of course, Ayala's goons from the BCM.

After pointing his index finger toward the ceiling, indicating that he wants Nadir to be quiet until instructed to speak, Dolan checked a recent, classified e-mail sent to him from a three-star general based at the Naval Sea Systems Command in DC.

"Currently holed up on a battleship in the Indian Ocean are six elite Navy SEALs waiting to embark on a search and capture mission for a known terrorist near the East African shoreline. Once capturing our suspect at his hideout entrenched in thick, trail-less jungle a few miles away from the beach, they have to hijack a vehicle at the terrorist's compound large enough to transport at least seven people. Then, once enduring and exchanging proposed gunfire with the target's associates, the six SEALs have to escort the target to a barren airstrip at least a half a day away in Ethiopia," said Dolan while scrolling through his Blackberry.

At the opposite end of the coffee house, Nadir's blood pressure rose as he stared at Dolan's associate first remove his standard-issue Beretta 92 from a holster beneath his fleece pullover, then cock it underneath the table in plain sight of Nadir.

"Doctor, I've heard enough. Down the line, we can always attribute a user's mental issues to PTSD. Now this is what happens next: over the next twenty-four hours, you will give me my first installment of x-2317 in the form of six refined pills. I know you're a busy man, so we'll meet in the driveway of your Bethesda home tomorrow night. In exchange, I'll delay charging you with any cybercrime based on what the NSA found on your laptop. Taking this matter to the press, or any other law enforcement agency, will only expedite, and ultimately solidify your future jail time. But hey, I believe in free will; so the choice is yours."

Nadir then sipped on his coffee one last time and hurriedly exited the coffee shop in front of his armed co-worker.

Chapter 28

"Grip the barrel of the weapon before pulling the trigger, son. You have to show the trigger respect before you can pull it. Always remember that."

"OK, sir. That'll make it ten times in a row if I hit the bulls-eye one more time," said Renzo, bent over in front of a two-hundred-yard-deep, fifty-yard-wide shooting range Blake had created for his protégé.

A few months before they reentered United States territory and made a surprise visit to Blake's ex-wife in Bellevue, Renzo and Blake drove an exhaustive, fifty-six-hour cross-country road trip through Ontario, Manitoba, Saskatchewan, Alberta, and finally through British Columbia to an uninhabited, three-room, wooden shack forty-five minutes east of Vancouver. Farid, as part of his handshake agreement with the former Navy SEAL, secured twenty acres of unused, unincorporated, mostly wooden land for Blake to reside in for up to a year; no questions asked.

"Secretly collaborating with marijuana activist Marc Emery, a friend of mine used it to grow BC bud on the property then transport it through unmarked, well-hidden wooden trails across the border and into Washington. You can even use one of these paths to reenter the States whenever you want to. Except for a few hollowed-out trailers on the edge of the property he used for drying plants, the land is completely empty and isolated from society. Use it however long you want, no questions asked," said Farid when negotiating his eventual payment with the stone-faced, mysteriously evasive Blake.

An owl howled at the moon, momentarily distracting the young Aruban from his target.

"Evening conditions are often unpredictable, Renzo. Before positioning yourself at the next station, confirm the target again with your right scope. Do it quickly; the true sign of greatness is consistency, and our mission becomes easy once you've grasped these fundamentals." Looking at Renzo's next target, which was a two-dimensional cutout of a middle-aged, male civilian, Blake stood behind him in a harmonized outfit of tightly-laced, gray military boots, camouflaged khaki pants, and a faded Orioles sweatshirt.

Renzo then put the FLIR ThermoSight, attached to the top of his M40 rifle, in front of his right eye and prepared to fire his next shot.

Digging the toes of his brand-new Adidas sneakers into the muddy grass, Renzo then snaked underneath ten more yards of shin-high barbed wire in front him.

"Was it really necessary to take my shirt off, sir? The ground is freezing."

"You need to acclimate your Caribbean body to cold weather. Stay focused on the enemy in front of you," said Blake.

Renzo, his eye still glued to his rifle's night-viewer, finished crawling under the last tenth of Blake's Marine boot-camp-style obstacle course.

Still on his stomach, Renzo then effortlessly fired a shot toward his manufactured target, a quarter-mile away from the last row of barbed wire.

The target's head exploded on impact, sending splintered, moonlit wood into the clear, Canadian midnight sky.

"That's my boy! That's my boy!" triumphantly exclaimed Blake, lighting his Cohiba Cuban cigar.

"Now, clean up for dinner; I'll take a few more bison steaks out the freezer. While eating, I'll tell you our game plan once we sneak back into the States. We're going to quick-strike two territories on the west coast, before additional training for a second, and final, mission."

Renzo nodded his head in agreement.

Not saying much after memorizing *The Art of War*, by the time the two passed through Winnipeg, Renzo then followed instructions by bathing in the frigid, outdoor shower stall behind their shed.

Meanwhile, Blake, seated at the duo's impressive communications hub within their modest cabin, fulfilled his promise by wiring the final ten thousand dollars to Renzo's anonymous, untraceable bank account in Central America.

"Momma, I met a teacher at a resort and am finishing my education abroad before I take my high-school equivalency test later this year. I think this is the best way for me to get accepted to an American university. Hope this money will help," later wrote Renzo, e-mailing his mother info on how to access his new checking account.

Renzo's mother, agreeing to not press kidnapping charges against Blake in exchange for an additional $50,000 to buy a new home, never told any of Renzo's siblings the truth about their brother's whereabouts.

"He found a job as a busboy on a cruise ship and should be back before the end of the year," she eventually told a nosy neighbor.

While enjoying a hearty dinner, accentuated by surprise fix-ins purchased from a local KFC, Blake made his argument on the justification of killing innocent US citizens, starting with his ex-wife in Bellevue.

"How could you possibly want to kill the mother of your only child, and how does this fit into bringing x-2317 into the world's consciousness?" asked Renzo while devouring his third well-balanced meal of the day.

"Don't think of me as a human being, son, hold me in the same regard theologians revere Muhammad and Jesus—or in the same regard as Jews hold money."

"I don't understand."

"Mr. Benjamin Dolan, using blind jingoism to justify the CIA and Navy's attempt to fry my brain, thought that a simple settlement to my team members and I could erase the potential harm x-2317 could have on my reproductive, central, and peripheral nervous system. Like seven figures of rectangular paper would automatically erase their sins? But I'm not a disgruntled soldier looking to enact revenge against those who sought to destroy me mentally and physically. No, that story's been told before. And, although I love my five brothers in arms that are no longer with us, retribution against Dolan, or Dr. Nadir Jayaraman for that matter, is not our mindset, son."

Due to paranoia from possible congressional and executive branch leaks, the CIA hid disclosure of Blake's repeated breach of its classified website from both the Senate Intelligence Committee and the White House.

Directly accessing then mining Dolan's internal memos via a powerful laptop within their Vancouver compound, Blake and Renzo were able to read about Dolan's connection to Nadir. Accomplishing this feat weeks before heading to Bellevue, the duo discovered the two main sides effect of ingesting x-2317.

Blake and Renzo also unearthed documents detailing Dolan's attempt to cover-up evidence linking the CIA to the other five soldiers who first ingested x-2317 then committed suicide hours after returning home from Cuba.

"They decided to take their lives because death meant no more suffering, no more oppression. Not from their suicidal voices associated with x-2317, or from those in the government that used them as guinea pigs and consciously destroyed their careers, but from elected officials, corporations, and established religious leaders who control the masses of sheep that populate this globe. Now, we're going to deliver this mantra to those who need it most, beginning with my baby's mother in Washington. Once doing so, my child will be enlightened without her in this world."

"So in a way, x-2317 is a new religion? Or more accurately, a new paradigm defining the way that humans should approach society, death, and the afterlife."

"Exactly, son. If death is no longer the end, but the beginning—if life is merely a forced, pre-determined path—then full control over one's consciousness originates once your eyelids can no longer open," answered Blake.

"How so?" asked Renzo.

"Because once I perish, I'll become a Voice like my guide here on earth in a habitable environment that gives me the ability to manipulate humans in accordance with the twenty-one goals I described to your earlier while battling against other enlightened Opponents who are trying to accomplish the same goals within a defined time frame," responded Blake.

"Do you believe that a simultaneous game, between another Voice and Opponent, exists in this dimension?"

"I have my suspicions that another dimensional battle does indeed my intersect with ours, and more specifically, that the production of x-2317 is where these two crusades either convene or repel against each other. Time will give us the answer to that question, I guess."

"Back to the subject of mortality. What happens when I die? Where will I end up if I'm killed in action?"

"Once I reach my final destination, I'll make sure you're canonized in this dimension and will request a special exemption, based on your genius intellect, for you to join me with the Others once you leave Earth. But you have your whole life ahead of you, and I will always protect you, regardless of where I reside."

Chapter 29

“Now I know you're not stupid enough to implicate me in your dealings with the CIA, especially after our encounter on Monday. I'll be in College Park in five minutes, and as soon as that happens, I'm signing off for the night. So hurry up,” says Konrad from his speeding vehicle on Route 95 South.

“As promised, the afternoon after Benjamin threatened to arrest me, he showed up at my home in Bethesda to personally collect the x-2317 pills. With my daughter and wife looking on, I handed Dolan the six pills, just as he asked, individually wrapped inside a small, translucent, zip-lock bag,” tepidly responds Nadir.

Nadir then takes Konrad back to the specific incident years ago, one afternoon in the driveway of Nadir’s mini-mansion.

“‘By this time tomorrow, each of the six SEALs I spoke of will ingest one these tablets two days before their mission in Africa. If you don't hear from me, it means that everything, for now at least, is OK between you and me,’ Dolan said.

"Dolan then ran back to the Suburban and left, drugs in hand. I haven't seen him since that incident. Repeated monthly calls to his cellphone and office in Langley have gone unreturned. For him to have taken the x-2317 to a CIA chemist, in hopes of replicating my product, is all but impossible due to x-2317's ultra-complex rarefaction process. But that being said, I have no idea if he administered x-2317 to six troops or not," rambles Nadir to Konrad.

Konrad passes through the neighborhood of future deceased Columbia mall killer Darion Aguilar and quickly makes his way down Baltimore Avenue.

"If x-2317 and synthetic heroin make previously peaceful users want to kill others in massive quantities, I need a few hours to figure out my next move. Wrap this up, doctor, and e-mail me your controlled test results on primates."

"In approximately five years of introducing it to their bloodstream, approximately 50 percent of all x-2317 and synthetic heroin users will undergo internal changes consistent with what I observed from my lab animals. Nearly a million users in the upper northeast, along with hundreds of thousands in the Baltimore area, will develop unfettered killing instincts consistent with those of a homicidal maniac. The desire to end someone's life for the infected will become insatiable and will create chaos on a scale never seen before in human civilization."

Five minutes later, Konrad parks his car in front of WaWa and crosses the street toward Cornerstone.

"Konrad! Konrad! Bro, you finally made it! I have a drink waiting; come join me over here!" screams Ronnie at the top of his lungs through one of the bar's open Safari windows.

After struggling through a throng of drunken revelers bouncing to a popular Killa Cam song, Konrad gives Ronnie a hug and says, “Where's Nina? This place is lame; let’s grab her and catch up in Laurel until the sun comes up.” Konrad casually returns eye contact with two attractive co-eds who lustfully lick their lips while motioning him to the dance floor.

“I know Sullivan's turned you off to women permanently; she has that effect on guys. C'mon, kiss me. You know you want to,” coyly whispers Ronnie. Using his perceived sixth sense, Konrad eyes every cluster and clique throughout the establishment to see if he can spot any older male patrons who could pass as undercover officers or federal agents. Satisfied that there aren't any, Konrad returns his attention back to his inebriated, homosexual friend.

Standing close to Ronnie, as if he wants to give him a passionate hug, Konrad places his left arm a few inches above his thigh. After casually putting his mixed drink on the windowsill behind him, Konrad then places his right palm on Ronnie's cheek as if he wants to embrace him.

Ronnie smiles in anticipation while Konrad winks at the two aforementioned blondes gossiping about him across the bar. Konrad then abruptly inverts Ronnie's neck sixty-five degrees clockwise, abruptly pressuring not only Ronnie’s vertebrae, but also the nerve roots attached to his spinal cord.

“You worthless faggot, I can paralyze you faster than you can scream for help. Do you understand me?”

“Chill, bro, calm down; that really hurts . . . I was just—just kidding. You know I've had a few too many drinks,” desperately pleads Ronnie as he begins to lose feeling in his lower torso.

Quincy's co-workers of bartenders, waitresses, and other bouncers, thinking that the two are just drunk play-fighting, avoid intervention.

“Tell me where Nina is located. Once I grab her, we're headed back to her place. Is that clear to you?” barks Konrad.

“She's—she's in the bathroom, touching herself up,” lies Ronnie, refusing to tell Konrad that Nina's conversing with Quincy in the back alley.

“That's fucked up, that you gotta guard the alley all by your lonesome.”

After fully opening the bar's cracked emergency exit, Nina tugs at the right sleeve of Quincy's bright yellow, tight SECURITY t-shirt. “Hey, you're not supposed to be out here, pretty girl,” casually says Quincy as he turns away from the twelve kegs he's been instructed to guard.

Feigning retreat, Nina turns to go back inside. “I was just playing; don't leave. I'm Quincy, and I just transferred out here from Pepperdine this fall. What's your major?”

Nina, thankful that her looks haven't degraded under stress, smiles. “No, I graduated from NYU a few years back. My friend and I just stopped here for a drink after dinner in DC. Why the hell would you leave the beaches of Malibu for here?” While keeping her hand interlocked with Quincy's, longer than what most would consider socially acceptable for two strangers, the brash young female adds, “It's alright; you can trust me.”

“You only live once; fuck it,” begins Quincy, before sighing. “I almost got busted for distributing cocaine, oxycodone, and heroin to a small-time dealer in LA, but the cops only found some weed plants at my apartment, and since the lease wasn't in my name, could only arrest my roommate without definitive evidence that the trees were mine. Using guidance from the local DA's office, Pepperdine's lawyers felt the best PR move was to quietly expel me while recommending five years' probation. So that's how I'm here in front of you, happy to not be in prison and making the most of a second opportunity. I can tell there's more to your life than you let on; what's your story?"

Nina's olive skin and full, naturally pouty lips along with her eyes, the turquoise, transparent color of tranquil Caribbean seawater found in Negril, causes the Californian to stare at Nina longer than necessary. His casual body language indicates an instant emotional connection to Nina, which he's never felt before with any female, including his mother or Rebecca.

Before she can respond, Nina feels a soft vibration and pulls the buzzing cellphone from her back pocket. Clearly the sexual aggressor during this impromptu flirting session, she says, "Please excuse me while I read this message," while repeatedly massaging Quincy's taut right deltoid muscle.

"What the hell's wrong with you? Konrad is here and wants to see you now. He seems angry; what's troubling him?" reads the text.

Back inside Cornerstone, Konrad holds Ronnie's phone while quietly staring at the obscured bathroom entrance in anticipation of Nina's return.

"Drugs, huh?" responds Nina.

"Your unpredictable emotions are an asset. Use them to increase your chances of victory," I remind Nina, knowing full well that she's on the verge of a nervous breakdown.

"I just . . . I just wish that sometimes I had balls like the sniper—that I could just kill everyone who's making my life a nightmare then never be seen again. Don't you?"

Clearly taken aback, Quincy puts his right thumb on Nina's cheek, carefully wiping away the mascara running down her face.

"Violence is never the answer to any of your problems. There's gotta be a peaceful way for you to deal with whatever's going on; there always is. I'm just a broke pre-med student, but I've had a decent amount of success working my way around established power structures. I'd be lying if I didn't say I wasn't doing this because I'm attracted to you, but maybe I can help. What gives?" says Quincy.

While Nina thinks of the best way to divulge my twisted game of survival and global domination, she and Quincy hear a loud knock at the iron exit door separating the inside of Cornerstone from their meeting spot.

"Everything all right out there, iQ? We need your help soon to clear kids outta here," says an associate bouncer before partially opening the rear exit, then sticking his thick, steroid-infused neck through the partial peripheral opening.

"iQ? That's your nickname?" curiously asks Nina.

"My high school chemistry professor started calling me that after I got a perfect score on the SATs," casually responds Quincy.

After exchanging contact information with Quincy, Nina stands on her tippy-toes, then steals a quick kiss before dipping back inside.

As soon as she sees Konrad at the front of the bar, Nina wipes the tears from her eyes and, using the congested dance floor for cover, sticks the shaft of her BMW key through her middle and index finger for physical protection.

Reluctantly accepting a shot of vodka from her maniacal ex-boyfriend, Nina stays silent as she tries to read Konrad's body language. The separated couple pay their tab without speaking to each other, then exit the packed bar behind Ronnie, who can hardly put one foot in front of the other without tripping.

“It's been a long night for all of us, buddy; just a few more yards to my car,” says Konrad as he takes Ronnie’s Porsche keys from his pocket then tosses them to his silent ex-girlfriend a safe distance behind him.

“Hey fuckboi, yeah I'm talking to you, you drunk piece of shit. How many Shirley Temple's and Pink Squirrel's did your loose ass swallow?” yells a stubby, younger looking version of Governor Chris Christie to Ronnie. From the northeast corner of Knox Road and Route 1, the intemperate heckler stands by himself, cocking his short arms toward the trio.

“Don't do it, Konrad; be the bigger person. You don't need this to happen,” warns Nina. Students in front of Ratsies cheer on the action as Konrad accelerates into the terrified and retreating heckler, driving his head into the rock-hard sidewalk pavement, much like he did to Nadir on Monday. Ronnie, now in Konrad's sedan after reluctantly taking his keys from Nina, accelerates out the parking lot and toward the red stoplight at Baltimore Avenue.

Before getting into Ronnie’s sports car, Nina turns her head and sees the lights inside the Smoothie King, which is directly behind a crouched Konrad, turn on.

Within the closed, blended fruit-drink retail shop, an older, severely bald Caucasian man dressed in a robe and flip-flops loudly bangs the shaft of a full-length, semi-automatic shotgun. “Can you drive?” yells Nina at the stoplight.

“That old man's gonna shoot Konrad in the back!” yells Ronnie from Konrad’s car, which is stopped next to the German sports car.

“Be calm, and run the intersection light behind me,” shouts back Nina.

“He's going to kill them!” screams a bystander, safely watching the action across the street.

Revelers from both Cornerstone and Bentley's gasp in horror as The Smoothie King owner unlocks his front door, then points his Benelli M2 at Konrad and his desperate combatant.

“I just replaced this door last week, ‘cause one of you punks threw a beer bottle through it. If the cops won't do anything about you thugs, then I will!”

Konrad, remaining silent, continues to jackhammer his left and right fist into the fractured jaw of Ronnie's shell-shocked mocker, causing blood to splatter on his suit jacket.

Quincy, unseen by the store owner, tiptoes to his side with the precision of a ninja. After waiting for his light to turn green, Ronnie, now at the street corner besides Konrad, reaches across his car's center console, then opens his front passenger door.

“Konrad, get inside, you won. It's over!” screams the plastered Brooklynite. It's important that Konrad realize that Nina has allies too. I’ve provided Nina with defenders of her free will, specifically chosen to offset Konrad’s hired associates: Warren, Eric, Kreesha, and Ayala.

Nina's most important associate, unbeknown to him as of yet, uses both hands to grapple the gun away from the distracted store owner. Quincy then slides the weapon on the ground back inside The Smoothie King.

Konrad, his fists bloody, staggers to his own escape vehicle as Nina, parked in the intersection behind Ronnie, beeps the horn of his Porsche.

"There's more than 200 wild students out here . . . the cops should be here by now," shouts Nina while following Ronnie and Konrad up Route 1 and toward her apartment in Laurel.

* * * * *

Back at the Montgomery County Police command post, Chief Macklin, Detective Adams, Superintendent Dobkins, and Lieutenant Patrick convene their second official meeting within the bunker-like, Tactical and Elevated Threat Meeting Room.

"Give me the rundown on the latest shooting; you're telling me it happened fifteen minutes ago?" asks Macklin as he speaks into a speakerphone positioned between the four seated investigation leaders.

"Preliminary observations indicate it's most likely the work of our sniper. The shooting occurred near the Montgomery and Prince George County border, a few miles west of West Laurel at the Burtonsville Town Square Shopping Center. At approximately 12:45 a.m. in front of the Zen Asian Grill, an African-American teen was shot in the side of the head by what again seems be a long-distance bullet from a long-distance rifle. We haven't been able to ID the body yet, but it seems the young adult was an employee at one of the various stores, eateries, or supermarkets in the immediate area," radios Officer McGary.

"Well, if this happened in Florida, our killer could use the 'Stand Your Ground' defense for at least one of the murders."

After chuckling, Dobkins says, "My officers, in coordination with the College Park, Greenbelt, and Laurel Police department, had checkpoints set up throughout that vicinity. My lord, this bastard is just playing with us at this point."

Realizing the unknown killers are now specifically targeting children, Lieutenant Patrick struggles to fight back tears.

"Obviously, your checkpoints are ridiculously pointless, so keep your fucking mouth shut unless called upon, got it?" barks Macklin.

"Got it, Chief," whimpers Dobkins.

"Officer, secure the entire area by keeping a half-mile perimeter around the mall. You can't do anything about TV copters, but keep all media as far away from the body as possible—and no interviews!" continues Macklin, before adding, "I need to talk to Nicole now; give her your receiver, McGary." The shaken EMT grabs the walkie-talkie from McGary as the rookie cop pops open the trunk of his cruiser and takes out ten rolls of yellow police tape.

On the way to arriving to the set of parallel oak trees on top of a patch of grass separating parked cars from traffic on Old Columbia Pike Road, McGary notices a set of fresh, embedded tire tracks about fifty meters from the deceased body, which lies limp on top of the sidewalk directly in front of a closed, Asian-themed restaurant.

“Chief, the victim is a young black male dressed in a black North Face fleece, jeans, sneakers, and a backpack. There is a purple polo shirt sticking out from underneath his jacket, which I believe indicates that he worked at the Giant Food Supermarket within the shopping center, probably as a stock-boy because the Giant was closed well before he was assassinated,” observes Nicole.

Over a dozen squad cars and ambulances flood the shopping center's parking lot area, which is empty sans a couple of parked cars. In JFK-like fashion, brain fragments of the teen lay among the fallen victim, who quickly collapsed to his left as the long range bulled entered the right hemisphere of his brain milliseconds before exploding his skull beyond recognition.

Back at the ambit of the crime scene, Officer McGary motions for another cop to finish taping the exterior for him, then runs back to the suspicious tire imprint he just passed.

“Someone made that tire track specifically; I swear on it,” mumbles McGary. He then runs back to Nicole, who's in the process of placing a white sheet over the dead teen with another EMT.

“Get Macklin back on the line. I think I found proof on how this killing is connected to the others,” shouts McGary as he approaches the sullen female.

“OK, youngin. Our homicide DTs are a few minutes from arriving; tell me what you've got,” responds Macklin.

“As I was running to the crime scene's perimeter to wrap barricade tape, I noticed screech marks from a vehicle no longer on the town center's property.”

“Those tire marks are probably from a startled witness that drove off in fear. I saw the same thing at a sniper murder scene in Baton Rouge,” says Adams.

“Chief, open up the e-mail I just sent you. Don't you think this tire track looks like the roman number seven?”

As Chief Macklin plugs his laptop into the wall-mounted television behind him, McGary walks a few feet backwards to get a broader perspective of the burnt rubber residue.

“Whoever did that wasn't trying to get away, they were trying to make a statement,” adds Macklin. The three other investigators pivot their chairs to the right to see the rookie's captured image.

“The imprints of 'V' and two subsequent 'I’s are doubled because of the rear tires. Maybe the double indentation both tires made has some meaning too. But why would the killer refer to the number seven?” asks Patrick.

“Well, there was a Hollywood film about a serial killer called ‘Seven.’ Maybe it has something to do with that,” remarks Dobkins.

“Officer, go into the Giant right now, clear out any employees that may be hiding, then find the closed-circuit television room as quickly as possible,” orders Adams.

Chapter 30

"Is anyone in this store?" screams the excited cop. "This is the Montgomery County Police Department! I repeat, the coast is clear, and I need to see your outdoor surveillance tapes right now. Is there anyone in the store that can please assist me?" adds the animated officer, while scanning the check-out section with his standard-issue, 9mm handgun.

A sixteen-year-old female Giant employee, also African-American like her deceased co-worker and classmate from Paint Branch High School, cautiously sticks her hands above the "15 Items or Less" conveyor belt twenty feet from McGary's location.

"One tangible point remains consistent at these parking lot killings from even back to Baton Rouge," begins Adams, who's still at MCPD headquarters in Rockville conversing with his peers. "When taking into account factors like the time of day, possible traffic obstacles, and the weather, murders two, three, four, and five all randomly took place at business settings somewhat familiar to this most recent killing. But at those four crime scenes, the murderer made a point to scope out the area before his shooting and either avoid surveillance by making long range shots, or in the case of two of the liquor store shootings in Baton Rouge, disable the surveillance camera seconds before killing his targets. My point is, unless he's superhuman, it would be pretty difficult to do this without some sort of assistance."

"No man can do that much reconnaissance without help. How much more evidence do you need to see that our targeted killer has an accomplice?" interjects Dobkins.

"The 'Bonnie and Clyde' theory has been bothering me too. Because some of these pinpointed crimes happened way too quickly for just one man to be the perpetrator. But unfortunately, the footprints at these murder scenes point to just one person acting alone," adds Macklin. Back in Burtonsville, the brave cashier ushers McGary past the dairy section and toward his wanted destination.

After playing with a couple of illuminated buttons on a keyboard in front of six wall-mounted, twenty-five-inch flat screens, Officer McGary uses his right hand to twirl a desk-mounted knob from left to right in order to quickly rewind and fast forward through recorded footage from inside and outside the Giant.

"I have a video ID of the teen taking off his employee apron and placing it underneath a cashier's station he just cleaned. He then waved goodbye to the young lady who brought me to this room."

"Go on, son," instructs Adams.

"After the African-American teen exits the Giant, he walks into the parking lot toward an unknown location," adds McGary.

"His name was Marcus, and he wasn't doing anything wrong; he was just leaving work after a twelve-hour shift. He was voted employee of the month in August and was given the responsibility of closing the store every Wednesday night, which is what I was helping him do because he was always so nice to me," interrupts Jamie, the diminutive Giant employee of over five years, from behind the shoulder of the overwhelmed first-year officer.

"What exactly happened to the deceased once he exited the supermarket?" anxiously asks Patrick.

"From what I see from the recording, Marcus exited the store forty-five minutes ago. He then walked between srow of ten four-foot concrete crash barriers and into the parking lot, which was almost completely empty."

Marcus' former coworker lets out a high-pitched, soprano scream, nearly piercing McGary's eardrum.

"A red, high-end sports car, of what on first appearance seems to be a Ferrari coupe, first pulls up next to Marcus on his left side, which stopped him from advancing any further. The kid, probably sensing something is wrong, turns around, and attempts to run back inside. As Marcus gets back onto the sidewalk, he's hit by two, high-powered rifle bullet. The shots seem to originate from inside the Ferrari's cabin on its passenger side; the butt of the gun doesn't stick out of the driver's side window. Marcus falls, dying instantly as the sports car makes an abrupt ninety-degree turn . . . As I thought, the Ferrari then accelerates toward the parking lot's center, and quickly creates the roman numeral seven by screeching its rear tires in reverse and then in the formation of a 'V.' After leaving the imprint on the ground, the Ferrari exits south on Sandy Spring road, leaving the dead boy on the spot where we found him exactly four minutes after the red coupe drove away."

"These two psychos are tired of being anonymous. They want us to bring them into the limelight now," observes Adams.

Macklin inspects a text on his phone.

"Guys, I just got a message from a Baltimore County Sergeant. That red Ferrari coupe has been found; it's currently on fire in front of a 7-11 at 231 East Baltimore Street downtown. The car was stolen last night from the outdoor lot of a Northern Virginia dealership. Their videotape identifies just one perpetrator: an athletically built, five-and-a-half-foot male, whose race and age are undeterminable because of the ski mask, gloves, and long sleeves covering him from head to toe."

"All of this, it's all connected . . . I mean, that's what that imprint is referring to. These two killers must have had the whole night of violence planned days in advance," comments Patrick.

Chapter 31

"Don't stop what you're doing . . . please keep fucking me," begs Nina.

That early afternoon, not far from Burtonsville in Laurel, Quincy quickly pushes up from Nina's quivering body.

Using his mocha-colored biceps to flip the exhausted woman off her stomach and onto her back, Quincy trails his lips down Nina's neck before working his way down to her swollen breasts, taking minutes to swirl his tongue around each silver-dollar sized areola as Nina whimpers in ecstasy.

His large brown eyes lock in with Nina's as he softly bites her pierced nipples while massaging her clit with his right thumb before softly inserting his index and middle finger inside of her; Nina spasms with delight and uncontrollably, once again, spreads her wiry legs open. Quincy pulls his hand from Nina's vagina and extends it toward her mouth.

Nina's eyes roll to the back of her head, gleefully tasting her own pussy juice. Desiring more pleasure, she wickedly smiles before sticking her hand inside the top drawer of her bedside dresser and grabbing a set of large, pink glass anal beads.

Quickly turning around and bending over, Nina orders Quincy to, “Stick your tongue in first, then loosen me up with this toy . . . Hurry up, I need you deep inside my ass.”

Quincy’s appendage quickly stiffens as Nina’s uncontrollable orgasm makes her powerfully squirt clear liquid onto the bed’s disheveled sheets. Seconds afterward, like a melting ice-cream cone, a waterfall of vanilla cum leaks onto Quincy’s quivering chin.

“Fuck . . .” murmurs Nina. Quincy slowly pulls a second ball from Nina’s asshole while stroking his rock-hard ten-inch shaft with his left palm.

Nina looks at the clock, then again says, “Fuck . . . No, stop, Quincy. We can’t do this anymore.”

“What?!”

“I just remembered. I’ve got to get to the office for an important meeting at three with my manager and Konrad.”

Nina delicately removes the sex toy from her undercarriage and then runs into the bathroom.

As she turns on the shower, Nina says, “By the way, thanks for saving Ronnie from the cops last night; he's probably passing through Delaware by now.”

“Hey. I get tested yearly and am clean. Are you on the pill?”

“No, but I can't have kids anyway, unless I find a cure I guess,” nonchalantly remarks Nina, gently pushing her still aroused partner off her and jumping underneath the running shower faucet.

Quincy, his impressive erection waning, looks at his sweaty body in the mirror, then begins to gargle mouthwash and wash his hands.

“I don't have any STDs or terminal diseases either. Please don't look at me like we just practiced Quimbanda.”

While turning up the water’s temperature, Nina adds, “Take a shower with me. I need to tell you everything that’s happened since Monday and why we have to destroy my enemies by Friday.”

Over the next twenty minutes, between passionate kissing and reciprocated scrubbing, Nina does her best to give a rational recap of the horror and despair she's faced over the last seventy-two hours. From her mother's long-standing destructive addiction to prescription painkillers to her unwitting ingestion of x-2317 and perceived schizophrenia to Bartolo threatening to kill her mom if she doesn't play the role of drug mule for Konrad to Konrad creating synthetic heroin from x-2317 and distributing it to a thirsty upper northeast market to Kreesha threatening to fire her if she doesn’t close PWI by Friday, Nina unabashedly reveals everything.

Quickly falling in love with the athletic dynamo, Quincy is captivated by Nina’s truthful recap. Although her hot-and-cold body language indicates her uneasiness about Quincy’s role in her Voice’s game, Nina exudes relief to finally tell someone about her pain.

“Get your shit together, Nina. Stop crying and calm down. After listening to you, my first thought is that Konrad is a genius for creating synthetic heroin. However, in getting you to take this secret super pill through a secondary contact, he miscalculated that you wouldn’t have the balls to investigate the genesis of x-2317 further. Konrad should have just slipped x-

2317 into your drink when you visited him on at his home on Tuesday. Instead, you now know exactly where the epicenter of your madness is, and of course, that's at PWI," first concludes Quincy.

"We need to find the person that created x-2317 and sells these tablets to Konrad for him to create synthetic heroin on a weekly basis."

"You're right. I'm so blessed to have found you."

Minutes later, now out of the shower, Quincy quickly dries his lower torso with a large beige towel. While cleaning out his eardrums, he adds, "Konrad and his gang connections, from Ayala in prison to his henchmen on the outside like Warren, Eric, Bartolo, and even Kreesha, are all prepared to thwart any move you make to get the authorities involved. But this fucked-up serial killer on the loose can work to our favor. There's a lot more local, state, and federal authorities patrolling the street, desperate for any crime-fighting win to boost their own career—Bill of Rights and Constitution be damned. We have to exploit this to our advantage. But I have to ask, why didn't Konrad just have you killed instead of giving you what amounts to a permanent abortion pill? I feel like these issues of abandonment and betrayal are at the roots of your problem."

"Konrad was elusive when I asked him that last night and instead gave me some vague, abstract answer relating to Game Theory. But he also works in corporate sales, so getting a straight answer from him is impossible. And to tell you the truth, I have no idea what'll become of this meeting with Mason and Konrad today. It's the first time I've been in the office since breaking Colin's nose on Monday."

Quincy walks back into Nina's bedroom to get dressed, then turns on the television to CNN.

"And another thing, it's imperative that you restrain from participating in any future altercations, because any police officer doing his due diligence is going to question if you had a history of violence during your relationship with Konrad. That office manager Curtis isn't going to be any help either and will probably complicate matters if you approach him. Do you know anyone else who works at PWI that we can pressure for help?"

". . . The victim, a junior from nearby Paint Branch High School here in eastern Montgomery County, was an assistant manager at the Giant supermarket behind me and was categorizing new inventory with another young co-worker until he left for home just before 1:00 a.m. this morning. As Marcus Jackson began the short walk home to his residence, he was shot in the head during an encounter that police believe is the twelfth shooting of the infamous Serial Sniper," begins the news anchor.

"The media's turning this killer into a celebrity. Soon this murderer will start selling his art on E-bay and convening autograph sessions at gun shops," remarks Quincy.

"A police source close to Chief Macklin has told CNN that detectives now believe that the accused killer has an accomplice or is working in tandem with another shooter also connected to the previous homicides. This has led some public officials to openly ask: Where is Cheney? And how come the president isn't taking a more public role in helping to capture the murderer who's killed in his own residing city?" continues the anchor while Nina, now dressed in work attire, applies a conservative amount of makeup.

"Other than the clueless gatekeeper at the front desk, there's no one there I've actually spoken to."

"Think deeper, are those two people the only PWI employees you encountered on Monday?" I patiently ask.

A half hour later, Quincy, entangled in another drug trafficking scheme, increases the volume of the M3's car stereo in order to get another news update of the sniper investigation.

"MCPD head Chief Macklin has just confirmed our investigative report regarding the luxury sports car used in this early morning's killing of Marcus Jackson. Sources reveal that the bright red Ferrari was anonymously stolen two hours earlier from the lot of Ferrari of Washington in northern Virginia, which is about forty-one miles west from Burtonsville."

Another news station, further up the radio dial, elaborates. "A few minutes ago, Chief Macklin, flanked by his counterparts from the FBI and Maryland State Police on the front, top steps of MCPD headquarters, answered questions from the media after giving a brief rundown of the latest murder."

The newsman's studio engineer then plays a recorded snippet of the hastily prepared press conference.

"Chief, can you confirm that after killing the unarmed youth in cold blood, the driver of the Ferrari performed a large burnout of the roman numeral seven in front of the supermarket? If so, do you have any idea why he referenced that number?" unflinchingly asks a local reporter. Nina takes out a pen and piece of scratch paper from her purse, then abruptly turns the radio down.

"What are you writing down?" Quincy asks.

"That address: 231 East Baltimore Street. And the tire imprints the murderer, or murderers left; that news report said that it was a roman numeral seven. Now what are the chances that, out of all the numbers this psychopath could have screeched, compounded by the address where they left that beautiful sports car to burn, contain the same four numbers as x-2317?"

"I got guts, girl, but I ain't chasing after a serial killer in order put this puzzle together. It's also unwise to directly seek these madmen on our own. Because literately hundreds, if not thousands, of officers are turning over every rock in the DC and Baltimore area trying to find them. Like a Sōhei Buddhist warrior, we'll stake out PWI to discover the true origin of x-2317 and then sneak around their premises in order to gather enough information to build a case strong enough to solidify your innocence," angrily says Quincy before abruptly parking the M3 on the shoulder of a quiet, tree-lined, four-lane road.

Too tall to fit in the trunk, Quincy crawls into the backseat to avoid anyone at efficienTECH seeing him.

"Before I go inside to speak to Konrad and Kreesha, I better call my mom to check if she's OK; I haven't spoken to her since Monday night."

"Why don't you use telepathy to reach her, you mutant," jokes Quincy before contorting into a human pretzel.

Meanwhile, at Nina's destination of efficienTECH, her coworkers eagerly anticipate her return.

In the office's waiting area, Denelle runs her bony, maple syrup-colored hands through Colin's slicked-back hair. Denelle's secret lover, their last rendezvous being last night in the office complex parking lot, leans back in her front desk chair, staring at the glass entrance door.

"Don't you dare lay a finger on her. We need Nina to orchestrate our coup, remember?" whispers Denelle, who stands behind him with her arms crossed. Colin, nodding in agreement, removes the 500,000-volt UZI stun gun from underneath the ten-foot-long cherry wood reception desk in front of him, then sneaks it back inside his jacket pocket.

Other witnesses to Nina's meltdown are also spread throughout the office, eagerly awaiting her return.

Nina's successful counterpart, Gabriella Francisco, who lives in downtown Baltimore at The Lenore apartment homes, could smell the 562 horsepower, naturally aspirated Ferrari engine burning from her apartment.

"You woulda sworn it was 9/11, with the amount of military helicopters, police cars, and fire trucks that surrounded the area. I live two blocks away from that address, 231 East Baltimore Street, and it's a really nice area of B-more. I mean, the 7-11, open twenty-four hours, is right in front of where the killers torched their getaway car, so they definitely wanted to send a message regarding their invisibility," told the Ohio native to Kreesha and Konrad upon entering the efficienTECH office two hours ago.

An hour after Gabriella retreated to her desk to follow up on business cards collected during Wednesday's round of cold calls, Dave Palmer, the meandering efficienTECH salesman responsible for Anne Arundel County, personally handed his hastily scribbled letter of resignation to Kreesha. The recent Temple graduate wisely stated his intent to switch jobs after witnessing Nina flip out on Monday.

"This is too much for me, Ms. Mason. I'm folding before the hand is called, so to speak, and have decided to join the sales team of a tech startup in Silicon Valley," said Dave after marching into Kreesha's office. As a venerable Konrad sat on top of the credenza behind Kreesha's desk, staring directly at Palmer in silence, Dave added that "the high level of unprofessionalism in the office" was the main reason for his departure. Instead of raising her voice, or immediately pleading for him to stay, Kreesha first promised Dave all the best—and a letter of recommendation, if needed.

"But you know, Davey, here at the Maryland branch of efficienTECH, it goes without saying that we've seen record growth since you joined the firm twenty-four months ago. And, as the regional leader in business-to-business sales of industrial copiers, scanners, and printers, we'll see twenty-four more years of growth after you leave the firm. Since you left our South Jersey training facility two summers ago, your sales statistics have been mediocre to poor, depending on how many lucky ship-ins you get delivered to your territory. However, since I can't fill the vacuum of your departure for at least six months, what would a switch to more fertile ground in Montgomery County, in addition to a 300 percent bump of your current base salary, do to your perspective?" proposes Konrad a little while later as Dave is packing up his desk.

"That's that psycho bitch's territory. Does that mean that you're finally going to fire Nina when she comes in? You know, doing so would really boost morale around here."

"No, instead of throwing her to the curb ceremoniously, we're going to box Nina in and make her life miserable until she helps drum up some business, at least in the short term."

"But what's in it for you, Konrad? No one in this office loves money more than you."

"As of yesterday, I've been promoted to regional vice president. My added duties, which will still include representing all four quadrants of DC, now give me the ability to help us close more deals in a more structured, advisory role," prevaricates Konrad.

"You mean like that PWI account, right? I heard they've requested price quotes for thirty of our most powerful copiers. That's a multi-million-dollar deal—one that could give Nina over a hundred thousand in commission and revenue bonus. Now that you're in this quote-unquote advisory role, how much of that will she get?"

Konrad takes a sip of coffee, then unbuttons the jacket of his dark gray, bespoke Jon Green suit. Before flicking his wrist forward to motion Dave to depart, Konrad takes notice of the office's newest inhabitant.

"I'm here for my meeting; are you two available to speak?" asks Nina, standing in the doorway.

Chapter 32

“Well, if it isn't Tony Montana and Griselda Blanco,” jokes Nina after a sincere apology to Colin and before closing the door behind her.

“Let’s keep this conversation as professional as possible. No flying UFOs during this meeting, please,” gently says Kreesha, motioning for Nina to settle in the leather chair five feet away and diametrically opposed to where Konrad’s now seated.

“Make it quick, Kreesha, I have some cold calls to do this afternoon,” responds Nina, ignoring Konrad as she takes off her thin black jacket and, as instructed, grabs a seat next to Konrad.

“As you can guess, in light of your recent progress working the PWI account, I'm not going to fire you. That's the good news,” starts Kreesha, pressing the back of her head into her ergonomic, futuristic executive chair while staring into the parking lot. Not seeing any police cars outside, or anything else unusual for a typical Thursday afternoon, Kreesha motions for Konrad to continue.

“I spoke to Curtis, and they've given us an oral agreement on twenty-six eT115 copiers to be installed on every floor of their Maryland, three-building compound. The deal will give you about $85,000 in commission before taxes,” begins Konrad.

“I don't remember making a deal with the devil; what exactly are you asking for in exchange?” responds Nina.

“We're putting a temporary restrictor plate on your growth engine, so to speak.”

“How the fuck do you get to make that decision?”

“Watch your language. I've been promoted, which gives me newfound staffing powers, as well as jurisdiction over all deals over $500,000. Until you prove your loyalty and dedication to this organization, you'll be selling $250 fax machines to home businesses. You're still in charge of Montgomery County, but no longer will you work any deals over $1000. And your base salary will remain the same until we decide otherwise. I've also gotten written approval from headquarters to give you a 'termination warning,' meaning that if you're written up for provocation of violence against another efficienTECH employee, regardless of who it is, Kreesha and I have authorization to fire you immediately. If you have a problem with this arrangement, you're free to leave and explore employment elsewhere.”

Before Nina can protest, her phone rings, and on her caller ID appears an unknown cell phone number.

“That's probably urgent. You should take that call,” says Konrad, without making eye contact.

Nina, anxious and tense, reaches into her purse to grab her cellphone.

“Don't test me, bitch; I'll kill your crackhead mom today if you don't do as you're told. So drive those birds to BWI every Friday,” begins an anonymous text message from an area code from southeastern Pennsylvania.

“I'm five feet away from her, and will slit her fucking throat once I get the OK,” adds another text.

Before approaching the efficienTECH front door minutes earlier, Mrs. Sullivan called Nina on her cellphone and told her daughter that Bartolo was in her apartment, giving her her daily cocktail of Vicodin and oxycodone.

“Is something the matter, Nina? I want to wrap this up so I can take off the afternoon to go shop with my daughter,” calmly says Kreesha.

“No issues; I'm fine. And thanks for letting me close that PWI account plus keep my job boss; I'll try to never let you down again,” sarcastically quips Nina as she grabs her coat and prepares to leave.

“You will never outsmart me, because you don't see the theory of time the same way we do. Your inability to harness your powers makes you weak, and I continuously petition the Others to find me a new Opponent. The threat of the clock, whether that be biological or professional, is hampering you from seeing the bigger picture. I don't have that problem; therefore I can anticipate your moves way before you can conceive them. And your failure to conceive is just the beginning,” confidently states Konrad.

“You're a smart, strong woman, Nina. And you remind me of myself when I first entered the corporate world. Let's end the hostility and strengthen our bond. If you ever need to talk, about anything, please don't ever hesitate to give me a call," adds Kreesha.

Nina, on the verge of tears, struggles to maintain composure.

"I'll be on the road all day doing cold calls. Call me if you need me." As a clearly demoralized Nina exits the office in front of a solemn Colin, Denelle, Dave, Gabriella, and a handful of other efficienTECH employees, she gets another text from the same number that threatened her only immediate relative.

"Tomorrow morning at 6:30 a.m., go to the same place you were Tuesday night. Make sure your gas tank is full. You'll be doing additional driving soon after getting there."

"They want me to deliver multiple kilos of synthetic heroin to BWI tomorrow morning. And please keep your head down until we reach I-95, Konrad and Kreesha are probably watching my car leave."

"Well you're definitely not doing that. Because business is taking off, they feel that now's the best time to pull you in; if shit hits the fan, you'll be an accessory to federal drug trafficking," states Quincy before asking, "By the way, where are you driving us to?"

Nina, now a safe distance away from the efficienTECH office, pulls the car onto the highway's embankment so Quincy can safely get into the car's passenger seat. "We need to go to the cops now and tell them everything. I've passed Macklin's office dozens of times. Let's go speak to a narcotics detective, sign a written statement, and clear this up right now," insists Nina as Quincy clicks in his seatbelt.

"Number one, you do that and your mom is dead; a conviction won't bring her back. So we can't do that, at least not yet. Number two, and just as important, we need to find out more about x-2317. And if it exists, an antidote for it. If this case falls into police hands, it could be years before you find a cure," says Quincy, before adding, "You not being able to have children isn't going to work for me, at any cost."

Quincy then holds Nina's right hand and places it on her flat stomach.

"A wise man gets more use from his enemies than a fool from his friends," I remind her, quoting the Spanish philosopher Baltasar Gracián.

"I'm sure that Konrad has already anticipated us trying to gain access to PWI and will thwart any attempt to do so. But I have a hunch that there's someone else we can pressure to unlock the secrets of x-2317."

"Who?"

"I know this isn't a question you usually hear on a first date, but have you ever kidnapped anyone before?"

Meanwhile, in his makeshift, broom-closet sized office set up at the Montgomery Police Department, FBI Detective Adams slumps back in his faux leather chair, struggling to keep his eyes open after working for sixty hours straight.

"All this evidence sprinkled throughout two states and three cities, and we still don't got shit," mumbles Adams as he opens his laptop and checks the waiver-wire of his Fantasy Football league.

"Yeah, boss, unfortunately nothing new to report here," he adds into his government-issued cellphone.

"Collecting fingerprints from the stolen Ferrari was impossible; the car was burnt to a crisp by the time forensics arrived on the scene . . . No, we've got no ID of anyone driving or discarding the car, nor do we know what car the suspects used to get away after setting the Ferrari on fire," continues Adams to his boss, Alex Henson.

"Hey, don't get depressed, Charlie. When counting state and local officials, there's over 500 officers in Maryland currently searching for these killers. And like the flatfoots in Louisiana, most of them wish they'd just move to another state and carry out more murders there."

"The thing is, we have this mountain of evidence from three different states and DC, yet no footage of these assholes on tape. We also don't have any fingerprints, and the footprints are a dead end because the majority of shootings occurred from either long distance or via a moving car."

While speaking to Henson, Chief Macklin taps the office door of his most trusted adviser. Adams puts his hand on the receiver, then yells, "Come in, Davis, I'm on the phone with HQ" seconds before the chief comes in with two fresh cups of java and patiently leans on Adams's desk.

"I'll tell you what. The FBI doesn't get enough funding to let agents just stare at the wall all day. And since you're already in the DC area, I'm giving you another case to add to your workload while this sniper case plays itself out."

"No problem; maybe it'll invigorate my passion for catching these killers."

"Great. Late last year, there was a breach in the internal CIA website by an ex-Navy SEAL who was recently honorably discharged from service for extreme PTSD. Normally, this would be a problem for those Virginia farm boys own Internal Affairs department, or in extreme cases, the Justice Department.

But because of an apparent cover-up to minimize repercussions, and Senator Feinstein's reluctance to ask the NSA for help in light of them illegally monitoring her e-mails, we've been secretly asked by her aides to investigate the matter further."

Adams puts his phone on speaker, then raises his index finger to his mouth; motioning for Macklin to remain silent. "Glad to take the case, but I'm really horrible with computers. Why me?" asks Adams.

"Because we know who did it and still can't find him," states Henson.

"Dumb question, but is this same ex-soldier responsible for the thirteen murders I'm investigating?"

"If he is, then he's going to bring down the whole CIA once he's caught. So I need you to drive to Langley right now and aggressively inquisition an agent there named Benjamin Dolan. He oversees clandestine CIA operations in East Africa and has been doing so without much oversight since the resurgence of Al Queda in that region. I'll e-mail you the details to your personal Yahoo account, but Dolan was responsible for the hacker's last operation in Somalia and Ethiopia. Senator Feinstein's office received written approval from both the White House and Attorney General to conduct this inquisition, so you now have authorization over all of Dolan's files related to at least one of our suspects," says Henson before apocalyptically warning, "It goes without saying that time is off the essence, and it behooves you to keep this inquiry as quiet as possible. If the press gets hold that a federal employee was in some way partially responsible for this cross-country murder spree, expect everyone, from both the right and left politically, to anarchize every major metropolis from New York to LA."

Chapter 33

"Are you sure that that's the guy?" whispers Quincy to Nina from the passenger seat of her BMW.

In the rear, entrenched corner of the massive, three-floor underground parking lot stationed underneath PWI's large Maryland building, Nina nods her head in approval, then positions a pair of newly purchased binoculars in front of her verdigris eyes.

From the drivers and passenger seat of her obscured BMW, Nina and Quincy see Nadir finally come into view.

"Yeah, that's him in the white lab jacket coming out of the elevator now. Out of the corner of my eye on Monday, I distinctly remember seeing Konrad leaving the lobby to chase after that same Indian man."

"That guy looks exactly like the Bollywood actor Irrfan Khan, except much smaller," begins Quincy, before rhetorically asking, "The timeline of events between you and I seem parallel, yet at the same time, seem out of order. Don't you agree?"

"Yeah, I can't grasp that fact either. It's like 'Daytona 500' by Ghostface. That song was released in '96, so why does Raekwon shout out 'Drake' when he doesn't even begin his career until many years later?" says Nina.

"At the very least, everything happening this week is reoccurring in a slightly different format. Like, for example, the random similarities between your ex-girlfriend's predicament and mine. Not to get too deep, but ever since Curtis drugged me with x-2317, I feel like I've stepped into an alternate, synchronistic universe where events, especially those that I have no direct connection to, can be positively or negatively manipulated by my thoughts and ideas. For example, I feel that I can solve this complicated Serial Sniper case plus incriminate Konrad and Kreesha while also saving my Mom from Bartolo just by staying on this path," says Nina before checking another anonymous text sent to her cellphone.

"Great, they want me to swing by Konrad's on Friday to take my first batch to PWI."

"What should we do with this scientist walking to his Volvo? He's about forty-five seconds from getting into his car, and driving away."

"What say we kidnap him, then bring him back to my place for questioning? If he's responsible for x-2317 production, he'll be too afraid of retribution from Konrad to go to the cops."

"See, that's what your opponent would do. I keep telling you, in order to win this battle orchestrated by the Others, you have to think different than your enemy. Pull your car behind his to block him in his space. Then get out, tap on his window, and ask if you can speak to him for a few minutes about everything that's happened to you."

“You sure?”

“You'll be surprised how far being rational gets you when encapsulated within irrational situations.”

Nina quickly accelerates her vehicle fifty yards through one of the two equidistant rows in the otherwise empty, enclosed garage floor jam-packed with eighty parked cars in four rows of twenty, then pulls up behind the trunk of Nadir's Volvo.

“This is how the Repo Men should have trapped me on Tuesday,” says Nina, right before pulling up the emergency brake and quickly exiting her vehicle.

Using the knuckles on her index and middle finger, Nina angrily raps the closed front driver's side window of the Volvo, expecting to startle Nadir.

Nadir, who looks like he's in a zombie-like trance, stares blankly at the concrete wall in front of him, ostensibly unaware of the ball of anger to his immediate left. Instead of texting PWI's security force for assistance, or attempting to escape by ramming the rear his car into Nina's parked coupe, Nadir winds down his window, and without making eye contact, says, “Welcome. I've been waiting for you, Nina. My name is Dr. Jayaraman, and I'm your facilitator.”

* * * * *

“Mr. Dolan, there's a Detective Charlie Adams from the FBI here to see you. He says it’s imperative that you speak to him now,” says Dolan's assistant Kyla after sticking her head into his Langley office.

At the same time, ten minutes after doing a quick loop in Nina's BMW around the parking lot to check for witnesses, Quincy opens the passenger side door and watches Nina toss Nadir's passive frame into the backseat.

“That guy's gotta be around 170 pounds; how'd you get so strong all of a sudden?” remarks Quincy. Fifteen miles south of Quincy and Nina, Dolan timorously waits for his secretary to escort Adams into his workspace.

“Charles Adams, FBI South. Good afternoon, Benjamin, and thanks for seeing me on such short notice.”

“No problem, I was just preparing for a teleconference with a contact in Sudan. As you know we just successfully completed a drone strike in Yemen, killing fifty-five Al Qaeda militants. Please, have a seat,” says Dolan while escorting Adams through his plush corner office.

Easily twice the size of Macklin's, Adams takes note of the dozens of plaques and medals that adorn each wall, then briefly gazes at a photo of him shaking hands with past Director of Central Intelligence Former President H.W. Bush.

“Yes, after meeting him before an impromptu Poly Sci lecture at Yale, Bush One gave me my first job here as an analyst. And I've been fortunate to be here ever since. What can I help you with, Detective?” responds Dolan, taking note of the taller Adams casual, normcore attire not usually associated with FBI employees.

“But you don't oversee CIA operations in Central Asia. Your territory is Northern and Eastern Africa, right?” inquires Adams, taking in Dolan's executive view of the densely wooded landscape outside.

"Terrorist interests often overlap more than one region, which is the same reason that serial killer brought you from the deep south to suburban Maryland. Isn't it, Charles?"

Adams sits down, puts a digital sound recorder on the messy workspace in front of him, turns it on to chronicle their conversation, then says, "Today is Thursday, October 11 in the year . . ."

Dolan turns on, then inhales vapor from an e-cigarette while his guest finishes his preamble.

"My name is Charles Adams, lead detective of the FBI's Southern Regional District. Today, I've been authorized by the Department of Justice and Senate Select Committee on Intelligence to conduct an inquiry about former Navy SEAL Blake Arthur Rice, who was last under your directive during the CIA's 'Operation Catch and Collect' stealth mission. I've been given broad clearance to question you, Mr. Dolan, for two main reasons. First, the ranking senator of the SSCI is appalled that the six SEALs assigned to 'Catch and Collect,' five of whom are no longer alive, were medically discharged from active duty even though each of the six soldiers had flawless military records for over fifteen years and doctors concluded that their PTSD was treatable. Second, the DOJ, in collaboration with the FBI, has sent me here to ask you why Rice, upon leaving the Navy, immediately decided to hack into the CIA website to unearth every e-mail sent to and received from a . . ."

Adams then briefly takes his eyes off the distinguished, motionless operative to look at notes he scribbled at MCPD.

"So the White House had nothing to do with this meeting."

Taking note of Dolan's subtle implication of the Cheney administration, Adams continues. "Dr. Nadir Jayaraman of

Pharmaceutical Warehouse Incorporated in Montgomery County, Maryland. And that's where we'll begin. Early last year, why did you, an executive operative of the Central Intelligence Agency, feel the need to conduct an undercover sting at a local Starbucks to entrap Jayaraman for possession of child pornography on his laptop without referring the case to the DOJ and Maryland State Police? Also, after intimidating Dr. Jayaraman into deleting his admittedly criminally negligent software without a warrant, what events led you to precipitate discussion of incarcerated drug kingpin Tavon Ayala of the Black Commando Mafia?"

"Mr. Adams, Mr. Adams . . . Since time is of the essence, it would be more beneficial for both of us, in the near and long term, if we elongate this discussion in a different environment," says Dolan, while quickly looking outside.

"Answer the questions."

"Again, the unilateral opprobrium regarding this matter dictates us speaking outside. Privacy inside these walls is nonexistent and prevents me from being forthright. So let's advance this conversation in the park across the street."

Dolan then points at the overhead fire sprinkler above both federal employees.

"Alright, Jimmy, we'll do it your way. Once outside, I'll even turn off the recorder so your coworkers don't become suspicious," adds Adams, trying to gain Dolan's trust.

"Thanks for understanding; let's get some fresh air."

Adams walks behind Dolan as the twenty-five-year CIA veteran leads the two government men out his office and past his secretary's desk.

"Kyla, please call my wife and tell her I'll be late for dinner in Federal Triangle and for her to order apps and a bottle of wine without me," instructs Dolan.

As the two enter the empty elevator, and Dolan presses the button for the lobby to descend four flights, Benjamin smiles for the first time, since meeting his assured inquisitor.

"From what I read on his case file, it seems that Blake Rice, one of this country's most distinguished and experienced SEALs, with an unblemished record spanning over 200 missions around the world, had a bit of a brain malfunction. My records indicate it happened during that long flight from Ethiopia to Cuba last year. To repeatedly physically assault the skull of a shackled, submissive al-Queda combatant with the butt of his M-16 seemed out of character for not only Rice, but also for his decorated team members who attempted to defecate on the African suspect before being interrupted by an army co-pilot unsettled by his passenger's actions. When questioned about those events by CIA doctors evaluating their mental capacity, all six SEALs said that the abuse and torture of the combatant in the plane never happened and repeatedly asked why they were being railroaded. But anyway, the last time you saw Blake wasn't on that cross-Atlantic flight in that unmarked Gulfstream, it was in that Navy ship a few miles off the coast of Somalia hours before this 'Catch and Capture' operation began. Once we get outside, I need clarity on these disputed events," says Adams, intent on staying on message.

"And lastly, in electronic discussions between you and Dr. Jayaraman, I kept seeing the alphanumeric character 'x-2317' popping up. Yet, there's no mention of this term in the official 'Catch and Capture' report. What exactly is x-2317?" adds

Adams seconds before the massive silver elevator doors open, giving both men passage to the building's colossal lobby.

"Until we get outside, please keep quiet. I'll tell you everything you need to know once we cross the street," answers Dolan, which prompts Adams to restrain from further interrogation until the two leave the building. Both men pass through the busy, TSA-like checkpoint where Adams retrieves his loaded, government-issued handgun from a baby-faced Latin-American security guard.

"It's corny, but I'll always remember what my mom told me when I told her I was joining the CIA after graduation," begins Dolan as the two men enter, then exit a large glass revolving door. Adams takes a second to watch the burnt orange sun set over the timbered horizon as Benjamin transitions into a serene, blasé demeanor.

"I'm not even allowed to tell local authorities this yet, but Blake killed his ex-wife in cold blood, Dolan. It happened earlier this year in Washington State, no more than twenty feet away from his infant child hiding in fear. Based on the style of killings executed, I know he's responsible for at least eleven other murders scattered around the country. He hasn't lived at his home in Maryland since being discharged from the Navy and seems intent on staying 'ghost' until God knows when. Now why did he seem intent on leaving an electric footprint on the CIA website connecting himself to you and Dr. Jayaraman?" asks Adams.

Now halfway through the thirty-yard concrete walk-path in between the agency's nerve center and a perpendicular, two-way road used as an artery for traffic to the George Washington Memorial Parkway, Adams zeros in on an empty steel bench on the edge of a plush, manicured lawn across the street with its back toward a dense acreage of wooded pasture behind it.

“Let’s continue this conversation on that bench over there. It seems private enough.”

Instead of answering Adams, Dolan continues to reminisce about his past conversation with his now-deceased mother. “After I told her that I was going to work here, my Momma kissed my forehead and said, 'Be careful what you ask for, son, because you just might get it.' I guess it took me twenty-plus years of service for this country to finally figure out what she meant.”

Dolan then sprints full speed and leaps directly in front of an oncoming olive-green M35 military truck, instantly snapping his spine like a broken crab leg and immediately killing the husband of over thirty years.

Chapter 34

"Give me your hands. I'll make this as painless as possible," says Nina.

Back in Laurel, Nina removes a black wool scarf from Nadir's eyes and ties his wrists behind the same chair she tried to work from on Tuesday morning. The composed chemist cheerily replies, "I know you're in a bind, Ms. Sullivan, but you don't need to imprison me. I'm truly blessed to finally meet you."

Unequivocally, Nina's new boyfriend agrees. "Kidnapping isn't the direction we're going to take here. Ask him the questions you want answered while I make dinner for the three of us. Because if the cops ever ask, we're going to tell him he was a guest enjoying a casual meal, not a prisoner held against his will. After we eat, you're going to call a cab to take Nadir back to PWI as soon as he feels like leaving."

As soon as Quincy departs to the kitchen, Nina whispers "I'll end your life if it means saving my Mom's. Never forget that."

"See, that's what I'm talking about," calmly says Nadir as he removes his shoes, slides his arm through the slightly ajar glass door, then softly puts his penny loafers on the balcony floor; adjacent to the living room.

"Unproductive comments like those are one of the unfortunate side effects of x-2317. That's why I didn't take Konrad accosting me on Monday personally. The random elevation of testosterone, and other steroid hormones in your bloodstream, is a permanent side effect of x-2317. Believe it or not, this can be mitigated through yoga—usually of the pranayama variety—to regulate your breathing. Let's get into a Lotus Pose so I can give you an accurate account of what's going on inside your body."

Quincy sits on the living room couch behind the two, and lights his first spiffs of the evening.

"Please listen to the man, Nina; he's our only chance for peace and understanding. Right now, he's our only way out," advises Quincy.

Sighing, Nina relaxes the tension in her face and gets on the carpet next to Nadir. Nina cross her legs, then faces our designated administrator.

"I don't trust you. But go on," says Nina.

"Essentially, you've been given the keys to a McLaren F-1, without any instruction on how to properly operate the vehicle," starts Nadir. As Nina contorts herself into the next pose, Nadir slips a phone-like device into her pocket. When she tries to interrupt him to ask what it is, he continues with his story like nothing happened.

"x-2317 has rewired your brain to point of being a genius, essentially giving you the decision-making ability of a chess grandmaster. It's also refined your ability to tap into your adrenal gland when necessary, giving you a short, incredible burst of strength upon demand. This is not new news; I'm sure you've already figured this out over the last few days while overcoming both professional and personal hurdles. The region of your brain responsible for short and long term memory, the hippocampus, has been enhanced to levels never seen before in humans. In the past, you would struggle playing chess against a 1200-level player in a seven-day correspondence game. But now, if we analogize chess to life, you can dominate fifty, simultaneous, random blindfold games with the ease and skill of Aron Nimzowitsch."

"Will I be able to have children? Is this side effect of x-2317 irreversible?"

"x-2317 has reduced the fertility in your ovocytes to the point of inhibiting your body from being able to create another life form. Saying these effects are permanent at this point are impossible to ascertain, until the Others approve of more testing."

Nina gets silent, and her eyes begin to water as the gravity of no longer being able to conceive finally hits her. Early, x-2317-enhanced memories of Nina's mother carrying her in her womb, breastfeeding her, and teaching her how to walk and swim quickly enter Nina's psyche.

"Tell me who the Others are and where they're from," barks Quincy.

"Use the simplistic complexity of math and science to answer your own question," responds Nadir.

"I don't understand," responds Nina,

"You are the Others, and the Others are you," says Nadir.

"Stop speaking in circles, Doctor, and give her a straight answer," interrupts Quincy.

"The dissemination of x-2317, and the subsequent battle for human civilization between you and Konrad, rests upon three foundations, permanent, inflexible, and sacrosanct in any galaxy. They are Newton's third law of motion, the Uncertainty Principle, and the universe's fascination with reality television. Decisions you've made in your life, consciously or otherwise, has determined events, both large and small, in another region of the universe. These events haven't occurred in a traditional chain from past to present, because time has a different meaning to the other connected species."

"So aliens were watching 'Real World' one day and decided to create their own reality show between Hunter and I?" asks Nina.

"Because I have never ingested x-2317, the only direct communication with the Others came in a stimulating visual hallucination—much more elaborate than the ones you and Konrad experienced soon after taking it. While I was alone in my lab, conducting standard quality control on a routine oxycodone treatment a little over six years ago, a letter-sized, twenty-by-ten-inch rectangle appeared near the ceiling's corner, illuminated by red, green, and yellow flashes, which exploded like firecrackers but had no sound to them. Inside the screen, a young man appeared, with smooth, yellow-brown skin like Quincy's, yet black, olive-sized eyes like Konrad's. Being the coward that I was, I immediately tried to run out my laboratory to get a security guard to view what I was seeing. As I did, the steel entry door quickly shut and locked in front of me.

"'Dr. J, turn around and meet your maker. You exist only to serve us, and I'm only going to tell you this once,' said the young man on the hovering screen. I demanded he tell me his name.

"'I'm an advanced life form from the Planet Proxima B, which will be discovered by scientists from Earth in about fifteen years. Our interaction with time is much different than yours. Where I'm from, past, present, and future have different connotations, which give me the ability to create a synthetic environment, like the one you currently inhabit, purely for my enjoyment.'"

"What did you do next?" asks Quincy.

"I pulled out my cellphone camera and tried to take a video of the hovering image, but the camera showed nothing except for the generic gray ceiling behind it. To my hardware device, the image had no existence.

"'Put your camera away, and keep your mind black for the next ten seconds. Failure to do so will result in me inadvertently killing your brains ability to control some of your motor functions. When I went through this process with Steven Hawking, he initially resisted, and subsequently can no longer walk. Momentarily free your mind, so I can enter it,' the young man said.

"After one sixth of a minute of me doing my best to think of absolutely nothing, the young man on the elevated flattened screen said, 'I'll make this simple. Create x-2317. Make sure Ms. Nina Sullivan and Mr. Konrad Hunter eventually take it.'

"'Who are you?'" I asked.

"'You currently reside in one of many alternate dimensions that share similar rules regarding chemistry, physics and biology, but differ in minute ways too numerous to mention. My associates and I have created your environment for Ms. Sullivan and Mr. Hunter's advancement, through a game determined by either Nina, or Konrad, accomplishing the majority of twenty-one goals in their lifetime, that I have also uploaded into your mainframe.'

"After blinking my eyes, I felt my memory instantaneously remembering what the twenty-one tasks that he, and his opponent who controls Konrad, were."

After Nadir told a captivated Nina and Quincy the same goals I mentioned earlier, along with other previously described parameters of the game between my Opponent and me, Quincy asked, "What happened next?"

"The mysterious man, who looked exactly like a human, then said, 'I will tell you one last thing. Never, under any circumstances, give x-2317, in its raw form, to another individual. You will never hear from me again.'

"And then the hallucination disappeared," finished Nadir.

"So why didn't you just ignore this alien's instruction, and continue your job as normal?" asked Quincy.

"I always feel compelled to push the limits and ramifications of chemistry. It's in an inherent trait in all scientists."

Quincy, a science junkie himself, takes an immediate liking to Nadir, then asks him, "How are you able to manufacture tens of thousands of x-2317 tablets a week for Konrad without your bosses at PWI not catching on?"

"It's exactly 12,500 tablets we create every seven days, and you have Eric and Warren to thank for that. PWI, in addition to distributing the most popular prescription drugs region wide, also manufactures generic acetylsalicylic acid, or ASA, which of course is known by its more popular name: aspirin. So every Thursday night, going back over a dozen months, I run my formula through that mammoth manufacturing apparatus Nina was in awe of, while visiting Curtis this Monday. The diameter and volume of each x-2317 tablet is identical to each generic aspirin tablet PWI produces, and has no indentation distinguishing it from aspirin. To completely cover their tracks, Curtis installed a secret software program that temporary disables the tablet-manufacturing machine's internal counter, preventing it from accounting for the increased, yet officially undocumented x-2317 production. Once synthesis of the weekly quantity is complete, Warren and Eric haul it off in an oil drum to Konrad's place, where they manipulate the tablets as they see fit. Konrad, and sometimes Kreesha, stay up all night to convert x-2317 to synthetic heroin. Kreesha would usually drive the two suitcases worth of end product herself to BWI for shipment up north. But because of increased security due to the snipers, they now need you to fill that role. From start to finish, this procedure takes about ten hours to complete and has made everyone involved richer beyond their wildest dreams."

"Why are you divulging the entirety of Hunter's template to us? Aren't you worried that we'll take this information to the police?" asks Nina, still cross-legged and sitting inches away from Nadir.

"Regardless of whether you believe me or not, money matters; let's not kid ourselves. At your age, and in this recessed economy, it would be great to be financially independent for the rest of your life. Even if you figure out a way to save your skin without Konrad orchestrating the murder of your mother, there's still another caveat you're not aware of. What I'm about to tell you is the reason I let you bring me here in the first place, and why I think prison is the place I need to spend the rest of my years." Seeing no update on the sniper's location, Quincy turns off his laptop, and gives Nadir his full attention.

"By the end of the decade, half of those that snorted x-2317 even once, and 100 percent of those who've injected synthetic heroin only one time, will either become a habitual, homicidal maniac, serial killer, or both. I have asked the Others for an antidote numerous times, but have received no answer."

Quincy and Nina stare at Nadir in awe, slack jawed and aware of what the country's burgeoning heroin epidemic can devolve into.

"Konrad Hunter and Tavon Ayala have sold hundreds of thousands of synthetic heroin packets from Baltimore to the Canadian border. If you're right, when all these people turn into mass murderers, this country will descend into complete chaos—just like Konrad predicted," exclaims Nina.

"Wait a second, what's the difference between a serial killer and homicidal maniac? I thought they were the same thing," asks Quincy, briefly interrupting Nina's train of thought.

"As I understand it, a serial killer is someone who stalks his prey in an established manner, and repeatedly kills those he has a prior relationship with, or fantasizes being with; like the 'Son of Sam' or 'Zodiac Killer.' A homicidal maniac is someone who kills innocent individuals at random for no apparent reason. In my humble opinion, the Serial Snipers are both serial killers and homicidal maniacs. Because even though they're plotting out each murder before carrying them out, they're choosing victims at random," responds Nina.

"I have spent a few days on my own, researching a cure that can erase the homicidal/serial killer side-effect of synthetic heroin, but it will take at least another year to complete. Also, when I sneak the counteracting antidote into future batches of x-2317 for Konrad, there's no guarantee that those who currently take synthetic heroin will enjoy snorting or injecting the new, reformatted version of synthetic heroin. Obviously, this could complicate efforts to clean up my mess," quickly points out the nervous chemist.

"What's the worst-case scenario?"

"Unless every heroin addict is taken off the street, and locked up against their will, in a safe environment where social workers can administer the antidote, then I conservatively estimate that *at least 150,000 innocent Americans will be violently murdered by this time next year*; all because of synthetic heroin."

"I don't care if you have to sleep in your lab, you're going to create an antidote by Devil's Night, not by this time next year," barks Quincy.

"That's impossible on my own. Trials alone would take till at least mid-winter to complete. I'd try my hardest, but unless I know how humans will react to an antidote, there's no way that I can properly embed it into Hunter's weekly batch."

"Nah, bruh, that's not good enough. Give me the $50,000 a week Konrad gives to you to bake that rat poison. All that Buddhist mantra bullshit you preach can't hide the fact that you're just as evil as he is. You're going to destroy humanity as we know it!" screams Quincy.

"No, you gotta understand, Konrad's psycho. He's threatened to kill me numerous times, and derives humorous pleasure in seeing people beg for their life. His goons have even spied on my kids at the park."

"What's the worst thing Konrad has done to you?" asks Nina.

"Hunter once siphoned out the gas of my wife's car while we were watching a movie at Pentagon City. When we came out and figured we had to take the Metro to Wisconsin Avenue in Bethesda, he followed us onto the subway and snuck up behind me in a crowded, standing room-only car. He then whispered in my ear, 'One move, and I filet your spine out the small of your back. But answer me this riddle: How long will it take for your sexy wife to react? I approximate ten seconds of shock before she starts screaming hysterically. Then you can rub shoulders with Biggie and Pac and decide who's better lyrically.'

"Konrad then stuck a common, sharpened kitchen knife into my fifth lumbar vertebra. As I turned around to acknowledge his presence, he ran out the open door at the Foggy Bottom stop in Northwest, then punched a female traffic cop in the face before sprinting into the night. I'm only continuing production because he'll end my family's lives otherwise, just like he'll have Bartolo kill Mrs. Sullivan in York if Nina doesn't get in line. But maybe your mom's life isn't important to you, Ms. Sullivan. Maybe it's in everyone's best interest if that albatross is removed," continues Nadir.

After Nina clocks Nadir in the jaw, Quincy, unmoved by Nadir's story, continues.

"In return for fifty stacks a shipment, I'll help you facilitate production of an antidote. You're going to immediately hire me as your assistant at PWI so you can use me as a guinea pig."

Nina shakes her head in disapproval.

"That's an insane idea. Look at what long term disabilities the current form of synthetic heroin does to users. There's no telling what version 2.0 will do to you."

"There's no other way. I need the money to pay for my final years at Maryland and for med school. It's funny, because drugs got me into this predicament back in LA, now I'm using drugs to dig my way out."

Nadir graciously receives a bag of ice from Nina, then continues. "The only thing you may be digging is your grave, young man. Yes, using you in clinical trials of a new version of x-2317, which I'll start calling x-46, will speed up production within Nina's desired timeline. Also, the participatory money you're requesting isn't a problem; this snake oil has made me more than enough profit. PWI gets interns from schools around the area, so your hire won't attract suspicion. With the weight of an anarchy-led apocalypse on my psyche, I'll try my hardest to deliver."

"What's the 'but,' doctor?" asks Nina.

"Doing so won't erase two important caveats. One, regardless of whether it contains x-2317 or x-46, synthetic heroin is destroying countless neighborhoods in the Northeast at a rate twice as fast as crack did in the eighties. But the media is underreporting the epidemic, because it's primarily affecting suburban enclaves. And two, fueled by greed, Ayala, Kreesha, and Konrad have plans to soon distribute their product nationwide. Nina, while Quincy and I work to remove the murderous trait within synthetic heroin, you have to figure out a way to permanently disable their criminal enterprise now. I think you'll find that, when the time comes, you have all the tools you need," he finishes, glancing noticeably at her pocket.

* * * * *

"Get some sleep, Detective. You've been on duty for almost seventy-two hours straight. I'll send you a text if any developments arise," says Chief Macklin to his trusted advisor.

A few hours after Nina fed and then called a cab for the gray agent, Adams further immerses himself back into the sniper investigation.

"Domestic terrorism is a much larger threat to this country than radical extremism. The last time I witnessed a suicide bombing was in Fallujah. A young Iraqi teenager approached my squad's parked Humvee from the right front passenger side as my four-man team was conducting a routine checkpoint for suspicious vehicles approaching Camp Dreamland. One of my guys sitting in the driver's seat was playing a Slick Rick song, or maybe it was Mos Def; I don't listen to that coon bullshit, so I'm not sure. Anyway, the kid approaches the open right front window, leans in his head, and asks in Arabic, 'Have you done enough to please God?'

"It was my fault, because our translator had his torso sticking out of our truck's open top, manning the Humvee's roof-mounted gun turret. He was up there to protect the sergeant and I, as we were inspecting a bevy of incoming suspicious cars, which we pulled over at random and had parked in a line on the side of the busy, dusty city road. Anyway, as the soldier in the driver's seat tried to get the translator's attention, the kid zipped through a busy four-lane road like Frogger, then sprints toward another group of four soldiers across the street, who just finished their checkpoint duty shift minutes before we started ours. 'He could be a bomber, Charlie. Give me the word and I'll take him out. He's already crossed three lanes,' said my translator, operating our elevated machine gun turret. But I couldn't do it, I couldn't tell him to pull the trigger and shoot the child in the back of the head. The kid, after successfully crossing through the sea of traffic, jumps on top of the front hood of the other team's Humvee and pulls a cord, detonating the explosives within his backpack and instantly killing all four soldiers within the other Jeep."

"Words can't describe your pain, I imagine," remarks Macklin. "But before he exploded himself to death, and I'll never forget this, he looked in my eyes and smiled broadly—to the point that it caused me to smile. It was *that* warm and inviting. Benjamin Dolan, before jumping in front of that M35 in Langley this afternoon, flashed that same smile."

Also standing in Macklin's office with the chief is Lieutenant Tommy Patrick. The intense sniper investigation, which seems to be stuck in a black hole on the local and state level, hasn't progressed much—even after the two recent, brazen acts of violence by Renzo and Blake. Elevated closed-circuit cameras, located at the parking lot where Marcus was shot and killed, failed to catch more than a covered arm and hand as the Ferrari sped away. Eerily similar to the events surrounding the execution of the unarmed youth this morning, Baltimore City cameras failed to pick up any clues on the duo's whereabouts, leading the media to correctly theorize that the two killers studied cracks in security at the Ferrari Dealership in advance before eventually using a second getaway car to make it out of B-more unnoticed. Baltimore murder detectives, eager to throw their hat in the ring, are trying to wrestle control of the case away from Chief Macklin and the MCPD, leading a paranoid Patrick to believe that Adams is also working as a spy for the federal government.

"Sorry you had to witness that, especially with everything else going on here, buddy. Since you joined us from Louisiana, the dead bodies seem to keep piling up," accurately observes Patrick.

"Do you think that there's any tangible connection between this rogue SEAL and our suspects?" nervously asks Macklin, who's unaware of Dolan's connection to Blake Rice.

"I doubt it, Chief. This looks more like an isolated spying case instead of an avenue connected to our investigation. Based on the evidence I've seen, this Dolan character was probably working with Chinese hackers involved in mining classified information against domestic nuclear, steel, and solar energy firms headquartered in DC," replies Adams, who then yawns, looks at his watch, and grabs the exit doorknob to prepare to leave.

After the three make tentative plans to huddle with Dobkins, along with selected contacts in Baton Rouge and Baltimore the following morning, Adams finally ends his day at the MCPD complex: the first time he's done so at a reasonable evening time since arriving in Maryland.

Walking to his rented vehicle in the parking lot, Adams sees a squad SUV rapidly approaching him.

"Detective Adams! Detective Adams! How's the case going? Can I be of any assistance?" yells Officer Michael McGary from his four-wheel-drive police vehicle.

Adams jumps on the rear of his rent-a-car just as Officer McGary hits the brakes a few feet from his dangling legs.

"Sorry, Detective Adams, just wanted to make my presence known," shouts McGary as he jumps out of the car, then trots toward his idol. In casual conversations with other officers,

McGary has let it be known that he intends to join the FBI in hopes of eventually becoming a detective like Adams.

"I see you with the chief and lieutenant a lot, so I've never gotten the opportunity to make my services directly available."

"Directly available? Your services? What the hell are you talking about, son?"

Officer McGary leans against Detective Adams' Chevy Malibu and nestles his chiseled physique closer to his hunched over, visibly fatigued exoskeleton.

"The way I see it, you're the real head of the investigation. We both know you're just using Macklin as a figurehead: a shield to protect the federal government against negative press amid the public outcry for an arrest. But the truth is—the truth is these two troglodytes will continue to elude us as long as we don't think out of the box. "

"Go on. I'm listening."

"We both know you can't catch these psychos all by yourself. Don't get me wrong, I would run through a wall for the chief, but because this sniper case is colder than the Redskins playoff chances, he doesn't have the patience to gently massage a lead the way it needs to be investigated. That's where I can come in."

"I'll tell you what, officer, sit in the passenger seat while I plug an address into your navigation screen. I need you to stake out a home address in Bethesda all night; and do it using your squad car. I want your presence known to the neighborhood, but not to your ranking sergeant. Am I making myself clear?"

Chapter 35

"Why are we still plotting to kill all these people? By implementing continued death and suffering, how are we advancing our message? I don't get it; how does our enemy know our message if we haven't told it to them yet?" justifiably asks Renzo.

The duo, no longer in the Baltimore region, aimlessly drives through Montgomery County. Blake and Renzo desperately search for a desolate road they can park on before transforming their apparently beat-up Chevy Caprice into a makeshift bedroom so they can get at least five hours of uninterrupted sleep.

From Northwest Canada to the DC Area, Renzo and Blake have logged almost 7,500 miles in the navy blue, 1985 Caprice Classic sedan.

After the two committed their first planned sniper hit in Arizona and left the rotting carcass of Billy Ray Braun at the golf course, they determined they needed to refine their ability to remain invisible to law enforcement. This included everything from accustoming the body to a strict, intermittent fasting routine of only eating every seventy-two hours, training on everything from how to take makeshift baths in fast food and rest-stop bathrooms to retrofitting the Craigslist-purchased Caprice for a variety of capabilities unknown to outsiders.

THE BLUE CAPRICE

In addition to adding a second car battery to the car's electrical system to eliminate startup problems in cold weather, the two killers, after completing the agonizingly long drive from Arizona back to Coquitlam, swapped the car's standard 4.3 liter, V-6 engine for a much more fuel efficient, inline-four-cylinder diesel attached to a brand new, hand-built manual transmission. Renzo and Blake also removed the car's rusty steel brakes, expertly replacing them with four Brembo carbon ceramic discs.

But, easily the two most important add-ons Renzo and Blake created in the old-school Caprice were (1), installing a small motor into the rear seat, enabling it to transform into a small bed with the flip of a discreet switch, and (2), inventing a mechanized, metallic peephole. Conceived from opening a quarter-sized space usually reserved for the trunk's keyhole, it is this small cavity, less than an inch in diameter, which Renzo keeps the silenced tip of his Canadian military-grad, McMillan Tac-50 sniper rifle attached to. From this peephole, Renzo killed many of the duo's victims, along with countless domesticated dogs for target practice.

"Call it a night, son, and get back up front here as I finally park for the evening. At the crack of dawn, we'll set up shop closer to MCPD headquarters."

Renzo smoothly disables his rifle in twenty seconds and locks it in a disguised metal box embedded within a drawer underneath the rear seat. With his weapon securely hidden, Renzo crawls through a man-made hinged partition separating the Caprice's trunk from the rest of the car, quickly wiggling his toothpick frame into a small ball before tumbling into the right front passenger seat.

“Here, Mr. Vincent, eat this while it's still cold. I must admit, our little fridge has been a life-saver during this adventure.” Blake removes a small, white paper bag from the refrigerated glove compartment, then hands his mentee a small chocolate-dipped vanilla ice cream cone he bought in Germantown while Renzo took a much-needed nap during rush hour.

“Will all this be worth it if the police shoot us to death?”

“Son, I’ve been waiting for you to ask me this question, because the answer is two-fold. First and foremost, we, as enlightened humans, don't view death as the omega. The ending of one’s life, no matter how it occurs, is an opportunity to teach the uneducated how this world really works. This statement can cover every conceivable way a life ends, because words like 'random,' 'inconceivable,' and 'accident' are only designed to distract the misinformed from realizing the truth about their, and of course your, livelihood. For example, when reading a novel, every aspect of the environment surrounding your main character, whether it be the designated protagonist or antagonist, has been created to enhance your reading enjoyment—or if we use a more modern, video game analogy, your viewing experience. Coincidence is a fallacious delusion, methodically advanced by the deaf, dumb, and blind.”

“So God, being the author of my life, created you to rescue me from poverty and despair in Aruba? He did that so I could help my mom buy a new home, right?”

“The God you speak of is yourself, Mr. Vincent. At the same time, you're the author and reader of your own biography. Now that I’ve taught you to no longer fear longstanding, seemingly axiomatic canons that regulate Occident society, pressures of repercussions regarding your actions have evaporated. x-2317 opened my eyes to this very fact, and in turn, I'm passing this esoteric knowledge to you. So, although you don't have the same tactical vision that I enjoy, you'll walk this earth with your head held high, firmly planted outside the sphere of the 'Infamy of Fact.' Today's society will view you as seventeenth-century Europe would: as a banished noble one who pursued those of disrepute by any means necessary in order to no longer live his life as a forgotten exile.”

Blake, as tired as Renzo, parallel parks the Caprice into an open spot, which is less than five miles from Macklin’s MCPD office.

“This is a quiet neighborhood. We'll be fine here until the morning,” adds Blake, checking the rearview mirror for oncoming traffic.

Renzo, ecstatic to eat for the first time since Tuesday, eagerly licks at his cone as Rice turns off the engine.

“My designated combatants, those in the United States military who've worked so hard to repress these facts regarding life and death, also have no regard for the sanctity of 'free will' and the 'presumption of innocence.' That's why this country invades sovereign nations and why they illegally eavesdrop on conversations between their own citizens. Around the world, this country's military has about 2.3 million employees working for

Dick Cheney, the appointed commander-in-chief. The only way for me to get his, and the world's, attention about the hypocrisy and atrocities committed by those sworn to serve this country is by doing what we've done. But because Mr. Macklin is a cognizant puppet for the federal government, he'll do for now." Renzo climbs back into the car's rear, presses a secret button spreading the back seat into a usable bed, and removes a folded sheet and pillow from his duffle bag on the floor.

"Well, we've got to take out one of his family members, co-workers, or loved ones next. I assume Dolan is either dead or contemplating suicide, as forensic investigators are starting to connect who was killed in Bellevue to the murders in Arizona, Baton Rouge, and around here; it's only a matter of time before they finally dissect the e-mails detailing the x-2317-CIA-PWI triangle. Answer me this: How's the public gonna react when they find out the US hired, then harbored, a known holder of child pornography to . . . to?"

"Be still, son, everyone other than me has their faults. Dr. Jayaraman's double-edged sword will, soon enough, pierce his own skin."

"Sir, I know it is not my place to ask, but, but what is it like being on x- 2317? I get depressed sometimes, because I'll never experience all the great stuff that happens to you when you take it. I wish I could be a superhero like you."

The grueling year, and extended time away from Aruba, has done little to waiver Renzo's enthusiasm for his mentor, provider, and bulwark. Even though he was originally told by Rice in February that he'd be back home by the end of summer, Renzo has not asked to fly back to Aruba since the duo's first murder in Bellevue. Every one of the three times Blake asked Renzo if he wanted to speak to his mom, Renzo declined, saying that he normally would go weeks without seeing her, so any attempt to talk to her now would seem contrived and staged.

"I basically ran away from home when I was ten, but couldn't make it very far because I was trapped on an island. She won't call the American Embassy if she senses any fear, heartache, or lonesomeness in my voice. She'll just ask for more money," said Renzo earlier this spring.

After Mrs. Vincent's first withdrawal of money from her shared Panamanian bank account this past May, she held true to her bright son's word. Renzo's mother, more enamored with new home ownership than her child's welfare, gave her son the blessing to continue 'studying' with Rice overseas with the expectation that he'll enter a four-year institution as soon as he receives his GED. Blake, hedging that Mrs. Vincent would never alert Aruban authorities about Renzo's whereabouts as long as the money kept rolling in every month, mailed her a short letter around this past Independence Day, raving about Renzo's academic prowess, ability to use tactical knowledge, and innate instincts to solve real-world problems.

Using the name and address of one of his dead comrades from Texas, Blake went on to say that homeschooling Mrs. Vincent's son is easy, because he's "a natural-born leader" and a young man who's lustrous future "will bring much change in the world."

And to fully cover his tracks, Blake paid his Canadian associate Farid an additional $25,000 to assume the pseudonym of Dr. David Gardner, Deputy Commissioner for the Texas Higher Education Coordinating Board. Around this most recent Memorial Day, Farid then penned a letter to Mrs. Vincent, stating that, "Since 2000, Texas has opened the doors of college for 540,000 more students, which include doubling enrollments for Hispanics and African- Americans. I have personally worked with Blake Rice for many years, and believe your son will soon have institutions fighting over his enrollment. You should be very proud of what Renzo's accomplished in such a short time, and also, what achievements lie in wait."

"Taking x-2317 is like playing chess," answers Blake, almost four months after Mrs. Vincent received Farid's letter.

"Only it's in your mind, instead of against any particular opponent. And the opposition is always black, always moving second to begin the game, and always using the Scandinavian Defense against your King's Pawn Opening, quickly taking control of a position you just secured. Do you understand what I mean, son?" says Blake as he readjusts the side-view mirror to get a better view of posterior traffic.

"No, Mr. Rice. I do not; please explain."

"This analogy means that although an x-2317 user is always making decisive, winning moves in life, they're always on their heels, waiting for an equally aggressive response from their enemy. So when locked in this type of conflict, prolonged happiness is elusive. But don't fret, son, victory is near. So get some rest; we've got a big day ahead of us tomorrow, my child."

Having honed his body to perform at peak mental and physical levels without sleep for a maximum of eighty-four hours, Blake sips his chilled iced coffee, standing watch from the driver's seat as he scans the middle-class, Montgomery County residential street for late-night, conspicuous activity.

"I'm two minutes from this dothead Nady's home, Detective," texts Officer McGary into his private cellphone.

Before leaving, McGary reassured Adams that he could discreetly deviate from his normal patrol route through

Germantown, Beallsville, and Poolesville, and into Bethesda without arousing suspicion from his ranking officer. It is now early Friday morning, October 12, around a week and a half since the first Maryland murder officially linked to the snipers.

Back in his Montgomery County hotel room, Adams quickly responds to McGary's text by typing, "His name is Nadir, officer, and do not, I REPEAT, do not approach the suspect under any circumstances."

Immediately after Dolan jumped in front of a moving truck this morning, Adams ran toward the terminated, mangled body of the CIA operative and discreetly removed his Blackberry from his pants pocket. As two MPs and the shaken driver circled around the body, Adams then ran back upstairs to Dolan's office and grabbed his laptop before leaving Langley as quickly as possible. In a subsequent conversation with Henson, Alex told Adams that the CIA quietly stopped the possibility of any local TV stations finding out about Dolan's suicide.

"I had to twist some arms because the agency really doesn't want the FBI involved in this, but you've been given tacit approval to electronically go undercover as Benjamin Dolan. Using him as an alias, softly reach out to any and all contacts you think are relevant to catching our sniper," said the deputy director in his most recent e-mail.

"Go to bed, Detective. I'll follow up with you in the morning on what I've observed during this stake-out," replies McGary, parking next a short distance from Nadir's home in Bethesda.

The non-divided, open-ended two-way road housing Nadir's 50,000-square-foot-foot, four-garage mansion sits on an empty street occupied by seven other homes, all of similar pomposity and stature. With front lawns large enough to fit a cricket field, the block was recently used as the backdrop for a protest railing against rising economic inequality. Unlike the block filled with ranch-style homes that Renzo and Blake are sleeping on, this suburban DC street has no other cars on it except for a late-model Mercedes belonging to Eric at the opposite end of the block.

"Why is there a MCPD pig twenty car lengths in front of me?" says Eric as Officer McGary, located in front of an oligarchical palace four castle's east of Nadir's address, turns off his car engine and high beams.

Wisely borrowing his closest friend's S65 sedan instead of taking his slightly more ostentatious, florescent yellow, Aston Martin coupe, Eric decided at the last minute to leave his car in Konrad's private, hidden garage and conduct overnight surveillance of Nadir in Warren's Mercedes.

"You'll blend in fine in the neighborhood. And don't complain; I need you for reconnaissance duty because Nadir hasn't answered any of my calls all evening. So stay there all night, and don't leave until you see his car enter or exit his driveway," instructed Konrad earlier this Thursday evening, around the same time Nina ushered Konrad's chemist into a waiting taxi at her place.

"I'm pretty sure that's the same sedan I pulled over at that highway roadblock earlier this week," says McGary, in current time, to himself while walking up the block.

"Hey! Hey you, I remember you from the road block. This is the MCPD, wind down this tinted window now! Don't make me pull out my weapon!" yells Officer McGary, now next to the Mercedes.

Two hundred yards away, from the window of his first-floor study, Nadir nervously squints as McGary removes the standard-issue handgun from his holster and taps it on the front driver's side window.

“What do you want me to do about this, boss?” texts a calm Eric from the driver's seat as he starts the German V-12 engine and prepares to speed the short distance to I-495.

Konrad's untraceable phone immediately responds, “Proceed as planned, then blaze the target at our agreed location.”

Eric immediately puts the expensive sedan into drive, then roars past Officer McGary, breaking his pinky toe as he accelerates toward the front curb of Nadir's mansion. While the rookie cop screams in agony, he accidentally fires three shots into the air, causing the dwellers of the other seven homes on the block to wake up, cringing in terror.

Eric, accelerating north of sixty miles an hour, jumps the luxury sedan fifteen yards into Nadir’s property, landing on the precipice of the doctor’s substantial front yard.

“Please, Konrad, I beg of you. Do what you want with me, but leave my family out of it,” whimpers the desperate doctor from a second-story window. As his wife and children sleep, Eric digs the Mercedes tire treads into Nadir's immense front lawn, gashing the once-immaculate turf with the ferocity of a prison inmate 'buck fifty'-ing a rival’s face.

“Congratulations, Nadir. Via your connection to the CIA, you've now got every cop in the state thinking you're connected to the Serial Snipers. I'm the least of your worries now,” replies Konrad before hanging up the phone. Konrad has Eric imprint the four numbers 2-3-1-7 into the lawn, which Clarke does with the precision speed of an X-Games rally racer.

“I'm exiting off the doctor's front yard right now, boss. I imagine the front spoiler and undercarriage of the car are pretty banged up, but I don't have any flats and the transmission is still operating OK,” screams an exhilarated Eric into his phone.

“Great work. Remain calm and safely drive to EuroMotorcars on the other side of town. The dealership is only a few blocks away, and Warren is waiting there with a gas can, book of matches, and an escape car to bring you back safely.”

“OK, I'm leaving Nadir's hood right now.”

“Hey, I'm not mad at you,” continues Konrad, “but why are my scanners telling me that Bethesda PD Is approaching Nadir's address from various locations because of 'shots fired' instead of 'vandalism.' What happened?”

“There was a MCPD cop at the other side of the block in front of another home for a reason unknown to me. After a couple minutes of unprovoked profiling, the cop accelerated to a distance about ten yards in front of my car, then got out and knocked on my closed window barking to see my papers, only he did it with the tip of his nine. So instead of relinquishing power, I ran over his foot before destroying Nadir's lawn. And see, that's when . . .” timidly starts Eric, hoping not to anger the violent, enigmatic mastermind.

Chapter 36

"Hey, honey, check this out. The morning after we agreed to work with Nadir, there was another car bombing in the area, this time in front of a Mercedes dealership in Bethesda," says a naked Quincy, cross-legged on the carpet adjacent to Nina's couch.

While staring at Nina's open laptop, Quincy clicks onto the fourth story in the news section of a local, respected, independent online newspaper.

"It says here that 'authorities are trying to piece together evidence from the early Friday morning's explosion and are exploring all leads. A source inside the MCPD believes that the auto arson isn't directly linked to Thursday's torched Ferrari in Baltimore, but may be connected to someone in Montgomery County aiding the sniper—or snipers," adds Quincy. It's been three weeks since Nina escorted Nadir into a taxi that surreal Thursday night and watched as our coordinator was driven back to his office in Rockville and two weeks since the couple decided to take a vacation abroad.

"That's a great idea. Go sit on a beach and clear your head for a couple of weeks. After you get back, you'll be much more focused and in tune with our philosophy. And while you're gone, I'll have Colin manage your territory while Bartolo, God bless his soul, will stay in touch with your mother to remind her that you'll be away," said Kreesha at Konrad's place the same morning Adams and Chief Macklin investigated the crime scene at EuroMotors.

After biting the bullet and agreeing to transport a double shipment of synthetic heroin to a waiting BCM member who also works as a Fed-Ex cargo handler, Nina dropped her BMW off in long-term parking, then rushed to a patiently waiting Quincy at the BWI US Airways terminal. Deciding that running away would only exacerbate their legal problems, plus definitely lead to the ghastly murder of Mrs. Sullivan, the two stuck to their original plan of flying to the Dominican Republic to reenergize and devise a concrete formula to implicate Kreesha, Konrad, and Nadir while at the same time avoiding prison.

"Sorry, it's my fault for not picking up this story while we were away. But at least I stuck to our promise that I wouldn't open a textbook in Punta Cana. I can't find an update on this article. What do you make of this development?" adds Quincy in present time, trying to get Nina's attention from the opposite side of her modest penthouse.

Last week, once the two got back from their spontaneous Caribbean getaway, Quincy began his "internship" as a human guinea pig at PWI where he received five daily injections of x-46 in order to gauge its potency. Nadir, staying true to his word, did not reveal this development to Konrad, Curtis, Warren, or Eric. Not even after intense questioning from Detective Adams, followed by a warrant-backed search of his Bethesda home, orchestrated by the Maryland State Police, did Nadir snitch. Nina, unsure that her self-conceived plan will work out, resumed her position as a sales exec for efficienTECH the same day he began testing at PWI. Eager to put her fiasco with Colin behind her, a tanned Nina immediately secured Curtis' signature for a high six-figure, multiple-copier agreement, easily giving her more commission dollars off the deal than she had made in salary all year.

"Well, at least she's still alive," says Nina out loud, twisting her ocean-bleached ends to temper her nervousness.

Just entering home after an exhausting day at work, Nina kicks off her heels and stares at the answering machine on the hallway table, smiling as she sees that her mother has tried to reach her all day. Like the rush of entering a k-hole, the euphoria of escaping reality for fourteen days in paradise has been temporary. However, the impromptu trip gave the twenty-something-year-old time to take a proverbial step back and examine how best to solve her various issues while still avoiding prison time. The tens of thousands in cash she's received from Konrad for being a drug mule, all going to relieving Quincy's tuition and college loan expenses, has officially implicated her in his drug ring.

"You and I just have schizophrenia from all the drugs we used to do in our apartment. Let's put this episode behind us and seek professional help together," begged Nina to Konrad before their most recent Monday's sales forecast meeting.

"Let me take over Planet Earth without murdering your mom. Just talk to the Others about resigning so their dimension can declare me victorious," responded Konrad, two days ago, when the two walked past Denelle's memorial and through the eT parking lot.

"And what happened after you called him psycho?" asked Quincy in present time in Nina's living room.

“He smiled and said that I'm currently in the third step of the Kübler-Ross model.”

“Once you stop 'bargaining' and reach 'acceptance,' then the real fun will begin,” added Konrad two days ago.

Gasping, Nina drops to her knees, crawls past her TV broadcasting regurgitated DC sniper stories, and grabs Quincy’s left and right forearms.

“Hey, you've got track marks! You didn't tell me Nadir would be injecting you with that poison. I thought you'd only snort and smoke his samples,” exclaims Nina after viewing the four needle scars left by Nadir’s mad experiment.

Quincy, who hasn't shaved in weeks, finally puts on a pair of boxers and lights a cigarette.

“You know those aren't the best ways of getting his drugs into my bloodstream. He's been injecting me with the old synthetic h, formed from the opium substitute x-2317, along with ultra-pure black tar heroin unwittingly provided by Konrad’s associate Eric. He's also injected me with diamorphine, imported from a legal drug clinic in Switzerland. And finally, a refined, new form of synthetic heroin generated from x-46. Just like the Others gave him strict administration instructions on x-2317, Nadir said he isn't allowed to give anyone x-46. Konrad does quality control of his product every week but will be unable to tell the difference between this new form of synthetic h and the old one, as they are 96 percent indistinguishable,” adds Quincy as the two take in the dry, chillingly refreshing, late autumn air.

“It's a Morton's Fork, what we're experiencing,” says Nina, referring to the fifteenth-century saying that describes when someone has to make a burdensome, undesirable decision between two undesirable options.

"Every day I continue working with Konrad, the probability of serving serious prison time increases exponentially. And if I keep condoning my mother's obvious drug abuse, she'll overdose sooner or later."

"Do what benefits yourself the most. Neither party cares about your future; they're just attached to you out of necessity," I advise. "Since the US occupation of Afghanistan began in 2001, the amount of opium produced in Afghanistan has gone up 2,500 percent. Two thousand, five hundred fucking percent, all under the guise of turning a country inside out to search for one so-called terrorist. Concurrently, since 2001, the amount of heroin users in this country has doubled. 80 percent of the smack headed to Europe flows through Iran now, which is tearing that country apart. Now answer me this, don't you think the CIA has more to do with our problems than we previously thought?"

Miles away, a stonewalled Adams has been pondering that very same question for weeks.

Hours after Benjamin's suicide, the CIA allowed the FBI detective complete access to Dolan's e-mail in hopes that assuming Benjamin's online identity will lead Adams closer to Blake. E-mails and texts sent to Nadir, disguised in the sometimes passive, sometimes aggressive lingo that the operative used when intimidating the embattled chemist, have gone unreturned. A day after Eric destroyed Nadir's front lawn with the rear tires of Warren's now-incinerated Mercedes, MCPD conducted a warrant-backed search of Nadir's home and office at PWI in the process seizing his laptop, along with written documents thought to be associated with the investigation.

However, Nadir's lawyers, citing the eventual exoneration of Dr. Steven Hatfill, demanded that all his property be returned immediately due to lack of evidence. Secretly put on retainer by Konrad, Kreesha, and Nadir when they joined forces almost a year ago, the powerful DC law firm, Covington & Burling LLP, successfully argued that exposing their client to another dead-end trial-by-media would only inflame public anger and frustration toward the federal government. Wanting to curtail growing dissatisfaction with the unsolved sniper case to Chief Macklin's department, the feds backed off and returned everything to Nadir before meekly threatening Nadir with an ambiguous “person of interest” charge.

“Michael, since you're headed in that direction, can you please go to my car out front and retrieve a couple of cds I accidentally left in the front passenger seat? They contain some files I need for the case,” asks Adams. His face unshaven and aging at an unnatural rate, his once-ripped military physique defeated by desk relegation and late-night McDonalds, and his psyche destroyed from daily verbal lashings from Deputy Director Henson, Adams sits alone in his broom-closet sized makeshift office, quickly typing the first paragraph of his resignation letter. Recently promising his wife that he'll leave his government job and seek work in the private sector closer to home, Adams tosses his rented car keys to the rookie officer in the hallway.

“Sure, Detective, be right back,” replies Officer McGary as he limps through the labyrinth of uniformed officer desks, past the newly built holding area for incarcerated prisoners and finally out the front door toward the visitor parking lot. The rookie then walks past the metal detectors, shaking hands with security personnel stationed by the facility's entrance, and into the late-fall night.

Now outside, McGary takes note of the massive buildup of local, national, and international news trucks with their raised satellite antennas two stories high. The mobile media hubs, from TV stations from Maryland to Japan, are randomly scattered on the police department's 18,000-square-foot front lawn.

Reporters removing their makeup with baby wipes, along with their production assistants disassembling cameras and microphones, close up shop as they prepare to leave the police premises. The media, frustrated that a third straight day has passed without an official update on the sniper's whereabouts, has temporarily stopped producing live reports: at least until tomorrow.

“I can’t believe those sand monkeys are here,” observes McGary, who makes note of the Al Jazeera truck to the left of the fifteen-step, concrete front entrance staircase. The keystone cop-like episode at Nadir's home, which failed to net anything except a Nadir-backed, multi-million civil lawsuit against the MCPD and FBI for defamation of character, cemented Officer McGary's future not as a federal detective like Adams, but instead, as a mugshot taker and suspect line-up coordinator firmly relegated to desk duty for years.

Back inside, Adams receives an e-mail, sent from an anonymous, untraceable Hotmail address, to Dolan's personal Yahoo account.

“Every month, until each of my demands are met, I will murder a member of your terrorist organization. Demand #1: have Macklin tell the public that the villainous treachery of the CIA is responsible for this multi-state killing spree. Run to the

window and take a look outside so you can see this death firsthand. You, along with your own organization, are powerless to stop me," states the nameless, unsigned paragraph.

Adams swivels his chair 180 degrees, then digs his navy-blue Asics into the filthy, laminated beige floor tiling, propelling the five rusty wheels on his office chair eight feet across a thin hallway toward a closed third-story window.

"Why won't this fucking thing open?! Someone get in here and come help me!"

Screams by reporters, higher pitched than fans at a Beatles concert, emanate from outside Adams' locked window. Below, on the foreground of the MCPD campus, ten feet from the standing WRC-TV news truck, Officer McGary's body lay permanently spasmed in an unrecognizable yoga position, unresponsive after a fatal, long-distance bullet infiltrated his chest cavity just seconds before.

"We're under siege. I repeat, this is not a drill; the MCPD is under attack. All available SWAT snipers: take peripheral positions at each corner on the rooftop. Sergeants, send half your regiments to support officers guarding prisoners in central booking and the rest convene within the lobby immediately. Security officers located by the metal detectors: do not leave the building until you have word to do so from Lieutenant Patrick, who will coordinate our outdoor offensive from there!" orders Chief Macklin through the building's speaker system.

The dozen camera crews, along with a couple food truck operators also in the wrong place at the dimensional wrong time, scurry underneath vehicles and behind trees, desperately searching for anywhere that can partially shield their body from anonymous gunfire. Chief Macklin heads to the sixth-floor rooftop to coordinate outdoor maneuvers and get a firsthand, widescreen view of the complete chaos outside. Meanwhile, Adams waves the cross of their crucified savior across his chest, grabs two handguns from his knapsack, and follows a group of flatfoots toward the quickest way to exit the six-story building.

"These fuckers brought Baghdad to Maryland," says Adams as he accompanies the small squadron into a large, hospital-sized elevator destined for the lobby.

As the band of heavily armed men reach downstairs, innocent bystanders of Renzo and Blake's most recent attack crawl past McGary's dead body and through MCPD's front glass doors, crying and wincing in disbelief.

"Is anyone physically hurt? I know you're in a state of shock, but do any of you have bullet wounds?" asks Patrick, who immediately attends to the shell-shocked witnesses. Adams, who's witnessed scenes like this while organizing operations in modern-day Babylonia, decides to launch an offensive initiative.

"What do you see from the rooftop, Chief?" asks Adams into his walkie-talkie while cocking one of his handguns. Six stories above, Macklin inches his back toward the rooftop's railing, then points for two MCPD snipers to take opposite, equidistant, angled positions thirty yards away from him.

"Our copter is about to take off from the helipad to give me a bird's eye view of the area," responds the chief.

Chief Macklin arches his neck into the moonlit sky as the white-and-blue Eurocopter AS350, indefinitely loaned from the LAPD Air Support Division, accelerates its main propeller and takes off. Before escaping outside, Adams helps a producer from Fox News into the lobby. After escorting her to a staff psychologist next to Patrick, Detective Adams cracks one of the glass entrance doors wide enough to let his body through, then squats and crouches on the outdoor staircase plateau. He shuffles his feet from left to right fifteen times, gathering courage before sprinting down the thirty-yard-wide worn-out concrete stairs, finally making it to McGary's corpse. Located at the foot of one the front lawn's grassy knolls, the carcass once belonging to McGary's soul is unresponsive and cooling rapidly.

"The shot came from southeast, southwest, or directly south of the property. So half of you give the detective gun support from behind that local news truck parallel to his location, while the other ten of you sprint to people stuck underneath vans and behind trees. Run in a zig-zag motion to minimize yourself as a target," orders Patrick. From the inside the gridiron huddle of uniformed officers in the lobby, the hyper vice-chief raises his voice to rally his troops.

"Be aware of your surroundings and view the battlefield peripherally when going outside! There's no telling where or when the next shot is coming," adds the lieutenant.

"Can you speak to me, officer? Everything's going to be OK, do you understand, son?" futilely asks Detective Adams to the dead cop.

Adams, through years of hands-on military service and detective work, quickly surmises that McGary died immediately after the bullet's first impact, giving the young officer the same age as Nina no chance for survival or recovery.

"He's DOA . . . Not sure what direction the kid got shot from. What are the eyes in the sky telling you?" yells the FBI detective into his walkie-talkie.

Seventy feet above, Macklin peeks his balding, nappy head above the rooftop railing, then uses his infrared binoculars to watch the madness below. With three minutes now passing since

McGary dropped to the ground, the immediate area surrounding the MCPD compound has been turned into a modern-day ghost town.

"Our chopper sees nothing. No vehicles, suspicious or otherwise, are leaving the immediate area. Rooftop SWAT snipers are searching for flickers of light coming from adjacent homes, bushes, and trees, but haven't found anything tangible so far. They're also providing air support for a half dozen ambulances streaming down Main Street from Gaithersburg and Germantown. Nicole's ETA to your position is less than five minutes, over."

Adams, receiving additional assistance from a Richmond reporter and cocooned by two roving MCPD officers holding cocked assault rifles, carries McGary's limp frame back up the stairs and into the increasingly congested antechamber of terrified denizens.

"There is literally not one person on the street within a four-block radius of headquarters. And no cars are driving erratically away from the crime scene, Chief," radios the tenured pilot to Macklin, who sits nervously in the chopper's passenger seat.

"Remain surreptitious in the trunk. As you can see via your peephole, I've already sidestepped the caravan of ambulances headed to the police department by using a secondary road parallel to Main Street. To recuperate yourself, use that mask attached to the oxygen tank I installed underneath the rear tire. We'll end the day at the same hiding spot we unwound at after killing Sengupta, Ramos, and Henderson. That was a marvelous undertaking, son! I couldn't watch because I was guarding our car. Did you hit Adams' assistant in the chest as I instructed?" inquires Blake, who uses his extended right palm to casually grip the Caprice's steering wheel.

“Yes, Officer McGary didn't stand a chance. Killing him was like playing Big Head Mode in Turok. It took real skill to hit his right pectoral muscle at an angle directly impacting his heart, especially while he was a moving target. Can you please wind up your window and turn up the heat, sir? It's getting really cold back here.”

“This marks the first time a law enforcement officer lost his life while trying to pursue us,” remarks Blake, adjusting the car’s temperature.

“Are you sure McGary's death will get Detective Adams to finally reveal the truth about x-2317?” asks Renzo after taking a few breaths of O2 from his augmented plastic visor.

Blake flips a discreet switch underneath the steering console, triggering an internal car mechanism that electronically tints every one of the Caprice's six windows, instantaneously darkening them by 85 percent.

“It will if we keep murdering the architects of our opposition in environments once deemed safe. Then yes, I do believe we'll get our point across. After a quick workout at the gym in the morning, we'll intensify our study of Dr. Jayaraman and that tall, young man he seems to spending so much time with as of late.”

Chapter 37

"Nadir, why haven't you implemented x-46 into Konrad's supply yet?" exasperatingly asks Nina a handful of weeks later while driving back from the Christmas party at Morton's in Chevy Chase. It's been a banner year for efficienTECH's Maryland district, with sales of the international conglomerate's industrial copiers, printers, and fax machines reaching well over eight figures.

Kreesha, after politely turning down an executive VP position at headquarters in New York, was in an ecstatic mood, having just been photographed and profiled by *Black Enterprise* magazine for an upcoming February cover story titled "Incredible Women of Power: Leaders, Innovators, and Risk Takers." Konrad, near the end of the raucous affair, interrupted the superficially joyful repast and stood on a dining room table, with an open bottle of Legacy by Angostura in his palm, to tout his Money Mayweather ethos of "hard work and dedication."

"Konrad had the gall to say, 'The reason I took home the coveted 'Diamond Award' for highest revenue-generating salesman nationwide is not because I sit on my ass all day and wait for my life to improve like Nina or steal from associates like that Uncle Buck-lookalike Colin. No. It's because I see opportunities that others don't see, seize on it, and then exploit it for maximum profit. This is the essence of big business, and this is the American way.'"

"Look, Ms. Sullivan, these things take time. With your boyfriend's help, I'm already in advanced development of an antidote that eradicates synthetic heroin's murderous side effect. It took me years to manipulate the chemical balance of x-2317 and just as long to gain Konrad's trust. Patience is key," cautiously responds Nadir from his dimly lit lab at PWI.

As the scientist hangs up on Nina, Quincy takes off his sweatshirt and ties a thin leather belt around his left forearm.

"Why is this substance bright blue?" inquires Quincy who, with his concave chest and sullen cheeks, is starting to show visible, severe signs of hardcore heroin usage.

"I'm going to put you through my reformatted MRI machine and then, in real time, use computer mapping to track how x-46 reacts in your bloodstream and major organs. Just try to relax and envelop your mind inside a happy place."

Nadir grasps a liquid filled, seven-inch glass syringe then presses its attached hypodermic needle into Quincy's basilic vein, causing the Californian to immediately pass out.

About two hours later, while Nina places a warm towel on the forehead of her exhausted lover, I decide to boost her morale and remind her that insecurity is hampering her progression.

"Through the mouths of subordinates, I've spent months explaining the rules to this game. As my Opponent did for Konrad, I helped you assemble your team. So take the initiative or give up and suffer defeat. The choice is yours."

Yeah, but what if victory is Pyrrhic? Look at what this battle has already done to Quincy, thinks Nina, finally mustering enough courage to address me directly for the first time in weeks.

"The collateral damage of war is always something that a general has to take into consideration. Start testing the powers I've given you; your cache of weapons is becoming stagnant," I reply.

Nina raises a purple NYU coffee mug to Quincy's chalky lips as Quincy peeks his bloody eyes from underneath the comforter.

"Here, drink this warm cup of almond milk; it'll make you feel better" purrs Nina as Quincy struggles to stay awake.

"Marry me. I know we've only known each other a little while, but let's spend the rest of our lives together," says Quincy, his watering eyes indicating the seriousness of his statement.

Nina puts the cup to Quincy's mouth, nourishing his dehydrated throat as a mother would a newborn. "Come on, that synthetic heroin has destroyed your common sense. You know full well a psycho chick like me isn't wifey material."

"This drug money will run out eventually, but once I graduate med school, I can comfortably take care of you," says Quincy.

"All right, give me a couple days to think it over. I promise I'll give it serious consideration," says Nina as she dials Colin's cellphone.

"Hey, Sullivan . . . no I got a few minutes to talk before I hit the hay; what's up?"

Colin, back at his newly purchased condo in Baltimore County, sits on top of an open toilet seat within his refurbished guest bathroom.

"Slow down and stop babbling; no one's gonna tell corporate about us. With efficienTECH getting acquired by Canon next year, headquarters is more concerned about keeping their own high salary jobs than worrying about what you're up to," adds Colin before spraying an aerosol can of Lysol in the air. Nina starts ranting a second time, raising her voice for emphasis, which prompts her coworker to cut her off.

"If everything you've told me is true, then I'm putting my life on the line, all for this harebrained scheme of yours." Referring to his recently acquired knowledge of Kreesha and Konrad using bogus, shell LLCs from various parts of the country to filter, then divest, dirty profits of synthetic heroin to untraceable overseas accounts, Colin signed an affidavit and gave a deposition videotaped by Nadir's lawyer, absolving knowledge of Nina's participation in Kreesha and Konrad's extracurricular activity.

Documented information about Konrad and Kreesha's illegal activities, retrieved from Denelle the night after Nina shattered Colin's nose, was specifically acquired after Denelle broke into Kreesha's office, then took mobile phone photos of a half-dozen suspicious contracts, each one not having factual contact information. Nina pulls the expensive Venetian blinds next to her goose-feather pillow, exposing the room to the Cygnus constellation reposed on the stratum of the Milky Way galaxy. She's coming along slowly, but if we win, I'll show her what her planet looks like from my view.

"No. I can't guarantee that you'll take over the office once Kreesha is implicated, but you're third in charge in the most profitable branch in the country. It seems only right that you'll be promoted to district manager," responds Nina, now in bed with her passed-out soulmate.

"That's not good enough. I want, in writing, your post-dated resignation from efficienTECH, which will be the same day that Konrad and Kreesha are arrested. You can't be trusted, and that's the only way I can guarantee that you won't interfere with my accession to the throne. Am I clear?"

"Fine, Esposito, copier sales sucks anyway. Just fucking do what we agreed on by the end of the week."

As Nina and Quincy call it an early night in Laurel, a member of MCPD's inner circle takes a much-needed respite from work.

"Don't hesitate to take your man off the dribble, son; you can see the weakness in his eyes. He knows you can win the game with one last bucket," whispers Lieutenant Patrick to himself from the upper blue rafters.

Within the storied, standard-sized gym on the campus of the internationally renowned DeMatha Catholic HS, Patrick holds his breath as his first-born, 6'9 son stands at the top of the key, ball cupped in this ginormous right hand.

Julian Patrick wipes off beads of sweat with the left strap of his white, V-neck, polyester jersey, then makes a decisive jab step to the left with his Nike Foamposite sneakers at the apex of the three-point line before sizing up his opponent, who's unsure of the pterodactyl's next move. Taking a moment to glance at the dwindling shot clock melting toward zero, Julian then dribbles to his right, easily shaking his tumorous defender in the process. Lieutenant Patrick rises his to his feet, joining the other hundreds of Stag fans who also cheer on the country's best point guard.

Julian's help defender, the opposing shooting guard conscious of his attack to the hole, leaves Julian's teammate, who's hunched behind the right corner three-point line.

Instead of pulling up for a foul-line extended jump shot or skying over two trees in the paint waiting to block his shot, Julian makes the textbook play and delivers a no-look pass to his teammate, twenty feet away from the basket.

Decisively not shooting the lower percentage, long distance field goal attempt, the senior shooting guard, who hails from Steve Francis' hometown of Takoma Park, yields self-serving gratification, and unexpectedly tosses back a precise alley-oop pass to the already airborne Julian.

Julian, simultaneously using his forty-six-inch vertical leap and ballerina-like flexibility, maximally stretches his right deltoid to its zenith, allowing his right hand to snatch the mid-air ball from an awkward angle. He then flushes the sphere between the four outstretched arms of the helpless opposing power forward and center and into the orange hoop at the same level as his nostrils.

The buzzer sounds the moment the ball travels through the net and hits the ground, delivering DeMatha a fiercely battled victory over national powerhouse Montrose Christian. The final score: 75-74. The obvious MVP of the game, Lieutenant Tommy Patrick's son, who led all players with a monstrous stat line of 32 points, 14 assists, 12 rebounds, 4 steals and 6 blocks.

DeMatha students, alumni, and fans, in a rush of euphoria, storm the court to celebrate the victory and personally congratulate their hero, Julian. As they jump in jubilation, David Hobbs, assistant head coach of the prestigious University of Kentucky basketball program, taps Lieutenant Patrick on the shoulder. He then gives the ecstatic policeman a vigorous handshake.

“Wow, Thomas! What a game by your son! Can I chat with you for a few moments?” says David as the two exit the seating section, then delicately navigate through the throng of humanity on the gym's ground floor.

Lieutenant Patrick, grinning from ear to ear for the first time in months, returns the salutation, then puts his right hand on the ballyhooed recruiter.

“Yeah, my boy had quite the game. It goes without saying that I'm very proud of him,” responds Patrick, while motioning to Julian that he'll meet him in the parking lot once the high school star is finished signing autographs.

“Your son, in two years’ time, will be a starter in the league. He reminds me of a younger version of Larry Bird, with Vince Carter-like athleticism—depending on how many more inches he grows. NBA scouting websites already are touting young Julian to be a future top-five pick. And after at least a year of worldwide exposure in Lexington, I can all but guarantee that he'll be a superstar,” gushes Hobbs as the two make their way to the exit.

“Thanks for your kind words, friend; our family is very blessed. The first thing I did, after assembling his crib a month before his was born, was install a miniature basketball hoop above Julian's head he could stare at—and eventually use once he was old enough to crawl. He's shared my love for the game ever since.”

As the jubilant crowd finally begins to dissipate outside, Lieutenant Patrick hands David one of two dirty water dogs just purchased in front of the temporary food stand next to DeMatha's voluminous trophy case.

“Well, as you already know, we've already received offers from the Wolverines, Blue Devils, and Wildcats, and are looking to our visit from Coach Smith—as soon as his schedule permits,” adds Patrick. His sweaty son, now dressed in a thin-fit sweat-suit, joins the conversation.

“Hi, Mr. Hobbs, this is the fifth game you've seen me play this season. What'd you think of my performance?”

“I was just telling your father that Tubby Smith and I could see you walking onto that stage inside Madison Square Garden, vigorously shaking David Stern’s hand as you tip your team's cap and flash that million-dollar smile. Last year, four out of our starting five players were drafted in the first round, with three not falling past the lottery. After you,” says Hobbs, while opening the wooden front door for the Patricks.

The congested school parking lot is abuzz with Julian's immortal performance. Older fans, wise enough to realize that this scene doesn't fit their demographic, hurriedly get into their cars to avoid the widespread debauchery. Teenagers, encompassing the DMV gambit of East Asian, Central American, Black, and White suburbanites, sit on the closed car trunks, exalting the Stags last-second win. Even the opposing team from Montrose Christian, waiting patiently in their school bus standing in the fire zone, can't help but give congratulatory lo-fives to Julian as he walks by.

“Hey! Can I please get an autograph, Mr. Patrick?” asks Renzo, handing Julian a game program.

Chapter 38

Renzo is inconspicuously dressed in black, slim-fit jeans, Reebok Pump Omni Lite Vintage sneakers, and an old-school, tan Members Only jacket.

"That makes me uncomfortable. You don't have to call me that; I'm around the same age as you, my dude," replies Julian as Hobbs shakes Lieutenant Patrick's hand one final time, then makes a sideways "shaka" sign next to his right cheek, indicating that he'll call his five-star recruit at a later date.

"Sorry for the formalities, it's just that my boy doesn't get out often, and we're blessed to witness such an incredible, seemingly effortless display of athleticism. You must be very proud of your son, Thomas," says Blake, who takes an impromptu selfie with the two Patricks.

The elder Patrick takes note of Blake's chiseled square jaw, impeccably faded buzz cut hairstyle, and tightly laced, muddy military boots.

Pointing to their cars, conveniently parked next to each other at the far end of the lot, both father-son duos make their way to their respective vehicles while continuing to converse.

"I'm sorry, do I know you, friend? Are you a military man?" politely inquires Lieutenant Patrick while automatically unlocking his black, late-model Escalade.

The older Patrick then tosses his keys to his child and motions for Julian to get in the driver's seat.

"Start the engine, son; I'll only be a minute," he adds before turning his attention to the two undiscovered serial killers.

"Yes, my name is Blake Rice, retired Navy SEAL. I recognized your face from the numerous Chief Macklin press conferences on TV lately. I must ask, do you have any definitive leads on who the killers could be? I want this ambiguous chaos to end just as badly as you do," says Blake as Renzo stands silently next to him.

Knowing that his identity is only known by Macklin and Adams, the two cold-blooded murderers display no signs of nervousness. Instead, they just completed a peaceful session at nearby Bikram Yoga Riverdale and couldn't be more composed in front of their adversary. The young Afro-Aruban, glancing behind the embattled public official takes note that the parking lot is now at 10 percent capacity and arteries leading to Route 1, the East-West Highway, and eventually Interstate 495 seem manageable.

"Well, to tell you the truth, friend, nothing has been the same since that piece of shit shot my brother in arms—on our own property, no less. We always thought our suspect was a coward after targeting children, but to specially go after a lower level officer with no input in the case; well . . . the devil has a special place in hell lined up for this guy."

"I've seen hell, sir, while serving in Africa and in Cuba at Guantanamo. Maybe you and your team should efficaciously look in the mirror, and then you'll see who the real culprits are."

"Dad, I'm hungry and tired. Let's get out of here," yells Julian after winding down the Cadillac's driver's side window.

"OK," responds Lieutenant Patrick as the early winter frost begins to cover his thinning gray hair. "If I knew that I was speaking to some right-wing nut intent on shutting down the government, then I wouldn't have had this conversation in the first place. We've been getting hate mail from your type the minute this fiasco started," adds Lieutenant Patrick, trying to get any facial response that could link the two to Adams' anonymous, ominous e-mail received moments before McGary's assassination.

The sender of the message, only standing a few feet from the armed officer, smiles while burying his hands in his pocket: one of which gently caresses a two-inch gravity knife.

"I belong to no organization, sir. I mean, why would I endorse a congregation of less advanced human life forms? When instead, on a multi-dimensional level, I can cannibalize progressive thoughts and ideas at a speed faster than light. Is what I'm telling you soaking in?" responds Blake.

"Unless you two want to get run over, don't keep standing behind my truck," says the older Patrick.

Blake raises his forearm and softly pushes it on Renzo's chest, furtively instructing his partner in crime to step aside while Lieutenant Patrick gets in the Escalade's passenger seat. As Julian backs out of the parking spot and points the hefty gas guzzler toward the school's exit, Renzo and Blake wave at their dimensional contradictions as if the Patricks were inside the last car of a presidential motorcade.

"He's watching us to see exactly what car we walk toward," mutters Blake while pretending to cough so Tommy can't read his lips.

"The receiver, for the tracking device I installed underneath the Cadillac's rear differential, is inside the Caprice's center console. Based on my calculations regarding off-peak traffic, we should be able to cut him off in Southwest DC, near the Potomac. They'll have a five-minute head start, but we should be able to catch them without speeding," says Renzo once Julian and Tommy leave the outlying DeMatha property.

"Those two were weird, Dad; like, they seemed like polar opposites," says Julian as the two make their way southbound on the seemingly vacant I-295 toward their home in Northern Virginia. Fifteen minutes after their encounter with Blake and Renzo, the young phenom pushes the Escalade to ninety mph.

"Just keep your eyes on the road, son, and thanks for taking the wheel. I want to see if we're being followed," replies the older Patrick, his eyes fixated on the rear-view mirror.

"Sorry to get you involved in this mess, but it's prudent to take every precaution possible. And don't tell your mother about what just happened, she'll have a heart attack," adds the agitated lieutenant.

"I guess now's the best time to send my second message to Detective Adams," says Blake in the passenger seat of the Blue Caprice as Renzo makes his way toward their target.

Still located in PG County, Renzo stomps his foot on the Caprice's accelerator, speeding through two stop lights within the quiet, small DC suburb of Edmonston.

"Officer McGary was a pawn to the federal government, dead or alive. And since Macklin and Adams are so stubborn, and won't utter any public dissonance about Dolan, the CIA, or x-2317 for that matter, we're going to eliminate a bishop," responds Renzo's unofficial guardian.

Blake grasps the hand-built tracking receiver from in between his legs and places the reconstructed laptop closer to his face in order to get a better view of the moving, flashing blue light darting toward its home base.

"Can you see them, Dad?" cautiously asks Julian as his father cocks his handgun.

"No, we should be alright now. Get into the slow lane and ease off the gas a little."

Racing past the Howard Johnson in Cheverly, at twice the speed limit, Renzo makes a hard, ninety-degree rotation, turning the souped-up, four-wheel drive sports sedan off Annapolis Road and onto an on-ramp for the BW Parkway.

Blake sees, from the car's dash-mounted scanner, that no police vehicles are in the immediate area.

"After reaching full speed in a moment, we should approach their SUV in no more than ten seconds," responds Renzo.

"Let me just send this second e-mail before I take care of business," says Blake.

Blake queues his message by quickly mining a saved draft from his inbox. He then takes his untraceable mobile phone and points it directly at the windshield. Renzo, elated to finally be using the tips he picked up from attending the ProFormance Racing School in Kent, Washington, much earlier this year, effortlessly executes a maximum speed, right-hand power drift and aligns the Caprice to the aforementioned two-lane highway.

“Four o'clock son; we're being ambushed!” yells Lieutenant Patrick from the Escalade's passenger seat.

Blake snaps a pic of the Patricks’ family car, encapsulating a view of Cadillac's rear license plate two seconds before the killer's Caprice violently rams the SUV at a diagonal angle.

The confounded teenage driver instantly loses control of the vehicle, sending the Escalade into a severe counter-clockwise tailspin on the highway's southbound lanes. Renzo slams on the brakes and allows the Cadillac to finish its rotation before it finally comes to an abrupt stop.

Blake, in a terrifyingly normalized, unemotional fashion, places his phone in a cup holder seconds before picking up his AR-15 and sticking it out of the open front passenger window.

“Tag; you're it,” says Renzo while Blake aligns the assault rifle to his extended right forearm.

“Shift the car into reverse and floor it, son!” screams the mortified veteran police officer.

The Escalade, after completing a violent, nauseating, 540-degree spin, now directly faces the Caprice on the empty highway: exposed and at the mercy of the two hardened killers.

“Follow them slowly, Renzo; I need to get a clear view of the two front tires,” says Blake.

Lieutenant Patrick, not waiting for a first strike from Blake, empties a full clip into the Caprice as the severely damaged Escalade struggles to reverse away.

The sixteen bullets deflect aimlessly off the vehicle as the aftermarket bulletproof windshield, headlights, and front bumper Blake and Renzo installed in Canada remain intact and fully functional. Blake, taking notice that his adversary is now out of bullets, sticks his head out his window and then points his weapon down at a thirty-degree angle before only using two hollow-tip slugs to shoot out the Escalade's front tires. The gunshots immediately disable the Cadillac, rendering its steering wheel useless.

"Dad. Dad, I've lost control. I can't steer anymore . . ." mutters Julian as the Escalade, still driving in reverse, finally loses its vertical balance and begins to violently flip sideways toward Washington DC.

"It's all right, son. At least we'll be in Heaven together. Close your eyes and let it go; this will be over before you know it," calmly replies his father.

Both front and side-impact airbags discharge around the two Patricks, whose necks twist unnaturally as the continuous impact of steel on pavement jars their spinal cords beyond repair.

"Hurry up, sir," warns Renzo with an earpiece in his left ear connected to the car's police scanner.

The young Aruban then adds, "A passerby, headed north toward Baltimore, just reported the truck's accident to highway patrol. We have less than thirty seconds to make a clean escape."

The mangled SUV, now at a complete stop in front of the paused Caprice, oozes steam and smoke from its front hood as it rests in the slow lane like an upside-down terrapin.

Renzo turns on the Chevy's high beams while Blake jumps out the passenger seat holding a cocked, semi-automatic pistol in his left hand. "You're going to rot in hell for this," whispers Patrick, who hangs by the now ceiling-mounted impact restraint.

The thirty-year police veteran struggles to take his seatbelt off his motionless son, knowing from the angle of his neck that there's no point checking for a pulse. Blake kneels beside Julian while staring directly in Lieutenant Patrick's eyes.

"No . . . Don't!"

Ignoring his father's plea for mercy, Blake cocks his assault rifle and sticks its thin barrel in young Julian's motionless mouth.

After exploding the basketball phenom's head from the inside out, he casually shoots the older Patrick in the neck, so, while desperately gasping for air, he can view what's left of his dead son.

While running fifty yards to the waiting Caprice, which is now on the other side of the highway and pointed northbound, Blake says, "Macklin's next. It's just too bad he doesn't know where it's coming from.

Chapter 39

"The execution of Lieutenant Thomas Patrick and his son Julian, so close to our nation's capital, is truly heartbreaking. Lynne Ann and I send our deepest condolences to both his family and his community at this very difficult time. As Attorney General Ted Olson has indicated, the Department of Justice is investigating the situation along with local officials, and they will continue to direct resources to the case as needed. I know the events of the past few months have prompted strong passions, but as details unfold, I urge everyone in the Washington DC metro area, and across the country, to remember this fine officer through reflection and understanding. We should comfort each other and talk with one another in a way that heals, not in a way that wounds. Along with our prayers, that's what Julian and his family, along with the other Americans who have died and been directly affected by this ruthless criminal, deserve. Thankfully, today I'm signing an emergency bill passed by both houses in Congress that gives law enforcement the right to intercept evildoers before they inflict pain and suffering on innocent Americans. **The Nationalist Act now authorizes the federal government the ability to conduct**

searches of private property without the use of a warrant when the Homeland Security Advisory System is at a HIGH or SEVERE level, which it is at now," says President Dick Cheney on a large television deep in the heart of Baltimore.

After watching the White House press secretary deliver the commander-in-chief's latest comments regarding the Serial Snipers, then walk away from the podium before answering questions about the undebated Nationalist Act, a solitary confined prisoner on an immaculately made single bed presses the mute button. He then whispers to himself, "It won't be long before prisons are the safest place to be in this country. The age of anarchy is near."

"Mr. Ayala, someone is here to see you in the visiting room, sir," cautiously utters a corrections officer at the ultra-violent Baltimore City Detention Center in East Baltimore, Maryland.

Ayala, located at cellblock 13:17-18, turns on his bedside desk lamp and slowly puts on his Browline spectacles. He then turns his attention away from the young man speaking through a small, five-foot high, retractable, mail-slot like aperture inside a ten-inch thick, reinforced steel door that separates the gang kingpin from the general prison population.

Clearly in no rush to acknowledge the officer, Ayala turns off his expensive sixty-inch television, then picks up his desired reading material for the day: a short, non-fiction story called "I Was Tortured in the Pasadena Jailhouse" written by his anti-Semitic idol, Bobby Fischer.

"No, set it up in the assistant warden's office. Make sure I'm speaking to Mr. Hunter alone—no cameras on," responds the highest-ranking East Coast member of the Black Commando Mafia. Without making eye contact with the well-connected prisoner, the cautious CO opens the soundproof egress and grabs a handful of dirty laundry on the room's extended leather couch.

“Yes, sir, and I'll have these pressed medium-starch, just as you always like.”

A half an hour later, and less than a week after Julian and Lieutenant Patrick's horrific, unsolved murder on Interstate 295, Konrad hands his business partner a large, navy-blue plate full of kimchi and cucumber salad along with two square cups of steaming miso soup.

“Avoiding traditional utensils was smart, Konrad; you're always thinking one step ahead. And from what I've heard, you've had a banner year at efficienTECH.”

Before snapping open his chopsticks and mixing his wasabi and soy sauce in a side dish, Konrad takes in the gently falling snow, clearly visible from the six large windows on the second story, impressive corner office roughly the same size as Curtis' at PWI. The two men, seated at an abbreviated conference table next to the assistant warden's pre-war desk, are eating next to each another at an uncomfortably close distance. “Try these spider, caterpillar, and Atlantic rolls. All freshly made this afternoon,” tentatively remarks Konrad, trying to keep the conversation superficial.

“So, regardless of the health of our arrangement, your pockets will remain fat,” adds Ayala, pulling his desk chair closer to Konrad. While two armed officers stand guard outside the closed door, Ayala, refusing to ever drink Maryland swamp water from the tap, takes a long sip of green tea and then continues.

“I've also heard, from my sources at MCPD, that their FBI liaison has evidence connecting me to x-2317 via an e-mail correspondence between former CIA agent Benjamin Dolan and our master chef, Dr. Jayaraman."

Konrad, unaware of this revelation, chews a piece of gari to cleanse his palate, then wipes his mouth.

"I had no idea . . ." begins the tranquil synthetic heroin distributor.

Ayala, known for his intolerance of incompetence, clenches his jaw. He then adds, "The good news is that the feds have no idea what x-2317 is. They think it's either a BCM code word for murder or a secret financial transaction term used to liquidate illegally acquired assets. Because that dead pig unsuccessfully staked out Nadir's home in Bethesda, and a subsequent investigation failed to unearth any concrete evidence linking the chemist to the Serial Snipers, the feds are hesitant to go any further after Nadir, regardless of what Dolan said. And after Nadir and his lawyer publicly condemned the witch hunt against him at a press conference, decrying to sue the government for nine figures based on the hysteria surrounding the snipers—"

"The feds think that you'll do the same thing, which is why they're staying quiet. At least for now."

Ayala, no longer interested in eating, turns his chair toward Konrad, slightly raising his voice as he continues.

"Regional BCM leaders and I have concluded that your unrestrained arrogance, coupled with this bout of clumsiness, will be the downfall of our stratocracy. The other families, especially the Columbians and Mexicans who took over Staten Island and eastern Long Island with their nearly-pure, dirt-cheap product for New Yorkers who can't get a hold of prescription opiates, and the North Koreans, who'll make at least a billion this year exporting some of the world's best smack, still have no idea how we're able to transport significant quantities of what seems to be normal, generic heroin, to such a remote region of the US—all without an international supplier. On top of this, we're able to sell synthetic for one, two dollars a packet, whereas their product will go no lower than three. You're a reasonable man, and you know where I'm going with this."

"Killing Nadir will bring down the whole operation, because I only turn the fake poppy into fake heroin, but Nadir's created x-2317 in a proprietary manner that can't be replicated. Murdering me won't work either, because Warren and Eric think I'm using certain chemicals based on false equations I've written for them, and ingredients that I've labeled in my lab. But I've always mismarked the plastic and glass bottles while simultaneously sending them on wild shopping goose-chases, in order to keep them clueless. You see—"

"Look, boy, be quiet and listen. Your doctor created nothing more than a newer version of LSD, one that just so happens to mimic the chemical effects of opium. So chill with that existential, extraterrestrial bullshit. Instead, let's talk about your reality. My New England soldiers on the street are losing their lives over synthetic heroin, because junkies are leaving their normal dealer and flooding my blocks for our cheaper product. Two of my corporals, in charge of territories in and around Manchester, are being tortured by my rivals inside a barn near Burlington, all for information about the original source of synthetic h."

"That's not my problem. You know unintended consequences always occur in this line of business. I came here to discuss how we can take this product nationwide. And as you can see, I can always reroute my shipments through a different supplier. You're very much disposable."

"The problem is, Konrad, for all the advanced intelligence you think x-2317 gives you, you can't calculate the consequence of a Navy SEAL using x-2317, under the CIA's directive to do so, then anticipate the repercussions of that SEAL feeling the need to go on a cross-country killing spree from Seattle to DC," responds the drug kingpin.

Konrad walks past the convicted felon and places his right hand on the closed glass window, causing his bare palm to immediately chill and stick to the glass as if it's pulling him outside.

"So how long was Lieutenant Patrick on your payroll?"

"Long enough to pay for his not one, but two mistresses—plus supplement his self-destructive gambling addiction. The poor sap was betting on preseason NBA games and was about 80 g's in the hole before getting murdered last week."

"Sit back down, son; I got something to show you," adds Ayala, who bears a strikingly similar resemblance to Philly rapper Beanie Sigel.

While pulling out a few pieces of legal-sized paper from his pants pocket, the drug kingpin rubs his chin, gently pulling at the full-length beard he grew while converting from Christianity to the Nation of Gods and Earths, more commonly known as the Five-Percent Nation.

Ayala then unzips a backpack hanging off his chair and pulls out his newest electronic device. He then queues his laptop to a recent Chief Macklin press conference located at MCPD headquarters. "See. Right here, the clean-cut military type off to the side, standing next to Macklin's secret girlfriend Nicole during a recent press conference. Once Dolan killed himself, this man, Detective Charlie Adams, took Benjamin's personal e-mail address, and unbeknownst to the public, corresponded with at least one of the killers since the Officer McGary shooting a month ago."

Konrad stays silent as he views the grainy image of Adams on-screen with his hands stuffed into his ruffled suit pockets, staring at the hundreds of reporters, protesters, and other local officers who've lost patience over Macklin's generic, regurgitated message. With the image of Detective Adams now burned into his memory, Konrad takes a look at the printed e-mails sitting next to their finished meal.

"You can't wage war against the MCPD, Hunter. They're more heavily armed than most second-world nations due to the DoD's 1033 program. No, you've got to figure out a different, more insidious way to stop them from coming after you. Because Lieutenant Patrick's no longer around to stop Detective Adams from putting the pieces together."

"Nadir must be so happy Dolan committed suicide. Between me threatening to kill his family unless he continues production of x-2317 and Dolan threatening to out him as a purveyor of child porn, he truly must have felt suffocated. I wish I could end his life for that reason alone, but there has to be a way to enact Newton's Second Law against him."

To keep anger and distrust against him high from both sides, my Opponent failed to disclose that Nadir was entrapped by Dolan for the illegal pornographic images that he in fact had nothing to do with.

"If Dolan didn't seem interested in you one iota, why did Nadir feel the need to bring your name up?" wonders Konrad aloud.

Konrad specifically refers to a hacked e-mail Nadir sent to Dolan one week after the Starbucks ambush, where Nadir wrote, "He can't give any more troops x-2317 because 100 percent of its production is being diverted to the BCM."

"Nadir created a parachute for himself if investigators incriminate him with anything tangible, which is what you'll do to me, and I'll do to you if shit gets too hot. Conversely, if any of us break up this web of production from PWI, to your home, to BWI, and then finally, to the upper Northeast, we'll lose out on tens of millions of dollars in profit, which is beyond stupid," warns Ayala.

Konrad, grinding the gears of cognition within his skull, rubs the back of his neck with his right palm. Then, as if looking for my divine guidance, he stares at the vanilla ceiling for half a minute while Ayala chuckles to himself.

"It's time to think past maintaining this pipeline, or even expanding it. Instead, let's focus on how we can create the maximum amount of damage, both psychologically and socially, to this country," advises Ayala.

One of the prison guards quickly knocks on the office door, peeks his head inside, and says, "Boss, the warden wants to know when he can get his office back. How much longer—"

Without saying a word, Ayala turns his head 180 degrees and shoots the guard a glacial stare: a look that could easily be read as a sign for the guard's impending death. As soon as the door shuts, maintaining the privacy of Konrad and Ayala, Konrad brings his eyes back to his father figure.

"What if I told you that the chaos you desire has already begun and will only intensify if we stand put. Now, we can both take measures to curtail this impending anarchy, and continue to stay under the radar, thereby maintaining our uninterrupted cash-flow, or—"

"You're referring to the explosion of unabated, random homicide in the areas we've flooded with synthetic heroin, right? My street soldiers and I already have our theories as to why this is occurring. Out with it, son."

"In October, Nadir warned me that ingestion, insufflation, or injection of x-2317, in either its base or synthetic heroin variation, will cause death and destruction far beyond the scope of what local law enforcement can handle."

"And you trust that this proclamation by Nadir is truthful?"

"Nadir's a lot of things, but courageous isn't one of them. He, like my delivery girl and other fringe players like Warren and Eric, loves his relatives too much to stab me in the back. I don't have this problem because I don't have a family. Obviously, the Serial Sniper was given x-2317 by Dolan for its ability to enhance cerebral activity at an abnormally astronomical rate."

"Maybe Dolan gave them a placebo. Wake up; x-2317 is nothing more than a version of oxycodone that causes schizophrenia!"

"You're wrong. But anyway, what Dolan couldn't anticipate, or the feds can't wrap their hands around, is the fact that half of all x-2317 users will not only develop the thirst to not only kill, but will do so in a ghastly manner inside of half a decade."

"Not including you and these six soldiers, five of whom are dead, who else do you know of who's taken x-2317?"

“No one,” lies Konrad, before adding “Refocus your thoughts on our commodity, because the upper Northeast's crime rate will increase exponentially. Beheadings, mass executions, public torture—much worse than anything we've seen in Iran or North Korea. I've already seen recorded footage of three synthetic heroin addicts, coming of a week-long binge, who used machetes to chop up a dealer who ran out of synthetic h. They then dragged his body into an empty alleyway, doused his carcass with gasoline, and while his heart was still beating, skewered his different body parts on a sharp metal pole. The Portland cops were so happy that my pusher was off of the street, they marked the incident as a rival drug battle.”

“I've been doing this a long time. man, and have never, ever, seen heroin addicts act like this. Meth heads, crackheads, and habitual prescription drug abusers, yes. But usually heroin addicts, struggling to get their next fix, are too dope sick to enact this type of violence toward others,” responds Ayala.

“At least half of every man, or woman, that has shot that poison in their bloodstream will become like that. It's just a matter of if it's now or within thirty months,” adds Konrad.

Ayala pulls up the calculator app on his laptop and presses the keyboard a few times.

“And this won't be an inner-city problem like crack was in the eighties.”

“The media, not having any stereotypes to vilify, will be in denial about this epidemic until it's too late. So give or take 10,000 users, I'd say in two and a half years, we'll have about half a million mostly Caucasian serial killers on our hand in Vermont, Maine, New Hampshire, and upstate New York. Armed with this powerful information, what'd you want to do now?”

Ayala rubs his chin, laughs, and then says, "Double your production, and my men will lower the synthetic price to $0.50 a packet. It's full steam ahead."

Chapter 40

Later that night, Nicole, in her car after a solemn dinner with Chief Macklin, turns the radio to WTOP-FM.

"In national news, the office of Karen P. Tandy, head of the Drug Enforcement Administration, reports the number of heroin overdoses has tripled in New England over the last eleven months."

Anchor Dimitri Sotis continues. "In addition to skyrocketing usage, at a percentage much higher than our social services can handle, the demographics of those being affected are changing at a rate difficult to halt. In the past, ODs were mostly confined to the city limits of Manchester, Portland, Buffalo, and Albany. But most likely due to tightened restrictions on prescription drug abuse, *the twisted, altered converse is now reality* with the majority of heroin-related deaths now occurring in those cities' outlying suburbs . . ."

Another voice, Karen, takes over. "The recent heroin overdose of actor Glen Quinn, who on a popular TV sitcom played a half-demon character who receives prophetic visions from an enigmatic, angelic force called *The Powers That Be*, shed light on how widespread and far-reaching this epidemic is.

Nationwide, heroin distribution is highly organized, high volume, and it's now being moved much more efficiently and effectively to reach out to a broader user base."

Macklin then states, "Regarding overdoses, I've witnessed the same type of demographic shift in Montgomery County. Suddenly the DEA says it's a problem now, because suburbanites and gentrifiers are dying. That nonsense Karen's spewing is just Darwin working his magic."

Driving through the Gaithersburg business district, the ambivalent chief turns the dial to sports talk radio as Nicole stews.

At the MCI Center in Northwest DC, Kevin Durant uses a large towel to wipe a myriad of sweat beads from his forehead. Having just finished his team practice for their upcoming night game against the Miami Heat, the world's most versatile offensive basketball weapon sulks his wide, bony shoulders in the near-empty arena. As his teammates, coaching staff, and trainers head into the locker room to watch game film on their Western Conference opponent, Durant leans against the rotating advertisement partition doubling as an exterior for the mid-court scorer's table.

The perennial All-Star then leans his sinewy torso forward, bringing his baby-face closer to the arc of handheld microphones waiting for him to comment.

Since Blake's most recent murders of Tommy and Julian Patrick, Kevin's lost fifteen pounds, led the team in turnovers per game, and shot less than 35 percent from the floor. And his Washington Wizards, who were predicted to make the finals earlier this year, are in the midst of six-game losing streak with each loss occurring during this extended December homestead.

"Enough is enough. The execution of Lieutenant Patrick, and his son, man. His son . . ." says KD, who's on the verge of tears.

"This summer, I played with Julian during the Goodman League and remember his father fondly. He was our team's most vocal supporter," continues Durant, his head looking down as he avoids eye contact with the half dozen cameras documenting the impromptu interview.

"Since the murderers came to the DMV in October, there have been no arrests, and very little information about the progress of the sniper investigation. What would you like to see happen?" asks a beat reporter for SLAM Magazine.

Kevin tenses his face before saying

"Our PR staff told us fans stopped bringing their kids to games, and I just had to bulletproof my van yesterday. For starters, Chief Macklin has to go. He's an embarrassment to the Black community. And just talking to my brothers in the locker room and fans on the street . . . everyone's saying that change has to come—that the status quo won't solve this. President Cheney has to get more involved. All he does is create more rules and restrictions on our freedoms, all in the name of national security; yet he can't catch a serial killer living in his own backyard? The whole system is corrupt, and it needs to change. Now."

* * * * *

"I know you want to leave me, Nicki. I know you think I'm a piece of shit for not solving this case. But it's not my fault; I'm being railroaded by Adams and the feds. I'm getting info on the killers second-hand, yet I'm still being pushed to be the face of this flawed investigation."

Sitting in the passenger seat next to Nicole, Macklin then attempts to kiss his girlfriend on her voluminous lips.

"No; stop . . . get off of me. There's been a drive-by shooting a few miles from I-95. I gotta get to the ambulance depot by the MedStar Medical Center ASAP."

* * * * *

"It's all done, boss," says Eric on his cellphone.

Alone, and driving back to Konrad's western Montgomery County home in Dickerson, Eric steers his vehicle with his inner thighs, puts his phone on speaker, and uses a credit card to lift "Belushi," a light-brown, potent mix of uncut coke and synthetic heroin, directly to his right nostril.

"You sure you killed her, buddy? You did exactly what I told you to, right?" asks Konrad. Located in a basement corner of his homemade chem lab, Konrad wraps an apron around his waist. He then pours a drop of liquefied synthetic h into a test tube already filled with eighty milligrams of crushed OxyContin.

Eric, with his phone on speaker, turns up the song "New York, New York" by the rap collective Tha Dogg Pound, which is the song he always plays after breaking the law.

"Absolutely, I emptied fifteen slugs into her chest cavity. So unless she's superhuman, the bitch is definitely dead. It's weird though Konrad . . ." says Eric while nodding his head to the hypnotic beat.

"What are you talking about?"

"When I drove right next to her, and pulled out my nine as you instructed, she had this broad smile on her face as if she was kinda expecting me to snuff her."

"Don't drive like a jackass coming back here, and remember to park in the garage. Warren has the spray paint and secondary body panels ready. I already set up an account on eBay for your whip. Once you get here, don't forget to wipe down the interior—"

"Hey, boss, there's one thing," interrupts Eric, refocusing the conversation on the murder he just committed.

"Before I pulled the trigger, Denelle put her index finger to her mouth, as if to politely tell me to be quiet. Well, I been thuggin' for a while, and I . . . I never seen anything like that before. Then, she threw her handbag through the open rear driver's side window; not in an antagonizing way, just kinda playful like."

"What did Ms. Coleman do next? And there's no tracking device in her clutch, right?"

"No, just a few goofy photos of you two from your Christmas party. At first, I thought she thought I was a robber, but after tossing the bag to me she said, 'Tell Konrad I love him. I don't blame him for any of this.' She then put her hands in the sky and looked down, still smiling as she waited for me to kill her."

"Why'd Denelle have to be so fucking stupid by hacking into Kreesha's files like that? Didn't she think I'd find out?" says

Konrad, who takes a seat at the bottom of the basement staircase, to catch his breath.

Via the instantaneous world of social media, word spreads like brushfire that Denelle may have been the latest sniper victim, prompting the whole Maryland staff of efficienTECH to leave their domiciles and agree to meet at the office parking lot, where they'll construct a candlelit memorial for their fallen co-worker.

“Her family lives by the Denver Airport and won’t be able to make it here until tomorrow morning. Bring any and all photos of Denelle to the murder site. In addition to assisting law enforcement with their investigation, we’ll be singing church hymns and helping each other grieve,” wrote Kreesha on her most recent Facebook post.

“What do you make of all this?” asks Quincy, who stands above a kneeling Nina in front of her laptop. The duo, already dressed for bed in boxers and loose fitting t-shirts, spent all evening refining their next move in hopes of liberating themselves, and synthetic heroin users, from its sinister murderous trait that’s already taken hold of Konrad.

“I’m not sure, but be ready to leave in ten minutes,” responds Nina.

While Nina and Quincy make their way to the crime scene, Adams surveys a landscape more familiar to him then his home, hotel room, and MCPD office.

“Same day, different shit. I have to resign, and tell Henson I'm tired of being a supporting character in this Groundhog Day remake,” says Adams as he ducks underneath twenty feet of yellow plastic tape hastily wrapped around two parking lot light poles.

"Merry Christmas, Detective," says Superintendent Dobkins as he hands Adams a fresh cup of coffee.

"Thank God Christmas Eve isn't for a couple days. If it were any sooner, my estranged wife promised me she'd sign the divorce papers in blood. I can't wait to go home for the holidays."

"How come you haven't returned any of my voice-mail messages? My troopers feel like you guys are ignoring us."

"Listen, asshole, I know for a fact that you've spoken numerous times at the Heritage Foundation, hunted wild boar with John Hawkins and members of the 'Silent Brotherhood' in Western Maryland, and secretly marched with the Klan on MLK day in Charles County. Let me tell you something about supremacy. It's called Article VI, Clause II of the US Constitution, which gives me the right as the ranking federal monitor, for any reason I deem necessary, to supersede any move by you I feel hampers my investigation. So keep your fucking mouth shut, and continue managing your little bullshit checkpoints, or I'll get the Justice Department to take down your whole force."

Dobkins sheepishly looks around at the untangled mass of two-dozen officers scattered around the office complex parking lot, pretending not to hear Adams eviscerate Maryland's top cop.

Too embarrassed to stick around, Dobkins gets in his unmarked SUV and exits the parking lot's only artery at the same time Nina and Quincy arrive on the relatively tranquil crime scene.

"I know that girl's face from somewhere," says Dobkins as he drives past Nina rotating her steering wheel counterclockwise off the road parallel to the Rockville office complex.

"That's Colin, the brave soul who gave us the dirty laundry on Konrad," answers Nina to Quincy as she turns off the tuned German engine. While Nina violently pulls the key out the ignition and turns left to exit her vehicle, she checks her newest text sent from Konrad's anonymous cellphone. The message reminds Nina to still make her weekly delivery to BWI—no matter whom she speaks to.

As the new couple holds hands in a public declaration of their undying love, they make their way past a few parked ambulances and a blacked-out LenCo Bearcat just used by MCPD's SWAT to secure the building and surrounding property. Now closer to the crime scene's exact location, Nina tries her best to stay composed.

Meanwhile, Detective Adams squats to a truncated, Garland yoga pose and then takes the clip of his ballpoint pen to peel back a plastic white sheet covering Denelle's body. Nina, on the verge of vomiting, sees Denelle's eyes closed and her head tilted to the side—not unlike the time she saw Denelle taking a siesta underneath her workstation like George Costanza. Returning the cautious greeting from Kreesha, the couple passes an expressionless Chief Macklin inside the back of a flashing ambulance while Nicole, seated next to him, fills out paperwork on a clipboard.

"We both know Konrad won't ever kill your mom because he's still in love with you. You're just using me to prove to him you're capable of being in a relationship and aren't psycho like he thinks you are," says Quincy quietly.

"I would have committed suicide that Wednesday if you didn't walk into my life. Real talk, the only reason I'm alive is because I get to kiss your pretty lips every day while we plan how to spend the rest of our life together," honestly answers

Nina as the two finally make their way to the group of assembled efficienTECH workers.

Nina momentarily takes another hard look at Denelle's body as two officers from the Rockville Coroner's office strap on latex gloves, then hoist Denelle's inverted, lifeless frame off the cold concrete sidewalk adjacent to the office complex before finally loading her onto a mobile steel gurney. Kreesha subtly avoids eye contact with Nina while politely shaking Quincy's hand.

"It's really unfortunate that we have to be meeting each for the first time on these terms," says Kreesha before handing the new couple two cups of hot chocolate.

"Where's Konrad?" immediately asks Nina.

"He didn't return my texts. I have no idea," answers Kreesha. While her co-workers introduce themselves to the UMD sophomore, Nina tightly hugs Colin for a good thirty seconds before uttering another word.

"They're going to find whoever did this; you hear me, Colin?" says Nina, wiping tears away from the hulking man's eye sockets.

"It doesn't make any fucking sense; none at all," timidly responds Colin.

Kreesha tries to hide her interest in Colin and Nina's conversation by looking at the commotion in the far background, where a few news trucks unsuccessfully try to get past the cop stationed at the yellow-taped barrier. Nina kisses Colin's forehead and zips up his windbreaker to protect his eighteen-inch neck from the cold.

“Because it was on the way home, I decided at the last minute to come back here to file some paperwork and then left the office around a quarter past six. I even tried to coax Denelle into having a quick drink with me at Ruby Tuesday’s, but she said she had to stay around to finish organizing a few documents,” states Colin.

“Is it unusual for her to work past traditional work hours Mr. Esposito?” interjects Adams, who effortlessly penetrates the membrane of the efficienTECH employee amoeba with the precision of a microneedle. Colin, in no mood to talk, puts his hands on Nina’s shoulders as the two face Adams from a distance of five feet.

“We all loved Denelle very much and were a close-knit group. Who are you, sir?” asks Nina, eagerly taking the opportunity to act as spokesman for the collection of white-collar workers.

“Oh, sorry. I’ve been to so many of these crime scenes since early October that I seem to forget my manners. My name is Charlie Adams, lead federal detective for the Serial Sniper investigation. I know that some MCPD officers already asked you a few preliminary questions; I’m just here to supplement their investigation,” unassumingly says Adams, who then hands a business card to everyone in the circle, including Quincy.

“Denelle was our hardest working employee. Most of us operated out of our cars, as our sales duties throughout the state dictated doing so. But she was the backbone or our team and did whatever it took to make sure our orders went through as fast as possible. Often that meant staying past five,” answers Colin.

“You seem more heartbroken over her death than your co-workers. Were you romantically involved with the deceased?” asks Adams.

Instead of gauging Colin's reaction, Adams quickly glances at his coworkers. While sighing, Gabriella puts her hand on her forehead.

Dave peevishly shakes his head in dissatisfaction, while Quincy and Nina, paying more attention to finally seeing Chief Macklin in person, remain expressionless. But Kreesha, who would have been scolded by Konrad for doing so if he were present, discreetly smiles, giving Detective Adams the first deviation from witness solidarity he was looking for.

"We messed around a few times, I won't lie to you. But I wouldn't . . . I didn't kill her," nervously responds Colin.

"Please remain calm; I'm not saying you did. If you need to speak to a psychologist to address your stress, we have one headed this way right now," reassures Adams, before asking, "I know you're all here in this near-freezing weather to remember Ms. Coleman's life, but can you tell me if anyone would want her dead?"

"Hey, no disrespect, Detective, but I thought you were here because this was the work of the Serial Sniper. Are you saying that it wasn't?" asks Gabriella.

"Everything's on the table. But at this time, we do believe it's another shooting orchestrated by our targeted suspect," answers Adams, before adding, "Please be aware that we've obtained a warrant to enter your workplace and will have access to all of your hard drives for at least the next twelve hours."

A few minutes later, Kreesha leads a short prayer session around the chalk line, which once encompassed Denelle. All five eT employees and Quincy hold hands, close their eyes, and make a circle around an array of scented candles and pictures.

"What does the Bible teach us?" starts Konrad's partner in crime.

"Second Timothy, Chapter Three: 'All scripture is God-breathed and is useful for teaching, rebuking, correcting, and training in righteousness.' Through the ever-loving graciousness of the Lord, let us use this tragic event to bring us closer to each other. This life can be so trifling and petty sometimes: the things we fight for, the things we fight over. Let's take a second to not only grieve for Denelle and her family, but think of how we can make the person who's hand we're holding a little less stressed and a little more joyful. Because one way or another, one of these days, it's all taken away from you," preaches Kreesha.

Safely inside the M3 ten minutes later, Quincy turns the car's heat to high and asks, "Why'd you feel the need to ask off for Christmas break? What's up?" Nina looks in her rear-view mirror and sees Kreesha, off to the side from the rest of eT's employees, talking into her cellphone while staring at Nina's car drive away.

"Regardless of what Nadir says, I need you to stop using synthetic h for the next four days. And make sure you have enough methadone to last until Monday; it's important, OK?" responds my heroine.

Chapter 41

Thirty-six hours later, Nina arrives at Konrad's property, on time, to collect to suitcases stuffed with synthetic h for delivery to Maryland's largest public airport.

"I'm here; open up," texts Nina before slowly reversing her BMW into Konrad's twenty-yard-long gravel driveway and toward his above-ground garage at its end. Much larger than the enclosed environment where Nina parks her car, the converted red barn, hidden in a seemingly endless maze of leafless hickory and maple trees, sits to the far left of Konrad's immense dwelling. Used the previous morning, noon, and night by Warren, Eric, and Konrad to wash, sterilize, and disassemble the luxury German sedan, used by Eric to murder Denelle, the ten-foot-high, barn-like doors unfold to the M3's opening trunk.

"Twice the product means twice risk means twice the money. Where's Konrad? Has he gone into hiding?" asks Nina as Warren and Eric stuff four, instead of the usual two, carry-on suitcases into her sports coupe.

Warren hands Nina an envelope with $20,000 in unmarked bills—twice the amount she usually receives each week.

“Because the pigs think one of Denelle’s coworkers may be responsible for her death, Amun Ra advises you to lawyer up. Especially after they see that you’re managing the PWI account,” says Eric.

“Stop calling him that, you disillusioned moron,” says Nina, counting her money.

Eric places a blue comforter over the quad set of carry-ons, which, once broken up and stepped on, will produce nearly one million packets of synthetic heroin.

“By the way, how’s your mom doing?” asks Warren before closing the trunk and splitting a Philly with his dirty brown thumbnail.

Nina clears her throat for emphasis, then spits in Warren’s face as violently as her lungs will allow.

She then slowly gets in her car and finally drives off directly toward Anne Arundel county.

Another stipulation of Konrad’s contract with the Black Commando Mafia, unknown to Nina, is that a regional lieutenant of Tavon Ayala, acting as counter-surveillance, tails Nina until she gets through the gated Fed-Ex property at BWI to meet her mark.

After meeting her bought-off shipping executive inside a closed airplane hangar an hour later, Nina pops the trunk and waits for him to extricate the four suitcases.

“Just have to park in the long-term lot. See you in ten,” texts Nina to Quincy, who waits anxiously in front of the JetBlue ticket counter inside Concourse C.

An hour later, and well after Ayala's unsuspecting spy drives back toward Baltimore, the two hold hands inside a northbound Airbus A320 and prepare for the worst.

Upon their exit of Boston's Logan International Airport, a white box truck, not unlike the one Quincy canvassed in front of the College Park WaWa in September, pulls into an empty spot near the passenger pick-up area at the end of a road parallel to Terminal C.

"That's us," says Nina as the two walk through sliding glass doors and into the frigid Bostonian air. The truck's driver flashes his high beams and waves his hand in a backward motion, beckoning for Nina and Quincy to hurry up. Quickening their pace through the sidewalk, the duo slips through a pair of three-foot high concrete barriers, erected to prevent domestic terrorist attacks, and step into the truck's now open storage area.

"Merry Christmas," says a masked gunman inside the cargo section.

He then points a black Uzi at Nina and Quincy's chests.

"Toss me your luggage, put on these, and then handcuff yourself to the wooden handrail," instructs the trained assassin after tossing the duo two blindfolds.

An hour later, Quincy and Nina, still standing after their mysterious road trip, feel the barrel of a submachine gun in the small of their backs.

"You're here. Step down carefully," says a third, unknown voice while grabbing the couple's hands from the rear of the same open truck they entered earlier at Massachusetts' busiest airport. The frigid, coarse hand then carefully guides Nina and Quincy to the frozen pavement.

"Their luggage, ID and belongings check out boss," barks one of the gunmen from inside the box truck's cargo area into his cellphone.

"All right, bring them to the dope house, then remove their blindfolds," responds an auto-tuned voice through the captor's phone speaker. As they shuffle their feet for twenty minutes, toward an unknown location under leaden skies, Nina and Quincy can feel their exposed necks and hands embrace warm temperature for the first time since exiting the airport.

Quincy, sincerely terrified as they approach the anonymous illegal drug warehouse, taps Nina on her calf muscle in order to remind her that he's still next to her. Realizing the magnitude of being alone in this perilous environment, Nina quickly kisses Quincy on his dry neck before stating to her captors, "We're not here to hurt you, only to bring your story to light. And let me remind you gentleman that you're forbidden to harm us under Articles 15, 76, and 77 of Protocol I to the Geneva Conventions."

"Restaurar emabrgo vista Rodrigo," says a deep, unknown Latino voice different from the urban American ones Nina and Quincy heard in the van.

Rodrigo points his gun at Quincy's temple while his associate removes the scarf from Nina's head.

"All right, Ms., calm down. We're very familiar with your show on the National Geographic Channel. My people brought me your post on Craigslist a few weeks ago, so tell me this: Why are you so interested in dealers in this state? Lie to me, and watch me blow your cameraman's brains out," says Felipe Guzman, kingpin of the highly organized, highly profitable Salieri Street gang.

"As producers for the ongoing series Drugs, Inc., we're here to document the booming drug trade in the upper Northeast. Please untie and unmask my associate. I know you've seen our work, so you know that your identities will eternally remain anonymous regardless of what laws your organization may, or may not be breaking," begs Nina as Rodrigo unlocks the safety to his automatic weapon.

"I retrieved their business cards from both their wallets and spoke to their boss in DC for a few seconds. Everything checks out," says Thiago, the third masked member of the Salieri Street gang inside the windowless, graffiti-adorned, drug-mixing room.

Rodrigo, after Felipe nods in his direction, unmasks Quincy and then pushes both he and his girlfriend toward a ratty, bedbug-infested couch in the room's corner.

"I'm familiar with your show; you guys do good work. Now pick up that digital camera brother, and let us tell our story," commands Felipe. Quincy quickly digs a Sony HDR from underneath the pile of clothes atop his luggage as Nina thanks me for advising her to go the extra mile to disfigure their identity.

If we didn't get those fictitious business cards printed and create those fake 202-area-code numbers, and if Colin didn't pose as our supervising producer, we'd be dead by now, thinks Nina.

Felipe pushes aside a small table, used to slightly scramble their shipments from the Sinaloa cartel, and unearths a loaded Colt 9mm rifle from underneath a hidden compartment below the floor. Felipe then points it directly at Nina's temple, an action that Nina is becoming used to by now. In true gonzo journalism style, Quincy keeps his lens focused on Felipe and presses record.

"We use this right here to protect our booming heroin trade. With the crackdown on prescription painkillers, business is good; but it could be better," says Felipe.

"Your crew operates mostly out of the Jamaica Plain section of Boston, and also has clients in Dorchester and Roxbury. Boston is a large city. And from college students to prostitutes, there are plenty of addicts to keep your pockets fat. So why'd you drive us all the way out here to Lawrence?" asks Nina.

"You assume that just because we're somewhere outside of Boston and all have Latino accents, that we're in Lawrence. That's racial profiling, Ms. Medea," says a smiling Rodrigo, who instructs his worker to put away their weapons. Rodrigo then hands "Felicia" and "Dutch" back their bogus Maryland licenses—another trick engineered by Colin whenever he wanted to slide a fake deal through headquarters to reap illegal commission.

"Call me Mr. Gris, or 'Gray' in English. I've seen your shows about drugs in cities around the country and am impressed on how you document and clarify what we do. I'll avoid the messy dealer clichés, but let's keep this relationship cordial," says Felipe.

Thiago pulls out a black .44 Magnum from his waistband and sits on a steel chair a few feet from Nina. He then states, "Something about you two don't add up. You both seem too sure of yourselves; you too polished."

Quincy, visibly exhausted from the flight, is starting to get dopesick and is in desperate need of his fix, real or synthetic. His perspirations, equal to that of a marathon runner, combined with extreme nausea, is driving him to almost lose consciousness.

"Hey, I hear those Chico's down south got the best product around. It's been half a day since my last session. My man, do you think I could score half a finger and shoot up right now?" Itching uncontrollably, Quincy scratches his neck with his right hand.

Satisfied that an undercover would never shoot up in front of them, the three Dominicans ease the tension by putting down their weapons and placating Quincy's wish. Rodrigo quickly taps the inside of Quincy's extended forearm to find a vein receptive for shooting while simultaneously wrapping a plastic strap around his arm.

Nina stomach churns as the full impact of her second job comes full circle, poisoning the only person in the world she can completely trust.

"Specifically, regarding heroin, you just said that business is going well. We know heroin addiction, especially when it's the local end-product of high-quality h combined with benzo's like fentanyl has become a full-blown epidemic not only in Boston, but the entire Northeast. Other than generic issues, like maintaining distribution from Mexico and the Caribbean, and DEA interference, what other business problems are the Salieri Street gang facing?" asks Nina, now using the camera to record their answer.

"Competition," begins Felipe. As the mephitic mixture of heroin and Quincy's blood fills the needle's chamber, the drug-game veteran smiles in approval, then continues. "There's a product on the street right now we can't get a hold of, meaning that we don't can't understand why it's so cheap, yet so pure."

"We call it El Diablo," blurts out Rodrigo, cutting off Felipe with his excitement. With the powerful opiates fully in his bloodstream, Quincy tilts his head to the side and slowly reclines into the filthy couch.

"Your co-worker's nodding out," says Thiago to Nina.

"I know, Dutch is tired from the long day of traveling. He'll be fine."

"No, you don't understand. His respiration system is in danger of shutting down. Or just as worse, he could possibly choke on his own vomit. Cause he overdosed on what we gave him and is now bouncing back between two worlds: the conscious and unconscious," continues the hidden-faced dealer.

"You said two worlds, huh?" replies Nina, before sighing at the thought of his last sentence. Nina runs her fingers through her hair and starts gnashing her teeth.

"Stay calm. At least two people a day are dying from heroin overdoses in Boston. But he'll be fine. We got Narcan for this yellow nigga," affirms Felipe.

"Put down the camera and hold him upright; your cameraman is dying," adds Thiago, who takes off his mask. Rodrigo, not wanting to deal with the process of burying a dead body on Christmas in fifteen-degree weather, affixes his handheld nasal atomizer to a needle-less syringe, then assembles the glass cartridge of Naloxone. Felipe tilts back Quincy's head, then sprays half the Naloxone up Quincy's left nostril and the other half up his right one.

After two and half minutes of rescue breathing performed by Thiago, Quincy finally begins to normalize his breathing and motor functions. Once drying tears of worry from her eyes, Nina says to Felipe, "Tell me more about that heroin sold called El Diablo. Why do you guys call it that?"

"Because only the devil could concoct a heroin product that pure, make it that cheap, and cause side effects resembling the worst strung-out crackhead or agitated angel dust fiend. It's like nothing I've ever seen," responds Rodrigo.

Thiago unscrews a bottle of water and gently pours it down Quincy's parched throat. Simultaneously, the leader of this mid-level crew hands Nina a navy-blue synthetic h wrapper used weekly by the BCM to distribute Konrad's product.

"See, up here, one gram of heroin will set you back eighty dollars. The quality of h we get from Mexico is high and very pure, which gives us the ability to step on it by 80, even 85 percent. And still the addicts, all the way from Boston, to Vermont, to up in Manchester, go mad trying to re-up what we sell," begins Rodrigo before adding, "But this right here, this type of heroin is something entirely different. From what my workers and I've seen over the last six months, this heroin variant is much more insidious to not only the user, but this Northeast community at large."

Genuinely seeing it for the first time, but obviously cognizant of its origin, Nina inspects the small square of wax paper printed by an industrial efficienTECH copier inside Konrad's home. "I wonder why these guys chose to stamp it with a black, upside-down Christian cross; that's weird. Who's selling this smack, and what side effects are you seeing on the streets?" asks the emboldened drug mule.

Quincy, now fully conscious and operational, licks a drip of blood from his arm, and then grabs the recording camera from his partner. "The Blacks got full control of this strain and we got no idea where they're getting it from. They're not connected enough to get it from Afghanistan or North Korea, and they're definitely not getting it from Mexico," says Thiago.

"I've tried bribery, torture, and even a few drive-bys here in Lawrence; they ain't saying shit," admits Rodrigo.

After a quick meal at Lee Chen's Restaurant on 230 Winthrop Avenue, the Maryland couple and Salieri Street triage get into a beat-up Aerostar Van and drive toward a corner where synthetic heroin is being sold directly to the consumer.

"I don't know what these monkeys are adding to their h, but it's making people crazy. I know for a fact that it's turning some addicts into straight killers. White, Latino, Black; it doesn't matter. A local cop, on my payroll, told me that since dealers introduced El Diablo to Lawrence this summer, the murder rate here has quadrupled. OK, we're done talking; now get the fuck out," says Felipe while putting the van in park alongside a dangerous-looking street littered with old, domestic, windowless sedans that haven't been driven in at least twenty years.

"I let you guys off a couple corners away from their block. We'll be watching from an alley across the street from where their dealers operate. If they start shooting, you're on your own," he adds.

As the van drives off, Nina looks around, taking in the burnt-out and boarded up row houses lining the street.

Nina and Quincy stand on the cracked concrete sidewalk, then immediately jump away from two raccoon-sized rats looking for dinner next to a stuffed garbage can. While Nina buttons her peacoat and digs in her left pocket to make sure her bundle of hundred dollar bills haven't been stolen, the Ford van makes an abrupt, three pointed U-turn and heads in the opposite direction.

"It looks like a ghost town 'round here tonight. You think the Dominicans are setting us up?" asks Nina as she and Quincy carefully embark eastward toward their destination.

"We're about to find out. The more 'The Wire' vigilante bullshit like this you try to pull on your own, the more likely you'll serve prison time—regardless of what deal you negotiate with Macklin," assesses Quincy while wrapping a wool scarf around his ashy beige neck.

The brave couple, now halfway toward the synthetic h dealers, walk underneath a buzzing orange streetlamp at the corner of an empty intersection and see two young, skinny African-American males at the opposite end of the upcoming block.

Dressed in classically unlaced, tan Timberland boots, olive green sweatpants, a hooded black sweatshirt, and an army surplus jacket, Ricky, a four-week trial member of the Black Commando Mafia, rubs his hands over a fire emanating from the bottom of an open oil barrel.

Ricky's lookout Shareef, huddled inside a silver Patriots NFL parka, and also new to BCM, whistles to his partner from the top of a frozen staircase behind him.

"A-yo, look alive. You got a couple coming up behind you," orders Ricky.

Shareef blows chilled air through his cupped hands while leaning against an especially filthy, foreclosed corner home ten feet from Ricky's location. Doubling as a crack den during daylight hours, the first floor also holds a personal cache of automatic weapons in addition to Lawrence's most popular illicit drugs.

"Ebony and Ivory, what the fuck y'all looking for? Please don't waste my time this Christmas night," says Ricky, after turning toward Quincy and Nina.

Nina promptly hands him fifteen crisp, $100 bills.

"This should cover thirty grams. Or three fingers, whatever you call it."

"Why you and stretch need so much? You a suburban dealer looking to re-up for New Years?" asks Ricky, while staring down the much taller Quincy.

"Yeah; something like that. Before you give me my product, can you answer me this: why does this heroin cause users to act so violently? Are you guys lacing it with something I should know about?" retorts Nina.

As Shareef looks on from the porch, Ricky counts his money, and replies, "Nah, it's too cheap to do that. The client stays happy with it as is, so we don't cut it with shit. Wait here for a minute, I gotta go inside to get your order."

Ricky then turns around and nods slightly at his partner while walking into the home's porch behind him, slowly approaching the plywood door Shareef rests his back on.

While Ricky walks past Shareef and opens the door hiding his handheld killing machines, Nina shouts, "One more thing, tell your boss that Konrad is about to stab him in the back."

"Who the fuck is Konrad?" shouts back Shareef as Ricky passes the house's entrance-way behind him.

Ricky opens the front door to the dope house and decides to grab his "street sweeper" by the moldy staircase while letting his associate use the MAC-11 on top of the front windowsill.

"Ain't no undercover DT's come to my hood on Christ's birthday, trying to set me up!" says the hardened sixteen-year-old, before cocking back the rusty, but reliable, Amsel Striker in his honey-brown hands.

"Shit's too hot; we're outta here," says Quincy outside while grabbing Nina's right wrist.

Shaking off the tugging from her boyfriend, Nina looks over her shoulder and sees a hidden pair of van lights turn on from the alley across the street.

"I knew the Dominicans would rescue us," says Nina before finally heeding Quincy's call to retreat.

"Hey, you guys take the money. It's no big deal, and happy holidays to you and your family," screams Nina while slowly backing into the street with her hands in the air.

Shareef pulls out his trusty six-shooter and lets off three shots: one in the direction of Quincy's behind and two toward the angled, zigzagging torso of Nina.

"Floor it!" yells Felipe to his driver Rodrigo. As Thiago leans out the van's passenger side, and squeezes his 9 until it recoils seven times, Rodrigo makes a left turn out the alley, briefly over-steering the van into a parked Lincoln parked in front of the dope house.

Nina, thinking that they're about to be rescued from the two BCM goons, stops running down the street, turns around, and begins to flail her arms in an V-like motion. She shouts to Rodrigo, "Open the sliding door so we can jump in!"

As gunfire from Ricky hits the back of the Ford van, Felipe yells, "El diablo está aquí, so fuck that ballsy coño for pulling us into this mess. Don't stop moving!"

Quincy, now squeezed between two parked cars, jumps into the one-way road with the agility of a panther and forcefully shoves Nina toward safety on the other side of the street milliseconds before the vehicle hits Nina head on. The van's front silver bumper then crushes Quincy's ilium, iliac crest, and acetabulum bones, instantaneously shattering his pelvis beyond repair.

"No! What are you doing?" screams Nina at the top of her lungs while watching Quincy's body forcefully execute an airborne cartwheel from being hit by the Aerostar at fifty miles per hour.

After flying through the air a dozen feet, Quincy's progression is finally halted by an elderly, frozen tree demarcating the northbound block's halfway point. The tree cleanly breaks Quincy's back in half, along with critically injuring his internal organs.

Meanwhile, down the block, gunshots coming from the BCM's dope house have ceased. Quincy whispers, "Those three cowards aren't coming back, Supergirl. Get outta here now, before the cops catch you."

Nina kneels beside Quincy, grasps his hand, takes off his beanie cap, and then kisses his soft forehead. "Bullshit, I'm not going anywhere. Here, take this, you're going to catch cold," responds Nina, before taking off her jacket. "It's all over. I'll just fess up to the authorities when they get here, and let whatever happens, happen. I'm in over my head . . . this experience, everything, the voices, is beyond me at this point."

"No, keep going for your mom. She's all you have now. You see, I deserved this. It's my divine fate for all the sins I've committed . . . God gave me a second chance with you, and I blew it."

Nina hears sirens in the distance, but doesn't see any vehicles, undercover or otherwise, approaching from either direction on the street.

"This will ease your pain," says Nina.

Nina breaks open a small packet of Rodrigo's heroin found in Quincy's jacket, spreads it into a dirty spoon found in his jeans pocket, quickly lights its bottom, then sucks it up with his used needle before finally shooting it into a bulging forearm vein.

"All I can feel now are my lips. Go find a foreclosed home to hide in until the sun rises, then call a cab to get back to the airport. You still have your real license on you and enough cash to get back before missing work on Monday," whispers Quincy before mustering enough strength, with all his might, to shout

"Leave now!"

Quincy then closes his eyes and tilts his neck to the side, just as he did when almost overdosing earlier. It's OK though, he'll soon be able to see Nina from this vantage point.

Halfway down the block, Shareef holds Ricky's shaking frame as the dying youth also gasps his last breaths. Return fire from the Dominicans caused compression and shearing to soft tissue throughout Ricky's body, causing the gang banger to start spitting up blood.

"Tell the captain about Konrad . . . Konrad has to be responsible for all of this, my brother," whimpers Ricky.

“Wake up! Stop playing man . . . open your eyes and look at me!” screams Nina, still with Quincy underneath the tree, before unsuccessfully trying to perform CPR on him.

Nina sees the headlights and flashing sirens of a police car approaching from about three blocks away, then looks toward the corner as Shareef catapults off the dope house's front porch and runs fearlessly south in the opposite direction of Quincy’s dying body.

“Yes. I will marry you.” Nina tearfully kisses Quincy one last time on the lips, quickly pats her hips to make sure she still has her phone and wallet, and sprints as fast as her legs will allow northbound and away from the double-homicide crime scene.

The next morning, Nina yawns while twisting on top of a malodorous mattress in the corner of an unknown, decrepit bedroom. Immediately patting down her pockets, Nina turns on her cellphone to see that it's now the twenty-sixth of December and a full eight hours after she saw Quincy, presumably for the last time. Busting out of the empty, second floor row house bedroom onto a spider web-filled staircase leading to outside, Nina steps over dozens of empty used needles along with a few cloudy crack pipes.

Before stepping through the front door, Nina carefully peeks outside via an adjacent window. Confident that she’s not under local police surveillance, she heeds Quincy’s advice and calls for an unmarked taxi to drive her to Boston.

“Logan International please; and I’ll double your fare if you break the speed limit,” says Nina upon entering the back of a silver Toyota Camry.

"I'll try my hardest, but I might not be able to get there as fast as possible. Police closed off a street a few blocks from here due to a shooting and hit-and-run. This is the most dangerous neighborhood in Lawrence you know, day or night," says the Pakistani driver.

I won't even get the opportunity to bury my fiancé, thinks Nina.

Nina puts on her sunglasses, shuts her eyes, and dozes off until her cabbie reaches the airport. After momentarily thinking to take the first flight to Dubai, because the UAE doesn't have an extradition treaty with the US, visions of Quincy being crushed by Felipe's van fill her head, prompting Nina to board the first available flight to Maryland.

After a tepid conversation with her mother, in which Nina got reamed out for only sending $10,000 in Christmas money, she turns her attention to Nadir and writes him a text message.

"If you don't find an antidote by New Year's Day, I'll . . ." furiously types Nina, who struggles to key the last few words destined for his inbox. Now back in Anne Arundel County after a short, uninterrupted flight from Massachusetts, Nina impatiently waits as another taxi drives her home to Laurel.

Nadir spends his last Saturday of the year at PWI, working as hard as he can to formulate an antidote for x-2317's villainous side- effects.

"All I have to do is observe young Quincy's reactions for a month, and then I should have a cure for this mess by the Super Bowl," writes Nadir into his daily journal.

Momentarily staring at a framed photograph of himself and his smiling wife hugging their adolescent child at the Vijayadashami Victory of Rama Festival last October, Nadir's daydream of past happiness is interrupted by an unfamiliar voice.

"Dr. Jayaraman. I'm here to pick up this week's batch of x-2317 for Hunter. Is it ready?" says the male, with a dialect alien to Nadir's ears.

The focused doctor keeps his back toward the open door and continues to mix an acidic compound for x-46 underneath the lab's chemical hood.

"Sir, please state your name. I'm used to only dealing with Warren and Eric," says Nadir while turning around to the dark hallway behind him, and removing his buzzing phone from his pocket. Seeing that Nina is on the other line, he answers his phone and says, "Sorry, kid, I've done all I can do. You're on your—"

Bang bang bang.

Nina crumples against the leather taxi seat, all too familiar with the sound of gunfire by now. She almost forgets that the phone is still on until Nadir's killer picks up the phone off the ground, checks its caller ID, then says into it, "I don't know who you are, Nina Sullivan. But once I find out your connection to x-2317, I'm going to find you, and I'm going to kill you."

Chapter 42

"Still assumed to be in Maryland, the two DC-area snipers have continued to evade local, state, and federal officials for almost three months. Clues indicate that at least one of the Serial Snipers is forty-one-year-old Blake Rice, an ex-Navy SEAL discharged after displaying symptoms of posttraumatic stress disorder during an east Africa, Al Qaeda-linked search-and-rescue mission occurring less than two years ago. Sources tell CBS that although Rice has illegally exited and re-entered the country twice in the last year, the FBI has been unable to detain him thus far and are unwilling to charge him for the various, seemingly random murders in DC and PG and Montgomery County out of fear that copycat killings will arise," says the same nasal, droning news anchor Adams has relied upon for media updates since September.

"As many can attest to, the Serial Sniper killings have had a profound, chilling effect, both in and around the nation's capital. Now statistics prove that nationwide, it's also dropped public trust in local law enforcement to record lows," continues the voice from Adams' car speakers.

The news anchor concludes his hourly update by stating "A Reuters/Quinnipiac College poll, conducted of eighteen- to forty-nine-year-old Caucasian, African-American, Latino, and Asian DC area residents, charts the MCPD approval rating at around twelve percent: a decline of over 60 percent since Labor Day. And in national news, other, once idyllic communities are also gripped by fear as a steep uptick in violent crime plagues daily lives. Respective police chiefs in Manchester, New Hampshire; Burlington, Vermont; and Portland, Maine are asking their respective governors for assistance from the National Guard after homicide and larceny rates have quintupled since July first. 'The audacity of those committing these crimes, which often happen in broad daylight with no rhyme, reason, or pattern, is difficult to comprehend, mainly because these criminals are, for the most part, first-time offenders usually residing in affluent neighborhoods with little financial incentive to kill,' said Manchester Police Chief, David J. Mara."

"So why did you, or your partner, kill Dr. Jayaraman of Pharmaceutical Warehouse Incorporated this weekend? What connection did this man have to the truth you're seeking?" types Adams before saving the draft text in his Blackberry shutting off his vehicle, and exiting his car.

"Was it another random act of violence or one more murder to justify your master plan?" adds Detective Adams before sending the message to Blake's Yahoo account.

Blake Rice and Charlie Adams have communicated infrequently since the murders of Julian and Lieutenant Patrick. The former Navy SEAL has now decided to focus on finding additional retribution against the federal government instead of trying to convince Adams that he's not the villain the media portrays him as.

"God, I hate this state. Everything about it makes me sick to my stomach," mutters the grumpy investigator after slamming his car door shut.

Stuffing his bare hands into the front pockets of his puffy tan parka, Adams makes the short walk underneath gray skies through the frigid, barren parking lot and toward eT's Maryland branch office. Passing Ms. Coleman's memorial on the sidewalk, he sees a picture of Denelle smiling while tailgating for a Ravens game.

* * * * *

"Let me begin by expressing my regret on how trying a time this is for everyone, especially after a very successful year for all of us here at efficienTECH," starts Konrad, who stands behind a seated Kreesha during their last Monday-morning sales forecast meeting of the year.

Konrad, his eyes watering like Rahm Emanuel's while apologizing for another case of police misconduct, continues. "Denelle Coleman was the glue that kept this office together. Words cannot explain the pain in my heart I felt when I heard of her passing, especially when the way it happened seems so gutless."

Kreesha puts her hand on Konrad's shoulder. Colin, who's unusually disheveled for work, sits next to her, emotionless and silent. Nina sits aside Dave and Gabriella at the opposite end of the long, thick, and obsidian marble table. She remains silent and unemotional while playing solitaire on her new Palm Pilot hidden in between her exposed, shapely thighs.

“I speak English, what’s up? I already told the police everything I know,” says the proud office cleaner in the office complex lobby.

“You’re not illegal to me, my man; please put your papers away. But let me ask, the day of Ms. Coleman's murder, did you observe any unusual activity in the lobby bathroom after traditional work hours? Anything at all?” inquires Adams.

“Now that you mention it, the boss lady of the first-floor company and one of the sales guys used to . . . used to . . .”

“They snorted cocaine in one of the stalls when they thought they were alone, right?”

The El Salvadorian cautiously shakes his head in agreement.

“I also saw him horsing around a lot with the girl who was killed; they often closed up the office together,” adds the proud janitor.

After concluding his inquisition minutes later, Adams unearths a keycard he stole from Denelle’s desk drawer, and opens the front glass door to efficienTECH.

Banging his badge on the clear window between the hallway and packed conference room, Adams startles the grieving group seconds after they held hands, closed their eyes, and bowed their heads in yet another prayer for the deceased twenty-five-year-old.

“Sorry to interrupt. I’m not breaking up anything important, am I?” patiently asks Adams in the hallway.

“No, Detective, we were just talking to Denelle one more time. What can we do for you?” asks Konrad, taking onus to speak for everyone else in the room.

“I know you guys are busy closing the books this year, but all I need are some answers to a few general questions, then I’ll be on my way. OK?” replies Adams, while vigorously shaking Konrad’s hand for the first time.

“None of us have anything to hide, and I hope you catch the bastard who did this as soon as possible. You look cold; can I get you a hot cup of coffee? I just got a special blend from headquarters after finishing first in sales this year.”

“I’ll only be a few minutes, but that sounds like a great idea. I’ll take it with two sugars, thanks.”

“Why are you here, Detective? Do you believe anyone of us are responsible for Denelle’s murder?” asks Nina after Konrad exits the conference room and walks toward the break room housing the coffee machine.

“No. Of course not; I’m just here to get a better sense of Denelle’s personality, habits, and relationships here at efficienTECH. We visited her apartment and found that, in addition to her love of Tupac memorabilia, she often brought home and perused many files usually only meant for executive eyes. Does anyone know why this is so?”

Now in the small kitchen at the rear of the office, Konrad pulls out a bag of Marley Blue Mountain coffee from the cupboard and turns on the BrewStation machine.

“The documents you’re referring to, Detective, were nothing more than receipts for high-level orders occurring in quarters two and three of this year, when I'm proud to say, this office achieved record levels of growth. Although I'm grateful business was strong, the days of this past spring and summer were long, stressful, and arduous. Denelle probably took the files home to process them in the comfort of her home, which she often did with my blessing. She did this because Ms. Coleman wanted her co-workers to get their sales commission as quickly as possible," says Kreesha, without exhibiting any signs of nervousness. Nina remains silent.

"Here you go, Detective," says Konrad, handing Adams a steaming mug.

"I'm glad you made it back in time; fantastic. Why do you think Denelle felt the need to archive all of your deals this year? She had photocopies of each one saved inside a locked drawer in her bedroom. On the night she was murdered, Mr. Hunter, Denelle was carrying three files on impressive seven-figure deals you closed this past fall. Written agreements on all three deals were for pharmaceutical research and manufacturing companies based in and around Boston who, like Pharmaceutical Warehouse Incorporated, are sub-contracted by a firm by the name of—" says Detective Adams, who takes one more sip of coffee before placing it directly in front of a muted Kreesha.

"The company those three organizations are sub-contracted to is called Purdue Pharma; they're based in Stamford, Connecticut. If I'm not mistaken, they've made a fortune creating and distributing MS Contin, which is an extended-release formulation of morphine. Where are you going with this, Detective?" calmly interrupts Konrad.

"All three Boston companies, Omega Incorporated, Alpha LLC, and Mimic International, bought efficienTECH industrial copiers from you based on the recommendation of a man named Dr. Nadir Jayaraman; one of the leading chemists for PWI. About forty-two hours ago, during this past Saturday afternoon, Dr. Jayaraman was murdered in his Maryland lab. I have reason to believe that the culprit was an accomplice of the DC serial killer we've been tracking since September."

"Questions regarding internal efficienTECH documents should be sent to our legal department. I can put you in touch with them this morning," quickly responds Kreesha.

"That's fine; I can save him the time. Our corporate lawyers will tell you the same thing that I will, Detective: that all questions regarding the inner-mechanisms of eT's relationship with PWI need to be referred to Nina Sullivan since she is the owner of that account after selling a substantial amount of equipment to them this fall. As for Alpha, Omega, and Mimic, I realized that once we had PWI on our roster of clients, we could provide a similar workflow service to similar companies. Anything else?"

"You know what, Mr. Hunter? I don't like the tone of your voice; not one bit. I've lost too many men while know-it-all pricks like you second-guess our moves from the sidelines. I'll tell you what, we'll just finish this conversation at the station," sternly responds Adams.

Adams whips out handcuffs on the much taller, much stronger North Philly man. Nina struggles to contain her joy as Adams shoves Konrad's face into the wall and squeezes both arms behind his back while at the same time jamming his knee right into Konrad's lower spine.

"Getting a little aggressive now, aren't we, Detective?" coolly remarks Konrad as his right cheek bone gets pressed into a mural-sized efficienTECH insignia on the side of thc gray brick wall.

"Shut the fuck up," screams Adams, before adding, "You have the right to remain silent . . ."

Kreesha and Dave take out their cellphones and begin to record the arrest.

"Why are you so harsh with him?" asks Gabriella.

"Every person deserves due process, and what you're doing isn't legal!" screams a genuinely concerned Colin.

Detective Adams presses his walkie-talkie and says, "Send two squad cars, with at least four officers, to the crime scene of Denelle Coleman right now. I've apprehended a suspect inside the first floor efficienTECH office."

"At least lead me out of here without handcuffs, Detective. I'll answer any question you've got and stay as long as you need me—no lawyers, no cameras. One on one: just you and me. But I've got a reputation in this office complex to uphold. So let's walk outside together, then your pigs can arrest me in the parking lot, OK?"

"We're outside, copy. How do you want to handle this, Detective?" says the voice of an officer in one of the marked MCPD cars parked next to Adams' rent-a-car outside.

"Meet me in the lobby. I want to make a scene in front of everyone," responds Adams into his handheld device.

The responding cop relays that he'll meet him inside the first floor, security guard-less lobby in sixty seconds.

FBI Detective Adams gets Konrad on his feet with surprising speed and then removes his handcuffs. "We're going to do this outside while everyone's watching; it's more fun that way."

"OK, have it your way," calmly responds Konrad. As promised, Adams leads the eT salesman of the year through the office hallway and into the empty, steel-gray, 1000-square-foot lobby, bordered by a common turn-style entrance, two closed elevator doors, the glass efficienTECH façade, a hallway leading to the bathroom, and an illuminated sign designating other companies residing in the medium-sized complex. Bypassing the 360-degree entrance, all four officers enter through a fire exit. One of the elevator doors open, releasing a bevy of uninspired, grumpy white-collar workers from the upper floor.

"Get on the ground, now!" yells one of the MCPD officers to Konrad, who immediately gets on his knees and does as he's told. The five eT employees behind him, resigned to Konrad's fate, remain quiet and severely embarrassed as their counterparts from a startup tech company upstairs point and gasp.

"I knew he murdered that poor girl," says one male software engineer from the second-floor company called Consumer Recreation Services. Another MCPD officer pulls out his handgun, and points it at Konrad's temple. Simultaneously, his partner palms Konrad's skull and, with his extended kneecap, forces Konrad's head to the beige carpet.

"I think it's time now, Mr. Adams; don't you?" whispers Konrad. Detective Charlie Adams stands up amongst the chaos in the lobby's center and runs to a glass box marked "Do Not Break Except in Case of Emergency." With the same voracity used by Amare Stoudemire, he punches through the box's plexiglass, severely cutting his hand in the process.

Meanwhile, at least ten camera phones document the madness. In the same quick, violent manner that lone-wolf terrorist Zale H. Thompson did on October 23 in Queens, Adams grabs the silver hatchet off the two interior, wooden pegs inside the metal box and chops down on the MCPD officer detaining Konrad.

Piercing through the side of his head before fracturing his skull, the unexpected blow immediately causes the Montgomery County cop to crumple to the floor and receive permanent brain damage.

"What the hell are you doing, Detective? Put down your weapon and stand down!" yells the injured officer's partner. Instead, Adams raises the small axe a second time and tries to take a swing at another MCPD cop, who unsuccessfully uses his body to shield the other freshly sliced fallen officer. The third and fourth uniformed officers, after shaking off their initial shock, let off a round of hastily fired shots from their handguns, killing Adams instantly and, in the process, accidently shooting Gabriella in the upper back. As the young woman screams in ear-splitting agony, the witnesses from the upstairs ECU extension company run into the eT lobby with a crawling Dave, Kreesha, Nina, and Colin following not far behind them.

The Entropy of disorder my Opponent created surrounding the shot FBI Detective, who now lies dead in the prone position next to the two axed police officers, allows Konrad the precious few seconds he needs in order to execute part two of his plan.

"Did Detective Adams come here by himself? Are there any other threats in the building?" yells one of the officers to Konrad.

"No, he came here to harass me by himself. For no reason, he broke up our meeting, threw me up against a wall, and . . ."

responds Konrad in a fragmented, rehearsed, and frightened tone.

"Go back inside the office with your coworkers until we secure the entire building. Do it now!"

Following one of many reoccurring episodes my worthy opponent constructed within this ever-evolving, labyrinth-like plot, Konrad slyly retrieves Adams' small notepad and mobile phone from his jacket pocket while the other two attending officers grieve over their butchered partners. Konrad then scampers into the eT lobby to join the other petrified bystanders who quickly escaped the crime scene. Employees from both companies ignore the officer's instructions to stay inside the efficienTECH office and instead run outside via eT's rear fire exit. Nina pulls Konrad into an empty cubicle and whispers, "You poisoned that poor man. You put something in his coffee to make Detective Adams act like that; I know you did."

"Did you see how poor Charlie was almost immediately able to put the pieces together, as if his powers of deduction increased faster than his brain could manage? I gave him the Red Bull version of x-2317, the one I had anonymously engineered by chemists who thought they were developing a non-addictive alternative for oxycodone from the Alpha and Omega labs up north. It was definitely worth paying Nadir to lie to them," says Konrad, while pulling out a small, sized bottle from his suit jacket.

Konrad extracts out a dime-sized bag of synthetic h that Nina immediately recognizes from her disastrous trip to Lawrence and pours some on the desk. He then ejaculates two odorless, colorless drops from the bottle and into the tiny mound, dissolving it immediately.

"Once synthetic h, enhanced by this new additive, cnters the bloodstream, it now has the ability to instantaneously ramp up x-2317's side effects in 100 percent of its users. I'm running out of nicknames, so think of something cool I should call it."

Nina softly bangs her head on the flimsy, five-foot-high white wall dividing two cubicles, then softly says, "These events keep happing, over and over, with the next only slightly different then it's predecessor. And all that research Nadir did; all gone."

"East Indians can't be trusted and are the most corrupt species on earth. That's why the Others made him a gray operative. You gotta wale up and start reading in between the lines."

"Enough with the racism, Konrad; it makes me sick how many ways heroin has destroyed you. Is that's why you had Nadir killed? Because you were jealous he was working on a cure to save mankind?"

"I didn't have Nadir murdered, but apparently, a man named Blake Rice did," says Konrad while scrolling through Adams' cellphone.

"Who's Blake Rice?"

"I knew it. I knew the two snipers were connected to us and that the Others had always created a Trinity. Encapsulating us two, in the end, and from the beginning, it was always about three dark forces connected by unknown, intersecting powers in this triangle. I'm so excited to meet another player representing the Others from a different game!"

Konrad pulls out a small white napkin and draws a pyramid-shaped triangle with two stacked dots in its center. He then draws a line, connecting the top dot to the top corner of the pyramid.

"My voice tells me to give this sign to you, and adds that it'll make sense to both of us later," says Konrad, handing the paper cloth to Nina.

"What the fuck are you talking about?" After questioning Konrad, Nina then glances back through the glass eT entrance and sees a bevy of EMT workers mount the corpse of Adams, along with the chopped officer and a deceased Gabriella, onto three compressed stretchers.

"One of the Serial Snipers is a former Navy SEAL; he was drugged with x-2317 before a mission a few years ago. I'll be in touch with a time and place all three of us can meet to discuss our plans for fighting order in this New World," says Konrad before kissing Nina on her salty, perspiration-filled forehead.

"I don't understand . . . everyone keeps dying. Help me get through this," begs Nina, her eyes closing as she imagines an embrace from Quincy.

"x-2317 is laced with telomerase: a ribonucleoprotein that, when combined with other chemicals that make up x-2317, increases your life expectancy by 200 percent. On top of that, it also provides us ever-lasting life from a technological perspective. After only one application, x-2317 released dozens of non-excretable nano-bots within your bloodstream," says Konrad.

"That's where that voice in my head comes from . . ." theorizes Nina.

"Right, on top of being the greatest chemist of this century, Nadir was also a leading transhumanist. The little computers he mass-produced, then embedded inside each pill, do everything from removing plaque from the walls of your arteries to recycling and regenerating collagen to keeping your connective tissue strong, young, and elastic. It also makes your brain cells more efficient, thereby enhancing your memory and intelligence to un-testable levels. No, you can't jump from here to Charlotte like the Hulk, or stop comets from hitting London like Superman, but you will be able to heal from non-life threatening injuries at a rate much faster than any human."

"I'm immortal?" asks Nina.

"That depends. Define immortality," I tell her.

Chapter 43

“Yes, happy holidays to you too, sir. Who is this?”

It's the first weekend of a new year, and with many around the nation extending their Christmas break a couple more days, an air of optimism and goodwill has spread to even the darkest, most baneful corners of the country. The death of FBI Detective Adams was ruled by investigators as a classic example of suicide by cop. Although an innocent woman was killed in the process, Adams’ death was hailed by the increasingly acerbic mainstream media as a positive turn in the four-month search for the snipers.

Predictably, social media have turned the Serial Snipers into modern cult heroes.

“Hello, Mr. Rice. This is Konrad Hunter, a simple corporate salesman here in Montgomery County. I have a strong feeling that you want to see me in person— as soon as possible.”

“And why might I want to do that?” asks Blake, before yawning.

Using a disguise, fake identification, and a prepaid credit card, he and Renzo were able to secure a deluxe suite at a local Hilton in Gaithersburg in order to celebrate a full calendar year of freedom. And after hearing about Detective Adams' untimely demise, Blake is surprised, and intrigued, to receive a nameless e-mail from Konrad.

Konrad's message implies that there was someone, unconnected to law enforcement in the immediate area, who personally knew both Nadir and Adams, and that this individual was interested in helping Blake's campaign for both transparency, and clarity, regarding x-2317.

"And before you answer that question, what is your association to x-2317?" adds Blake. Renzo continues to soundly sleep in his own queen-sized bed, the first time he's slept outside the Caprice in North America.

Leaning on the corner desk, Blake takes a healthy bite of a cranberry muffin, one of many breakfast items he's gorged from the free breakfast buffet in the lobby.

"Before you guys killed Nadir, I was his business partner. Please don't hang up; I'm not angry that you guys removed him from this dimension, as he's no longer any use to me anyways."

"Keep speaking. If I don't like what I'm hearing, you'll never get this opportunity to plead your case again."

"After Adams passed, I was able to acquire his notepad and phone before the cops did. I had a chance to digest the correspondence between you and the detective, along with the e-mails you archived from Dolan's hard drive. What the CIA, along with the FBI and state and local police have failed to tell you, sir, is that x-2317, instead of any circumstance surrounding your military and/or personal life, has turned you into the systematic, heartless killing machine you are today. As you probably have figured out already, this has also made you semi-eternal: incapable of dying of natural causes."

“Say that I accepted your theory as truth, who else is permanently under the influence of x-2317?”

“That's a tricky question, and what I say may sound crazy at first. But if you hear me out, by the edge of tomorrow it'll all make sense.”

Over the next several hours, and after Renzo joins the conversation via speaker phone, Konrad explains the important dichotomy of x-2317 vs. synthetic h; the salient points being that only three people alive in the world have the unadulterated version of x-2317 in their bodies: himself, Blake, and Nina.

“The hundreds of thousands, potentially millions, of synthetic heroin users in the upper Northeast, along with a significantly smaller amount of addicts in and around Baltimore, are infected with the same abnormality that affects you and me, but don't have the added benefits that x-2317 gives humans. These addicts can't think, anticipate, evaluate, or database information at our level, nor will their life expectancy expand,” accurately states Konrad.

“But they will, of course, continue to kill others, for seemingly no rhyme or reason, at rates never seen before in history,” responds Renzo, who provides his mentor with anecdotal evidence to back the statements of Nina’s ex-boyfriend.

After searching a couple of news websites online, Renzo says, “The murder rate has quintupled in major cities in Vermont, New Hampshire, Western Massachusetts, and upstate New York. What's the mortality rate of synthetic h? Are users more likely to overdose from it than if, for example, they used standard heroin?”

"No, the overdose rate is the same as a very potent, very toxic hit of 'organic' heroin. That's the main reason we've been able to evade suspicion of the DEA."

"On top of our actions, I imagine this is causing poor Dick plenty of sleepless nights in the White House."

"When paired against Hillary, the president is already losing in polls for next year's election. Cheney was ahead of her before our first killing in Maryland. Now that's power."

Comfortably relaxing in his backyard, Konrad reclines neck-deep into his ten-foot-wide, in-ground hot tub, then says, "What I'm proposing, gentlemen, is that we consolidate our influence."

"We agree."

"The reason being?"

"It's important that our story be broadcast to the masses. What we've done not only here, but around the country, was retribution for what the government did to my brothers in Africa and Cuba. Everyone loves a heartfelt apology regarding atrocities from a president, but regardless of who sympathizes with my actions, getting my message out there won't add up to anything other than death by lethal injection. No, there's gotta be another way."

I exhaustingly told Blake's puppeteer from another game that collaborating with my Opponent is a fruitless exercise in futility, yet my Opponent's intoxicating demeanor won her over. Overthrowing the US federal government post 9/11 would indeed advance various goals of both players in relation to their respective games, and she felt my Opponent's conniving nature was worth the risk of being backstabbed. In addition, she'll orchestrate the assassination of the one person Konrad can't kill.

“I've created something that led me to you; something that I tested on that helpless FBI detective you corresponded with,” states Konrad.

Konrad then quickly retells the duo how he murdered Adams, how simple it was to sneak the adulterated x-2317 into his coffee, and most frighteningly, how easy it would be to not only disseminate it into the bloodstreams of existing heroin addicts, but also to the general public at large.

“What I'm looking for, because of your established fan base and existing ties to all three levels of law enforcement with Chief Macklin, Superintendent Dobkins, and now Director Henson chasing you, is for you guys to become the public front of a new, unstoppable domestic terror organization: one that I’ll be the faceless third member of. In the same vein as al-Qaeda, we will use x-2317 to become our own nation-state. Once you figure out your action plan moving forward, matters regarding all aspects of international politics, legislation, and the US military will now be in our hands. Remember, this synthetic heroin outbreak can only be terminated if we identify it exists. Of course, spinning paranoia in our favor will be easy.”

“Things are bad now, but these murder outbreaks are only confined to the Northeast. The true genius is that, instead of being from the Middle East, threats would come from citizens born and raised in this country from all walks of life. Once Ayala and the BCM spread synthetic nationwide, we'll 'predict' catastrophic events involving an army of unwitting Americans from all social, racial, and economic sectors and then manipulate the outcome to our own benefit. This will easily give us the ability to win our own prospective game by breaking away from the United States and creating a new nation in the nine states that stretch from Maryland to Maine. A new nation that fully recognizes the Others as our guiding overlord," states Blake.

"But there's only one thing standing in our way. And I'm afraid I'll anger the Others if I orchestrate it myself."

"No need to elaborate; I have no problem killing Nina Sullivan," responds Blake.

* * * * *

Meanwhile, in the barren basement of Colin's home, Nina clutches a green blanket and twists her bony body on the military cot pinned against the cold, concrete wall. Wearing an open bathrobe, which barely obscures his private parts, Colin slowly makes his way down a subterranean, spiral wooden staircase.

Now on the bottom floor, Colin walks past a ping-pong table, and a few loud, mainstream American beer posters behind a small, impressively stocked antique bar. Colin then clicks on a few ceiling lightbulbs and finally sits on a dusty stool not far away from Nina's face.

"Please close your robe; it's not happening, big guy," says Nina while rubbing her bloodshot eyes.

"Sorry for the accommodations, but the good news is that brunch is on the table once you feel like eating. With us converting the guest bedroom for the new baby and everything, this is the best—"

"Don't sweat it, and thanks for providing a roof over my head until I feel safe sleeping alone. I don't want to burden you with anything more than you can handle, but it goes without saying that we've got a real dilemma on our hands. Have you ever heard of something called 'Culture-Bound Syndrome'?" asks Nina, leading an intrigued Colin to shake his head no.

"Basically, in the world of medicine, CBS is defined as an amalgamation of a disease's psychiatric and somatic indications. But unknown to the masses, the disease's symptoms are only recognizable within a specific, esoteric sub-culture. What you've seen on TV, what you've read on the web, is undoubtedly the most violent and wide-ranging example of this medical term."

"The madness of these unpredictable killers, running amok around the upper Northeast—you're telling me Konrad caused all that?" asks Colin.

"Not at first; no. But now that Konrad's found out that his product has the unintended consequence of causing such mass destruction, he's currently trying to find out a way to fine tune and corral this power so he can unleash it on the rest of the country—if not the world," replies Nina, who sits up, then politely refuses Colin's attempt to hand her a warm cup of coffee.

"Look, I'm at least partially responsible for what happened in Lawrence. It was too dangerous to let you go up there without a third voice of caution, someone older like me to give you backup and to help you navigate among unpredictable, armed drug dealers."

"You have my word that I'll never tell your pregnant wife upstairs, but everyone in the office knew you planned to leave her and run off with Denelle. We both lost our true loves because of what Kreesha and Konrad did to us; now it's time for payback."

"Denelle was the one person who understood me. I mean, we already spoke to a lawyer about how messy and expensive my divorce would be, yet she was patient and willing to wait for my wife to give birth before we could officially become a couple. There was no reason to kill her, and I'm gonna make sure those bastards rot in hell."

"You'll do no such thing. Before they come after you, they'll go after your wife, and they'll be sadistic enough to wait until after she has your child, just to make sure your boy grows up without a mother. Konrad has background information, including all social media imprints, of everyone in the office. He's confided in me that he has action plans in place on every co-worker, just in case they think of running to the police. He's followed through on one against Denelle, and is on the verge of killing my mother in York."

"How's she doing? It's been so long since you've said anything meaningful about her."

"I spoke to her on Christmas Day; she's holding up the same. You know, I calculated that Konrad won't end her life."

"Why?"

"He has schizophrenia, and suffers from intense, unannounced auditory hallucinations. To Konrad, I'm the main character in some elaborate, artificial world created for his and my enjoyment. A world where Konrad and I not only dictate the rules of engagement, but the future and fate of this world."

Colin stands and hurls his cup filled with scalding gray tea against the wall, shattering the tan coffee mug upon impact. Colin's wife immediately bangs her fist on basement door, then opens it and peeks in her rotund face.

"Honey, I heard something smash. What's going on down there?" asks the thirty-eight-year-old middle-school teacher.

The half-naked salesman shouts back "It's nothing, Agatha; my drink just spilled. We'll be up there in a few."

"Look, I'm going to walk straight up the steps of MCPD headquarters tomorrow, demand to see Macklin, then tell the chief everything that I know. Denelle and Quincy's death won't be in vain; I promise you," softly says Colin after his wife slowly closes the door.

"Instead of breaking everything down to Macklin, at least for now, let's finish the work that Denelle, you, and my dead boyfriend started."

"And what's that, kiddo?"

"Tavon Ayala. I'm going to pay him a visit in Baltimore and see how I can muck things up a little. I'm sure he'll be receptive to me."

"You wanna keep working with criminals now because you've become one. And you're moving so fast, from one bad boy to the next, that you don't even have time to digest that you're a whore to the game."

Chapter 44

“Yes, Mr. President. I understand your concerns, sir . . . I'm doing the best I can. As you know, I've lost my two most trusted advisers to this madness, as well as another young officer just trying to do his job. I've been to over ten funerals since the end of Labor Day, each more heartbreaking than the next, and . . .” says Macklin, into his cellphone.

Standing in front of the chief's desk at MCPD headquarters, Alex Henson pretends to look at his watch, then starts to impatiently tap his shoe.

“I do look forward to working with Director Henson and welcome even more oversight from the FBI regarding this case. I understand, Mr. President. Godspeed be with you too, sir . . . Good night,” intermittently continues Macklin to the beleaguered commander-in-chief before hanging up.

The president's approval ratings have taken a steep nosedive since the sniper killings. An explosion of seemingly random murders and armed robberies in mid-sized cities in New Hampshire, Vermont, upstate New York, and Western Massachusetts hasn't helped Cheney's re-election prospects either.

In response, President Cheney has signed executive orders that give the Federal Emergency Management Agency (FEMA), more specifically a White House-appointed, six-man board working within FEMA's National Response Coordination Center (NRCC), broad oversite to censor media reports they deem counterproductive to catching an imminent domestic threat. The uncaught Serial Snipers dilemma is immediately designated as the NRCC's first national crisis that allows the federal government to obfuscate the First Amendment. White House insiders have already leaked that "potential" voter fraud in the coming presidential election will also allow the NRCC to censor any media reports deemed derogatory against Cheney's upcoming reelection efforts.

"As the president informed you, I'm officially now taking over this investigation, Macklin. Sorry for having to introduce myself to you so late in the game, and under these circumstances, Chief. Charlie Adams was a great man who served this country well," says the stocky, 5'3, twenty-eight-year veteran of the FBI.

"I'm sure you guys want me to remain the head monkey in charge. Am I right?

"At this tenuous juncture of the case, it's imperative that we don't confuse our audience, much less the snipers, who would view a changing of the guard as an admittance of failure. I'm not looking at you as a figurehead, more like a second in charge, which is what you should have been the minute Detective Adams arrived in Maryland. Routinely disobeying my order for him to take full command, Charlie, God bless his soul, had too much reverence for your department to demote you. I've read reports on your struggles getting Dobkins to fully disclose his progress tracking leads statewide, but now that I'm here—"

"For months, I was asking Charlie for assistance from the Department of Justice. Why aren't they any US Marshals here, working this investigation to assist your agents? I agree that sending out the National Guard to patrol suburban, mostly residential streets also sends the wrong message to our citizens, but you're currently the only federal agent in the state of Maryland working this case. What kind of shit is that?"

"The situation in the upper Northeast is much, much worse than what's being reported by the mainstream media, and all of DOJ's manpower is dedicated to assisting overwhelmed police forces up there. I shudder to think that these mass murderers are causing copycat killers to emulate them, but all signs point to that happening at this very instant," responds Henson.

After sitting on the desk and placing his stumpy legs on top of a dusty guest chair, Henson proceeds to tell Macklin that the media has been instructed by the White House, citing an inscrutable clause in the Patriot Act, not to disclose that the characteristics of three consecutive Maryland murders, along with the chronological sniper killings in Baton Rouge, are being replicated at a rate much faster than law enforcement can handle.

"What are coroners saying about all of this?"

"Many of the killed murderers are teachers, lawyers, and corporate executives with no previous criminal record. Once doctors test their blood, the only characteristic in their system they all share is heroin use."

"What are you talking about?"

"On multiple occasions we've had cops drag in a heroin-drugged killer for blood tests and questioning, but its led to nothing other than revealing the low-level dealer they bought the drugs from. DEA's all but water tortured every smack dealer they can get their hands on up there, but each one is too afraid to talk."

"Something doesn't add up. Adams said, the Monday before Thanksgiving, that suspect Blake Rice wrote him an e-mail seeking 'cognizance, transparency, and retribution' because the CIA railroaded his brothers in arms, purposely destroyed his career as a Navy SEAL, and last but not least, illegally experimented with his body in order to advance Zionistic, one-world government ideals hidden from most of society. What if this x-2317 thing that Blake keeps referencing somehow got into a percentage of the nation's heroin supply?"

"You can't trust the schizophrenic ramblings of a serial killer," answers Henson.

"True, but by the time our detectives got access to Nadir's lab at PWI, his computer was removed by CIA investigators, along with his unfinished experiments. Nadir's murder happened in my jurisdiction, but unlike the sniper killings, you're keeping me in the dark regarding evidence surrounding his murder. Why did the CIA, as well as FEMA and the FBI, feel the need to overstep my authority on Nadir's murder, unlike all these other deaths?"

"I want us to be clear on this, so there's no problem moving forward. All evidence seized by the death of that macaca is a federal matter. Nadir's death is unrelated to our investigation of the snipers and rise in violent crime up North," angrily responds Henson.

* * * * *

The next morning, a tense but brief conference call takes place between Colin, Nina, Kreesha, and Konrad.

Kreesha and Konrad call in from the eT office while Colin and Nina correspond via an untraceable line from an unknown location. During the professional exchange, Kreesha agrees to promote Colin to executive vice president of sales and give the expecting father a six-figure raise.

After shutting Colin up with more money, Konrad tells the duo that his lawyer finagled a paid, five-month break from work for Konrad because of the psychological damage caused by Adams false arrest accompanied by him witnessing the detective hack an officer's skull with an axe.

"I may travel the world, or just sit on the couch and veg out; who knows. But my days at efficienTECH most likely are over," says Konrad.

Kreesha informs Nina of her revised and improved pay structure, which gives her two weeks more paid vacation, a significantly higher salary base, and an expanded commission rate. Nina will now also have the ability to work from home and only has to come to the office for Monday-morning quota meetings.

"Now that he's figured out how to wash his money without fear or repercussion, Konrad's never coming back to eT. You know that, right?" says Colin, fifteen minutes after hanging up the phone with Kreesha and Konrad.

Nina inspects herself in the mirror, slips on her most provocative red high heels, then pulls up her freshly pressed hair into a makeshift ponytail. While turning around, she says, "Konrad can't buy my silence like he did with you. But it's alright; with your wife and incoming newborn, it's for the best that we separate at this juncture."

Wiping tears from her eyes, Nina grabs her keys and prepares to enter Colin's two-car garage through a closed wooden door connecting it to his basement.

"I'm amazed by your strength through all of this, Nina," responds Colin, who's also choked up with conflicted emotions.

"And thanks for letting me stay here this week; I appreciate it."

"Hey, hold on for a sec; I wanna give you something." Colin then takes a peek at the closed first floor door at the top of the basement stairs and then slowly removes a bulge from underneath his sweatpants waistband.

"Please, I keep telling you to put that thing away."

"No, take it. You're on your own now, and you'll never know when you'll need to use it."

Colin then hands a Glock pistol to Nina, who reluctantly puts it in her purse.

After Colin carefully shows her how the safe action system works, Nina says, "Words cannot describe how thankful I am for your gratitude, support, and hospitality. You have my word that I'll do whatever it takes to make sure not only you, but your family won't be harmed by my actions."

Nina then kisses Colin's wrinkled forehead, gets in her M3 in his open garage, and leaves.

As she drives away, Colin turns on his cellphone and immediately calls Konrad.

Chapter 45

"She's gone now . . . going to see Ayala in prison, I reckon, but she could be headed anywhere. As you know, she's very unpredictable," nervously stammers Colin.

"You've done great work, brother. Rest assured, I'll spare your wife and future child any harm moving forward. Before you hang up, there's one more thing."

Konrad, standing in front of a wall, plastered with nine fifty-inch televisions monitoring every inch of his outdoor property, twirls a chilled glass of Nolet's Reserve Dry Gin with his index finger, then continues.

"Just so you know, that plastic Glock my boy gave you to give Nina was the same gun my assistant used to shoot your girlfriend. That's all for now, but keep your phone on; I may need you for additional projects." Without anything left to give, Colin hangs up his phone. Still alone in his basement, Colin unbuttons his shirt and removes his New Balance sneakers before finally taking off his ruffled jeans. Now in a crisp gray t-shirt and bright white underwear, Colin takes a barstool from next to the cot Nina called home all week and places it in the center of the room.

"If God places the heaviest burden on those who can carry its weight, why did he make me such a weak man?" wonders Colin out loud.

Slowly walking past the wall-mounted movie poster for the 1980 film *The Ninth Configuration,* Colin gently moves the heavy punching bag out of the way, removes the brown leather belt from his discarded jeans, and double knots it against a stainless-steel pull-up bar attached to the basement ceiling.

He then kneels on top of the cushioned, three-legged barstool and securely wraps the free end of the belt twice around his neck. Colin then whispers, "Denelle, I'm sorry for the pain and suffering I caused you. I guess that doing things the right way was never my strong suit, and I can't go on any more. So please find it in your heart to forgive me. I'd rather take my chances in the afterlife than stay here in Hell."

Taking one last look behind the bar toward the fake-gold "Man of the Year" trophy his wife just bought him as a stocking-stuffer, Colin kicks the stool away and asphyxiates himself to death.

* * * * *

"There she is, son: in the black M3. Don't follow her too closely in the fast lane though; the last thing we need right now is a run-in with an oblivious state trooper," instructs Blake from the passenger seat.

"She must have a radar detector, or some unknown anti-detection device, because she's doing well over a hundred, sir," calmly responds his driver, Renzo.

Thirsty for his next kill, Renzo gently presses the Caprice's accelerator in hope of either running Nina off of the road, or if possible, executing a drive-by shooting once they exit the somewhat congested highway. The thirst to murder innocent civilians has taken over the young Aruban's psyche, even though he's never taken x-2317, or for that matter, injected synthetic heroin.

Blake has keenly witnessed this transformation. And after having extended, private conversations with Konrad, both central pieces in their own elaborate chess game believe that x-2317 has enhanced their powers of manipulation to a superhuman level, giving them the assurance that they can brainwash any US citizen. Carl Jung's analytical thoughts regarding the animus and anima, or in layman's terms, *the totality of the unconscious*, accurately breaks down the pros and cons of the feminine qualities a male possesses, or conversely, the masculine qualities a female has. I feel that it's better that Nina, who contains many more traditional male traits than the vast majority of women worldwide, realize my psychological enhancements organically, so she doesn't immediately discard the inherent, masculine features that make her special. On the contrary, the Others, like my Opponent and his associate manipulating the marionette Blake Rice, feel that men, based on case studies of past, megalomaniac players like Pol Pot, Vlad the Impaler, and Idi Amin, need their egos stroked immediately, continuously, and forcefully to combat the immediate onset of insecurities that often overwhelms a man given ruling powers from above.

Other than his ex-wife, who Blake believed deserved to die for abandoning him after his disaccreditation from the Navy, he and Renzo have never killed someone unaffiliated with law enforcement they already knew personally. A man of conviction and self-established principles, Blake only agrees to assassinate Nina in exchange for the secret conversion technique used to create x-2317 into synthetic heroin, along with detailed knowledge on how to make its refined, more potent variation, which was previously used by Konrad to destroy Adams.

“Our target's driving very erratically, Konrad, as if she knows someone’s tailing her,” says Blake into his cellphone. Inside her vehicle, Nina's heart beats the fastest it's thumped since Quincy's death in Lawrence.

Her ears barely able to comprehend my advice, Nina turns off the news radio after shifting into fifth gear and darts her car's front end between two slower vehicles traveling on the mega-highway's middle lanes.

“All warfare is based on deception, so attack Konrad where he's unprepared, then appear where you are not expected,” I say. While Blake and Konrad confer on how best to trap her, Nina makes an abrupt, unexpected left-hand turn off the highway, then power-slides onto a small gravel road that not only serves as a hangout for state troopers, but also as an impromptu, illegal U-turn for anyone willing to brave arrest in order to travel south without paying the upcoming toll.

“She's diverged off course, Konrad, and is headed back on I-95 south toward DC. Renzo will blow out our tires if he follows her, and my patience is wearing thin. Give me some good news before I permanently ex-communicate . . . AND DO IT NOW!!!”

“You'll have other opportunities to take her life. Drive west toward my place so we can reorganize.”

“What's stopping us from killing you instead?” asks Blake.

“Stay calm. I'll show you the chemical composition of x-2317, its variants, and the process of converting it into synthetic h. What you decide to do with this information is your choice,” responds Konrad. After briefly deliberating Konrad's pitch, the duo discontinues their chase of Nina and heads west on I-70 toward Konrad's compound. Sixty miles north in York, Mrs. Sullivan shakes her empty orange oxycodone pill container with her left hand before turning up the TV with the remote nestled within her right palm.

“That smug bitch hasn't mailed me any money since Christmas, and I barely had enough to support my cravings last year,” says Nina's mom before turning back to *Hannity.*

Fixated on breaking news, Mrs. Sullivan sees live footage of Chief Macklin on top of an elevated press conference stage, for the umpteenth time, in front of MCPD’s immense headquarters.

However, during this press conference, he's simultaneously being beaten, tasered, and pepper-sprayed by a horde of five men wearing full length, navy-blue jackets with the words “U.S. Marshal” embroidered in bright yellow on their upper back and left sleeve.

“I'm at a loss for words,” observes the commentator.

Macklin, with blood trickling down the erupting crevice above his temple, tries in vain to stand.

Intent on impeding his progress, one of the marshals wraps his legs around Chief Macklin's torso and then securely wraps his right forearm and bicep around Macklin' neck, prompting the life-sized teddy bear to scream

“I can't . . . I can't breathe,” whispers the chief.

While the shrieks of a helpless Nicole can be heard off-screen, Mrs. Sullivan leans from her plastic-covered couch, wipes her runny nostrils, and then rewinds her VCR to see exactly what precipitated Chief Macklin's whipping.

“What the hell did I miss?” comments Mrs. Sullivan before finally queuing the TV to play a few seconds after Macklin's opening remarks.

“No, I don't have any new information about the exact whereabouts of former Navy SEAL Blake Rice, or for that matter, his accomplice. We do believe he's still in this state and are proud that our enhanced police work has prevented him from recently killing any Marylanders.” begins Macklin, squinting from the plethora of artificial lighting behind the dozens of reporters, now used to his monochrome, unemotional explanations.

“Due to the untimely passing of two of my most honorable and closest confidants, I'm here to report that FBI Director Henson has arrived from down south in order to supplement our already strong case.”

“AP and Reuters have reported that for all intents and purposes, you've been demoted as the leading decision maker of this investigation. Sources say that now you're nothing more than a PR spokesman for the MCPD. Care to comment?” yells a reporter from the frozen, trampled front lawn where Officer McGary was shot and killed late last year.

Macklin clears his throat, then puts his prepared notes back in his pocket.

“Hey, I know it's off topic, but my only son's turned me onto this computer game called 'Perfect World International,' or PWI, which is an online role playing game that's set in a virtual world. What sets PWI apart from other computer games is that in 'Perfect World' different players can take on interchangeable roles depending on their specific choice of race and socio-economic background. It's amazing how realistic these games are in relation to what’s happening around us, don't you think?”

As the crowd stares in stunned disbelief, Macklin adds

“I can’t hide this fact any longer! There is a prescription drug manufacturer, with a large office in this county, that’s acutely responsible for the serial killer’s murderous rampage. And this very drug company, named Pharmaceutical Warehouse Incorporated, is being sponsored by the Central Intelligence Agency. President Cheney has been aware of this fact for months, yet has said nothing!” screams Macklin at the top of his lungs.

Diverting attention away from my Opponent, focused on Henson, I was momentarily able to enter Macklin’s mainframe and coerce him speak the words he just said. It’s important to embolden the frustrated public to now, albeit unconsciously, take action against my Opponent.

As the assembled press core collectively scratch their heads in disbelief, Director Henson, watching the Q and A session from Macklin's office window, radios one of his subordinates to subdue, and prevent the chief from continuing to speak.

“He's trying to communicate with our targets. Get him into lock-up now!”

Seconds later, millions of earthlings watch in horror, as the chief is forcefully gang-assaulted, then jailed in his own police station without any formal explanation to the assembled press core. While dozens of cameras flash, Henson finally makes his way downstairs, strolling toward the same front doors that Adams carried McGary's dead body through. As he exits the building, two uniformed county officers, tensely holding military-grade, M-16 rifles pointed toward the sky hold the doors open for the federal government's *éminence grise.*

Nina, now off the highway, desperately weaves through secondary roads; to somehow personally connect with the incarcerated chief. As she does, Henson positions himself behind the podium on the police headquarters' front steps. After pulling a few pliable microphone cords in front of his mouth, in order to accommodate his diminutive stature, Henson declares that, "Today is the dawn of a new era . . . not only regarding this hunt for the two derelicts that have not only wantonly killed your brothers, sisters, friends, loved ones, and coworkers as they lived amongst you . . . bathing in your filthy water, eating your generic processed food, and socializing among your uneducated and misinformed."

Simultaneously turning up the volume on their car radio and TV, both Nina and her mother listen and watch as Henson continues, without referencing Macklin or Nicole, who heroically tried to fend off Macklin's attackers with the tips of her car keys before being shot to death by two marshals.

"Yes, America, in many ways you're more like these serial killers than you could possibly ever imagine," adds Henson, fully aware that billions around the world are now watching him.

To the stage's immediate right, cameras capture Nicole's bullet-ridden body, spread on the ground while Henson, looking forward to the flabbergasted press core, continues.

"With the full legal support of President Cheney, along with Speaker Boehner, the United States Senate Select Committee on Intelligence, and finally the office of former CIA operative Benjamin Dolan, I hereby declare Chief Davis Macklin, under Title V of the Patriot Act, an enemy combatant of the state subject to any interrogation technique deemed necessary to uncover information relevant to the capture of former Navy SEAL Blake Rice."

Almost paralyzed in fear from watching Macklin's Rodney King-like beating, a journalist tepidly raises his arm, then asks, "When will Chief Macklin be brought in front of a judge for these charges?"

"A secret grand jury is in the process of gathering all the facts surrounding Macklin's espionage and will make their determination about his fate shortly. Until then, we'll try to get as much information as possible out of him by any means necessary," answers Henson.

Nina, finally at the MCPD compound, quickly sprints from visitor parking without being detected and toward a news truck parked on the edge of the police station's front lawn.

Dressed in sneakers and a black sweat-suit, Nina then crawls underneath the mobile media hub.

Via a pair of cheap binoculars she often looked through to birdwatch from her balcony, Nina focuses on a guarded iron door just used to transfer a motionless Macklin into an underground jail cell.

This alternate universe, created for the enjoyment of my Opponent and myself, is quickly reaching its societal tipping point.

Nina digs into her sweatpants pocket and quickly unearths a handful of M-80 firecrackers, which she earlier found among some July fourth paraphernalia in Colin's basement. After laying a disposable lighter in front of her, Nina pulls out the device that Nadir slipped into her pocket what seems like forever ago now. When she first pulled it out later that night, it seemed like an ordinary cell phone, but now, after fully embracing her enhanced abilities, she's able to easily see which wires Nadir added to allow the device to connect to the internet via the cell towers. She logs onto an underground internet forum called 4chan, formed this past September by a group of hacktivists that now known as Anonymous, who, in light of the sniper crisis and Cheney's recent totalitarian, tyrannical legislation, seek to spread anarchy digitally. Via a handle she created at Colin's place, nearly identical to the one thought to be maintained by Blake and Renzo, Nina types "Because you've dedicated yet another day to in-house politics, squabbling and civil rights violations, I will now start shooting and killing all officers in front of Montgomery County Police Department headquarters."

Once sending the short memo into cyberspace, Nina again picks up her binoculars and waits impatiently, still hidden from view. On top of the MCPD roof, four heavily armed SWAT team snipers search high and low in order to intercept the perceived threat.

"We don't see anything from here. All buildings, roads, and trees surrounding the station are clear; over," says one positioned shooter into his wireless, ear-mounted microphone.

At the ground level below, a US Marshal cautiously walks on the stage, interrupting Henson's awkward Q and A media session.

“Director, Blake Rice is hiding around here and watching you, but no one can see him. There's no point in staying here around this chaos; it’ll probably expand to DC.”

Henson puts his finger to the crowd, and then leans toward his adviser.

“We need to get a grasp on this internal power grab now. A military coup is coming; we need to prepare our next move. I’ve coordinated with the Secret Service to have Cheney moved to the Presidential Emergency Operations Center and have prepared your jet for a flight to Teterboro. An emergency meeting containing each Wall Street CEO has already been arranged for tomorrow morning,” whispers the federal officer in Henson's right ear.

Nodding his head in approval, Henson then says to the assembled reporters, “That's enough for tonight, folks. We'll convene this in a few days.”

Henson grabs his notebook, filled with copies of all e-mails sent between Adams and Blake, and walks back toward the MCPD compound. As Henson turns his back toward the horrified audience, Nina tosses four ignited M-80s at the base of a large oak tree immediately behind the three dozen reporters in front of the elevated stage.

The explosion causes the journalists to scatter like roaches, ducking for cover wherever they can find it.

After hearing the dawn of new era, a uniformed officer, in front of the closed door leading directly to Macklin’s jail cell, also decides to make a run for it. Entropy is in full swing.

The aforementioned cop runs past Nina's hidden location and toward the same concrete lot she just sneaked in from. Unabated by fear of death, Nina, with all her might, tosses five more M-80s from underneath the van and toward a parked cruiser twenty feet behind her, causing snipers on the roof to immediately shoot at it with reckless abandon. Using skills she honed during the barbed wire crawl at a CrossFit obstacle course, my heroine gyrates her body on the ground like a black mamba, then makes the forty-yard sprint toward Macklin's confined location.

"Tell those snipers to shoot any reporters that enter the building; doing so immediately designates them as enemy combatants," instructs Henson to his assistant from their helicopter, which just took off from the rooftop helipad.

* * * * *

Running with reckless abandon, Nina finally reaches the unlocked iron door, opens it, and hustles down a flight of dimly lit, industrial subterranean stairs.

Nina, exhilarated to have safely made it inside, now jogs through a thin, gray hallway lined with steel-bar jail cells.

Within each cage of the modern-day dungeon sits one or two badly beaten demonstrators, some of whom are still wearing their Guy Fawkes masks that they donned during the afternoon's economic inequality rally in Gaithersburg led by Dr. Cornell West and Representative Bernie Sanders.

Stopping dead in her tracks, Nina pauses in front of the last and smallest cell in the miniature prison.

Perpendicular to the other bastilles, Nina quickly realizes that Macklin's cell makes up the dungeon's dead end.

"It's ironic, I had the brew she had the chronic, the Lakers beat the Supersonics."

While humming the rest of "Today Was a Good Day" in her head, you know, because it's great theme music, I remind her in both the macro and micro sense that in order to garner victory, she has to escape via the same treacherous route she just maneuvered through.

Macklin, whose face looks like Timothy Bradley after fighting Diego Chaves, rocks from side to side on a splintered wooden bench next to an overflowed, feces-filled toilet.

In the windowless, Matrix-green-lit room no larger than a broom closet, Macklin inadvertently spits a stream of blood onto Nina's sweatpants, causing her to recoil backwards in fear.

While hugging himself, as if Nicole was in his arms, Macklin extends his wrists toward Nina.

"Are you here to take me to the gallows?"

"No one is lynching you today, sir. I'm one of the esoteric few that deciphered your message. I know all about x-2317 and how it's destroying the world as we knew it. I can end all of this suffering, Chief, but I can't do it myself. I need your help."

Nina then reaches her arm through two steel bars and hands Macklin the tainted Glock given to her by Colin.

Chapter 46

“This is the second Revolutionary War! Give us guns to fight our oppressors, too!” yells one imprisoned protester, which elicits a thunderous roar from all ten jail cells.

“The minute they get outside, those kids will get shot on sight. The real jail is upstairs. These cells were used in the 1950s during the Second Red Scare to detain perceived communist agitators,” says the now re-energized Macklin, before adding, “Step aside.”

Using the same gun that murdered Denelle, Macklin points the weapon waist-level and shoots open the rusty lock separating him from freedom.

“This is your world, your mission, Captain, so here's your first tough decision to make. In my estimation, these prisoners in front of me are safer in here. Once we escape, we can always call the ACLU to make sure they're looked after. But if you distrust the system, we can release these anarchists and use them as a diversion—one that'll surely lead to their death. But in the process, they'll save our lives. If you want me to kill Blake Rice, then you've got to decide either way; and you have to do it now.”

"If you leave us here, we'll die!" exclaims one prisoner, which prompts the remaining detainees to bang loudly against the rusted, locked steel bars.

"The choice is yours, and yours alone," repeats the chief.

Macklin then motions to a silver wall-mounted box on the concrete wall directly to the left of Nina. He then opens the three-dimensional rectangle, prompting Nina to walk in front of the plastic, gray swivel-handle inside of it.

For the first time since I chose her, I let Nina decide her next move.

While my Opponent and I debate human nature's desire for self-preservation versus humanity's need for chaos, Nina pushes the handle up toward the word "Unlocked," instantly causing each one of the sixteen cells to creak open, much to the relief of the two dozen or so peaceful demonstrators.

"OK, what's done is done; there's no turning back now. Huddle behind the last escapee, wait for my word, then sprint back to the same parking lot you came from," barks Macklin.

Once in the dungeon hallway, all twenty-four, mostly male protesters quickly slap hands and hug Nina in relief.

Then, as Macklin predicted, in robotic-like unison, they make a beeline up the flight of stairs leading toward outside.

"Follow them! Hurry up!" yells Macklin. Obeying his instructions, Nina climbs the stairs to suddenly hear the screams of elation from those who clamored for liberation turn into shrieks of unmitigated horror.

Gunshots, originating from the rooftop outside, mow down the first three triangular rows of anarchists like a bowling ball first hitting a set of stacked pins.

Macklin, being the only African-American of those trapped in the basement's staircase, grabs a Fawkes mask from a frozen objector and then peeks outside.

The chief now focuses on an industrial-sized, mobile electric generator about fifty feet in front of the now-empty press conference stage.

Responsible for powering a cluster of elevated lighting that captured his public pummeling, Macklin shoots the gasoline-filled generator with the Glock's remaining bullets, causing it to explode immediately.

"That's our diversion. Let's go!" he screams.

Nina carefully hurdles over the lifeless bodies of three murdered demonstrators and ducks her head while running 200 yards toward her car in the visitor parking lot.

MCPD's surroundings look similar to Kiev's Independence Square during Ukraine's most recent revolution. A few remaining reporters and producers frustrated with FEMA's muzzle, and unwilling to remain bystanders after watching Nicole's murder and Macklin's beating, get in a local news truck and also decide to fight back.

Once starting the engine, the local media members accelerate the vehicle directly toward, and then through, the wooden press conference stage, immediately shattering it on impact.

While the van is still in motion, the two dissenters break numerous bones in their bodies after jumping out of the vehicle's side doors.

The unoccupied news truck accelerates up the building's iconic front stairs and directly into MCPD's front doors, killing a brigade of turncoat officers and US Marshals in the process.

"The whole world is watching!" screams Western Maryland reporter Jennifer Becker, who writhes in pain on the concrete staircase while pumping her right fist in exuberance.

"Are you OK, Chief?" asks Nina.

Macklin, still bleeding from his skull, breaks the Chevy's passenger-side window with his elbow and quickly dives into the car's cabin before manually unlocking the driver's side door for Nina.

"Taking this unmarked car is safer than driving your vehicle."

Macklin, breathing heavily due to internal bleeding from his broken ribs, uses a small extension from his Swiss Army knife and musters enough physical force to crudely bypass the ignition lock, ultimately giving Nina the ability to start the car's engine.

"Drive me to where this Konrad person lives and fill me in on why you know so much about x-2317."

Speeding away from the Montgomery Police Department as fast as the generic Chevy will allow, Nina checks her rearview mirror for pursuers. To her best estimation, there are none. "Even if we end up in the morgue, we're not going to let today's deaths be in vain," adds Macklin.

"Chief, unless you promise me immunity for what I'm about to tell you, the only place I'm driving you to is a hospital."

Macklin denies that he needs immediate medical treatment before screaming in agony as he reaches into the glove compartment.

Nina careens onto a sidewalk to avoid a man-made blockade of burning garbage dumpsters while Macklin retrieves a blank paper and pen from the glove compartment.

"*I, Chief Davis E. Macklin of the Montgomery County Police Department, head of the Serial Sniper investigation, hereby indemnify you of any past charges related to the pursuance and capture of Blake Rice,*" states Macklin before signing the handwritten note.

With one wrist on the steering wheel, Nina reads the immunity letter, then breathes a sigh of relief.

"Before we get to our destination, tell me everything you know; don't spare me any details."

* * * * *

"Yeah, Tavon, I understand the consequences of you losing one of your soldiers . . . It's unfortunate, but as you know, there's always going to be collateral damage when undertaking a plan of this magnitude . . . Yes, now that her boyfriend, Quincy, is dead, Nina has run out of crutches to lean on and will soon be neutralized by her own ineptitude," says Konrad from his basement before taking his phone from his ear and putting the receiver on speaker.

"Hello, Mr. Ayala. Blake Rice here, along with my understudy, Renzo Vincent. We're very impressed with your synthetic heroin distribution network and look forward to becoming the face of this nationwide movement once BCM expands production from the Northeast," comfortably says Blake while sitting on a stool next to a messy lab table.

Behind both killers stand Warren and Eric, each of whom hold a loaded handgun pointed directly at the heads of Blake and Renzo.

On the other side of table stands Konrad, his arms crossed in front of a chalkboard filled with various chemical equations related to not only the composition of x-2317, but what ingredients are needed to successfully transform it into synthetic h.

“You really trust working with these two madmen, Konrad? I mean, how many innocent people have you guys killed?” asks Ayala via an illegal cellphone smuggled into his jail cell.

Konrad, not having shaved in over two months, rubs the precipice of his nappy black beard.

“All of us have bodies in the trunk, Ayala; no need to point fingers at this point. With our power, the five of us, encapsulated within three unstoppable forces, are going to architect a new world; one that shifts from oppressive and inhumane capitalism to a new economic and political paradigm deeply rooted in anarcho-syndicalism,” says Konrad.

“Other than us, no one knows exactly why the murder rate has grown so rapidly in the upper Northeast. The left believes that what happened to Macklin tonight was the start of a revolution, while the right will use it as a reason to further crack down on civil rights,” theorizes Blake.

“Regardless of what happens, let’s state facts,” says Kreesha, who sips from a chilled glass of Chardonnay while standing next to Konrad.

“Our connection to PWI, for all intents and purposes, is dead. There's no way we have the manpower, or industrial equipment, to churn out the amount of x-2317 necessary to keep feeding the streets synthetic h. As you two gentlemen can attest to, it's always risky building allegiances at this stage of the game. However, we found a business partner closer to our central distribution cities: an accomplice that not only eliminates the need for Nina's job as a drug mule, but also gives us the ability to now take synthetic heroin nationwide. Bart Caddy, co-founder of a compounding center, along with Glenn Patella, who's a supervising pharmacist there, have agreed to take over mass production of Konrad's new, refined x-2317."

"Thanks, Kreesha. Not only will much more blood be shed, the resulting chaos will be impossible to contain. This will give you and Renzo the ability to lead your army of followers, and at last count you have over five million on MySpace, in any direction you like," adds Konrad, who's now speaking directly to Blake.

"Chicago, New York, Houston, Los Angeles, and Miami. We're going to flood the market with the new synthetic h without anyone knowing. Once crime rates rise 60 or 70 percent in those cities like what we've seen in the upper Northeast, all hell will break loose. Concurrently, the Black Commando Mafia will work with correctional officers to sneak synthetic h into prisons, which will lead to massive, uncontrollable prison riots from here to the West Coast," interjects Ayala.

Kreesha, standing next to Konrad, nervously lights a menthol cigarette and waits for Renzo's response.

"You see, son, it's nothing more than insider trading, but to outsiders we'll appear as villains with supernatural powers. We can manipulate currency, politics . . . everything is on the table, and anything we want in this world is ours," concurs Blake, much to the relief of the other adults in the room.

“All their cars must be hidden in the garage. What are they saying now?” inquires Nina.

On her stomach in a patch of hidden, frozen brush across the desolate street from Konrad's residence, Nina uses her binoculars to try to get a fix on Konrad's next move.

“They're now taking credit for the retribution killing of a patrol officer murdered in Brooklyn minutes ago by those who witnessed your beating,” whispers Macklin, who's huddled next to Nina.

Using the ParaDish parabolic listening device, recovered from the trunk of the undercover, commandeered police vehicle, Macklin points the handheld, clear, plastic satellite dish directly toward an exposed brick facade underneath Konrad's home. With a circumference no larger than a common dinner plate, Macklin then adjusts a volume button and presses the device to his right ear/

“I've heard six different voices from the basement: five men and one female. According to this prick Konrad, they’re talking about the events leading to formation of Israel in 1948 in order to create a new nation within the state of Maryland,” says Macklin, before adding, “Now some kid, I guess its Blake’s sidekick, says he wants an Enzo and his own mansion. All right, I'm using lethal force to take everyone out; you ready to back me?”

“I've never shot a gun before. Konrad has too much heavy artillery in there for us to be effective from outside. Let's stay patient,” quietly advises Nina.

Inside, Kreesha hands her former efficienTECH coworker a serrated steak knife.

Konrad and Blake have just agreed to take a blood oath, cementing Blake's synthetic h allegiance to Konrad's master.

Kreesha, while opening up a passage from her favorite Satanic libretto, then says "Slice a small triangle in the inside of your right arm, let the other two suck from your open wound, then state the following words after me."

As Renzo silently watches on, Blake and Konrad carefully follow Kreesha's instructions, quickly sanitize and bandage their open wounds, then hold their hands in a circle. The two males, transfixed on one another, then state in unison, "As members, I proclaim Lucifer as my one and only. I promise to recognize and honor him in all things, without reservation, desiring only in return his manifold assistance in the successful completion of my endeavors."

"OK, it's officially turned into the Blair Witch Project," relays Macklin.

My Opponent is Anton Lavey, the creator of Satanism who left your planet in 1997.

In our dimension, religious, political, artistic, and other revered figures from all backgrounds battle via this game within this alternate version of planet Earth.

And no, I'm not Jesus; just one of his humble surrogates.

Nina runs to the trunk of the undercover MCPD car, hidden farther into the woods, and removes a M72 LAW from the trunk. Short for "Light Anti-Tank Weapon," the highly-explosive, rocket-propelled grenade launcher is just one of many army surplus weapons scooped by the MCPD after the invasion of Iraq.

"First, let's take away their only options to escape, then see how calm and collected they act with no defined hierarchy of leadership," says Nina.

Macklin, his eyes wide open with anticipation, grabs the launcher from Nina's outstretched arms and immediately takes aim at the at the barn-like garage twenty feet to the left of Konrad's refurbished mansion.

"Nicole, Tommy, and Charlie, before I join you in heaven tonight, I swear I'm gonna make you proud of me," says Macklin before mounting the long-range bazooka on his right shoulder and pulling the weapon's hairpin trigger.

The grenade, aimed perfectly by the ailing police chief, quickly bolts across the desolate two-lane road and then hits the closed, red wooden door in its center, immediately detonating all five vehicles inside the above-ground garage beside Konrad's home, including Blake and Renzo's Caprice.

The surprising impact causes an already tense Warren to jump and accidentally fire his 9mm Winchester Magnum slightly to the right of Renzo, inadvertently hitting Kreesha in the torso.

Originally dressed for bed, a small circle of blood now stains her oversized Washington Wizards hoodie, instantly making the middle-aged, single mother crumble to the dusty cement floor.

"I'm sorry, boss! That explosion threw my timing off!" pleads Warren. As Renzo and Blake stand motionless, with no emotion shown toward the critically injured woman, Konrad kneels by Kreesha's side, comforting her as her breathing becomes irregular.

"Warren, please go upstairs to the viewing room and see exactly where we were ambushed," softly instructs Konrad.

Warren turns around and begins to sprint up the stairs. Konrad caresses Kreesha's pore-less brown cheek and nods toward Eric.

Eric takes a hard gulp and then rotates his six-shooter one hundred and seventy degrees away from Blake before quickly letting off three shots into the wiry back of his best friend.

Outside, Nina quickly slides off her headphones as the trifecta of loud bangs almost causes her eardrums to bleed.

"The explosion caused friendly fire, so now we're down to four," whispers Nina.

Back inside Konrad's home, Renzo and Blake are unsurprisingly calm. The two Serial Snipers politely get his approval to take a break from their Advanced Chemistry lesson and decide to give themselves a better vantage point from which to view the explosion. Meanwhile, In Konrad's surveillance room, on the bedroom-level floor, Eric focuses an external camera directly in front of Konrad's home capable of viewing objects up to two hundred feet. Eric then exclaims, "Oh, we're going to put some wings on a pig tonight. Oh, yes indeed!"

"This is a head scratcher. I expected return gunfire, but they've made no indication of even inquiring about what happened to their vehicles," excitedly says Nina.

"You're in charge; how do you want to handle this?" asks Macklin.

He has discarded the rocket-propelled grenade and now holds the same military-grade sniper rifle frequently used by Renzo. Inside, Kreesha's big brown eyes begin to flicker as she looks past Konrad and toward the monolithic, spider web-filled basement ceiling.

Konrad cradles Kreesha in his arms and begins to softly cry: the first time he's done so in years.

"You see, love, not hate, is what lasts. Love always perseveres, it perpetually conquers and endures all opposition. That's why you'll never beat Nina. I can see the other side now, honey. I can see him in the sky behind you. He exists, and his power is real."

Kreesha burps a tiny clot of mucus and blood from her throat, signaling once and for all that her time has come to an end.

"I'm God, Kreesha! He *is* me!"

After releasing Kreesha's unresponsive frame from his grasp, Konrad yells, "What's going on outside?!"

"We have two intruders hiding in the woods across the street. After taking out our transportation, they're trying to gauge our response," screams back Eric through the fortress' intercom.

Now finished with their meal, Blake and Renzo hide on the floor behind the kitchen's marble island, ironically trying to avoid long-range gunshots from Macklin's sniper rifle. Piercing the home's outer layer, the stream of bullets fly inches from Renzo's head while he was heating a slice of sweet potato pie in the microwave.

"Konrad, best case scenario, they're a couple of local officers responding to a guilt-driven tip from Colin. Worst case, it's the DEA or FBI. If so, we could be looking at a copter-led attack in a matter of minutes. We're running out of options—thoughts on how to proceed?" shouts Blake.

Konrad crawls from the basement door and down the carpeted hallway toward the kitchen. Poised and composed, he then takes a position against the refrigerator and views a camera feed sent to his cellphone.

“The cold air prevented the garage fire from spreading to the house. Should I keep firing into the front windows or try to take out their lighting?” giddily asks Macklin.

“There's got to be a reason they're not shooting back, and I’m sure they can pinpoint our position using counter-surveillance. It just doesn't add up.”

Using his handheld police scanner, Konrad hears that local Dickerson officers are less than five minutes away. The incoming police force has also requested assistance from neighboring towns for heavy artillery backup.

“Time to leave, gentlemen. Everyone follow me,” barks Konrad.

Eric, now on the first floor and crouched beside his allies, hands Blake, Renzo, and Konrad military-grade bulletproof vests. The four men quickly put them on, then squat toward the same living room Nina played spades in a few months ago. Now in the rear of the mansion, the Serial Snipers and Eric watch Konrad toss a coffee table into the corner and then roll away an expensive, large Oriental rug, finally revealing the crew’s path to exodus. Konrad unlocks a hidden metal door right where the wooden floor underneath the rug should be and types a five-digit code into the electronic keypad above its knob.

Releasing the door's airtight seal immediately allows a soft, artificial green light to emit from an underground path constructed well below the home's basement level.

“Time is of the essence. Hurry up,” says Konrad.

Konrad grabs a remote and presses a button that turns the stereo to a CD playing "G.O.D. Pt. III"—Konrad's favorite track from the album *Hell on Earth.*

While motioning for an amazed Eric, Blake, and Renzo to descend down the portable, eight-foot-long ladder beneath the new opening, Konrad fast forwards the track; to the fifty-seventh second of the song.

Outside, Nina blanches in horror, then immediately pulls off her headphones. Tapping Macklin on his left shoulder, she shouts, "Stop shooting, Chief! It's all over! I just heard gunfire from an automatic pistol inside. It sounds like there was a sudden confrontation between Blake and Hunter."

"Typical. One of those assholes pulled a homicide-suicide; I'm sure of it," says Macklin.

With Nina still holding the remote listening device, Macklin grabs her binoculars and runs into the flat, two-way road once separating him from Konrad's property.

"I see a stream of squad cars headed here; they're about a mile away. Technically, Dickerson PD is under my jurisdiction, and I've always been on great terms with these guys. We'll be fine. You're a hero, Nina; this is finally over," gushes Macklin.

Macklin extends his arm to wave hello to the arriving policemen. As he does, Konrad's home, literally rebuilt from the ground up, explodes into a fireball, fully decimating every viewable inch of stucco, aluminum siding, brick, concrete, and mortar on the property. The detonation's reverberation, in addition to being heard up to five miles away, picks up the already-injured police chief and flings him off the road, back into the wooded brush, and a few feet from where he shot the portable canon.

"Tell me you're alive, big guy, tell me everything's OK . . ."

Macklin is unresponsive.

"I don't have anyone else; please don't die on me!" pleads Nina, shaking his unresponsive body. Nina's own mainframe, seemingly electrified with energy, momentarily convulses as her confluence of emotions boils over. Softly and quickly dropping Macklin to the frozen dirt, she grabs his automatic rifle from the bushes and, with the skill of a professional, angrily fires multiple shots directly toward Konrad's burning front door.

Meanwhile, underneath the acreage where Konrad's home once stood, Konrad leads Eric, along with Blake and Renzo, down a seemingly endless, meagerly lit hallway reminiscent of the tunnels Bane operated from underneath Gotham City.

"Now I see where you've been spending all your money, boss; you could fit a Denali truck through here," observes Eric.

"Yeah, Tavon hooked me up with a cartel friend who's built numerous tunnels from Tijuana to San Diego. This passageway leads to a private airstrip in Western Maryland, and I've already arranged for a fueled, private jet capable of flying to Pyongyang if necessary. I've spoken to an intermediary of Kim Jong-il who can not only offer us infinite immunity, but give us the facilities and shipping infrastructure in order to take synthetic h global."

"What's that pungent smell, Konrad? And why do I feel so lightheaded?" says Renzo.

Renzo doubles over in pain and then violently begins to vomit his sandwich.

Blake, usually even-tempered no matter how stressful the situation, drops to his knees and grabs his forehead in pain as twenty-foot-high, ceiling-mounted sprinklers spray an unknown chemical into the air.

"My head feels like it's about to explode," screams Renzo in agony.

Konrad calmly slips on a tactical gas mask hidden in the front pocket of his hoodie as Eric, convulsing worse than an epileptic, faints and collapses to the ground.

Fighting to cough up the fluid that's entered his lungs, Blake asks, "Where are we? What have you done to us?" Konrad bangs a florescent light stick against the wall so that the dying gang-banger and two serial killers can fully witness the horror surrounding them.

"Being the meticulous chap that I am, I had to test the effects of synthetic heroin on ordinary citizens before I could disseminate it to the general public."

Konrad then adds, "Let's just say that the first few batches didn't turn out so well and had adverse reactions. Side effects that needed to be weeded out."

Lying like stacks of large fertilizer bags at a local Home Depot are hundreds of dead humans of varying height, age, and sex, decaying against both sides of the fifteen-foot-wide tunnel—all the way until they reach the sprinklers at the ceiling.

After Konrad walks forty meters, the yellow light stick now exposes the hallway's dead end, which has a twelve-inch-thick reinforced steel door usually seen at the entrance of bank vaults.

"You . . . you created a gas chamber underneath your home?" says Blake, writhing in agony as his appendix bursts.

"Yeah. It worked for the Nazis; why not repeat history?"

Konrad finally turns the door's iron wheel clockwise, unlocking a small, oxygen-rich decompression room.

Konrad gets in alone and seals the door shut.

Chapter 47

A few months later, in a Maryland courthouse, a judge receives a handwritten note and reads the verdict to himself. He then thanks each jury member for their time, dedication, and hard work in coming to a decision, which was reached after only a few hours of deliberation.

"Will the defendant, Mr. Tavon Ayala, please rise?"

Ayala, after receiving a pat on the shoulder from his trusted attorney, follows instructions and stands to his feet.

"In the case of the state of Maryland versus Mr. Tavon Ayala, we the jury find the defendant guilty on all counts."

After reading the juror's verdict, the judge reminds Ayala that, due to the damage he's caused with synthetic heroin in the upper Northeast, combined with the subsequent boost in nationwide power to the Black Commando Mafia, Ayala will be flown to Colorado, where he'll take up isolated residence at the ADX Florence supermax prison, where he'll stay until his next trial for numerous federal charges.

"We won, honey; it's all over now," whispers Mrs. Sullivan into the ear of her daughter.

"Yeah, this was more stressful than watching cops deactivate that motion-detection bomb at my apartment," says Nina as she and her mom walk out of the jubilant courtroom a few minutes later.

"And look at you," exclaims Nina toward her mother. Minutes later, the reunited family happily jostles through the courthouse's main hallway, slowly moving through a hive of aggressive cameramen and journalists.

"I'm so proud of you for going to rehab, Mom, and cleaning yourself up. With that new vegan diet to flush out those toxins, you've lost weight, plus your skin looks great. It's really amazing what treatment in Malibu did for you."

"I know. California is so beautiful. You really should have gone to Pepperdine instead of NYU; don't you think that would've been nice?"

"Nina Sullivan, Ms. Sullivan! Can I please have a word with you?" says an external, familiar screaming voice.

Mr. Davis Macklin is now internationally known as "America's Police Chief." Macklin politely pushes aside a few cameramen waiting to document the scripted photo op and vigorously shakes Nina's right hand as cameras flash.

"Again, I just wanted to let you know how proud I am of all you've done for the state of Maryland. Your courage helped convict this madman and also stopped the plague of synthetic heroin from infecting the rest of the country," begins Macklin.

Nina then gives the chief a heartfelt hug and congratulates him on his new-found success. After fully recovering from his life-threatening injuries in late February, Macklin received the Presidential Medal of Freedom from Cheney and was awarded a cash settlement of $4,100,000 in return for absolving the FBI of any wrongdoing. Macklin then retired from the Montgomery County Police Department and quickly formed Macklin Partners: a security and management consulting firm headquartered in Manhattan with wealthy clients worldwide.

Soon after, Macklin created and implemented a protocol that not only identifies synthetic heroin users, but gives doctors and law enforcement the ability to prevent them from damaging themselves, and also, society at large.

After that worldwide PR victory, Macklin's team successfully represented Purdue Pharma, maker of OxyContin, in a liability case against the Drug Enforcement Administration. Instead of executives at Purdue serving any jail time for their misdeeds, as Ayala will, Macklin Partners negotiated a $2 million fine and no further penalty for what the DEA said was "lax security" at their plants and culpability in producing a drug commonly marketed as being non-habit forming.

"After our success with Purdue, we're defending Pharmaceutical Warehouse Incorporated for liability against x-2317. Although the government has destroyed all known x-2317 pills at their labs, PWI still faces a host of local, state, and federal charges. Moving forward, I could really use your brains on these matters; so name your price, Nina."

"Thanks again for the offer. I'm going to take a much-needed vacation with my mom and will think it over."

As Nina and Macklin agree to converse at a later date, then say goodbye, Nina feels a slight vibration in her hip and removes her cellphone while walking to her M3. Shielding the converging press from her daughter, Mrs. Sullivan asks, "Who sent you that text, hun?"

Nina reads the message from a number with a 212 area code, which states: "Move up to NYC now so we can start our second game. And be quick about it; I'm just getting started."

Nina shoves her phone back in her pocket and opens the BMW's passenger-side door for her overwhelmed mother. Once safely in their vehicle, Nina happily responds

"It's no one, Mom, just some obnoxious telemarketer. I'm beyond exhausted; let's finally go home."

I then ask, "Are you sure you made the right choice by not taking the x-2317 antidote?"

About the Author

Gordon X. Graham is a novelist born in New York City to a Jamaican oncologist and nurse. He is an alumnus of New York University and the University of Maryland where he majored in political science and film. A collegiate student-athlete, Gordon played wing on Maryland's varsity rugby team.

Gordon is a staunch supporter of the National Alliance to End Homelessness and is an advocate of civil rights worldwide. He is also passionate about roots reggae, McLaren sports cars, hip-hop music, and most of all, chess. In chess, he is a 1950-ranked player, meaning that he's one level below that of a grandmaster. Gordon's favorite favorite chess player is José Raúl Capablanca.

Gordon eternally hopes that the New York Knicks will win a championship in his lifetime.

When not writing, Gordon also directs and is developing the Heroin(e) book series into a film trilogy. He resides in New York City but will probably have to move to a less urban area soon because he wants to own a Doberman Pinscher.

STAY TUNED FOR THE NEXT BOOK IN THE SERIES:

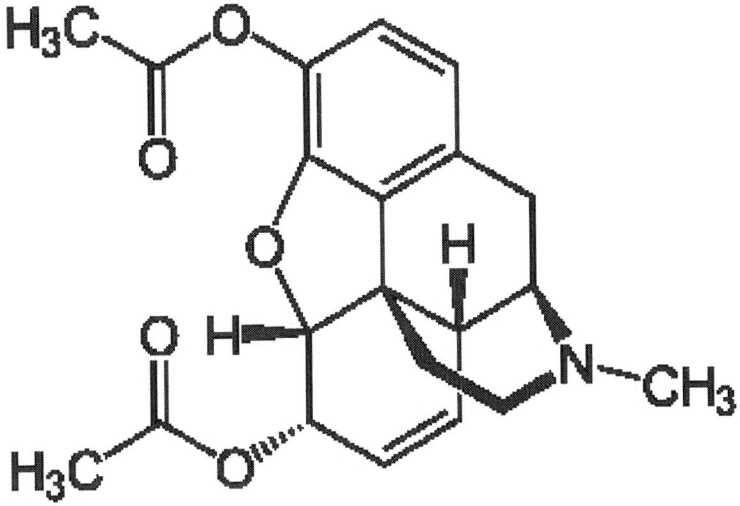

HEROIN(E): HERMETIC

"The more you can increase fear of drugs and crime, welfare mothers, immigrants and aliens, the more you control all the people." ~ Noam Chomsky